THE MATCHBOX GIRL

The MATCHBOX GIRL

ALICE JOLLY

BLOOMSBURY PUBLISHING
LONDON · OXFORD · NEW YORK · NEW DELHI · SYDNEY

BLOOMSBURY PUBLISHING
Bloomsbury Publishing Plc
50 Bedford Square, London, WC1B 3DP, UK
Bloomsbury Publishing Ireland Limited,
29 Earlsfort Terrace, Dublin 2, D02 AY28, Ireland

BLOOMSBURY, BLOOMSBURY PUBLISHING and the Diana logo
are trademarks of Bloomsbury Publishing Plc

First published in Great Britain 2025

Copyright © Alice Jolly, 2025

Alice Jolly is identified as the author of this work in accordance with the Copyright,
Designs and Patents Act 1988.

This is a work of fiction. Names and characters are the product of the author's imagination
and any resemblance to actual persons, living or dead, is entirely coincidental

All rights reserved. No part of this publication may be: i) reproduced or transmitted in any form,
electronic or mechanical, including photocopying, recording or by means of any information storage
or retrieval system without prior permission in writing from the publishers; or ii) used or reproduced
in any way for the training, development or operation of artificial intelligence (AI) technologies,
including generative AI technologies. The rights holders expressly reserve this publication from the text
and data mining exception as per Article 4(3) of the Digital Single Market Directive (EU) 2019/790

A catalogue record for this book is available from the British Library

ISBN: HB: 978-1-5266-8103-4; TPB: 978-1-5266-8105-8; GOLDSBORO: 978-1-0372-0222-3;
EBOOK: 978-1-5266-8107-2; EPDF: 978-1-5266-8106-5

2 4 6 8 10 9 7 5 3 1

Typeset by Integra Software Services Pvt. Ltd.
Printed and bound in Great Britain by Clays Ltd, Elcograf S.p.A

  Supported using public funding by
ARTS COUNCIL
ENGLAND

To find out more about our authors and books visit www.bloomsbury.com
and sign up for our newsletters

For product safety related questions contact productsafety@bloomsbury.com

This book is dedicated to my dear friend Clare Dunkel who was known to the world as the crime writer Mo Hayder.

She died of Motor Neurone Disease on 27th July 2021.

'How dare we predict the behaviour of man?'
Viktor Frankl
1905–1997

'Nature never draws a line without smudging it.'
Dr Lorna Wing
1928–2014

After My Death: How You Read My Book

History is not History when it is Happening. Do You understand? I hope You are listening? No, You cannot ask Questions. You can be sure that I will construct this Historical Record most accurately. I know because I lived through those Wartime Days. I saw it all and I recorded every detail in a Most Meticulous Manner.

Yet sadly my Notebooks were destroyed. However, I recreate them here with Absolute Accuracy. You might like to know my name. People prefer Stories which are Personal. My name is Adelheid Brunner although often they called me The Matchbox Girl. Please understand, I write for You now from my Posthumous Life.

Where most happily I have access to many documents such as Government Papers, Newspaper Reports, medical Files. This Information I may now view as from a High Tower, seeing all. (Such Information being clearly labelled within this Book.) Yet I must also write this Story as it materialised. Not saying – *with the benefit of hindsight etcetcetc.*

As Sister Viktorine told me, any Fool may be able to say what should have been done once the moment has passed. Hence, I will say only the Facts, drawing No Conclusions as many things are Misunderstood and I may inadvertently lead others to acts of spite against me. Personally, I am increasingly of the view that there is neither Past nor Future.

Only endless Present Moments appearing againagainagain, like Matchboxes laid out in a Collection, stretching forward into Eternity (regrettably resisting neat Categorisation). I cannot now remember Your Question. What I can say is that Dr A and I were watchers. We observed, noted, analysed. Yet I tell You now a Story of Blindness.

1.a. The Alchemy of Circumstance

I begin this Story on the day of 25 July 1934, a moment well known in the History of my Country of Austria. Personally, I do not remember that Day for the same reasons as do others. The World is so Extremely Busy, many things Happening all at once. (Adelheid – Do not go off down a Tram Track. Stick to the Facts.)

The Point is that on this day here is Adelheid Brunner (twelve years old) and she is arriving at the World-Famous Wiener Kinderklinik or Vienna Children's Hospital. She has in her pocket Franz Joseph, who is named after a Habsburg Emperor, but is a Rat. (I apologise if this Story sounds like a Children's Adventure. I have no other Words.)

Adelheid now walking up Lazarettgasse towards an Extremely Large and Tall Building on a small Hill. (Many towering parapets, pediments and knobs stacked topplingly high and many glittering windows tall as Fairy Tale Forests.) This Building being clearly aware of its own Importance not just in Vienna but in the Whole World ~

Adelheid is with her Oma and that Fearsome Lady is sharp and bristly as a Small Neat Hedgehog. She carries a Suitcase and says – *Come Along. Hurry Up. Stand Still.* (Adelheid bobbing behind, a kite on a short string, wearing her daisy-scattered summer dress, the strap of her Most Large Satchel pulling across her shoulder.)

As we step towards the Reception Desk, Rumour and Gossip scurry up the Pipes and across the Elaborately Plastered Ceiling as quick as Franz Joseph might run if he were not in my pocket. A pot plant saying – *That Brunner? The child's Grandfather? Yes, the journalist who worked for the* Arbeiter-Zeitung. *At the Karl-Marx-Hof. February. Ssssh.*

THE MATCHBOX GIRL

People – and Pot Plants – have been making remarks of this kind ever since Opa disappeared, which is five months ago now. Just a week ago we were told that Opa is Dead, having collapsed of a Heart Attack, just After crossing the border into Austria. Yet I know he is Alive and I am made most Angry by people telling Massive Lies.

Oma and I now being instructed – Go up to the Top Floor. See us now walking towards the stairs. (I shaped like a Golf Club – Straight and Thin with exceptionally Long Feet. Oma shaped like a Diminutive Christmas Tree. This being the least of our differences.) I should say that I have been to this Hospital before. Pneumonia when I was seven years old.

Those past days in the Hospital were a most Organised time of my Life. All the beds laid out in Matchbox-like rows and many people with Highly Organised clipboards on which to write their Notes. Opa read to me from *Das Kapital*, which is written by Karl Marx. Do You know much about Socialism and Communism? You might like to inform yourself.

Oma and I climb up-up-up many miles into the Sky and find ourselves at a half-glass Door. The sign says *Heilpädagogik* which You may translate as *Curative Education*. You may be sure that I will explain all Words You might not Understand. Although please remember some Words cannot be accurately translated. The cause of Many Difficulties ~

Oma rings the bell. A White Dove Nurse opens it and, after we have stepped over the threshold, locks the Door behind her and clips the key onto her belt. This Nurse has pinned her spider's-nest-hair under her tight-fitting white cap but spiders are still emerging above her ears. Saying now: You will be seeing Fräulein Weiss today.

Oma: Is she a Doctor?

Nurse: She is a Psychologist with long experience in her field.

Oma does not approve of women playing at Doctors.

Oma: Will she be available soon? I need to be back at the Café by midday.

The Nurse cannot say. A bench is indicated. We perch there like birds on a Telegraph Wire. A most strange part of the Hospital. Why is the Door locked? This wide Corridor-Reception is like a Sitting

Room, not a Waiting Room. From opposite the mellow pinging of music spills from behind a Door.

A plaque says Professor Hamburger. Next to another Door a plaque has been removed and a new one has Not been put in its place. One sees only screw holes where the plaque should be. An elegant Film Star lady bashes on a typewriter, her long legs in tanned nylons neatly crossed above Ruby-Red high-heeled shoes.

Occasionally she puffs on her cigarette, blows a smoke ring up into the towering ceiling while raising her eyes in Boredom or Despair. People move out of one Door and in through the next. In-out foot-tap forward-back-forward-back. This is a building of numerous Doors and interlocking rooms. Also windows of half glass through which much light can shine.

How might one navigate such a jumbled place without a Map? Adelheid – *Do not become Distracted. Focus on what you can See and Hear.* And yes, it is True, I see many things of interest from this Position. Also, I will be able to hear quite well. I have Excellent Hearing. This being Useful to a Person such as myself who likes to be Properly Informed. (One must be Properly Informed or how can one know What To Do?)

A Nurse appears with a basket of toys. How can she surmise I would be interested in these Childish Things? Such Spaghetti thinking. In the pneumonia days they gave you a number which was an Organised System for showing your place in the Queue. Hence why is this Nurse now indicating abacus, spinning top, gaggle of rag dolls with indigo wool hair?

Adelheid – *Keep your face blank and ignore this nurse entirely.* I would prefer to get out Adelheid's Notebooks. Yet Oma has spotted that Ever-Present Danger and says in a Voice Most Ferocious – *Don't touch that Satchel.* She has tried to stop Adelheid bringing Satchel-Notebooks-Albums-Envelopes to the Hospital.

Also, in a recent Shocking Incident she deliberately and callously burnt some of Adelheid's Writing. (Yet even after all these Many Years and Bitter Experiences I maintain the importance of Notebooks – either Actual Notebooks or Imagined in Your Head.) For where else may you put all your Questions when they have become too Big for Your Brain ~

Outside the heat of the day is climbing and Oma's temper is rising also. Today is Wednesday and the Surveyors from the Amtshaus (District Office) on Schlesingerplatz, opposite our Café, come to lunch on Wednesdays. Lukas has been left in charge. (Coffee in the gravy and red wine in the crème anglaise. Fears for the safety of the plush scarlet seats.) The spider-haired Nurse opens two long windows, the smoking lady complains. Oma: Excuse me but I really cannot wait. All I need is a quick word – privately. It is most difficult. The Funeral is next week.

The Nurse nods. The plants nod as well. Oma is in Danger of starting Fake Tears. The Nurse tilts her head to the side and nods, which is what people do when they are trying to indicate that they feel sorry about something. This makes Adelheid so Angry that I find it best to concentrate on Small Things which are Well Organised.

Also trying to notice the Differences in such Small Things. For as You know, a Million Blades of Grass are not the same as a Lawn. But there is no grass here therefore instead I will focus on Floor Tiles which go all around in the same (but not quite the same) zig-zag pattern. This Way of Thinking is usually good for keeping things in their place.

However, this Day is Different. Grass or Floor Tiles cannot save us Today. The air now shuffles and whispers. The City draws in a gasping breath. A loud bang leaps from below. Somethingsomethingsomething. I know my City of Vienna and I feel its Changing Moods. Out there in the Splendid and Decorous Streets is the Answer to every Question.

If you can only tell how to Translate, to Interpret. If you can only learn that Language. Now the Radio waves are crackling. High above the Trams the wires sizzle and fuse. Birds shriek. Orders are being issued, rifles are loaded, moustaches brushed flat, caps straightened. Prayers are said. Hands tremble and stomachs heave. Nonononono. Most Disorderly Times. Not again ~

Matchboxes. I recommend Matchboxes. Organised in straight lines and Clearly Categorised. Of course, Oma will not allow me to get my Albums and Envelopes out of my Satchel. Yet even in my head I can develop an Organised Plan showing what my Collection will finally be. Even despite the damage caused by the Incident of the Burning Notebooks.

(A small clarification needed here, which is that, when I say Matchboxes, I do not mean the whole Matchbox itself, only the Paper Cover from the Box. These Paper Covers being steamed off and put in Albums. Except mine not being Organised as yet but kept in Envelopes until I develop an Appropriate Plan to display them Elegantly.)

I assure You I am not going off on a Tram Track here. You do need to know. Happily, there are many different kinds of Matchbox in this my City of Vienna – the most common types are Solo and Rapid but you may also find rare examples made for export. The best come from the East, from Russia, the land of the Bears and the Bolsheviks ~

The Nurse says – *Fräulein Weiss will see you now.* Oma pokes my arm and stands up. Her silk jacket is smoothed by her gloved hands, her lips pursed, her eyes grow shrewd. She steps forward in the self-satisfied manner of one who is about to have her Position Thoroughly Vindicated.

The Spider-Nurse walks ahead of us towards high double Doors and pauses a moment before knocking ratatattat. A small woman appears. (Dark hair parted at the side and pinned back with a metal clip. High forehead, hooded eyes. Mouth small and tight with crooked lipstick. Eyes digging into my skin. Flat-chested with Bad Clothes but friendly smile.)

Fräulein Weiss: Good morning, Adelheid.

Did no one tell Fräulein Weiss that it is not appropriate to address Adelheid directly? Even at my School (the Much-Loathed Robert Hamerling-Realgymnasium at Albertgasse) this is understood. Oma is eyeing Fräulein Weiss with a smell-of-drains look. Why does the modern woman not understand that it is her duty to look pleasing?

Also, Fräulein Weiss is Prussian and Oma never likes the Prussians. *Most tiresomely Correct. We Austrians also know how to be Correct but we have a little more Style.* Fräulein Weiss is continuing to stare. Doesn't she know that is rude? Oma saying – *No Point in speaking to Adelheid. She doesn't speak.*

One Small Woman who would like to be Larger has met a Similar Type. Fräulein Weiss: Oh. Why does she not speak?

THE MATCHBOX GIRL

Oma dodges past that Question, switching on a sudden Gale of Charm and waving a clutch of Papers: Happily, this is a matter which can be dealt with quickly. The School has already sent a full explanation.

SchoolSchoolSchool. Samesamesame. I am always in Trouble there. The teachers assuming that I am an Idiot and not realising the Bad Behaviour of some others. Opa marching into the Headmistress's Office, smoke seeping out through the seam of the Door.

Opa soon emerging – the Headmistress singed and blackened. Opa saying to me – *Don't let the cattle get in the way*. Without Opa, I am Defenceless. Franz Joseph is wriggling exceedingly in my pocket. Oma lists my sins. *Just a total blank. Nothing there. Refuses to join in. Staring. Climbs out of the window and wanders through the City at Night.*

Adelheid – Do not listen. La-la-la-la-la-la-la. (Favourite Matchboxes: from India, printed on Canary Yellow Paper, a picture of an Elephant dancing on his hind legs, his feet landing neatly on a tiny stool. America: a wobbly man with a drooping moustache on a unicycle. Czechoslovakia: two-tailed white lion with crown and gold claws. Also Bears, Clowns.)

I currently own 561 Matchboxes therefore I still have 439 to collect. Unfortunately, I am so busy reflecting on Matchboxes that I have accidentally opened my Satchel. Oma is saying – *Adelheid. Put that away.* Yet Fräulein Weiss is wanting to take an Interest in me in order to demonstrate herself *Wonderful with Children*.

Saying: What a large Satchel you have there. You are interested in Writing? You could Write something for me about Yourself?

Write about Yourself? What is she talking about? I get out a Notebook. Adelheid – *ignore all attempts at communication to ensure such efforts cease.*

Oma: Only eating tiny pieces of soft bread, if you please. And heartless, absolutely heartless. No shred of Human Feeling in her. Her Opa has died and She Just Doesn't Care.

I wish Franz Joseph would keep still.

Oma: Such large feet. And her face blank. Quite blank. Cord round the neck at birth. Writing complete Lies. These Lies being addressed to her Opa even though he is Dead. God rest his soul.

Here she turns to look at me, yells: Right hand, Adelheid.

Fräulein Weiss: No, No. If she wants to write with her left hand—
Oma: Writing with your left hand is a sign of Bad Character.
Fräulein Weiss: No, No. I will speak to the School.
Oma is waving the Papers again.
Fräulein Weiss: We need to make a Full Assessment. In this Clinic we have the most Modern Testing Methods in the World.
Oma sniffs: Do you?
Fräulein Weiss: Sometimes a Parent can learn skills.

Most unwise to question Oma's Domestic Discipline or her skills in Child Raising. *Catholic values.* La-la-la-la-la-la-la. *Austrian values.* La-la-la-la-la-la-la. *Are you aware that I am the proprietor of the Café Stadler? Emperor Franz Joseph himself once ate la-la-la-la-la-la-la. One of the Old Cafés of Vienna, where you will not find any sauces thickened with flour.*

Fräulein Weiss: I do not have the Headmistress's Report but I do have Another.

Fräulein Weiss has drawn herself up to her full Diminutive Height and produces a File with the flourish of a card player who has just laid down the winning ace. Saying: Dr Josef Feldner, who works as an Advisor in this Ward, is also an Advisor in the Schools of this District. He notes that Adelheid's written work is Well Above Average.

Oma feels bitterly betrayed as Dr Feldner is a regular visitor of our Café.

Fräulein Weiss: Oh dear, Dr Feldner is not the best at Paperwork. What does it say?

I open one of my Envelopes.

Fräulein Weiss: Thank you, Adelheid. Marvellous. Yes, I see. Matchboxes.

Here she turns back to Oma: We would need to seek the opinion of Dr A, the newly appointed Director of this Ward.

Oma: Dr A? I know his father. An accountant in Burggasse? Can we see him today? A train has been booked and my friend Frau Vogt has agreed to take Adelheid. Today.

The lamps are beginning to shout, the Floor Tiles are laughing, Franz Joseph is biting me. My eyes fix on the Suitcase which Oma was formerly carrying. Why did I not apprehend of the Suitcase before? Here I am enjoying the Floor Tiles and now. Suitcases, Trains. Opa would say – *No Breadth of Vision.*

Fräulein Weiss: Some recent emotional difficulty?

Oma: Let me be Clear. I am not interested in Ridiculous Jewish Theories. You may perhaps be attracted by Herr Freud and his Improper Ideas.

I can leave Franz Joseph suffocating in my pocket no longer.

Fräulein Weiss: I am Not A Psychoanalyst, nor a follower of Herr Freud's. Here we build upon the work of Herr Erwin Lazar. Until recently he was Director of this Clinic.

Here Fräulein Weiss raises her eyes heavenwards and clasps her hands together saying: We return always to Dr Lazar's question – what gift is the child offering us?

Then she sees Franz Joseph ~

1.b. The Stupidest Clever Person You Will Ever Meet

I am alone. Fräulein Weiss has swept Grandmother away. The Door of her Office closes with a teeth-snapping click. Suitcases, Trains. Who is expecting me? Opa is saying – *Girl, stop dreaming and think-thinkthink* but I cannot. I need to get away but the Door is locked, the key on the Nurse's belt.

A Door opens and a boy is Staring at me. Sticks out his tongue – slow as a lazy lizard. (He is short, plump and has black hair oiled and slicked to one side. His face is round as a plate, his eyes shine like black marbles above fleshy cheeks.) I know this boy and he knows me. He also attends the hated Robert Hamerling-Realgymnasium although he is four years older.

He is known to be a Troublemaker. Now he is with another boy (most tall and pale with eyes both intense and vacant). Both lads are wearing white coats hanging down onto the floor, also holding clipboards as though they are Doctors. The Plump Boy is saying – *No Point in running. The Police will catch you.*

The Tall Boy speaks in a machine voice: Clearly a persistent Bedwetter.

I head towards a Door. There must be a Back Staircase.

Plump boy: Not that Door, Matchbox. Behind that Door is an Actual Dinosaur.

I look towards the long windows near the Reception Desk.

Plump boy: Sheer drop. But do not fear. I am the Führer of this Ward. We already have a copy of the Paperwork. Incidentally, this is my Business Partner, Gottfried. A Penguin, sadly, and damn boring, but useful. Possibly the stupidest clever Person you will ever meet. OK, Gottfried. Read it out. Only the relevant bits. None of that *limited social skills and lack of imaginative play etcetcetc.*

Gottfried says in that same machine voice: Inappropriate interest in Rats.

Plump boy: No. I said *not* that stuff. What are they going to do with her?

Gottfried: The Special Children's Home in Pressbaum ~

The Words hit the floor with the force of bricks dropped from Heaven. Plump boy shakes his head, crosses himself. Both juveniles downturn their mouths saying – *Time to get your affairs in order. Soon be boarding the 71 Tram.* This I understand. Wilhelm from the Fifth Form. Dead. Very Definitely Dead. He got sent to the Special Children's Home in Pressbaum.

Which was not surprising since he was ten and still crawling on the floor. Pneumonia? In Truth, he got pushed in a Freezing Bath and they held his head under the water until he Drowned. Children from our School saw him in his Coffin. Waxen and angelic with flowers in his tiny clawed hands. Halfway To Heaven But Beside Him A Sponge And A Bar Of Soap.

Plump boy: Honestly, Matchbox. What are you doing? Do you want to Choke on a Sponge? Collecting Matchboxes? That is no way to live. You need a Strategy. Now.

Just like Opa – *Thinkthinkthink*. Key. I move towards the Desk Drawers.

Plump boy: No Point. Sister Krämer has clipped it on her belt. Best chance is to stay here, right in this Ward. Problem is they don't admit many. Only around twenty and they don't want your General Bedwetter and Drooler. Their tastes are – how can I say? Specialist.

A voice calls: Boys, where are you? What are you doing?

Plump boy whispers: Create a Distraction. If in doubt, piss on somebody ~

The curtains and the benches are shuddering and shrieking. How would I actually piss on somebody? A rushing-and-running-and-rabbiting starts in the Corridor. A Person swallows a scream. This is Not Happening because Wilhelm is Drowning or because I will Drown. I feel our City and I know it. Something else – not just in this Hospital.

What Opa would call *the Alchemy of Circumstance* but should properly be called Causation. Meaning how one thing leads on Logically from another except it usually doesn't. I wanted a Distraction and the World is providing one. Fräulein Weiss appears from her Office, gripping the side of her face. Has she got toothache?

Surely despite her teeth she will help me? Which Door shall I choose? Perhaps the one with the missing plaque? The Spider-Nurse appears followed by Ruby-Red Shoes. A laundry cart rolls behind them, pushed by a Man who is mountainously large, with his head shrunk below his shoulder blades. His arms hang long and his dark hair is shaved close to his head.

He spins the laundry cart as though it has no weight. Says: Had it from a taxi driver. Trying to take someone to the Ballhausplatz but the area is now closed off. They stormed the building. An announcement on the Radio.

Fräulein Weiss's clipboard slides from her hand. I am swallowing Freezing Water. Opa, can you not help me? A siren sounds from the Street. *Hail Mary, full of Grace, the Lord is with You.* Garbled warnings are being whispered through the light fittings. My bones are turning to butter.

All will soon become Darkness and Chaos and Disorder and no gleam of light to be found anywhere. A Crack and a Bang sound outside. The vast encrusted facades of the buildings opposite will be shattered. The windows will splinter and blow out, showering glass across the Streets. Dustdustdust. A jagged hole revealing broken staircases, and tilted rooms.

Run, run. I will not be able to take my Satchel with me. I drop it on a nearby table. My Notebooks and Maps and Matchboxes are tumbling out. Nonono. I cannot leave them.

Laundry Man: At the Chancellery. They have taken Dr Dollfuß hostage. Not just taken hostage. What they are saying is – *Shot.*

People are speaking all at once: *Dollfuß was the only Man who could save us. The Italians? They will come to our Aid? You can wave goodbye to an independent Austria now. There will be another Civil War. Well, if you want to find out, I'd be inclined to ask Professor Hamburger. He'd be the one to know.* Laundry Man shrugs: Only a choice between our Fascists and theirs ~

1.c. A Dinosaur Defeated with Matchboxes

Did this shocking news from the Chancellery cause concern? Yes – but not as much as it properly should because in my Country of Austria someone is always blowing up some Person, or shooting them, or breaking their windows. Opa says – *Vienna, bloody powder keg. Guns left over from the War in every Cellar-Attic-Drain.*

Yet this current Story is so Extreme only a Fool would believe it. However, just as I know that Opa is Absolutely Alive so I also know that our Chancellor is Definitely Dead. But I have not a moment to consider this because it is now All Too Clear that I have chosen the Wrong Door. No back staircase appears, not even a cupboard in which one might hide.

I am trapped. Worse than that, this room is not empty. A tall Young Man – a Boy – is seated at a desk. I expect this Boy to look up but he doesn't seem to have heard any of the Extremely Loud Noise now taking place. Better to stay or go back? Against the wall is an Elephantine Bookcase. To the side a small gap between the Bookcase and the Wall.

I press myself into that gap. From here I can see both the Reception Area and this room. I will know if anyone touches my Satchel. A crucifix hangs on the wall. The legs of our Lord are broken and his feet are far below his knees. Outside in the Corridor, people and pot plant and Filing Cabinets are chattering.

Saying: *The Heimwehr are on their way with a force of many Men. They will storm the building and bring the Nazis out. The Italians will send troops to the border. They will defend the independence of our Fatherland. Just when we thought that we might have Peace. People will not accept this. Can we not put the Radio on ~*

The Professor Hamburger music-playing Door crashes open and a Man (sparse hair, high forehead, pince-nez and no lips) steps out. His chest puffs up like an offended parrot. His eyebrows shoot up and down, threatening those fragile lenses. Saying: Is this a Hospital or a Zoo? Staff will not engage in Senseless Gossip. Where is Dr A? Is the Man Deaf?

Dr A does not appear but the Young Man springs up, adjusts his glasses, gulps. He moves towards the Door. He wears a white coat which is too short over a saggy suit. His head is nearly touching the towering ceiling and on top of this lofty height he has blond hair in tight curls. His arms and legs hinge awkwardly, a strong wind would blow him flat.

He looks at me and our eyes meet. His Matchboxes are about to be torn up and shoved down the loo. *Idiot, Simpleton, deaf-mute.* Yet even in this moment of Fear, I see something which digs deep inside me and which I will not Forget. What I see is how this Young Man does assemble himself, putting on his Life as though putting on a coat.

Then taking a deep breath and instructing his bones to become steel. Giving Instructions to himself about how to *behave Appropriately*. All of this I Know, I Recognise. Yet seeing it Performed in front of me is the arrival of a Sudden Startling Truth ~

The Now-Assembled Boy strides across the room and pauses a moment before stepping out into the Reception Area. He steps forward with a slight bounce, a squeezed smile. He should be wearing short trousers but they have let him wear long ones today. His face has a trembling, rodent uncertainty. Regretfully, he has not noticed that the not-in-there Door has opened.

Young Man: Ah yes, Professor Hamburger. Ah yes. My apologies.

A Dinosaur appears and flaps his wings, squawks.

Young Man: Quiet. Immediately.

He says this rather loudly and forcefully while knowing that no one will listen.

Young Man: Quiet. Please. Ahem. As I have said.

The Offended Parrot has spotted the winged Dinosaur who is now flapping towards him. The parrot's eyebrows shoot to the ceiling. He says that he must not be disturbed again. He must make important telephone calls. Disappears back into his Office, slamming the Door. The Young Man sags. The winged Dinosaur has alighted on the top of a large cupboard.

Young Man: Is there a Problem?

The spider-haired Nurse reports that, indeed, there is a Problem. The Young Man is expecting her to comment on the Dinosaur. Clearly, he is a Person who can miss a Suitcase even if he has stumbled over it. The Nurse relays the news about the Chancellor. The Young Man says: Ah. Ah. Anyway, one shouldn't listen to Rumour and Gossip. Please continue with your work. We take no notice of Politics here ~

The Young Man thinks he has been saved from these Many Dangers but far worse is about to descend upon him. For Oma has broken out of Fräulein Weiss's Office. I was hoping that she might have stumbled into a Freezing Bath. First, she looks for me. Sniff, sniff. Yet she only glances at me briefly before continuing with her Strategy.

At the same time – this being the problem that too many things are Happening at the Same Time – a different Nurse appears. She walks with a tripping step and her eyes are full of Dangerous Enthusiasm. She is slim and neat, the wisps of brown hair which stick out from under her white-dove hat are soft as sheep's wool. A halo of light shines all around her.

She is clearly a Person who is *Wonderful with Children*. I particularly dislike such people, but the Cruelties of the World are such that, like a magnet, I attract them. I am Extremely Worried that this Angel Nurse will pull me out from where I am hiding but she is focused on the winged Dinosaur on top of the cupboard.

She begins to talk to him in a sweet and calming voice. The Young Man goes to stand beside her as though he is part of this rescue operation although in Truth, he is simply hovering, looking embarrassed, as well one might. Alas, he is woefully unaware that he has left himself open to Oma-ly attack.

Oma: Excuse me, Young Man. I need to speak to Dr A.

Young Man: Ahem. I am Dr A.

Oma is aghast. What can the World be coming to when a Dithering Teenager is allowed to become a Director at the Hospital? As the owner of a famous Viennese Café, Oma is able to Assess Most Meticulously the quality of a piece of steak and she is no less good at reading the Human Signs. Even the recent purchase of Quality Shoes cannot disguise the poor cut of his suit.

He may be considered Brilliant, he may have come top of every class at School and University, but Oma is not Fooled. The A Family. Sniff. Provincial people. In these troubled Times, how such families progress. Yet still the whiff of Agriculture hangs about them. This Young Man may have a salary of 120 schillings a month.

Yet his father, in the lowly Accountants' Office in Burggasse, earns less. No amount of Quality Shoes can disguise the fact he is still the Child that no one plays with in the Schoolyard. Easy to push a worm down the back of his shirt.

The Angel Nurse: A Diplodocus? Or a Tyrannosaurus Rex?

Dr A: Wings. Pterodactyl.

The Dinosaur is starting the descent from the top of the cupboard. Might he bring the whole structure crashing down? The pleading plasterwork wobbles and wavers. Oma knows that everyone is distracted now – the news about the Chancellor, the Dinosaur roaming loose, the swinging cupboard – all this she will exploit.

Oma: It has all been discussed.

Dr A: Ah yes. Ah yes.

Distractedly, he takes the Papers and walks towards the table, lifting a pen from the pocket of his white coat. Dr A's right hand curls around awkwardly as he reaches to sign – but then he stops. On the table in front of him is my bag – Albums, Notebooks, Maps and carrot peelings for Franz Joseph etcetcetc.

Dr A: Adelheid Brunner? Down the side of the cupboard?

Oma: Yes. Fräulein Weiss quite understands my Point. Arrangements have been made. Since my husband's Death. Sniff. I really cannot be expected. Next week it will be the Funeral. How can I take that Child to such an Occasion when she is certain to bring Shame upon me?

Strategy, Strategy. *Thinkthinkthink.* I step forward. Carrot peelings are no good when you need to save your Life. I do not have skills in the impersonating of Dinosaurs. I must put on my Life like a coat. Adelheid – Please try to remember what a well-behaved Catholic girl with Appropriate Community spirit would do.

Yet I can do nothingnothingnothing. Dr A stretches out his hand towards my Notebooks. Then his eyes fix upon my Matchboxes and he picks up an Envelope instead. Those Matchboxes do not have any problem in knowing What To Do. Immediately, they open their arms and pull Dr A into their Safe World. Neat squares, tiny territories, forever the same.

Mysteriously, Dr A knows that he must not attempt visual engagement or direct communication, yet he says: Marvellous, marvellous. A shame some have been damaged. Oil. However, only the envelopes, not the Matchboxes themselves. I am sure they can be salvaged.

This he says but the damage is Severe. All this being what ensued since the Incident which was caused by the phone call reporting Opa's Non-Death. Which I did write in my Notebooks. Oma then blaming me for everything, accusing me of *Writing Lies*. Burning my Writing and the oil being upset onto the Matchboxes ~

I need Floor Tiles. Yet I must focus on Dr A who has taken out the many sheets of Paper which I use to create my Matchbox Album Plans. He can immediately see how these sheets relate to the Matchboxes and understand the Planning I am doing. This being an issue of Categorisation how the Matchboxes must be best Organised.

Now he asks: Why all the numbers?

Oma sighs like a hurricane.

Dr A is leafing through the Pages: Oh, I see. Through to One Thousand? Quite a Collection you are planning. Our colleague Dr Frankl will be most interested. You are a serious Phillumenist, I see. (This word he uses meaning A Collector of Matchboxes.)

He stretches out a hand towards one of my Notebooks. Oma moves at the same time. She is thinking that she should have burnt all the Notebooks. Yet she is not quick enough to intercept even this one. She steps back, clears her throat like a lion roaring: I don't consider that it is helpful for people to encourage her.

Dr A: On the contrary, an interest in collecting is a normal childhood activity. We all have our little obsessions, don't we?

Oma releases another tree-felling sigh: I personally do not.

Dr A has his eyes fixed most intensely on my Notebooks.

Oma is saying: Absolute Nonsense. Cannot rely upon one Word.

Dr A takes no notice, continues to look, saying: Ah. Ah. Such Writings, Adelheid. Wonderful. I see that you like to make most detailed Observations and Reports. Clearly, you are a Scribe, an observer and chronicler of events. Writing can certainly bring some Order to the Chaos. Do you not think so?

Oma can Forgive Fanciful Nonsense coming from a Jewish woman but not from an upstanding young Catholic Doctor whose father is an accountant etcetcetc. She is so close to that train but what of red plush seats, coffee, gravy? Also, the front windows of the Café since they have been broken twice before.

Saying: Someone more senior? Professor Hamburger? I know his wife.

Oma has pushed The Wrong Button.

Dr A: We will be admitting Adelheid to the Hospital here for a few days.

Oma: That is not The Arrangement.

This she says but hurried calculations are clicking across her face. She may undoubtedly wish to be rid of me and yet the Truth is that she is also highly dependent on all my Domestic Work – although this she would never admit.

Oma: How long would she be with you?

Dr A: That I cannot say. The nature of our Observations. Usually a month.

Oma: Butbutbut. The train is booked.

Dr A: Frau Brunner. It is not for the school to decide, or for you to dictate, what happens in this Case. In this Ward, we never give up on a child. Never.

Dr A continuing in saying much stuff about our sovereign, Catholic duty etcetcetc. This is not a good route to take because in the game of Catholic v Catholic Oma will always out-Catholic any opponent.

The Dinosaur makes a loud snuffling noise – more pig than Dinosaur. Oma is brimful of righteous disappointment, wounded and struggling under so many burdens, but Dr A has remembered his lines now and he will not be stopped: I am the Director of this Ward. A decision has been made. Best reputation in the World. Success rate second to none.

All my strength has dripped away. I am tiredtiredtired. I need to find somewhere to hide. Dr A is asking if he may look at another Notebook. He is a Man who understands Observations, Reports and the Proper Ordering of the World. I push a Notebook towards him. With a slight bow, he stretches out his hand. His left hand ~

1.d. A Cupboard Full of Matchboxes

In the Writing of Books much time is being wasted on the repeating of The Same Information. Perhaps that is not such a problem in a Small Account but if I am to explain accurately all the oddities of the Curative Education Ward in the Children's Hospital of Vienna then this is a longlonglong work.

Therefore, in order to make my Account clearer I shall tell You of the things that are Always Happening in this Aforementioned Ward. You can then make an Assumption that this is materialising even if You have not been directly told. The most important Point being this Ward is meant to control Badly Disciplined Children and yet has No Discipline At All.

First, there is always a Child – I use that word loosely – engaging in Dinosaur and cupboard type *Inappropriate Behaviour*. Whooping, stumbling, pushing, hitting, babbling. Some freak banging their head on the floor, or wailing, or throwing a book, pissing-not-in-the-WC, biting a Nurse or another Child etcetcetc.

This Person will generally have big-ears-chewed-plaits-crooked-teeth-bent-back or high-up-shoe or leg-brace and is called Otto-Heinrich-Johannes-Kaspar or Liesl-Anna-Maria-Helene. These Children I do most thoroughly dislike and heartily dread. In particular, their sticky, sweaty, smelly skin and their hot close breath.

Anyway, I am not going into the details each time. You understand, I am sure.

Opa would say: *Last seen in the background of a Breughel painting.*

Or: *Hospital? I have seen better organised Bloody Riots* ~

Also, the staff of this Ward. First Angel Nurse who is called Sister Viktorine. She is always spreading her hands wide as though to catch all the Many Mercies which are dropping on us from God in Heaven. Saying: This is not a Hospital. Instead, a caring home where the Doctors and Nurses and the Children all live together happily.

This is the kind of Rot she says againagainagain. In addition, the other Nurses are rather the same. All in their dove-winged caps and starched aprons, clotting stockings, brick-like shoes. In some cases literally most similar to each other, there being three Nurses with spider-hair but different sizes. Are they actually changing size?

Adelheid – Do not engage in fanciful rumination. Yet they are, indeed, most like Russian dolls. Tall, medium, small. Their names being Sister Maria Krämer – who You have already encountered in this Story. The medium being Sister Elena and the smallest Sister Anna. Other Nurses are also called Sister Amalie-Frieda-Valentina-Birgit etcetcetc.

The Doctors being more complicated to explain. Dr Feldner is a Man I recognise as he comes to the Café and has also come to my School. However, he is a Man that I could not understand in my Actual Life and even now (with the help of many Dusty Documents, Records etcetcetc.) I am still quite unable to explain his many eccentricities.

Tall, thin, clumsy with a narrow face and not too much hair. A bulbous nose and a reputation for gambling. Can this be true? Perhaps it is for he is often doing foolish things such as organising a relay race round the School Room, the baton being a rolled-up pair of socks. Children stumblingfallingdropping the baton. When someone finally wins, Dr Feldner goes down on his knees, raises his hands to Heaven. Not *Appropriate Behaviour*.

Dr Frankl who is quite different but equally mysterious. (Small, neat, meticulous, watchful.) Generally, he is sitting on the floor, helping a child to play with building blocks. Dr Frankl builds the Tower and the child knocks it down – againagainagain. He suggests to build a Fort or a Farm but the child just keeps knocking down the bricks.

Or even throws them across the Room, or hurls them at Dr Frankl himself. Why does Dr Frankl not slap that Child? Yet it seems Dr Frankl does not care about the Fort or the Farm. Perhaps he is like me and sees how interesting Floor Tiles can be and also Blades of Grass. Certainly he just staresstaresstares and thinksthinksthinks.

In this Account I am writing many Watchers are Watching and Watched. Yet all are Blind. You will see ~

That first day I sit in the Meeting Room in a vast chair made of buttery velvet most pleasant to smooth with my hand. Often, I am apparently reading. I do have a reputation as a keen reader of factual books. Not entirely Untrue. But books are also useful for putting in front of your face so you do not have to talk to anyone.

Occasionally the Nurses come – *would I like to do singing?* Nonono. *Or play skittles?* Nonono. *Might I need books or drawing pencils?* Nonono. *We are rehearsing a play. Maybe I might take a part?* I keep my book most firmly in front of my face. *Shall I find a box for your rat?* That I do allow for poor Franz Joseph is also most exhausted.

That Meeting Room chair has a view down over the Garden. I did not know that a Garden would exist at a Hospital. This carefully tended Garden with many Blades-of-Grass-to-Count is at the back, in between the three blocks which make up the Children's Hospital. At the front being where the buildings of the Main Hospital are situated.

In those first hours, I keep my Satchel pressed tightly against me. But in the afternoon Sister Viktorine says I will now have a locker for my Possessions. I can keep hold of the locker key myself so I will not have to worry about people who may snoop, burn, upset pots of cooking oil etcetcetc.

I hear Sister Viktorine whisper to Sister Maria who is the largest spider-haired Nurse. *Don't try and touch her, don't take the bag, don't look at her directly, don't ask Questions. Also, you know about her Grandfather? Best not to say anything. Confused.* Not Confused, just tired from many nights of not sleeping.

Dreaming and drowsy now so that it becomes hard to know – what is Real and what Imagined. From close the clattering of Washing Up and the opening and shutting of Filing Cabinets. News exchanged about the Chancellery. Sometimes the distant ringing of sirens and shouts from the Streets. Maybe gun shots, maybe the exhaust of a car?

Later I recover, start to make some Observations in my Notebooks. So much to record ~

Sister Viktorine interrupting me to ask if I would like help with my Matchboxes. Perhaps we could find some new method of keeping my Matchboxes Clean and in neat Categories. Sister Viktorine comes with excellent cardboard Files. She also brings a kettle hence I can steam off the stained Paper on which some of the injured Matchboxes are stuck.

When it is supper time, I fear that I will have to eat with the other Children but Sister Viktorine says a tray can be brought to the Meeting Room. Medium-sized spider-haired Nurse Sister Anna brings the tray. Soggy vegetables and stringy meat. Undoubtedly sauces thickened with flour. The meat will not go down my throat.

I expect Sister Viktorine will say, as Oma does – *Stop picking at your food*. Instead she tells Sister Anna to fetch a bread roll. This warm roll has butter melting inside and I break it up into little pieces. Much better than pieces of meat which stay stuck in my stomach, the jagged edges of them pressing against me inside ~

Soon that same Plump Boy appears, introduces himself as Adolf Schreiber, saying: For God's sake, Matchbox. What are you doing? Sleeping is not a Strategy.

He is Quite Right. I must not fall into another Suitcase Situation. Yet how can I have a Strategy when I do not know the Rules of how this World works? I must at least establish fully where I am and how one may exit this building in a hurry. I might use one of my Notebooks to draw a Map.

Adolf says: Want me to show you around? Sister Vik says I can. Come on.

Saying then: First things first. You understand what is going on here? Famous place this. Visitors coming from all over the World. Because they study Cabbage Children. Or Mental Hygiene, or Moral Degeneracy. I know, weird. Really Weird.

He shakes his head mournfully, stretches out his hands, saying: You have already got yourself positioned in the Meeting Room. Good move. In general, Children are not allowed. One of the few places where you can get some Peace from the Cabbages. Also, most useful because the kitchen is right next door, meaning while you do Washing Up you can hear all that is said in the Meeting Room. You understand?

I most certainly do understand.

Adolf gestures then, saying: More important still. This alcove here – which can be accessed from the Meeting Room and the Reception Area – is where the Filing Cabinets are. Conveniently also right next to the kitchen. I personally find that there is much Washing Up to be done and it can be worth doing it twice. You understand?

Adolf is clearly a Person who understands Observations.

He is also saying: The Code around here is *I Have Lost a File*. You get what a Code is? Means the Doctors or Nurses want a private conversation. Stubborn stains on the plates. You need to be Properly Informed if you want to stay safe. Particularly now. More so than ever today. The Chancellery? You get my Point?

I absolutely understand his Point. Adolf is a Person Most Useful to me. If I do not have Opa to tell me What To Do, then Adolf may instruct instead ~

He then points to the desk where the Film Star lady usually sits: Fräulein Eder. Secretary to Professor Hamburger. Not a fan of mine, sadly. Of course, Hamburger is the Director of the whole Hospital and it is just bad luck that his Office chances to be here.

We move on and Adolf indicates a Narrow Door crammed at the end of a Corridor. Says: Back staircase. Vital, of course. Also, stairs to the Roof Terrace.

Roof Terrace? He is making that up.

He points from one Door to another: Nursery, Dining Room, School Room. Offices of the Doctors. You've already met the charmless Fräulein Weiss. Plus, Dr Frankl. Quiet chap. No Trouble. Interested in dogs. And Dr Feldner. Bigger delinquent than me. Then Erwin Jekelius. Most gracious. Popular with the Nurses. Nothing ever sticks to that Man.

He points now towards a Door which is near the entrance to the Ward. He explains that this is the Storeroom which contains bed linen, mops, all that Domestic Clutter. Here is a large Cupboard which is the kind of place where Matchboxes live. I can feel Matchbox 562 somewhere close, within my reach. Adolf tugs open the Cupboard Door. I am gasping.

A shelf full of Matchboxes. I don't mean Boxes of Matches. I mean, a Box containing maybe Hundreds of Matchboxes. Hundreds. All of them are shouting at me. *Take me, take me, take me.* Not just Matchbox 562 but 563, 564, 565, 566. Adolf takes a Matchbox, pushes it into his pocket, slams the cupboard. Says: Don't behave like a drooling Idiot ~

1.e. Dangerous Doors and a Nation Mourns

Nonononono. Medium-sized spider-haired Sister Elena is saying that it is now time to go to the Dormitory. How will I sleep? I do not enjoy being with other people. I like to be in my own bedroom with the Door Shut and the Window Unlocked so that – being on the ground floor – I may climb out whenever I want.

As we enter the long Dormitory, a terrible sight is revealed. Cabbages are everywhere. The worst is twin Cabbages who appear to be joined together. Only three legs between them. Adolf pushes these conjoined Cabbages, and several others, out of the way, so that they fall like dominoes. I hold on tight to Franz Joseph who is trembling in my pocket.

Thus, we make it through to the end of the room. Here I note that mercifully there is a Small Door (which I hope may lead to a back staircase). Adolf says: Not meant to use that Door. But you can. Stay down this end – with me and the Penguins. I do a good job of keeping Order. Been in and out of this place For Years.

I find that most fateful Suitcase placed on a bed near that small Door.

Adolf says: Let me introduce you to the Penguins. Gottfried, Anton, Elias, Thomas the Spaceship, Bruno the Book. Known as Penguins as they are always flapping. Good chaps. Follow Instructions. Boring as Shit but key to my Strategy. I make sure they stay here. Otherwise, you just get someone trained up and then they are gone. Disaster.

Adolf pulls a pair of silk pyjamas out of his bedside cabinet.

Continues: Anyway, as you can see. Different kind of Cabbages. Beyond the Penguins, the Sluts. Always rubbing their tits or licking their lips. Probably already got The Clap. Nice girl like you wants to keep well out of that. Then, in the even darker regions of this Dormitory, what can I say?

Adolf shakes his head mournfully. Combs his hair. Sprays himself with cologne. Turns back to me: Clearly, I myself am not a Cabbage. Or indeed a Specialist Idiot. I am just a Regular Delinquent and I'm only here until my mother gets a better job. Quite crowded at home. All down to good Sister Vik, God Bless her. Are you listening? By Christ. What is that ~

I fear he might seize Franz Joseph, but just at that moment, Sister Viktorine enters the Ward, claps her hands. Everyone is to be silent and stand near the foot of their bed as Dr A has an important announcement to make. Dr A comes into the Dormitory and shuffles uncertainly, stands erect, places his hands behind his back, says mournfully: Sadly, I must tell you that our dear Chancellor Dr Dollfuß has been taken to his Eternal Rest.

Jaws clatter to the floor. Eyeballs are similarly dislodged. Door handles shudder, the sheets on the beds press themselves down even flatter than before. I lose my grip on Franz Joseph and he jumps from my hands. Adolf watches him disappear under the bed but we neither of us dare move.

Dr A says: However. Ahem. Mercifully our noble Heimwehr have suppressed those rebels who were responsible for these acts of aggression against our Government. These Men of Violence have now been apprehended and Peace is fully restored.

Franz Joseph has skittered away under one of the bedside cabinets. I was Quite Right. The Chancellor has undoubtedly *boarded the 71 Tram*. If Opa were here, he would be phoning reports to London and Paris, maybe New York. Children are weeping even though I suspect that many of them do not understand what is being said.

The voice of Dr A continues: A State Funeral will take place this Saturday and Dr Dollfuß will be carried from the Ballhausplatz to the Stephansdom and from that Cathedral to his Grave. From there he will enter the Proud History of our Fatherland ~

Shocking news – but I am more interested in Franz Joseph. Is he still under the bedside cabinet or has he moved on? I am about to start searching when Sister Viktorine appears and shows me the bathroom where I am to get changed. I find it most elegant and temperate. Much better than the washroom at home, which is across the Courtyard, the water frozen in winter. But I have no time for bathrooms, and return to the Dormitory. Franz Joseph? Where? When I return, Adolf has changed into his much-too-large silk pyjamas and is examining a gap under the skirting board.

Saying from the floor: Died for the Fatherland? What the deuce. That's not what Herr Spellbinder told me. You know, Spellbinder? The Laundry Man. Says Dollfuß was shot in the head as soon as the Nazis got into the Chancellery. They wouldn't even allow him a doctor or a Priest though blood was gushing out of his Head. Six hours he was there – dead.

Adolf crawls across the floor to search under a wardrobe: Apparently, the Heimwehr offered safe passage to the border for the Nazis if they surrendered but then they found the body. Not even properly covered up.

Adolf raises his head now and addresses these next words to all around: Now apparently those Nazis will pay for the crimes on the gallows. Except that more Nazis are now in Styria and the Italians are massed on the border. And the Heimwehr? Not always possible to say exactly where their sympathies lie. The Nazis will take the City unless the Socialists stop them ~

One of the Sluts has arranged her hair in a glamorous coiffure and has rolled a piece of Paper into a Pretend cigarette. She says she is most glad to have been invited to the Funeral. A group of small Children are hidden under a bed blubbering etcetcetc. As I said, I am not going into the details Every Single Time This Happens.

Bruno the Book starts talking in a booming voice: *This is all the result of the War reparations. The German peoples must stand up to the bullying British with their Peace Treaties.* The way Bruno talks being an exact example of what is called a Tram Track. I do know as Opa goes off like this and once the Tram has departed nothing may stop it.

Bruno clearly being unaware that he will soon say the Wrong Thing and get himself in Trouble. Opa told me not to speak and I take his advice. Also, it is best for me not to draw Conclusions as they will too often be Wrong. Soon they will be burning Bruno's Notebooks and putting him on a train with Frau Vogt, our nasty old Caretaker.

Finally, I manage to get a grip on Franz Joseph.

Adolf barks: Shut up, Bruno. Just shut up.

Still Bruno is announcing: *One third of our population unemployed. One must ask if our poor little rump of a Country is economically viable? After the War, the Czechoslovaks got the coal, the Italians got the steel. How now can we live in these Times? A Great Empire of fifty million reduced to a mere seven.*

Adolf shakes his head, turns back to me. He is organising his hair in a neat quiff, talking over Bruno's toneless lecture: Anyway, they'll need a small coffin to put our Millimetternich in. What with him being so small. Don't want him rattling around in there. Personally, I never had any time for the Man. All Socialists where I come from.

We are called to the bathroom to clean our teeth. Adolf and the Penguins do not go and hence I stay with them. Bruno is still jabbering and blabbering. Adolf says: Bloody awful. The chap's a Nightmare. Just repeating the last thing he read againagainagain.

Small-Nurse Sister Anna tells us to hurry up. By now the bathroom is not crowded.

As I am leaving, in the darkness of the Corridor, I see Adolf and he is walking behind Bruno, pushing him towards another Door.

I know how this goes. *Idiot, Simpleton, deaf-mute.* Bruno is fighting, his hand twists, but Adolf pushes Bruno's fingers against the Door Frame and then pulls the Door sharply, making sure that Bruno's fingers are trapped. Bruno buckles but makes no sound. He knows not to tell.

Adolf saying: Now shut your damn mouth, will you? I have warned you before.

He sees me looking. His eyes calculate. Bruno has disappeared into the Dormitory, whimpering. I try not to look at Adolf. My fingers are screaming in Fear. Adolf hisses: Stop bloody well staring. Freak with Rats and Matchboxes. Maybe decide to see a bit less. Or only See what I tell you to See ~

The Dormitory is silent. The lights are out. Adolf is sitting on his bed, smoking. My fingers are aching where they are about to get crushed. Adolf says: You must understand. It's a full-time job keeping things under control here. Bloody Doctors and Nurses no good. New Man Dr A. Harmless drip. What we need is someone who cares about Discipline.

Adolf tosses Matchbox 562 up into the air, catches it neatly, says: I need people who have a Brain. Friday is the day when the Doctors have their Meeting. This Friday could be bad. If you are going to be transferred – to Pressbaum or wherever, or even just sent home – that is when they decide.

He leans towards me, holds the Matchbox close. I put out my hand but he snatches the Matchbox away. His hand grips my throat, pushes me down. The lighted tip of his cigarette is dancing close. I struggle but his hand is an iron claw. He fixes me with his blank eyes, says: Have we got a deal?

Even though he continues to grip my throat, yet still I nod my head until it is loose on its hinges. Adolf seems satisfied, lets go of my bruising neck, gives me a notentirelyserious Nazi salute, presents the Matchbox to me with a flourish, as though it is an engagement ring. The Matchbox nestles in my shivering hand ~

I cannot sleep. I can never sleep. This is why I don't know what is Real and what is Dreaming. Out in the Corridor, I hear the voice of Sister Viktorine. She is speaking to Dr A who is on his way to Mass. The churches are all open tonight as the Country is in mourning. *God bless Dr Dollfuß. We must pray for his Soul.*

I imagine Dr Dollfuß as I saw him in the newspapers. A Toy Soldier hardly taller than me and yet wanting to be taken seriously with his many medals and his military hat. Such an Important Man yet was there not something of the Music Hall about him? That silly moustache and his smile rather too Cheery? Can he really be Dead?

Later Adolf takes a blanket out of the cupboard and folds it tightly. He pulls back the sheets and organises the blanket into a sleeping-body shape. I have done this Childish trick often enough myself. Adelheid – Keep your eyes shut. Pretend to know nothing. That's what Opa says and I follow his advice.

After Adolf has edged through that small Door, I go to the Window, look out across our City. I see now below what You may also know. How Vienna grew like a tree in ever-expanding rings. So that within the Ringstraße exist the very same streets where Beethoven and Haydn played and where the United Rulers of Christendom met in the Stephansdom to give thanks for their salvation from the Turks.

That Old part of the City maintaining still that Fairy Tale glitter of Magic and Light – all situated less than a mile from where I now Watch. Green domes, yearning spires, skylighted roofs. A jewellery box piled high with paste diamonds and glass rubies. An optical illusion, both intricate and epic. All flimsy façade and gold leaf rubbed thin. A maze without a centre so that you turnandturnandturn again but you will never find your way in.

Yet all that Grand Past is finished and we are now the State Without Qualities. We exist in a World where everything has Already Happened ~

1.f. A Scribe Records the Friday Meeting

On Friday, I am ready. Gottfried will record the Meeting itself. This he will do by hiding in a good-size cupboard in the Meeting Room. I also am responsible for Writing. An excellent job for me as Dr A has most accurately recognised my abilities as a Scribe and Chronicler of Events. I am to wait in the Cloak Room at five o'clock.

After the Meeting everyone will come into the Cloak Room to get their coats. What is said in the Meeting is Important but what is said afterwards is the Meat of the Matter. I did many tasks of this kind for Opa. *Wait here. Keep watch. Don't say anything.* First, I take three Matchboxes out of the Store cupboards.

Numbers 563, 564, 565. That creates the problem of what to do with the Matches themselves. (Most Important to note that although they are called Safety Matches, they are Not At All Safe.) Mercifully, at this time, the Children are having milk and a slice of bread and butter and Fräulein Eder is not present.

A plant pot stands near her desk and so I tip the Matches into a gap between the plant itself and the tall china pot in which it stands. Then I flatten the Boxes out, therefore I can put them in my pocket. A moment later, I hear the Doctors coming, so I take up my position. Initially, the Doctors are talking about the Funeral which is taking place the next day.

Then the talk changes as the Doctors reach for their coats ~

Dr Frankl: Personally, I like young Dr A. A bit stiff but enthusiastic and basically decent. I'm not sure what aptitude he has for this work – but one may yet be surprised.

Dr Feldner: Good of you to be generous – under the circumstances.

Dr Frankl: Oh, I've no bad feelings. They were never going to appoint me. Can't trust the degenerate and perfidious Jew.

Fräulein Weiss reaches for her coat: Well, fine. Just as long as he knows he is actually working for you, not the other way around. If you had been appointed to the job, as everyone knows you should have, we wouldn't be obliged to have all these tedious discussions justifying what we are doing.

Dr Feldner: One always has such discussions. At least we can steer Dr A.

Sister Viktorine: He is undoubtedly a very well-meaning Young Man.

Dr Feldner: More than can be said for Jekelius.

Fräulein Weiss: Of course, but at least we all know what he is. And we know he's Hamburger's Man and we know what Hamburger is.

Sister Viktorine: Anni, dear. Don't. His Door is sometimes open.

Dr Feldner: I'm not so sure. I mean, Hamburger is certainly no Academic, no Doctor either. But the Man does have a genuine passion for social reform.

Fräulein Weiss: For God's sake, Josef, don't be so naïve. Hundreds of people are signing up for the National Socialist cause. It may now be illegal to be a Member, but supporters know that no action will be taken against them – and they are Right.

Dr Feldner: Surely not now? Not after this appalling Incident. Mussolini will not allow it. Thank God. As for Dr A, I'm in agreement with Dr Frankl.

Sister Viktorine: We should invite him to our Thursday evening Runder Tisch. (This referring to the Round Table Discussions of the Doctors.)

Dr Frankl: Yes. We should. We invite Jekelius.

Dr Feldner: Well, yes. But at least he cracks a joke.

The lights go out. The Doctors are all moving towards the Door which leads out of the Ward. I am pondering on their words. *At least we can steer Dr A*. I am most interested to know what exactly *steer* might mean. Clearly, not the same as threatening with a burning cigarette. Could I *steer* Oma? Or will we always finish up careening into the ditch?

Adelheid – Concentrate. You will need to Write This Down.

Sister Viktorine: I do think Dr A would like to be included. He perhaps feels that his situation is not entirely comfortable.

Dr Feldner: Of course. I would have invited him before.

He turns to face the group now at the Door of the Ward, puts his hat on, tilts the brim, raises his eyebrows: One can get on perfectly well with the Man as long as one regards him as a Patient rather than a Doctor ~

1.g. Please Understand the Times

Soon I am going to tell you about how I left the Ward for a day and went to a Funeral. Not the Funeral of our Chancellor which was attended by Five Hundred Thousand. Instead, the most Small and Fake Funeral of my Absolutely Alive Opa. Which was making me most Angry that I must attend, yet at least I have an opportunity to be a Scribe.

Yet before I tell you about the Incidents of that most Troubling Day, I must first explain to you the Politics of my Country of Austria. The Point being that I have already told you about the most violent shooting of our Chancellor but one must have *Breadth of Vision* and understand more widely. This may be best explained as a debate between Oma and Opa.

Such debates having gone on dingdongdingdong all my Life. Why does the child not speak? Why indeed? Debates most ferocious yet often conducted behind closed Doors. One must always be careful of Our Neighbours Upstairs. This being the girls Hildegarde and Gerda Winkler and, more importantly, their parents.

Since Herr Winkler is well known to be a supporter of National Socialism. The Danger being indicated with an upward rolling of Oma's eyes and a jerking back of the head. *I do not want any Trouble here* ~

Yet still all do know that Oma is a firm supporter of Dollfuß and the Fatherland Front. True enough Dollfuß may have suspended Parliament but what choice did he have? Austria was never a Democracy. It is an Imperial Nation. Was Dollfuß not right to suppress the Violent Reds? All that Childish talk of the wonders of Red Vienna.

THE MATCHBOX GIRL

Nowadays, every plumber wants to read Goethe. One has only to look at the Bloody Events of this most recent February. How could such Horrors happen in our City of Whipped Cream and Tolerance? Sighsigh. Sniffsniff. This being a reference to Violent Revolutions in the Socialist Housing Blocks (Karl-Marx-Hof etcetcetc). Socialists shot or put in Prison.

Oma – sitting in the Café with train-plotting Frau Vogt long after midnight when the City has descended into a most fidgeting quiet – would stress that Dr Dollfuß, a staunch Catholic, will surely bring Employment and Discipline back to the City. A Man pledged absolutely to keep Austria as an Independent Country.

Yet she also insists – wiry finger tapping sharply on the table – that nothing good can come of the World now that the Emperor has gone. (Not actually dusting the Emperor's picture, which hangs above the Bar, but you can understand my Point.) Another glass of Schnapps being poured. Frau Vogt and Oma shaking their heads dolefully.

Our dear Emperor was most skilled at suppressing the patchwork of insubordinate Slavs (Empire as Umpire) who all now want their own Tin Pot Nations. Savage hordes to the East – both Bolsheviks and the Infidel. We are the Bulwark which has Twice Repulsed the tide of Islam (1529 and 1683). The problem of Vienna that it is a Western City situated too far East.

Oma also stating her absolute contempt for the Nasty Little House Painter from Braunau am Inn. His ridiculous ill-fitting suits, his silly moustache. Playing at being Emperor. Yet has he not recently suppressed those who were engaging in murderous practices? That thug Röhm and his like. Has the House Painter not demonstrated himself to be a Man of Peace?

Convenient, certainly, to blame him in the matter of Dollfuß's Death but, in Truth, we have more than enough Nazis – that Word whispered as eyes are rolled upwards and heads jerked – on Our Side of the Border. Our Tragic Country squeezed between two Fascist States. We Austrians 7 million against the German 66 million.

Should we not defy the British and throw in the towel with Berlin? How much worse can the situation get? All Germans, though also Austrian ~

Oma may express her views only when decent folk are in bed but Opa says exactly what he wants to anyone and everyone. (He may insult the Austrians roundly with impunity, being himself Hungarian.) If we were to ask about the Murder of Dollfuß he would agree that it was indeed an Appalling Crime – but on no other Point would he find common ground with Oma.

Dollfuß was Shameful in throwing aside the Parliament and imprisoning the Socialists. The people of Vienna just want Work and Decent Wages. They want Peace and an Independent Austria. This Opa would say in his Newspaper Articles and at the Meetings of the Phillumeny Club, when they gathered in the evenings in the Café.

(The Phillumeny Club being apparently a group of Matchbox Collectors, including many old friends, such as the Stationer Herr Wächter etcetcetc. Yet also being a Socialist gathering which is safer if you appear to be looking at Matchboxes. *A Private Meeting, gentlemen.* Our Café being used as a Socialist post box and place to hide documents.

Do not be seen looking directly at the Atlas which lies on a shelf near the Newspaper Racks. Keep the rug in the hall laid out straight. The Atlas being where messages are left. It also being possible to lever up the floorboards in the hall where one might find much Paperwork, many Leaflets, Documents, Reports etcetcetc.)

At the Meeting of the Phillumeny Club, many drinks would go down, and diverse backs would be slapped, plus numerous patriotic songs sung, with reminiscences of the good old days of Red Vienna (the most successful Socialist experiment in Europe) when a New World was being built. The Great Struggle etcetcetc.

No good could ever come of Dollfuß – God rest his soul – and that limp rag Schuschnigg will turn out no better. The Fatherland Front may think they stand on the middle ground but they are stuck in No Man's Land, a strip of ground so narrow that one may hardly find room to place one's foot.

Now Dollfuß is Dead and who was responsible for this? Was it the Reds? It most certainly was not. Everyone worrying about the non-existent Red Terror instead of the all-too-real Brown Terror. *The Socialists would never have fought for Dollfuß. Never. And they will not fight for Schuschnigg.*

They will not rise. Even though the Nazis are at the Frontier. If Schuschnigg wants Austria to remain Independent, he needs the Socialists on his side because half of the City support the worthy Social Democrat cause. Yet so many are in prison or Dead. This is the problem of Austria. *The reaction always too little and too late, then too brutal, too violent.*

How can the good Socialists forget 1927 and the most recent closing down of Parliament or the Events of February? (In all of which events Opa has played his part, not only reporting but manning the barricades.) Glasses banged on the table and noble tears shed ~

Here I shall summarise much repetitive rambling about all the Violence and Insults that have been meted out to the good-hearted Socialists and Communists etcetcetc. Finally, Opa raising his glass high to declare: *Hear this. In truth, everyone knows that Schuschnigg has no Strategy for fighting the Fascists except to become a Fascist himself.*

Many opinions but what is the Truth of this situation? You might deduce that since I am most fond of Opa I would agree with all he says. But I do not, for although a Socialist Uprising is always expected and did, in fact, start to happen in February, the Truth is that the Socialists are struggling to organise even a Matchbox Club.

Opa himself admitting this when in a reasonable mood saying: If you have two Socialists, then you have three opinions. When the moment comes, they will not remember where they hid the Guns. Great talent for holding down a chair. Prefer to be morally right and powerless. Infected by the Great Viennese Vice of Uncertainty etcetcetc. ~

Having now understood this situation of my Country of Austria in the summer of 1934, you will see that it is Not a good idea to go to the Fake Funeral of a Man who is a well-known Socialist journalist. All the latest news being communicated to the Curative Education Ward via Adolf and the Laundry Man (Herr Spellbinder).

Also, that most talkative of Filing Cabinets. Much comment being focused on Professor Hamburger and *the important telephone calls he must make.* This I hear while Sister Viktorine places a neat black hat on my head. She has already helped me to put on a severe and sombre dress which Oma has sent to the Hospital.

The Dress was worn by Upstairs Hildegarde for the funeral procession of Dr Dollfuß. *Hildegarde looked most morosely elegant in it with her hair set in curls.* I care nothing for dresses and hats but old people in this City like Elegant Funerals. There being many to choose from in These Times.

Sister Viktorine now saying: Adelheid, I do understand that you feel strongly that your dear Opa is still with us. Of course, you are Quite Right. This the Church does fully confirm. The Funeral is only the Burial of a Body. The soul continues for all Eternity.

CatholicCatholicCatholic. GodGodGod. She must surely know, since he wrote about this most often, that Opa was an Atheist. I myself am a worshipper of Anubis. (Egyptian God with the Head of an Eagle who puts the Hearts of the Dead on his weighing scales. If your Heart is heavier than the Feather of Truth, you are a Liar and hence he eats up your Heart.)

A Fantastical Story but we can only hope it might be True. Yet not for Sister Viktorine. For even in my few days in this Ward, I have learnt how Useful she can be. Opa may tell me of the Great Struggle but that is no help in my Life. Also, Oma may tell me again and again that I must do what is *Appropriate*.

I hate that word. It is a club for which they never tell you the Rules and therefore you cannot join. What I need is to be told What To Do. Sister Viktorine does explain. *No Rats. No large Satchels. One Notebook in my pocket but no Writing. No wanderingstaringdawdling. Under no circumstances are you to leave Grandmother's side etcetcetc.* ~

Yet still there is one more Question I must explain. That relates to the issue of The Other Suitcase. I hope You are listening. The situation being that my Opa has not been seen for five months. Oma does say to me, and to everyone else, that six months ago he departed suddenly in the direction of Russia on some business to do with Bears, Bolsheviks etcetcetc.

She also says that on that day in February when the Karl-Marx-Hof was shelled, Opa was travelling to Salzburg for a Report on a blown-up railway line. This Information is repeated most often by everyone and reinforced by insistent nodding of heads. I shall not comment. Not at all. Beware of saying the Wrong Thing Freezing Bath, Drowning etcetcetc.

This being all that Oma and I knew for four and a half months. Until two weeks ago when Grandmother received a phone call saying that Opa had had a Heart Attack on his way back from Russia. Which may not sound Very Unlikely except for his Suitcase which is on top of the Wardrobe in the Bedroom.

The obvious question being – who would depart for Russia and fail to take their Suitcase with them? Also, Grandmother is not even a Good Liar. Even though the Police have come asking questions. Yet still she talks about Russia while Not Even Bothering To Take The Suitcase Off The Top Of The Wardrobe And Hide It Somewhere Else ~

1.h. Incidents in the Zentralfriedhof

As I arrive at the Zentralfriedhof (Central Cemetery), my concerns are not dresses, hats or even Suitcases. Instead, I am worried about Coffins and their possible contents. I remain Quite Certain that Opa is not actually Dead. Yet what can I do? I can only try to distract myself with the Sights and Sounds of this Place.

This being relatively easy as the Vienna Central Cemetery is, indeed, a magnificent sight. Situated in the Simmering District, it is a Vast City of the Dead containing the remains of nearly 2 million people. You travel here on the 71 Tram (hence the expression *taking the 71 Tram* which means Dead).

So many avenues and alleyways, marble memorials heavy with angels and crucifixes, gilt letters, cartwheel wreaths, curling iron benches and glades of sorrowful cypress trees. Opa tells me – *Every Viennese wishes to end up as a handsome corpse turning even his Death into a grand show for others to enjoy.*

Therefore, one should walk to one's grave with a large company of mourners. Oma and I are accompanied only by Frau Vogt, Caretaker of our building and Conspirator of the Train Plot. She is a woman with a face like bad carpentry and today she caws like a crow and hops in a cobwebby black coat. She and Oma are endlessly bound together in their Mutual Dislike.

As we come close to the corner of this vast Cemetery where the Fake Funeral is to take place, Oma's worst Fears are confirmed. No doubt many of her customers have sent flowers, notes etcetcetc., but they are not here now. Only the Altmanns are present. They live in the giltmarbleparquet top floor apartment of our building.

That apartment being even grander than the dwelling occupied by the Winklers. Oma thanks them heartily for coming and weeps on Frau Altmann's black silk shoulder saying what Good Neighbours they are etcetcetc. Even Lukas (barman) is not with us although he must be on his way.

Of course, the aforementioned Winklers will certainly not come to the Funeral. Oma rolling her eyes upwards and jerking her head towards the ceiling even though we are miles from our building. (In Truth, we are all enjoying the hope that we may hear a little less now from Herr Winkler due to the recent Violent Events.)

Oma weeps elegantly once again. If she is to be widowed, then she at least wishes to be widowed in some style. As a member of the von Fiquelmont Family, she should surely be entitled to Black Marble and Horses with Nodding Feathers? All this she might enjoy, were it not for the Times and the Mistakes of her Youth ~

Oma does have some cause for complaint as most of the mourners now arriving are from the Karl-Marx-Hof or the other Socialist Housing Blocks. A motley crew of downtrodden types picking their teeth and wearing flat caps. Their shoes not clean and some only in shirt sleeves and braces. Hotel porters, men who work on fruit and vegetable stalls. Even gypsies.

Oma does not talk to these people. They also do not approach as she is Otto's Stuck-Up Wife who would stop them drinking in the Café if she was not in need of their schillings. Many of them look nervous, their eyes fixed on the gathering crowd. One says: Half this lot are Police. Best we don't hang around afterwards.

Oma is moaning about Lukas and *all that she has done for that Man*. In Truth, Oma knows that Lukas will be lying in his narrow bed in the grimy, rubbish-strewn Streets of Ottakring, soaked in drink. When Lukas doesn't come to work, Opa goes around to that room, rants at Lukas, dips his lolling head in a bucket of cold water.

Holds his head down for a long time, pulls him up again, dunks him down. After that Opa takes Lukas's wages so he cannot buy more drink. His wages being, it must be admitted, pitifully low, but he is a Drunk so what can he expect? Without Opa, and the Bucket of Water, I don't know when we will see Lukas again.

Oma cannot run the Café without him, no matter how much she may blacken his already less-than-white name. (More people of the Wrong kind now gathering. A Man boxes the ears of a small boy. The day steamy, the air dusty. The sky low and suffocating. My dress sticky and prickly.)

Adelheid, Adelheid – Please remember how you must behave. I am counting now blades of grass, gravestones, silver birch. Socialist Types drinking from bottles of beer, punching their clenched fists into the air, shouting – *Freiheit, Freiheit, Freiheit*. (*Freedom etcetcetc.*) Also, smoking, which is most certainly *Inappropriate* at a Funeral.

However, no smoke without Matchboxes. Focus on Matchboxes. Lay them out in straight lines in my mind. Remember Sister Viktorine's Instructions. I have one small Notebook in my Small and Appropriate bag. Yet I may not write ~

Mercifully, here now is the Stationer Herr Wächter who does Definitely know the Truth which he will surely now explain. Other Scribes are arriving, including the Highly Reliable Mr Gedye who writes for the London *Times* and even for the newspapers in New York. Opa used to work as a String Man for him.

Oma pretendspretendspretends to the priest, saying: Yes, Adelheid is currently a Patient at the Kinderklinik. They often study Children who have Particular Abilities. All her Writings. Far beyond what they might expect for a child of that age.

Herr Wächter nods to me as he comes to join us at the graveside. Why does he not explain? Before it is too late? Allowing someone to be buried who is Not Dead? Unless, unless. Dr Dollfuß had a small coffin, so Adolf said. Opa was extremely tall. When everyone sees the Normal-Size Coffin they will know.

Yet the Coffin now being carried towards us is indeed Most Long. What does that mean? Could it be True? No. Anubis is suffering severe indigestion due to stuffing down too many Hearts. Please, please. I cannot stand this. I look over at that Herr Wächter. Why will he not help me? It is not True. IknowIknowIknow.

I need some Answers but Opa has always supplied the Answers. No Matchboxes or Notebooks can save me. Time has gone missing. The ground is at a Dangerous tilt. Trees, people, graves are all now jumbled together. The sky is shouting. The Coffin is going into the grave now. Is it full of bricks? Please, please can everyone Stop Pretending. Adelheid turns and pushespushespushes through the Crowds. Runs, tumbles, doesn't look back ~

I spend that afternoon walking through the City. My Last Afternoon on This Earth so why not drink in every detail. I do not have my Maps with me but I know every brick and beam. Every big-breasted marble lady with a bunch of grapes supporting a marble plinth. Every twisty iron lamp, elaborate frieze, clanking lift and vast frilled lampshade.

Cities stay in the same place and that pleases me. Today all is more than ever spectacular. Each towering Door and decorative window ledge weighed with some impenetrable significance. Everything flat but intricate. The Streets deep and tangled like a maze. All pomp, gilt, brass, stucco. Statues which have surely been poured rather than carved.

Yet also I know – know too well – how behind all this Glittering Theatre lie urine-smelling Courtyards and rat-residing alleyways. So many people crammed into shabby attics and even cellars. Even this filth I do enjoy. If only I could walk forever. I want to lose my Brain in Pattern and Sound and Scent. But the Knowledge does press in upon me.

The Freezing Bath is all that awaits. Opa will not now return, Herr Wächter will not tell the Truth. I am thoroughly ashamed of Adelheid ~

Eventually I go back to the Hospital. I knock on the Door of the Ward only because the rage of Sister Viktorine might be less fearsome than the rage of Oma. Therefore, imagine my surprise when Sister Viktorine throws up her hands and says how splendid it is that I have returned. Perhaps I might like to sit in the chair in the Meeting Room?

How brave I was at the Funeral, how wonderful that I managed so well. She obviously will not be saying that when she finds out the Truth. Yet I sit in that chair feeling most relieved and thinking that I absolutely do not want to say goodbye to the World, for although it has brought me so much Trouble, I have loved Every Element of it.

I am tiredtiredtired and I sleep. When I wake, it is evening. Sister Viktorine comes in and says that I am not to worry. Not At All. Everything has been arranged. Lukas has been found. Poor soul. He has been Most Distressed. Opa and Lukas are old friends, having fought together in the War. Friends have comforted Lukas and he will be at the Café tomorrow.

The only remaining Problem being that the Doctors wish me to stay in the Ward. Yet with the summer holidays arriving? Fortunately, Oma has agreed I should stay over the month of August. Is that Arrangement acceptable? This news is so unexpected and wonderful that I cannot make it fit into my mind. A Whole Month.

I do not mind any amount of Dormitory, or noise, or Penguins, or Sluts or Cabbages or would you not like to do this-or-that-or-the-other? Sister Viktorine must be Extremely Good at *steering*. Without a lighted cigarette, she has navigated clear of The Ditch ~

Adolf knows all that has unfolded saying: Nasty row. Bad luck. When your Oma arrived waving her clutch of Deadly Papers, she chanced upon Dr Jekelius. Of course, he likes to charm a woman and your Oma certainly told a Horror Story and oh-the-shame-the-shame. If you could just Sign Here etcetcetc. They should put her on at The Burg, they really should.

Adolf is enjoying the telling of this Story, continuing thus: All fixed up. You were to be sent to Pressbaum without delay. Until Fräulein Weiss said that Dr A and Dr Frankl had not authorised Any Such Thing. Fireworks then. Until it is established that you are quite sure your Dead Opa is still Alive, making you a Nutcase as well as a Cabbage. Good Strategy.

Hearing Adolf speak of my Opa in this way does make me extremely Angry. Yet I do not have time to think for he is telling me now that we can go up onto the Roof Terrace. *Come and see. Come and see.* I follow him through that small Door and down the narrow Corridor, then up tunnel-tight-stairs.

Until we emerge – gasping, blinking – onto an Actual Roof Terrace, which is extremely wide and spacious. Around the sides of it a Loggia hence you could sit there even in the rain. Adolf moves cane chairs so that we may balance on top of them and see far out over the balustrade. From there we can See Everything.

THE MATCHBOX GIRL

The roofs, onion domes, spires touched by flashes of sunlight. The big wheel in the Prater, the many Palaces to the South. The Woods beyond layered in grey and blue. Yet not only seeing the Big but also the Small. The same Streets that I had walked earlier in the day. How different when seen from above.

Neat and Ordered and arranged most carefully. Such a great pleasure to observe. For I have always believed that the Answer to every Question lies knotted up in the Streets, buildings, squares of my City. Once I might see all from above, then the Best Plan for the Matchboxes will soon be found. Everything Laid Out Straight ~

After My Death: The Burial of Body Parts, 2002

I hope You have looked most carefully at the Heading of this section. I did warn You that, although I understand fully the importance of Chronology in Historical Record, the Incidents of the Past also associate in other Patterns. Am I saying this Correctly? Please do not think this Historical Record is about Justification or Forgiveness. That is not my Point.

I have been waiting most exceedingly long to tell this Story but now I find it harder than I had expected. I hoped that an Author was a Person of great Authority but the Facts are most Unruly and will not be Glued Down. I am simply recreating my Notebooks (Actual and Imagined in My Mind) which were Sadly Destroyed. Do You Understand?

I admit that I may often be Confusing what I knew at that time and what I now know in my posthumous life (after reading many Dusty Documents and Paperwork). Indeed, I would agree that the level of Ignorance of my twelve-year-old self is most Extraordinary. Please affix Matchboxes to thick Paper. If not, the Matchboxes below may show through.

Adelheid — Avoid this Tram Track. I am trying to remember the Questions You did Ask. *Was Dr A the Man responsible for the discovery of what is now called Autism?* For many years, no Person was interested in what I might remember. But then, at a certain moment, it became clear that multitudes were beginning to enquire about Dr A ~

Many Things Have Been Misunderstood. Therefore, I now address certain Rumours which may distract from the proper telling of this Story. It is for that reason that we now travel to the Year 2002 and return once again to the Vienna Central Cemetery. Where a Memorial Service is Happening because a decision has been made to lay to rest certain Body Parts ~

Let us say Brains. This having been much reported in the Newspapers although not Most Accurately. It was this event which started so many Questions – and also much Confusion and Aggressive Comment. Therefore let me lay out the Facts of the Case. These Brains were of the Children from Am Spiegelgrund.

Let me be Quite Clear. Am Spiegelgrund had nothing to do with the Children's Hospital which I have just described. It was a new Hospital which was created during the War and was part of Steinhof which was then the Hospital for Mad People in Vienna and situated far away on the outskirts of the City.

During the War, the Brains of some Children from Am Spiegelgrund were stored in a Cellar, having been kept as they were needed for important purposes of Research. Most people in their Actual Lives had heard Rumours of such a thing but it was like Wilhelm and the Freezing Bath. No one ever thought it was exactly True.

However, it then turned out that these Brains Really Did Exist. Having been left in Glass Storage Jars in the Cellar of Am Spiegelgrund. You may still see photographs of them and a most horrible and curious sight they are – floating like white walnuts. Moon-touched, Intricate and Lonely ~

Thus the City Government decided in 2002 that these Brains should finally be buried. I cannot tell you who decided. The Political tides of our Country ebb and flow. Sometimes a conversation can be started, sometimes not. A Door opens, slams shut. As I have said before, I cannot offer any Analysis of these Events. As Opa makes most clear, I have *no Breadth of Vision*.

Therefore, I say only that a Memorial was built in the Central Cemetery. The engineers arriving first in vans bringing with them Paper, plans, spirit levels, tape measures, spades etcetcetc. Meanwhile a young medical technician was charged with taking the Brains out of the Bottles and placing them in Black Urns.

On the day of the Ceremony, all the High Officials of the City poured forth in their carefully ironed shirts, with their shoes polished.

The exceedingly few people still Alive from that Distant Time did also attend. Modern schoolchildren were asked to walk four abreast, carrying placards with photographs and white wreaths nearly as tall as themselves.

The Black Urns were laid down in the long trenches cut in the earth. Each of the mourners took a single white rose to drop into this grave. It was all most Properly Organised. Of course, the Schreiber girls were mentioned – Herta and Elisabeth. Since they had the same surname, you would have thought that they were related, but that is not the case. The mayor made a speech. Niemals vergessen. Never Forget ~

One would expect that the Dead might be left in Peace but sadly not all are Respectful. Some do not consider it is enough to create this Memorial. I do not agree. As a Person who has ample acquaintance with the Dead, believe me, they are best left in their graves. Not only are they Boring, they are frequently Destructive and Badly Mannered.

The main Point being that even now the Full Facts of the Case are not being Properly said. Because in our culture, You see, the keeping of Body Parts is standard medical practice. This being important for the curing of many Diseases. I am sure You understand. Therefore, we may return to the Main Part of the Story. The summer of 1934 ~

2.a. Pitschy-Patchy Moments of Happiness

What was it that Troubled me so Deeply in that time of my Youth in the long-distant Year of 1934? What was it that I wrote in my Notebooks? Certainly, Observations and Reports explaining all the Small Things which I perceived, many of which gave me Profound Pleasure, but more often lists of all the things I could not understand.

Some Questions I had been puzzling over for Many Years, but when I arrived in the Curative Education Ward, many further Complicated and Troubling Queries were added to the existing Befuddlement. The most Important being Questions of Right and Wrong, and Situations where you must make Moral Judgements and know the difference between Truth and Untruth.

Also, Theories of Causation meaning how things progress on one from the other. And whether it is more important to look at Small Things or whether one must have *Breadth of Vision*. In addition, what is meant by steering people and what is the Purpose of Friendship ~

Stick to the Point. During that summer I realised that the Doctors of the Curative Education Ward were also asking many Questions. Not so much about the World but about the Human Mind. They were Detectives but there was no crime, only the situation of being a Human Being. Hence I hoped that much that was Perplexing would soon be untangled.

That was my thought when I stood for the first time on that lofty Roof Terrace. Yet events did not progress in that way (how Causation does disappoint). For although Dr Frankl had been given that Notebook which Dr A did borrow from me, and although he did certainly read my Questions, he did not have any Answers.

Only looking at me with Searching Eyes and saying: Such vast Questions. Of course, you must appreciate that we can never know all the Answers. However, I feel that the Questions themselves are most important. Would you not agree ~

I did not Agree. All that Time spent watchingwatchingwatching and he had no Solutions. What then was he doing? However, my Frustrations did not last long and, indeed, all my Worries and Troubles did soon fade away. For the summer took hold of me. Such a summer. Quite unlike any other. No work to do. No work at all.

In the past I had travelled by train with Opa to St Pölten, Wiener Neustadt, Zell am See and once even across the Border to Brno (when the phone lines were down). Yet now I deduced that the exact meaning of the word Holiday is that you can do exactly what you want all day. (Some Children even stripping off all their clothes which I did consider Disgusting.)

Yet many other Freedoms I did greatly enjoy. In the early morning, I would go up to that much-loved Roof Terrace. There you could feel the holidays bursting and blooming. The stones were speaking of journeys by bus, car, train. Salzburg or Innsbruck, south to the Yugoslav beaches or North to the Rhineland.

Professor Hamburger has gone to Berlin, Dr A and Dr Feldner are in the Tyrolean Alps, Dr Jekelius in Bad Ischl, Fräulein Eder on the Italian Riviera. Only Dr Frankl and Fräulein Weiss remain (and even they take the afternoon off to swim in the Danube). The air sags, the days settle back in their comfortable chairs and ease off their tight shoes.

At that time everyone was joining the Fatherland Front. Even many Socialists. Adolf told me this and also Herr Spellbinder. All agreed this was our best Hope. Yet what Interest could I take in such matters once I had discovered the Garden? Finding there a Private Place. A Garden within the Garden. An enclosed patch of ground near the fence, close to the street.

Here I might spend long afternoons lying on the many Blades of Grass, with Franz Joseph in a box beside me, staring for hours at the patterns made by the clouds and by the swaying branches above. Later in the day Sister Viktorine would summon me inside and I would lay out my Matchboxes on the Meeting Room table.

Exploring my many Plans where I tried to establish how an Album might best be organised. A difficult question – by date? Or by Country? By Colour or Design? I tried many different variations. Sister Viktorine sometimes trying to help me in ways which were quite Useful but also making Stupid Suggestions about how some might be stuck at an angle.

Imperfection can be beautiful, don't you agree? No, I do not ~

During that summer holiday, Adolf was sometimes in the Ward and sometimes not. He apparently went home on some occasions to help his Mother. However, I do not accept that this Story was quite the Exact Truth. The Rumour was that he was also once arrested by the Police. Herr Spellbinder was the source of this Information.

Herr Spellbinder's Story may well be Correct. I say that partly because Herr Spellbinder lived in the same building as Adolf. Also, he himself was a Man known to trade in Black Market goods, therefore Informed in matters of the Police. Certainly, when Adolf was out at night, he was often in Herr Spellbinder's Storeroom in the Cellar of the Hospital.

When Adolf was present in the Ward, he was frequently at the Meeting Room table with Sister Viktorine for many hours. During those times the Door was kept firmly closed. Also, as You already know, Adolf was always busy keeping himself Properly Informed through the filching of Medical Notes from the Filing Cabinet.

I found this most worrying. The Paperwork was poorly organised even before Adolf rendered the situation yet worse. What I did also discover was that our Ward was situated near the main Records Room of the Hospital. One had only to go out of the Door of our Ward and climb five small stairs before one came to the low Door of this most Important Room.

I sometimes liked to stand outside that Door and imagine all the Notes and Papers therein. Everything inside that Room would surely be sorted most carefully. It gave me pleasure to meditate on this and often at night I happily dreamed of that Room and all the Magnificent Information which might be contained therein.

Surely in that Room would be Information much better than the Medical Notes which, I regret to inform You, were extremely rude. Not just Bedwetters but inadequate Mental Hygiene. Lack of Community Spirit and imaginative play. Neglected, Criminal, Psychopathic Neurosis. Sexual deviancy etcetcetc. ~

I did wish that the summer could continue so Peacefully forever but soon Adolf tells me – *Lounging in the Garden is not a Strategy, Matchbox. Offer them a Small Victory occasionally. Or your Grandmother will be booking a train*. I feared that Adolf's Warning was Correct. Other Children had visitors on Sunday but Oma did not come to reunite with me.

On Sundays I may catch a glimpse of her over the bobbing heads of the congregation in the Mass at the Piaristenkirche Maria Treu but the Children of the Curative Education Ward (Moral Degeneracy) must be kept at the back and in no way allowed to mix with the feathered hats, long leather boots and earth-green loden capes of the Proper People of this City.

In accordance with the Advice of Adolf, when Sister Viktorine suggests that I might like to sit at the Table in the Nursery with some of the other Children, I agree. Which is how I first see that most extraordinary room. Here are the same Floor Tiles and small lights shaped like Chinese hats hanging down on long wires from the ceiling.

But here also, at the very top of the walls, a frieze of happily dancing peasants. Plus long white curtains blowing in the breeze. Shelves are stacked with modelling Clay, bricks, musical instruments, fancy dress costumes. Tiny tables and chairs for small Children and miniature prams for the pushing of dolls.

In one corner is a dappled rocking horse with a silver mane, in another a doll's house so big you can nearly walk inside. Also, a toy kitchen with real china cups and saucers, all arranged neatly on a miniature dresser. Who would have such toys for Cabbages? The Nurses spend many hours playing with the Children.

Observing these games, I soon realise that what at first appears to be Chaos is actually carefully Organised. The Nurses nod to each other and make Notes. Occasionally, Sister Viktorine whispers an Instruction to a Nurse and that Nurse changes from reading to jigsaws. The Cabbages think that this is all just fun. It is not.

I sit at the table near the window with Gottfried and Thomas. Gottfried draws many butterflies and is most courteous to me.

Thomas says nothing but draws designs of spaceships which are most detailed and interesting to behold. Fritz is happily put in another room because he does start shouting for no reason and waving his hands.

Anton is occupied establishing an organisation called the Ancient Guild of Rescuers of Threatened Snow Globes and busily designing and distributing membership cards. (Dr Feldner sometimes helping him in this ridiculous enterprise, discussing the Rules of this Organisation and making suggestions on the Founding Charter and stated aims of this Guild.)

Also, Bruno the Book is sometimes present, taking one book after another from the shelves, turning the pages at extremely high speed. Then repeating Information in his loud and deadening voice. Always standing with one leg in front of the other and shifting his weight back and forth. Happily, Sister Viktorine sometimes moves him into the Corridor. Dr Frankl is often also in the Nursery, always watchingwatchingwatching ~

Fräulein Weiss suggests that I might like to play a game with her. I must offer her a Small Victory so we sit together in Dr Frankl's Office. Fräulein Weiss having no proper Office as she is a Psychologist which is not a real Doctor. This Office of Dr Frankl is most diminutive but has a window overlooking the Garden. The walls being decorated with watercolours of the Wienerwald.

On the desk flowers from the garden are arranged in a vase of watery green glass. Surely Fräulein Weiss is responsible for the comfortable arrangement of this Office as Dr Frankl does not seem a Man interested in Domestic Matters. Yet he does sit there with us in a comfy armchair, writing often on his clipboard.

The games Fräulein Weiss wants to play are Stupid. *Listen to a word and write down another that is related to that first word.* Like Tree, then Grass. Have I understood? She writes dog. I write iceberg. She writes flower. I write gun. Fräulein Weiss inscribes Notes and sighs. She knows this is a Silly Game.

I stare up at the cavernous ceiling, tap my feet on the floor, twist my hands in interesting shapes. Doing such things is not as annoying as talking incessantly and flatly and loudly like Bruno the Book but it can still be a good way of getting rid of people. Fräulein Weiss produces cards with pictures on them — silly Children's stuff like Bears and Cottages and Bicycles.

I am to write a Story based on the cards. I do not know what she is talking about. Where would a Story come from? Some things are True and some are Not. Why would you invent things which are Untrue? Since she clearly knows what happened with the Bear and the Bicycle then why doesn't she tell it ~

On another day, Fräulein Weiss is telling me that she is concerned that I do not speak. It can be Dangerous not to speak. What if I were to find myself at Risk? How would I alert anyone to this Situation? She has got this Wrong. It is Dangerous For Me To Speak. Opa has told me. I am a Person who may unfortunately provoke others to acts of Spite or Rage.

Sometimes as I leave that Office, I listen at the Door to hear what is communicated between Fräulein Weiss and Dr Frankl. The latter is saying that I seem to manage pretty well without words. Much communication is going on but not in the way we would normally expect. Dr Frankl then begins to talk about dogs (as Adolf has warned).

What is the language that the dogs speak? It is clear that they do communicate because they understand feelings most clearly. What then is their language? Are there not two different languages? One Logical and one Emotional. Dr Frankl having gone off on a Tram Track until Fräulein Weiss says: Oh really, Georg, do shut up about the dogs ~

The summer is such Joy yet I am not succeeding in my Mission to comprehend more about how the World Works and neither am I any closer to 1,000 Matchboxes because the Door of the Storeroom is currently locked. My best chance of new Information is the velvet Meeting Room Chair because it faces towards the window, hence people do not know that I am there.

Fräulein Weiss has a friend called Helene Deutsch who comes to visit in the evening. She is a Polish lady, older than Fräulein Weiss, and she sits by the wastepaper bin, smoking and scolding Fräulein Weiss most sharply: Really, why are you still working here, Anni? Have you no thought for your career? Lazar and his Pitschy-Patchy ideas.

Speaking then in large contempt: *Everyone knows that Curative Education is methodless, unoriginal, a mere mosaic made from countless splinters of other sciences.*

Anni is equally rude about Herr Freud who lives not three Streets away. Quoting what Dr A has said of how Herr Freud *overlooks everything divine and human.*

Still Helene Deutsch says: *Fine, fine, but you must attend Anna Freud's evening training sessions. Everyone who wishes to progress in the Medical World goes.*

Fräulein Weiss saying: *The one time I went, the women were all in the downstairs lobby wiping off their lipstick so that Anna Freud would not be offended. I mean really.*

They pour more wine, waft cigarette smoke around with a discarded newspaper, become friends again until Helene Deutsch says: *Anni, maybe you are staying because although you are always dismissive of Georg Frankl, yet in your subconscious you enjoy his attention.*

Fräulein Weiss shudders: *I do not. All that is finished long ago. Anyway, his ghastly mother has been scouring Vienna for years in search of a Suitable Wife.*

Helene Deutsch: *Why not you? I don't know you'll do better. Not At Your Age* ~

The next day Sister Viktorine and Fräulein Weiss ask me if I will assist with a Play. The Cabbage Children are most excited by this Planned Performance. The Nurses talk endlessly of the Fantastical Worlds Sister Viktorine creates. *Enchanted forests with astonishing, amusing and scary adventures.* Costumes which are *Fantastic Robes and swashbuckling finery.*

I most certainly will not help as I do not like plays. Grandfather took me once to The Burgtheater (most important Theatre in Vienna) but I did not enjoy it. Silly people Lying and Pretending to be what they are not. Fräulein Weiss explains that what she actually needs is someone to write down the script.

The play has been created through Improvisation but still it must be written down to enable the actors to remember What To Do. Fräulein Weiss tells me that I would be good at this job as I am most accurate in recording Information. Could I not help? Nonono. I hate Organised Fun. Anyway, what they request is quite impossible.

In the play many things are happening at the same time. How would one record such a jumble? I seat myself in the Meeting Room, in my velvet chair, place a book in front of my face. Regrettably, Fräulein Weiss is a most insistent Person and will wheedle a Child into submission whether they like it or not.

She sits down beside me: Adelheid, you are needed. Let me show you.

She produces then the script of a Play. It is indeed most clever, being set out in a way which shows only the words to be said. Here is a neat way of recording Information without repeating the same things againagainagain. I agree to assist.

Yet this is not as simple as I initially perceived because the Actors keep changing what is said and also not doing properly the Entrances and Exits. Also, the Story is most Silly. Dragons, princesses, swords, magic. Adolf plays the part of a Fearsome Wolf. Why would you teach Pretending and Lying to a group of Poorly Disciplined Children? I must copy many times before the script is Correct ~

This Script Writing I continue in the evenings. Listening also to the conversations of Sister Viktorine and Fräulein Weiss. They talk while savouring concerts on the Radio. Sister Viktorine darning while Fräulein Weiss sighs: Of course, there *is* change for women. The men may label me as pushy but women who don't push get nothing.

Sister Viktorine is uncertain: The Advancement of Women. Yes, of course. I do feel that my Profession should be taken more seriously but here we are lucky. Thanks to the ideas of our dear Herr Lazar the work of Mental Hygienists is recognised in all its aspects. If we advance too far, might we then lose those things which are Truly Feminine?

Fräulein Weiss: Change the whole system? I couldn't agree more.

Sister Viktorine keeps a tight grip of her darning needle: Such matters I leave in the Care of God. Our contribution is seen by the Almighty and will be rewarded in Eternity.

Fräulein Weiss commenting then in a provoking tone: Oh Catholicism. Catholicism. No one is fooled, dear Sister Vik. Everyone knows you're a Red at heart.

Sister Viktorine then becomes flustered and says that this is certainly not the case and she'll thank Anni not to say such things.

Yet the Filing Cabinet has made known that Sister Viktorine resides in the Socialist housing block on Alser Straße *but only because of her dear friend who is an invalid.* Everyone must be clear that *her name is not on the lease.*

Yet despite this, as the evenings slide into darkness, the lights in the other blocks of the Hospital now glittering, the two talk in hushed voices of Red Vienna. It is now their work to keep that spirit Alive. Even though we are surrounded by Fascists, yet the League of Nations will support us, also our friends the French and British can be absolutely relied upon ~

2.b. The Visit of an American

Dr A comes back from his holiday a week earlier than Professor Hamburger and Dr Feldner because he has much work to do. He brings boxes of Papers and Books. All were lent to him by Dr Frankl and he has discovered much which is exceedingly interesting. Particularly about Affective Contact (relating to the dogs, their language etcetcetc.).

The three Russian Doll Nurses, who all Gabble and Gossip, meet by the Filing Cabinet to discuss Dr A's return. *Got a spring in his step. Met a lovely lady friend while on his hiking holiday. Don't be so daft. You might as well get married to a coat rack. Hiking holiday? Is that what they call it now? I could certainly do with some hiking* ~

Adolf warns that just because there is no Friday meeting at present, that doesn't mean Children can't get transferred away. Plus, it is only one week now until everyone will go back to the School Room and then those Friday meetings will resume. Adolf raises his head, sniffs the air, shakes his head. Says: Wait until Hamburger is back. Then we'll see.

The twins who are stuck together? You remember them? In fact, they are not actually joined together but one of those twins only has one leg and a damaged arm. For this reason, his Brother always stands most close to help him walk. The Point being, they are departing. Not to a Children's Home but just their regular home. Still, that makes everyone nervous.

Their mother comes to collect them. Sister Viktorine later commenting to Fräulein Weiss: I never really understood why they were here. The situation is unusual. The problems were the fault of the School. Quite happy as long as they stay together. Three legs and three arms and they can walk along the road of Life most Happily ~

I consider how the twins' mother has come to take them home, which Grandmother most certainly will not do for me. Where then will I go and what will Happen? These Interrogations leading me to wander up onto the Roof Terrace and to write in my Notebook. As it is late afternoon, I hope that I may reside there in Peace.

Yet I have calculated Wrongly for unfortunately Sister Viktorine comes with some of the Cabbages. Time for gymnastics. They force us to do gymnastics at school and I always try to hide. Handstands and hoops and batons and ribbons. Sister Viktorine hands me a ribbon. Probably as many Idiots are made here as unmade.

Sister Viktorine also hands a ribbon to Dr A. He tries to look Charming and Enthusiastic but he just looks Silly. What he does most clearly enjoy, however, is watching Sister Viktorine and this is not perhaps surprising for she is extremely good at ribbon waving, being a Person who can move easily through the World and having much grace and lightness.

He would perhaps like to be similar to her, and so would I also, but we are not such people. Yet still I am interested in observing Dr A for what I understand is that, although you think you might learn from watching a Person who does a thing well, instead you have to watch someone who does a thing badly. Then You see the Mechanics ~

I can escape from this situation more easily than Dr A. I throw down the ribbons and open my bag, pull out my compass and Maps. Immediately he comes towards me and questions me about the compass. Do I know how to use it? I take the compass and line it up so that I have found north. Then I line the Map up in the same direction. He seems delighted.

He tells me about the Village of his Youth which is called Hausbrunn and is near the border with Czechoslovakia. He describes the empty emerald fields, a cream-coloured church with a russet spire, low white houses parading along the only road. (Should he not be embarrassed since no Cultured People live in such low-down Agricultural Places?)

He also tells me he has spent many summers climbing the mountains of the Wilder Kaiser and Dachstein, hiking in the Wachau Valley. He does indeed look like a rucksackandwalkingboots Man, isolated on some distant mountain, waving a pole which no one sees.

I stand on the chair beside Dr A and he indicates areas of the City. Of course, I know the position of Every Building and Street but still I like to be told. I also share with him my Matchboxes and Plans. As on that first day, he understands immediately, sees that the Matchboxes are sorted by Country. Yet this is problematic. Here is a Czechoslovakian Matchbox from before the fall of our Empire.

So where now should it properly be placed? Organise by date? Or Design? He stares for some long time but he also cannot see how they are best Categorised. I expect that soon he will tell me that I should go to bed but instead he settles himself in a wicker chair and asks me if I like the poems of Grillparzer. Grandfather used to read these poems to me.

I don't like poetry but I like to hear Dr A's voice, the words floating away across the City. And so it is, when we have finished with the compass and maps, he reads to me, and this soon becomes our habit during the many evenings of that late summer. Also reciting to me from Goethe's *Faust*. He likes the lines of Lynceus who is the Tower Warden. *Born to see, appointed to watch, sworn to the Tower, I enjoy this World* ~

Soon I have an opportunity to Consider Further these Questions of Categorisation and Observation and Evidence. A visitor comes to the Ward called Joseph M. Michaels MD and he is from Boston in America. He is coming to enquire into the Methods, Techniques and Philosophy of our Clinic. Gottfried reads this Information from a letter on Fräulein Eder's desk.

Adolf is particularly stimulated by this visitor: Maybe he will take me to America.

According to Adolf, everyone should go to America. He has an Uncle who lives there. Adolf puts on extra cologne, a spruce shirt, a red silk tie. In America there are many excellent business opportunities etcetcetc. I have Matchboxes from America (wobbly man on unicycle) as Grandfather did visit there.

In reality, Dr Michaels doesn't look much like the Americans in the films. He has no cigar clamped between his teeth but he does wear shoes which are two different tones and also a jumper which has coloured diamond patterns. He looks slightly Confused and Disappointed, which is Normal for Foreigners in our City.

They expect to find us all merrily waltzing to the music of the Blue Danube. Or hiking through the Wienerwald displaying our reputation for gaiety and Gemütlichkeit (homeliness). Instead, they find much Paperwork to be stamped, a prodigious quantity of bed bugs, blocked drains and a lack of the electric washing machines apparently common in other places.

Fräulein Weiss has several conversations with Dr Michaels. She is considering studying for a PhD and wonders what the possibilities in America might be? Dr Michaels is most informative and Fräulein Weiss records all that he says. After that Dr Michaels is occupied taking Notes on the people who are taking Notes ~

Later in the day Dr Frankl and Dr Michaels come into the Meeting Room together and happily I am hidden neatly in my Velvet Chair with Franz Joseph on my lap. Dr Michaels saying: I don't want to sound critical but what I've got to ask is – where is the actual Science here? The Diagnosis? This looks like a School or a Nursery – and not much discipline.

Dr Frankl: I see your Point but in essence it is all about Observation.

Michaels: That helps you make a Diagnosis?

Dr Frankl: Not exactly. Our main focus is not on diagnosis. Our approach is Practical. It is more important that we find the right way of Educating a Child. We need to understand the personality and we do that by Observing the Unconscious and Uninhibited Responses. Even an apparently insignificant gesture might give us a clue.

Michaels: You're not creating a test situation in order to register a certain reaction?

Dr Frankl: Generally not. That would be a Conscious and Inhibited reaction and we do not consider that Useful. Rather we Observe the Psychology of the Non-Essentials.

A silence follows, then Dr Michaels says: But you are looking to judge what is abnormal?

Dr Frankl: To be honest, we are not really interested in such terminology because that word is theoretically unclear and practically it does not help us. As Dr Erwin Lazar tells us *each one is different. Unique.*

Michaels: Oh. I see. Right. But in terms of Research?

Dr Frankl: Our feeling is that the specific external manifestations are only really relevant to the child who presents them. The idea of Mass Research into such manifestations in a large number of Children does not really seem to us to be helpful.

Michaels: Oh. Right. Interesting. And Problematic.

Dr Frankl: You have met Sister Viktorine? She is constantly telling her staff that they must Observe in the greatest detail. Even the way in which a child, when writing, screws up the muscles around the mouth. Even that can teach us something. Sister Viktorine instructs us to watch the whole child. Observe down to the tips of their toes.

Again, there is a silence. Perhaps Dr Michaels is not really understanding this.

Says: I'm not sure it would work for us. But one thing is certainly interesting here. You see Children from many Different Social Groups?

Dr Frankl: Oh yes indeed. Sometimes we see as many as 1,500 Children in one year. Many are referred by schools but also by the Juvenile Courts.

Dr Michaels: Ummm Yes. We tend to see only the Children whose parents can pay. Or we see Children who have already been placed in institutions. Maybe we miss something.

The American is packing up his briefcase now. He'll be back again tomorrow but now he needs some time to write up his Notes. A great deal to think about and he needs to get his clothes washed. Really, no washing machine? After he has gone, my Mind continues to be fully occupied by these Most Interesting Discussions.

Dr Michaels is right in this debate. Dr Frankl may explain most clearly but still he is Wrong. Matchboxes do have to go in Categories. For otherwise how can a Person have *Breadth of Vision* and draw Conclusions about the Entire Collection ~

The next day Dr Michaels comes to visit again but after that he is leaving Vienna. He says goodbye to Adolf and slaps him on the shoulder: A pleasure to meet you, Young Man. You are clearly a

Person who will advance in the World. I have no doubt I'll be seeing you in America before too long. And you, Dr Frankl. Should you ever come to Boston be sure to get in touch.

Dr Frankl: Unlikely, sadly. But I very much appreciate the offer.

Professor Hamburger comes out of the Office and shakes Dr Michaels by the hand. He says *what a pleasure* etcetcetc. but afterwards he says to Dr A that he finds Americans rather Primitive. *Dr Michaels stubbed out his cigarette in one of the Children's inkwells. Such vulgarity.*

In addition, he also says most forcefully to Dr A that he must take more care in Future. Dr Frankl should not show any more visitors around the Clinic. That job must be done by Dr Jekelius or by Dr A himself. Visitors must not receive the impression that this Hospital is infected by Decadent Jewish Ideas. Dr Frankl is not Properly Scientific etcetcetc. ~

2.c. Rats and Intelligence Tests

The holidays are at an end. Everyone must go back to the School Room (girls with white bows neatly tied in their hair). The weather is suddenly shivering and the cloudy colour of drains. Rain flattens the Garden. Floor Tiles shudder and Doors slam in sudden gusts of wind. Usually, Gottfried would write everything down at the Friday Meeting but he is weepy. Adolf says: Bloody drip. Matchbox, you can help. Just sit in the Cupboard.

I do not want to sit in the Cupboard. Once you are there, you cannot get out. I don't mind writing things in my Notebook since that can be locked away. But other writing? Oma has made it clear. I must not inscribe Information *which may get us all into trouble*.

Adolf: No choice. We need to be Properly Informed.

Unfortunately, I must admit that he is Right. My own Future is in question. Adelheid – What if you are despatched to the Freezing Bath Children's Home? Perhaps I should have made an effort to show *Community Spirit*? Engaged in more *Spontaneous Play*? In this Distorted World, you need to behave badly to stay but if you behave too badly you must leave.

Adolf tells me we also need Franz Joseph. Why? I cannot ask Questions. Inside the Cupboard all is cluttered and jumbled and dust sticks to my hands and clots in my throat. We leave the Door slightly ajar. A thin strip of light does run towards our cramped knees ~

The Doctors come into the Meeting Room. I am ready with my Notebook. Sigh, shuffle. The curtains at the window blow inwards. Talktalktalk. Thisthatandtheother. La-la-la. It is hard to discern what is said and I grow drowsy. Perhaps I can write this down in the manner of a play script? I jerk awake as I hear Gottfried's name.

Dr A: So — Gottfried. Ahem. Fräulein Weiss has given me the result of his Intelligence Test and, as we thought, feeble-minded. Such a shame when he has many good qualities. His manners, I have noticed, are exceptionally charming.

Fräulein Weiss: I'm wondering.

The men are bored by Fräulein Weiss and her wondering.

Yet she persists: Again, it is the Problem of these Tests. You see, he appeared not to be able to answer the Questions but then I realised he was distracted by the word Noun. When I said that it could be any Word, then he was able.

Dr Jekelius then intervenes. (I have perhaps not described this Singular Character who is most slick and dapper with neatly oiled black hair forming a widow's peak against his smooth skin. Also, appearing always elegantly situated as though posing for a photograph.) Saying now: Gottfried scored very poorly on the tests.

Fräulein Weiss: Yes. But sometimes the test results are not as interesting as the child's subjective approach to the Tests. Intelligence cannot be quantified by one figure on a scale of low to high.

Dr Jekelius: The tests have been carefully developed over many years.

Fräulein Weiss: Well, yes and no. Our former colleague Dr Lazar —

Dr Jekelius: A Test is a Test and the Point is that he Failed.

Fräulein Weiss: To condemn a child when he does actually know? I have written in my Notes. Perhaps you have not read?

Dr Jekelius: I have read.

Adolf looks across at me, rolls his eyes. What a Massive Fib.

Fräulein Weiss: Are the tests measuring the right things?

Dr Jekelius: Well, you should know. That's your work, isn't it?

Dr A is wriggling most uncomfortably due to these Scratchy Words.

Dr Frankl: To me there is clear Evidence of Autistic Psychopathy.

Dr Jekelius: Feeble-minded?

Dr Frankl: With all due respect, no. I'm sure you are aware of the ideas of the Russian Grunya Sukhareva, and Bleuler also? A Person who is locked up inside themselves. There is an Intelligence there although it cannot be easily expressed.

Dr Jekelius: Of course I am aware of Bleuler. I'm questioning the relevance.

Dr Feldner: Dr Frankl certainly has a Point. This is something we do not see often, therefore it is interesting to Observe, to try to understand further.

Dr A: Thanks to Dr Frankl, I myself have done much reading on this Question.

Dr Jekelius: What actually is there to understand? Fräulein Weiss tells us that he is Intelligent. His manners are exceptionally good. He tries hard to be helpful. Of course, he does lack Moral judgement. Copying out Adolf's schoolwork for him.

Everyone looks away. Almost as though they know that Adolf sees them.

Dr Jekelius: The other Children find him difficult. Well, you would do, wouldn't you? But Professor Hamburger has made his views plain. We need to assess briskly and move Children on. Is that not right, Dr A?

Dr A's voice is squeezed: Quite right. I would agree with you, Erwin. The boy could fit in. He needs to make more effort ~

Dr Feldner says that he will find that Interesting Paper for Dr Jekelius. Written by the Russian Grunya Sukhareva. *Most Fascinating*. He is heading towards this Exact cupboard. We will undoubtably be Drowned. Oh no. Oh no. Ohnononono. Adolf is raising his eyes heavenward as though the ceiling is about to fall. Which, in fact, it is.

Dr Feldner's rangy figure appears in the crack of the Door. I praypraypray that *the Alchemy of Circumstance* might yet provide Distraction. Dr Feldner pulls the Door open. His eyes travel over various Paperwork higher up the cupboard. Is it possible that he will not notice us? We have pulled our feet in as far as we can.

Not enough. His eyes drop down. He bends forward slightly. His eyebrows shoot up so far that they cast his glasses heavenward. He stares down at us through the slatted shelves. I am praying to the Catholic God, Anubis, Grandfather etcetcetc. Dr Feldner leans forward to lift a Box File from above, drenching Adolf and me with dust and Dead spiders.

The cupboard Door is shut. Shut, shut. Now we will suffocate and die dried out and crumpled like the spiders. Yet Dr Feldner is a most clever Man for he realises this problem. He must not be responsible for the suffocation of Children. We see his fingers appear above us again, positioning the Door exactly as it was.

Dr Jekelius: Thank you. Still my Point is.

Dr A clears his throat: Good. Well, thank you, Erwin. Of course, if that is Professor Hamburger's view. I think that we should discharge Gottfried. Ensure he is protected from difficult playground situations.

Adolf looks over at me and wags his head desperately. Who now will read the Medical Notes? Who will do Adolf's schoolwork? The Doctors have agreed on a pause while Sister Viktorine goes to get a jug of water. Dr Feldner comes and stands near the cupboard Door. Chance? Or is he guarding Our Position?

Fräulein Weiss moves to the window and stands in the breeze. Dr Frankl situates himself beside her. She raises an eyebrow at him, shakes her head. I am gasping due to the dust and the heat. How will the Ward function? Gottfried has always been Adolf's second in command. I am next in line. Next to be sent away ~

The Doctors come back to the table. Chairs creak, Papers shuffle. The Times are briefly discussed. Dr A says that we can now surely feel confident about the Future. This dreadful murder has brought people to their senses. No one can doubt now that what we need is a strong Catholic government. *I myself have joined the Fatherland Front. Much the best.*

The Meeting starts again with discussion of a boy called Klaus. Pressbaum. Definitely. Adolf shakes his head in Horror. Fritz? Yet more Disaster. He also must return home. Who will be left? Bruno the Book. We expect the worst but, on this occasion, Dr Frankl is most resolute and Dr A agrees. Bruno is relevant to Dr Frankl's work on Autistic Psychopathy.

Why? Of course, we all know that the Doctors are interested in curious obsessions. Such as spaceships, endless reading, butterflies etcetcetc. Except that, as Dr Jekelius points out, Bruno is not reading at all. He is just incessantly spouting random Information. Which is not too pleasant if you have to live with his voice burbling on all day.

Dr Frankl: I feel that there will definitely be a role for Bruno in the World.

Sister Viktorine: And Thomas with his lovely spaceships.

Dr A: Most interesting, is it not? Some of these interests can undoubtedly be useful. But what is anyone going to do with so many Fantastical drawings of Spaceships?

Dr Feldner: The drawings are technically very Correct.

Dr A: Yes. Maybe. But no one is going to the moon, are they?

Nevertheless, it is agreed that Thomas must stay and Bruno as well ~

Dr A: Adelheid Brunner.

Adolf and I glance at each other, then swivel our eyes away.

Dr A: Puzzling. My initial thought was that, looking at all this obsessive writing, this must be a case of graphomania. This is a condition I have seen in adults. The patient engages endlessly and obsessively in writing which has no sense or meaning.

All eyes in the room fix on the vast piles of Paper which sit around the table and particularly the Paper Mountain which rises next to Dr A. Dr Frankl: We don't often see that in a child. More of an adult condition.

Dr Jekelius: Simple-minded. Her Grandmother has already made that clear.

The water of the Freezing Bath is rising. Adolf is gripping his head. Fräulein Weiss: I disagree. She is good at Writing things down.

Dr A: Well, yes, perhaps. After all – the Notebooks.

Dr Jekelius: Full of rubbish.

He has never looked. May Anubis crunch up his Lying Heart.

Fräulein Weiss says: It seems she is describing things she sees.

Dr Feldner: Highly subversive.

Fräulein Weiss: Could she not also be a case of Autistic Psychopathy?

Dr A: Usually a condition found in boys? Am I right, Georg?

Dr Frankl: Probably. But at present, we understand so little.

Dr Jekelius: She has failed the Intelligence Tests. She cannot do even the most basic tasks, such as inventing a simple Story.

Fräulein Weiss: Actually.

Dr Jekelius mows her down: Clumsy and slow. A total lack of Gemüt. Nevertheless, undoubtably suitable for some level of Domestic Work. (Gemüt he perhaps uses to suggest Lack of Community Spirit).

Dr Feldner: Probably quite normal when in a room on her own ~

Adolf is trying to grab Franz Joseph. I am holding onto him tight. We wrestle silently, trying not to kick the Door or disturb the Files above. I understand what Adolf intends but is this the Right Moment? We have only One Rat. My mind is being battered by a Blasting Wind. The Cupboard is going to collapse and all the Files will fall on us.

Sister Viktorine: I feel that Adelheid is most upset about her Grandfather.

No one is listening because Sister Viktorine is only a Nurse. I cannot accept more Massive Lies about Grandfather. I shove Adolf aside. He stops battling as he knows that we are in agreement now. I put Franz Joseph down close to the floor. He is squiggling furiously and I release my fingers. He dashes for the gap.

All exclaiming and jumping up from the table. *Ahhhhh. Look, look. What? Where? God save us.* Sister Viktorine screams, pushes herself back against the wall. Dr A telling everyone: Please, please, keep calm. Herr Spellbinder will deal with this situation. Can we keep focused? Ah yes. Yes. Perhaps it would be best to reconvene.

Dr A is speaking to an empty room ~

2.d. Clay Models and Mincing Machines

It all unfolds just as was agreed in the Meeting. First, Fritz's mother arrives to transport him home. No one is sorry to see him go. Yet when I see his mother, I do wonder if Fritz might rather join Wilhelm in the Freezing Bath. For his mother is savage and spiky with scissoring fingers. She paces up and down the Corridor, gabbling at the speed of an express train.

Dr A greets her in the Corridor and recounts Fritz's progress but she is not attentive. Instead, she is organising poor Fritz and his Suitcase and his toy cars and his patched brown wool coat. Dr A says goodbye but she is booming Loud Instructions and does not hear. Dr Frankl appears but Fritz and his mother have already blown out of the Door.

Ah. Gone? I shall miss him.

Dr A: Yes, yes. I have just encountered his Mother.

Ah yes, his Mother. I am sorry to miss her.

Dr Frankl moves towards the window and peers down. Even from this great height we can often apprehend voices below most clearly. Dr A moves to join him and they Observe.

Dr A: Extraordinary. Is she not Most Eccentric?

Oh yes. Certainly so.

Dr A: You feel that it is Correct to let her take Fritz home?

Oh yes. Beyond a doubt. She is, in fact, the best Person to look after him. I have watched them together during our Various Exchanges. She never looks at him, never touches him, barks Instructions at him incessantly. Then one Observes more deeply and one sees how completely she understands him. She has been most Insightful in her assessment of him.

Dr A: She understands him?

Dr Frankl: Undoubtedly. Far more than we ever could. If one looks back through the History of that Family, one sees the same essential characteristics manifested in different ways across the generations. The Point is Fritz's mother loves him. Her love doesn't fit the pattern we expect in a Mother-Son relationship. But who are we to judge?

Dr A feels that his Matchbox Collection is a little more secure ~

Gottfried is weeping like a burst pipe when his Oma comes to take him home. He should consider himself lucky that she is ready to receive him. My Oma still has not come to visit me. Adolf paces up and down in a most Wolf-imitating manner. Says: Disaster. Why didn't Dr A tell that swine Jekelius to shut his trap? I need Gottfried.

The small Cabbage called Klaus is also being prepared for despatch. I never knew him. He was just part of a group of small Cabbages who were constantly tripping everyone up by playing Marbles or Räuber und Gendarm (Cops and Robbers). Sister Maria assists him with packing, brushing hair, cleaning shoes. Also, putting cake and sandwiches in his bag for the journey.

Klaus is simple but pleasant. He wears his best clothes – knee britches and a double-breasted jacket over a checked shirt. He is Excited and waves to us all most regally. Sister Viktorine places a flower in his buttonhole before Sister Maria leads him out of the Ward. Clearly, he knows nothing of Wilhelm the Drowned but I do. I need to thinkthinkthink.

Those words the doctors used are rattling through my mind againagainagain. Simple-minded. Notebooks full of rubbish. Failed the Intelligence Tests. Clumsy and slow. A total lack of Community Spirit. No doubt suitable for some level of Domestic Work. In the Meeting Room I lay out my Matchboxes and my Plans.

Perhaps if I find the Optimum Plan, the right Order, then I will be Safe? If not, how long until I am following Klaus? Oil might again be spilt on my Collection. My mind is sizzling, my hands are jingling as I move the Matchboxes again and again. Adolf shakes his head mournfully: Klaus will do fine. They don't drown them all ~

When Sister Viktorine requests me to join other Children in making models out of Clay, I make haste to follow her Instructions. *Show community spirit.* Is that the Right Strategy? Soon I make a family of Clay Rats. They look like Mountain Trolls and I want to slide away and hide. Sister Viktorine comes to help me. *Lovely in their imperfections?*

Sister Viktorine then tells me that we are participating in a project called Myself and that I could perhaps shape a model of me. What? Sister Viktorine says that she has some scrap material which is similar to my dress. If I create the model, then she will assist with the dress. Dr Frankl is Observing this conversation, his eyes fixed on me.

He disappears and comes back a moment later with a mirror. He stands this against a pile of books and then asks me to come and stand in front of the mirror. I see myself appearing there. My white hair cut short and curling inwards at the level of my chin. My face oval in shape, the nose wide at the bridge between startled eyes. My chin rather stubborn.

My hands also I hold up and examine. They are long and white and my fingers slice back and forth as I am thinking (the cause of me being called *Freak*). How strange this is. This is who I am. There is the Troublesome Adelheid, standing in front of me.

Dr Frankl: Now could you make a model of yourself?

Soon I have made a rather splendid model and found white wool for my hair. I have shaped my feet rather long as they are in reality. Sister Viktorine is ready with the miniature gingham dress. I am interested by Clay Adelheid. Could I turn her back into a lump of Clay and make a different Person out of her? Can you steer yourself ~

The rehearsals of the play are not progressing positively. Fräulein Weiss saying: Can you imagine how the Shopkeeper responds when the Dragon arrives? Can you imitate how a Princess might walk? What do you do when you are frightened? Can we all Pretend to do that?

She is explaining that this is called Improvisation but no one understands. Her Instructions go awry. Adolf is wearing a hearth rug and brandishing a toasting fork. Growlingclawingpacing. The small Cabbages wail and the rehearsal has to be halted ~

This ridiculous Wolf situation is soon forgotten because *the Alchemy of Circumstance* manifests even less predictably than usual. Gottfried has not even been at home for two days, yet he is back again. This news causes much groaningmooingteethchattering among the Cabbages and also many Filing Cabinet conversations.

Adolf: Some bastards put his hands in a Mincing Machine. Fingers sliced up to the wrists.

This is mainly True although not the bit about his wrists. Gottfried probably said something which infuriated people. He should know to keep quiet. Like me, he is a Person who may accidentally provoke others to acts of Spite or Rage. Gottfried is soon wheeled into the Ward in an Invalid Chair with his bandaged hands folded in his lap.

We hear his Radio-Reader voice: In these complicated circumstances, it would not be Appropriate to blame any particular Person or group. Gottfried has behaved Extremely Badly.

Adolf says: Damn and blast. Right out of order. A Mincing Machine?

The face of Dr A is Paper-pale and he moves restless as a spectre.

He speaks to Sister Viktorine: What is going on in this City?

One of the boys in his class has a father who is a butcher.

Dr A: Is this the kind of Behaviour that is now Acceptable?

Sister Viktorine: Shocking. I agree. Poor boy. He has been very brave. They think the damage will not be long term. Of course, his family situation is not Comfortable. His father has departed the Country. For our young people these are Difficult Times.

I am holding the tips of my fingers most firmly. Dr A the same ~

That night I lie awake, my mind crowded with those Waking Dreams which so often haunt me. I see Gottfried and the Mincing Machine. Youths are grabbing hold of his hands, pushing him and jeering. Yet now he is not Gottfried but has become Dr A in his short trousers in a village school in that distant village of Hausbrunn which he did describe.

That Village being flat and wide under staring skies and no place that one may hide from those Ignorant People and Agricultural Children. He being told – *Do not write with your left hand. Do not say Hans A likes reading. Instead, you must say – I like reading.* Trapped in that one-room School House, his eyes searching, darting.

THE MATCHBOX GIRL

He can't identify who Hans A might be. He is reading the poems of Grillparzer but no one will listen. He is waving from a high mountain top (or perhaps a Tower) but no one Sees or Hears. *Cabbage-Idiot-Neurotic.* He must Try Harder, he needs to learn to withstand some teasing and understand how not to alienate the other Children.

If only the vaporous and tranquil Viktorine would sit by his bed and wipe a cool sponge across his fevered brow, lay her hand firmly on his shuddering shoulder ~

2.e. Dr A Understands the Work of Dr Frankl

I must get out of bed or the Waking Dreams may strangle me. I look towards where Adolf should be sleeping. Anyone should be able to perceive that he is a rolled-up blanket not an Actual Boy. At least he will not Question me. This I think as I slide towards the small Door leading to the back stairs and out into the Corridor.

The nighttime shadows and low burning lights are malicious and finger-pointing. *Notebooks full of rubbish. Failed the Intelligence Tests. A total lack of Community Spirit.* I open my locker using my key and carry my Matchboxes up the tunnel stairs onto the Roof Terrace, lay them out on a wicker table. Concentrate.

Yet I have not been there two minutes when suppressed voices rustle in the stairwell. Dr A and Sister Viktorine are coming up to take the night air. As they emerge onto the Roof Terrace, both of them see me but strangely they do not instruct me to depart. Perhaps Dr A might like to use his compass to assist me in the drawing of my maps, as he has done so often before.

Yet instead he is attentive to Sister Viktorine. Her voice sounds as though it is being squeezed through a sieve. She sits on a cane sun lounger and he sits opposite, bending his head in order to appear understanding. She is saying as so often before – *Socialist housing block. I am not on the lease. I have nothing to do with Politics.*

Dr A answers most forcefully: I can assure you. Your Position here is secure. You are a Highly Valued member of staff. In all my conversations with our excellent Professor Hamburger, I have made clear that I cannot manage the work of the Ward without the highly experienced team that I have.

Sister Viktorine says how grateful she is for his support.

Dr A replying: I learn a great deal from you.

She: Oh no, sir. Surely not.

Dr A: Yes. You have such experience.

She: Well, thank you, sir. This work is my Life, this Hospital my Family. I was fourteen when I started Nursing and seventeen when I went to the Front. It was indeed most Difficult but I had Youth and Faith on my side. We all have our worries in these Times. Do we not?

These words solidify in the air. A whiff of smoke or even poisonous gas? Surely she has said the Wrong Thing. Dr A might take offence. He is the Director of the Ward hence he does not have worries. Sister Viktorine realises that she has perhaps taken a step too far and her voice stumbles, she begins to apologise.

Dr A cuts in saying: You are right. I feel most guilty about that boy. I should have insisted that he stay.

She: Oh, no. No. We can only do our best. So many Children. The need So Great.

Dr A: Yes, but we should be able to do more. I have been in this Ward now for some months and I have been finding my feet, assessing what we are doing. So much is highly impressive but, finally, we understand so little.

She: Yes, but you are a Person of great ability. You will take Time and Trouble for these Children. You have a Sense of what they Suffer ~

I am monitoring all that is said but I am tiredtiredtired and my hands move the Matchboxes without any thought. Czechoslovakia. Italy. France. Great Britain. America. If only I could stay here – on this Roof Terrace, in this Disorganised but Kindly Hospital – but I know that I cannot. How long? How long? What other World is there for me?

Dr A is saying: I have had many interesting conversations with Dr Frankl. Also, with that American. You remember? Of course, I respect the work of Herr Lazar and our friends Dr Frankl and Fräulein Weiss. And you yourself. These Runder Tisch discussions have been wonderfully informative. Yet I feel that if we do not Categorise, if we do not Diagnose.

Sister Viktorine: Yes, I know.

Dr A: It is difficult to make an Argument for these Children. To Fight for them when so often we don't even have any Names.

Sister Viktorine: But that is exactly where a Person such as yourself could make a Great Contribution. Dear Dr Frankl has done this work for many years but it is difficult for him to make his voice heard. The approach perhaps needs presenting in a way which can be more easily understood. I know that Fräulein Weiss is considering doing a PhD.

Dr A: Yes, and Georg has an interest in this idea of the Autistic Psychopath. But is that where the need is greatest? There are many Children worse afflicted.

Sister Viktorine: Yes, but a boy like Gottfried does present a particular problem. Some of our Children have obvious difficulties hence people do have patience with them. The problem with Gottfried is that he is Intelligent and he speaks well. But what are they to do with a Child who has no educational problems yet makes no contribution to the School Community?

Sister Viktorine waves her hand in my direction: Poor Adelheid, also. Of course, I know nothing of the Science, but to me it seems very worthwhile to invest time in such Children.

Dr A: That is Georg's area of work. I would not want to tread on his toes.

Sister Viktorine: Georg would not take that view. He is not ambitious, competitive.

Dr A: Ah, really? Well, then. I must raise the matter with him. I certainly find myself most interested. One sees a pattern. These particular boys. Thomas, Fritz, Gottfried ~

Does this mean that Dr A will soon be copying out Dr Frankl's work? Part of the reason Gottfried was sent home was because Dr Jekelius resented the help he gave to Adolf. The Rules for Adults are often Different. So much Inconsistency. I am so tired that my eyes are drooping, my head sliding sideways. None of my Plans make sense.

Dr A: I fear that the Times are against us.

Sister Viktorine: The Times are always against us. However, we have our faith, do we not? I believe that when our purposes are closely aligned with those of the Lord, when we honour some part of God's creation, some Person whose divinity is obscured—

Dr A is Observing her most Intensely and it is as though he suddenly spies some Distant Light. He turns, comes towards me, does not look at me but at the Matchboxes. Says: Adelheid, Countries are the approach you need. The Map as it is today. Don't you think?

He sweeps up that pile of Matchboxes which has so troubled me. The odd Matchboxes which have been left homeless by the shifting of many boundaries and the break-up of our Empire. His hands moving deftly to lay the Matchboxes in a new Constellation. All the tiredness of the day seems to leave his body.

He turns back to Sister Viktorine and speaks with a sudden fierce intensity: You believe it is possible to find Answers?

Sister Viktorine: I know it is. Through God's Grace. You would be able, I am sure ~

After My Death: Dr Wing in London, 1980

Once again we travel to a Different Time, a Different Place. I must check that You have read the Heading of this section Correctly. We have come to the Contemporary Age because it must be explained how, long after his Death, Dr A became a well-known Person and his once obscure Work widely discussed.

To understand how this happened, we travel to South East London in 1980 where lives a lady called Dr Lorna Wing. I am able to tell You about her as I have read all the documents but also because, being familiar with the Theatre, I may ask such questions as – what might a Person do in this situation? How might they behave? For this I thank Fräulein Weiss ~

Now Improvise Dr Lorna Wing who is sitting at her desk in this Far Distant South East London where it is ten o'clock at night. All is most quiet except for the occasional growl of a car moving in the street. Dr Lorna Wing's desk is toppling with so many Books and Papers spread upon it that the legs might surely buckle under their weight.

She is asking those same Questions which Dr A asked nearly fifty years before. She has just finished reading an article by an American Researcher but it doesn't help her. She now lays the Paper down, goes to make a cup of tea. As she waits for the kettle to boil, she stands at the bottom of the stairs. The house is lofty and narrow but Susie is only one storey above.

Dr Lorna Wing would hear if there was a Problem. Often there is a Problem. Mercifully, Candy, big shaggy Candy, is there, so all will be well. Dr Lorna Wing loves Candy almost as much as she loves

Susie – and her husband John. She goes back to the kitchen, pours the tea. It is June and the night is hot. Not as hot as Vienna but even in Distant London the nights can be Warm.

Lorna Wing opens the kitchen window, smells the garden. She has placed many plant pots on the terrace and now she breathes in their scent as she blows on her tea. She loves gardens, just as our own Sister Viktorine also loved gardens. Yet tonight Dr Lorna Wing's legs ache, her eyes ache. Everything aches.

She is fifty-two now and she doesn't have the energy she wants. That annoys her. She needs energy now more than ever. Briefly, she considers turning in for the night. She could open the window and lie in bed listening to the shuffles and settlings of suburban London – a fox in a dustbin, a beep of a car horn, the rattle of a distant train.

She could read one of the Detective Stories she so loves. She relishes their certainty. All the mysteries will be solved. Dr Lorna Wing should surely go to bed because she does not know what the night will bring. For the last twenty-three years – ever since Susie was born – John and she have never been sure of a good night's sleep.

However, Dr Lorna Wing's mind is a pendulum, endlessly swinging. She goes back to her desk and picks up that American Paper again then lays it down. She takes out her Notes. Again and again, she returns to these Notes. She remembers the day last year when some young male colleagues at the Maudsley Hospital had accosted her with this pile of Notes.

They hadn't known how to ask their Question. The words they needed did not exist. All that they could tell her was that they were concerned. They kept coming across Patients who they could not understand. Of course, they had admitted, in the World of Psychiatry you spend all day with people you struggle to understand ~

Dr Lorna Wing has worked in this field now for over thirty years and so much has changed. That first Doctor she had taken Susie to see had seemed sympathetic. *Really, there is nothing to worry about. Children develop at different speeds. All will be well.* But it wasn't. Later, when the Diagnosis came, there was nothing.

Dr Lorna Wing wanted Answers, treatments, drugs. The steps ahead. Nothing, nothing. Just shame. Doctors trying to tell her that she herself must be the cause. Even people who were meant to be friends had supported this idea. *She was overly ambitious, too well qualified. If a woman is not in the home, then it is inevitable that her Child will suffer.*

The role of the Mother in causing Autism was well documented. Research was being done in America. If Dr Lorna Wing wasn't interested in Motherhood then one might consider an institution? Dr Lorna Wing knew that this Assessment was Wrong but still she wept – in the loos at work, behind bushes in the park. She tried not to let John see but he knew ~

Then she stopped crying and decided: John, I'm going to become a specialist in Autism. John had been too exhausted to argue. He had said Yes, she should. Yes, together they would solve this problem. It was Science. There was an Answer. It was just a question of Research.

Lorna Wing, drinking her late-night tea, travels back now to those early days. Everyone says now – *Oh, how Times have changed.* Lorna could say that Times do not change of themselves. People change them. Oh, it was hard. Trying to care for Susie and then working endlessly in that basement Office.

Visiting every child in the Camberwell District of London who had an IQ below fifty. She and her colleague Judith Gould had assumed there wouldn't be many but they were Wrong, entirely Wrong. She found Susie again and again. The same Susies but also all different. Autism is a rare condition, she had been told, but it turned out not to be rare at all ~

Now she works with the Mothers. Exhausted women with rigid smiles. Some of them find it easier than she does. *I love it that he smiles but I just wish that he smiled at me.* She tries to sound professional, upbeat. She makes positive suggestions, although often what she is suggesting has not worked for her.

Sometimes the women who come to the Clinic have Children who talk. On a bad day Dr Lorna Wing might want to say – *At least he talks, at least he sees you. You have hope.* Yet in a way she finds it easier to cope with the other Children like Susie, who do not speak and perhaps never will.

What she finds most difficult are the Children who are at School. They are bullied – forced to eat tablespoons of mustard, heads pushed down toilets, arms twisted behind their backs. The mothers say – *He is so polite and Intelligent but he just does not seem able to Understand*. She can do nothing for those families.

The Children are merely eccentric, anti-social. Not ill. How can they be Organised and Categorised? They call this Autism but is there really just one condition? She has to believe that there is. Diagnosis brings safety. She thinks of Susie. How she has longed to cuddle her. The terrible pain she felt in the thwarting of her love ~

Things are better. Definitely better than they were. In this current year of 1980 there are now Schools and Academic Papers and Books and a National Society. But what actually is known? Nothing much. All that Dr Lorna Wing can say with certainty is that Categorisation is difficult ~ Nature never draws a line without smudging it.

Now this other puzzle, within the puzzle. She thought that their Camberwell Study would give them precise numbers and that would lead to Categories. But now her young colleagues are saying – *Why are these men in institutions? They can pass any number of Intelligence Tests and yet they cannot lead independent lives? Why?*

Briefly Lorna Wing drops her head into her hands. As she does so, her sleeve catches against a pile of Papers which cascades to the floor. Damndamndamn. She reorganises the Papers, remembers. She had asked John to Translate for her. Just the beginning, so she could get an idea. She hurries to his study and sees that he has indeed made a start. Bless him.

She carries the original Paper and the few pages of translation back to her desk —

She had found these Dusty Documents in the Cellar of the Hospital. Some obscure German. The name has been mentioned at International Conferences. She sits down in an armchair and starts to read. The text is impossibly difficult to follow. Is that a problem of John's translation or is the original Paper dense and incoherent?

She perseveres, stops thinking about the awkwardness of the language. Twenty minutes later, she hears John at the Door. He is the Director of the Maudsley Hospital and his job never stops. She hurries to the Door, waves the Papers at him. He is so tired that he's barely walking straight, his shoulder slanting down due to the weight of his briefcase.

Lorna saying: John, John. These Papers. I need you to Translate more.

John: Oh. Yes. Fine. OK. I can do that at the weekend. Don't I get a kiss?

Lorna: No. You don't. I need you.

John: No, Lorna. It is gone eleven. Have you checked on Susie?

Lorna: Susie is fine. John, please. I need this.

John knows that there is no way out: Half an hour. Only. Do you have any idea how hard this is? I don't actually speak German. I may have studied it at school but I've forgotten. It is not like French. The sentence structure. And this particular Paper.

Lorna saying: I know. But the Point is – this Man. Whoever he is. I mean, he's probably Dead. This Paper dates back to 1944. The Point is – he knew these people. He knew them.

John: Which people?

Lorna: You know which people. What is *Heilpädagogik*?

John: Oh that. There isn't a translation. Something between Medicine and Education. Maybe – Therapeutic Education? Curative Education?

Lorna: Autistic Psychopaths? Why would he use that word?

John is frustrated now: That's exactly my Point. You cannot make a straight translation from German to English. The word means something different in German. Plus, these things shift with time. The 1940s? Really? We must go up to bed. Are you sure these people exist?

Lorna: Yes. And I'm not the first Person who has seen them ~

3.a. Not Copying the Work of Adolf Schreiber

Now I finish the Story of Dr Lorna Wing and I return to the Curative Education Ward in Vienna in September 1934. Where Adolf is most determined that I must write his History Essay for him. This I must Not Do because this is Wrong Behaviour. Anubis is waiting but also one sees the Lesson of Gottfried. *Do not say anything at all.*

Also, the situation being even worse, for this Essay concerns the History of Austria which Adolf says I can just copy out of a book but, of course, History and Politics are closely knit, are they not? Oma telling me – *We do not discuss Politics in this Café* ~

Adolf speaks most grandly: Matchbox. I only ask because of Gottfried's hands. I simply do not have time. I'll be in a row with Jekelius. We have a deal, don't we?

For two days I avoid him. Then he traps me in the School Room when none of the Nurses are present. I try to move away but he tugs me back. I try to dodge out of the Door, but he shoves me against the wall so my head bangs, then he pushes the pen at me. I take that writing equipment but then force it back at him.

For Christ's sake, Matchbox. You spend all day Writing. Why not this?

The Lessons are commencing and Cabbage Children are pressing through the Door. This is like School. Leering faces. Worse here for there are Bedwetters, scab pickers, Children who eat their own poo. *Idiot, Simpleton, Moral Degenerate.* A compass will be stuck into my hand. My head slapped down onto the desk so that my nose is smashed.

THE MATCHBOX GIRL

Adolf says: Limited Intelligence? Brain damage. Is that your Problem?

Children are pushing, shoving, cheering. They are too close, too close. *She sees ghosts. Writes letters to her Dead Grandfather.* The zig-zag floor is scissoring. Books on shelves are flapping their pages. The lids of the desks are banging open and shut. Cracks are running across the ceilings. Adolf is a Liar. Why doesn't he do this work himself? If he wants me to Write then I will Write. Then he Will See.

I grab an exercise book and open a clean page. The Cabbages are hushed now, expectant. They want to see what I will write. Adolf also is now silent, watchful. I write the words large and certain, easy for all to read. *Adolf cannot read or write* ~

Like Biblical people or Fairy Tales, everyone is turned to blocks of stone or salt. Yet why are they shocked? They knew this Information. Of course they did. Everyone knew so why did they not say? A vivid energy has burst into the room and a bubbling Fear. Ripples of laughter, shrugs, all eyes on Adolf. His stinging hand slaps my cheek.

He is bursting out of his skin with Anger. His eyes are bullets. He shoves my shoulder: Shut up. Shut up. You wouldn't even be here if it wasn't for me. Everyone knows. Your Grandmother telling everyone that you are totally mental. Ghosts. Writing down how your Grandfather is Alive.

The lights are flashing, the windows and walls gasping. I hate Adolf. Stunted, pudgy, sweaty. I grab an inkwell and chuck it at him. The brick-like glass inkwell hits his shoulder, the black liquid splatters across his shirt, the well dropping to the floor with a massive clatter. Ink is dribbling and pooling. Everyone is silent. The Door of the School Room opens.

Dr Jekelius marches in. *Simple-minded, unable to perform the most basic tasks.* He wants me sent away and now he has reason. Nothing will happen to Adolf or the Penguins but I will ~

Too many Words and they are all getting out of control. They can no longer be laid out in straight lines and properly Organised. Instructions and QuestionsQuestionsQuestions. What is going on here? You, Adolf. Go and find Sister Viktorine. Adelheid Brunner, I have had enough of your insolence.

You will stay in this Lesson. Sit down sit down get on with your work we are studying Geography today why can you not do what you are told do you not hear what I am saying? If you cannot do this exercise then let us find something that you can do I hear that you are good at Writing Stories you certainly seem to spend plenty of time writing.

This is an exercise for Children far younger all you need to do is recognise these Story cards you understand what you have to do you need to write a Story organise the cards in a way which makes a narrative which makes sense and has a beginning-middle-end. My patience is really at an end if you really cannot do this then here is your Maths book.

You must finish these exercises you need to do that now stop staring into space are you able to hear me are you deaf is it surprising that both your school and your Grandmother are not able to cope you are causing a disruption and you have repeatedly failed stop staring at the floor you must go into the Meeting Room ~

Dr Jekelius may not have said all of those Many Things. All I know is that later Adelheid is sitting in the Meeting Room and the Story cards and her Maths books are in front of her. Sister Viktorine is bringing her a glass of milk and her Notebooks. The window is open and I suck in citrus-sharp air. If only I could squeeze the Clay up into a ball and make a new Person.

Yet the Truth is that in that moment no one is actually interested in me. They are all talking about Bruno the Book. *What is he doing? How could he know? It isn't possible.* Sister Viktorine saying: He isn't just turning the pages. I asked him – what is on page 220 of this book? He told me. Not the general idea. The actual Words.

Of course, Bruno is Actually Reading. Or at least he knows what exactly is in the book. Everyone knows that. Every actual Word. But why does this matter ~

Later, Fräulein Weiss comes into the Meeting Room: What is the matter, Adelheid? What are you doing here on your own? Fräulein Weiss goes to find Sister Viktorine and they whisper. *Punishment is not our way. What is he doing? Anni, I do not think you should question. I cannot be involved. I must follow the Instructions I have been given.*

Fräulein Weiss returns and sits down beside me and says: Never mind, Adelheid. You can do this work easily, can't you? Particularly the Maths.

She is trying to help but she is the same as Dr Jekelius. Too many questions. I ignore her and focus on my Notebooks. Fräulein Weiss is not pleased, takes my Notebook from me. I taptaptap my feet and stare out of the open window. Hope to get rid of her.

Sister Viktorine says – I wonder if this is really to do with her Opa.

Soon I will throw a bottle of ink at her ~

I am left alone but the problem of the Story and the Maths homework has not been solved. I could do the Maths but I am too Fatigued now and too Disarranged and too Disconcerted. All I can think of is how I will get taken away on a train, how I will Drown. Fräulein Weiss is talking to me again.

Saying things she has said most often before. Such as: We live within a Certain World, within a System. Sometimes we are required to do things which we do not want to do so that the System can work. We have to adapt etcetcetc.

All this I do know perfectly well. Everyone knows. Yet there is another Question. Of course there is. She knows that so why doesn't she speak the Truth? Since I am already in Trouble, it hardly matters what else I write now. I write in large letters – What is the difference between Pretending and Lying ~

Fräulein Weiss ceases speaking and Observes me. Considers me in Microscopic Detail. Looks, Frowns. Peers at me again. Her Clay Model has temporarily gone bendy and collapsed. Yet soon she gathers herself together again and says: Thank you for that Question, Adelheid. Thank you for Writing that down for me. How interesting.

How will she give me an Answer?

She considers for a moment and says: Well, as I have said, we all need to Pretend sometimes, don't we? Lying is different, isn't it? It is defined as deliberately saying something which you know to be False. The Point is we don't need to make a fuss over every Small Thing.

What help is that? What is a Small Thing and what is a Big Thing?

Fräulein Weiss does perhaps understand that she has not properly answered my question for she then says: Of course, there are moments in Life when we must speak the Truth. That is important. We must be Honest even if the Consequences are most Difficult. If such a moment arrives, then I think we will know. We will just know.

This she says – but how will we Just Know ~

She returns to Sister Viktorine in the Corridor and they whisper. *Just as I thought. It was always clear.* I am too weary to listen and lay my head on the desk. Until it is evening and Sister Viktorine comes to visit me again saying: I do understand, Adelheid, that you are Troubled by many Big Questions in this Life.

Of course, she has been talking to Fräulein Weiss. She continues: What I wonder, Adelheid, is whether you actually need the Answers to all these Questions? Are we really interested in how the World Works? Or do we just want to know how to Live more Godly Lives? It is our dissatisfaction with this World which is our Glory ~

Sister Viktorine is disturbed by footsteps ringing in the Corridor, the clanging of a Door. She is nervous that Dr Jekelius will return. I also am nervous but still I can do nothing. Evening comes and the light at the open window softens and haunts. At seven o'clock I hear a familiar voice. Dr Feldner saying: Not still here?

Sister Viktorine says in a most Proper voice: Adelheid needs to finish her work. She may not move from here until she has done it. Whispering then to Dr Feldner – *I don't know what to do. I've tried to persuade her. She won't. He'll be back soon.*

Dr Feldner sits down: So, Adelheid, what are we doing?

He peers at the books and wrinkles his nose as though they smell: Oh, come on. Let's not sit here all evening. This is Boring. If you don't want to write a Story, I'll do it for you.

Sister Viktorine gives him a warning look but he ignores her.

Dr Feldner takes up my pen and most strange it does look in his large hands. I do not think he will really write the Story for me but soon enough I see. I suppose he is going to make some effort to Pretend that his handwriting is mine. He doesn't bother at all. Plus, the Story he writes is Totally Ridiculous.

The Small Bear (who is good at riding a unicycle) has been sold by his Parents. He meets a Witch and then a Fairy. Also Talking Animals. Then through some magic he can go back to his comfortable home. A Silly Story, even by the standards of Silly Children's Stories, but that isn't the Problem. The Story has obviously been written completely in his Handwriting.

Sister Viktorine says: What if Dr Jekelius checks?

Dr Feldner shakes his head: Unlikely. Not really a Man for detail, is he?

Dr Feldner continues but his writing is not neat. I will get into worse trouble for the rubbish he is writing than if I did nothing at all. Or so I think – although perhaps it is possible that you can write any Nonsense at all and yet still it will be Categorised as a Story?

Dr Feldner stops, shakes his head: Oh dear. My handwriting is not nearly as neat as yours, Adelheid. Perhaps I can suggest some things for you to write?

So desperate am I to avoid this ridiculous situation, that I take the pen from him and start to record the rubbish he is telling me. Yet surely this only makes the situation worse? Now there is a transformation from his writing to mine. Hopefully, if someone only starts at the end then they might not see. Fräulein Weiss returns and also Dr Frankl.

Dr Feldner appears most pleased with himself and says: There we are. Problem solved. Look how quickly we are getting on. Adelheid has kindly given me a hand. I'm hopelessly slow – always have been.

Sister Viktorine smiles tightly: Thank you. But?

Dr Feldner: Refer him to me. Frankly, I don't care what he does. Dr A may not be prepared to stand up to the Man but I won't put up with this Nonsense. Now, Adelheid, try not to get into any more Trouble. You know I don't like Bad Behaviour.

Sister Viktorine: And the Maths?

Dr Feldner grabs the book: Maths. To hell with it.

He tosses the Maths book out of the window.

I am not making this up ~

3.b. Fräulein Weiss Explains Clever Idiots

Friday comes. Will any of us still be in this Ward at the end of the day? Seems unlikely. No escaped Rat will save us. Adolf is morose, shakes his head gloomily. He has not Forgiven me for the bottle of ink. Yet still we position ourselves in the cupboard. The Meeting begins with the normal stuff. *Instructions from above. Feeble-minded.*

Then Dr A says – *Adolf.* This is new. Usually, I never hear Adolf discussed and, of course, he does not allow anyone to read out from his own Notes. Sister Viktorine always protects him because she likes to help his Mother. Now we will hear whether we want to or not. Sister Viktorine sits up a little straighter.

Dr Jekelius says: The family situation would suggest Low Moral Character.

Sister Viktorine's cheeks have turned the shade of beetroot as she says: He does have many good qualities. He is very good with his hands.

Dr Jekelius: You mean, he steals?

Sister Viktorine turns pleading eyes on Dr Frankl.

Dr Frankl: With all due respect, I think that we need to stick to the Observations we have made. My impression is that over the time Adolf has been coming to us, he has made considerable progress. He has great Charm and he tries very hard in many respects.

Dr Jekelius says: Charm? Is that really enough?

Dr Feldner: Well, for some it certainly seems to suffice.

Fräulein Weiss looks down at her lap and tries not to smile.

Dr A: Ahem. Gentlemen, gentlemen, if you please ~

Adelheid – Do not look at Adolf. Do not look. But Adelheid can't be stopped. Adolf is close to me but his face is sliced in half by a dark shadow. Still, I know that he is furious. Everyone now knows that he cannot read and write. Then the bottle of ink. His essay still not written. He finished up Pretending that the inkwell hit him on the head.

Not True. Still he was put to bed like any other whingeing and Pretending Little Cabbage. No wonder he is Angry. How can he be the Führer of the Ward when he is treated with so little respect? Happily, the Doctors are now turning their attention to Bruno the Book and the tone of the Meeting changes.

Fräulein Weiss saying: Formerly, we did feel that actually he was not reading. Now we see he is. Even though he turns the pages so fast.

Fräulein Weiss is most excited: He said he had enjoyed the Book. I asked him which part in particular? He didn't know what I meant. Well, page 220? The book was lying there hence I picked it up. I turned to page 220 and he was replicating exactly what was on that page, just as Sister Viktorine reported.

That lady agrees: Repeating the Words exactly. Exactly.

Dr Jekelius: Yes, but we know that, don't we? We know what he says relates.

Fräulein Weiss: No. That's my Point. He Was Saying The Words On The Page.

Dr Feldner. The exact words?

Sister Viktorine: Yes, the Exact Words. I know it doesn't seem right.

Fräulein Weiss: But here Dr Frankl was most helpful. He can perhaps explain.

Dr Frankl: Well, my Point is only that this is possible. I saw something slightly similar once. In my childhood, I came to Vienna with my parents. We went to the Prater and there were various shows and stands. A fair. There was a Man there with prodigious mathematical abilities. I thought about it for so long afterwards. I felt there must surely be a trick. Yet there was no trick.

Dr A: Yes. It goes back to the work of Édouard Séguin in 1870.

Dr Frankl: Exactly. What he called an Idiot Savant.

The conversation goes on etcetcetc. The air in the cupboard is musty and bottled. La-la-la-la-la. My nose is tickling with dust. When will this end ~

Dr A: Adelheid Brunner?

Dr Jekelius: Disruptive behaviour. Ink pots.

Fräulein Weiss: Yes. Yes. But we know perfectly well that she had been provoked. If she would keep away from Adolf.

Adolf nudges my knee, grins.

Fräulein Weiss: I continue to feel.

Dr Jekelius: Undoubtedly capable of Domestic Work. Her Grandmother says the same. It really isn't our business to go against the preferences of the families.

Fräulein Weiss: We need more time. I have a strong sense. The questions she writes down. These are the thoughts of an Intelligent and Sensitive child. The thoughts of an unusual mind. Perhaps even Brilliant. As in the case of Bruno, we have to dig deeper.

Dr Jekelius: Fräulein Weiss, with all due respect. You are a Psychologist, not a Physician. While I'm sure your input is welcome.

Dr A says: Now, please. Please. Everyone. We must keep these discussions civil.

Dr Jekelius: Are we to entirely ignore the Instructions of Professor Hamburger?

A large iceberg is sailing past the window causing the temperature to plummet.

Fräulein Weiss: Dr Jekelius, I seem to remember that Dr A has already taken your advice on a similar matter.

Dr A: There is no need to return to that Question.

Fräulein Weiss: On that last occasion, a prediction was made as to what would happen and a boy finished up with his hands—

Dr Jekelius: I was not the Person who made that Decision.

Fräulein Weiss: Were you not? I fear your memory fails you.

Dr Jekelius: Fräulein Weiss, do you run this Ward or does Dr A?

The voice of Dr A wavers, squeaks. His Wolf impersonation lacks vigour. He may be wearing the hearth rug and waving the toasting fork but still he fails to convince as he says: Ahem. Ahem. I run this Ward. Clearly. I am most disappointed by the tone of this discussion.

Fräulein Weiss: I am simply asking that Adelheid Brunner be kept at the Clinic a little longer. Both Dr Frankl and I are engaged in assessments. This is important, is it not, Dr Frankl?

Dr Frankl: Yes. I would prefer that she stays.

Dr A: Good. Thank you, Georg, for clarifying. I myself recently looked at a Story which she wrote. Very odd. Bears on unicycles and so on. But not the work of a Child who is simple-minded. Adelheid Brunner will stay ~

Adolf and I look across at each other. He slaps my knee, silently laughing. The Meeting is ending. Dr Jekelius leaves first and then Dr A. As Dr Feldner is leaving, he looks across at Fräulein Weiss and punches the air, just as he does when the sock relay or some equally Silly Game is won.

Dr Frankl pulls Fräulein Weiss towards the window where no one will hear: Anni, please, be careful.

He is Quite Right. Safety Matches are not Safe.

Fräulein Weiss has no time for this: You men. I don't understand. Why don't you just tell him? You are vastly senior to Dr A or you should be. You have levels of experience and skill that he will never achieve.

Dr Frankl shakes his head, turns away.

Fräulein Weiss: I will not be pushed around. We have to be firm on these Matters. Just this morning I had news from my mother in Sagan. She is shutting up the Factory and leaving for London. Leaving our Family Home, our Whole Life. This is not *acclimatisation*. It is not *animals who change their coats for the winter*. You know this.

Anni, I am sorry to hear this.

Fräulein Weiss: I am not sorry. I am Angry. It is Not Necessary and I have told her so. She needs to challenge these Questions through the Courts. This is no time for weakness. No time to surrender to ignorant people who will do anything for their own advancement ~

3.c. The Choice Between Mops and Maths

I am an Intelligent and Sensitive Child. I may even be Brilliant. Fräulein Weiss has said so. I consider what she has told me about making an effort to Fit In. Of course, I have heard all this many times before but I do not have any ability in such Behaviour. Yet one can scrunch up the Clay and make a new model.

Or like Dr A, one can put on the coat of a Life and perhaps change for another garment when the need arises. Yet Dr A is not an entirely helpful model for me to copy. Perhaps I must behave like Upstairs Hildegarde Winkler for she is certainly considered a Proper Catholic Austrian Girl.

I shall start by completing all my Schoolwork. I have done little of it since I came here. Fräulein Weiss needs to be able to demonstrate my Intelligence and hence I sit down in the School Room and hurry through all the exercises that I have missed.

Adolf says: That's not a Strategy, Matchbox. If you are such a Very Good and Clever girl then what are you doing here?

Sister Viktorine and Fräulein Weiss say: Excellent work. Very well done. See what you can do when you decide to Participate ~

Just as I am considering this Question, *the Alchemy of Circumstance* presents me with Information which is most Useful to me. I am watching Dr A and he is collecting together various Books and Papers which are stored in the long cupboards of the Meeting Room. Dr Feldner comes in with his coat on, intending perhaps only to say goodnight.

Yet he does perhaps unwisely start talking to Dr A, saying: Hans, Hans. For God's sake. What are you still doing here?

Dr A: Ah. Reading. You know. And Paperwork.

Dr Feldner: But what of the lovely Hanna? Does she not require your company?

(Hanna – young woman on a Hiking Holiday with coat rack.)

Dr Feldner: I hope you were not discouraged by our Meeting today?

Dr A says that, of course, he was not in the least downhearted.

Dr Feldner is a most strange Person for although he is incredibly frivolous – such as sock relay races, allowing excited small Children to ride on his shoulders or his back, throwing books out of the window – yet he is also extremely good at guessing what other people think. Just like in a Play. Imagining how others might act in a certain situation.

He waits and waits and after some long silence Dr A says: Ahem. Actually, Josef. I am concerned. You have long experience in such matters. May I ask your advice?

Dr Feldner sits down: Of course.

Dr A speaks most quietly: I am worried that our colleague, Dr Jekelius. Well, you understand. In any event, I have been asked to go and see Professor Hamburger tomorrow and I fear that Erwin. He means well, of course. I have asked him before not to discuss matters with Professor Hamburger before discussing them with me. Then Fräulein Weiss.

Dr Feldner: Yes. Of course. I see your Point. Let me think. Firstly

Here Dr Feldner taps his finger sharply on one of Dr A's piles of Papers.

Says: Hans, let me just say. Dealing with Hamburger is not a question of the right Paperwork. That is not the kind of approach that interests Hamburger. The Point is – what do you need out of this Meeting?

Dr A says something about priorities la-la-la.

Dr Feldner takes no notice: Flattery. That is what I recommend. Tell him the Story about Bruno's reading. He'll like that. He will be able to share that with many colleagues and with his superiors. It demonstrates absolutely the value of Curative Education.

(I personally am bored of hearing about Bruno's reading.)

Dr Feldner continues: And your PhD, Hans. Your Research. Georg was telling me that you've made a decision. Tell him about that. Autistic Psychopathy. The Man loves to be seen as a scientist.

Dr A sounds uncertain: Ah. Ah. Perhaps not. The Point is that this new field of enquiry is not really scientific. I have tried to explain to Professor Hamburger before that this Ward is not so much interested in the science as the individual case.

Dr Feldner saying: No-no-no. Don't say that. Always present your work as thoroughly scientific. I know that Man. He loves plenty of talk of science and numbers and Evidence.

Dr A: I don't want to say anything that is less than True.

Dr Feldner: Of course. The Truth is of paramount importance. That is clear. But Presentation. That is the key. He will see the interest of the Research. I am sure.

Dr A: I see your Point but there is also the question of staff. I am worried about Sister Viktorine and others. In such troubled Times. We can't work without these people.

Dr Feldner: Tie it all in together. Say that you cannot carry out this new and important direction in your work if you don't have the staff. Come, Hans, have courage. Professor Hamburger could have appointed Jekelius to this job and he did not. You just have to present this in the right way ~

Presentation. This is a Startling Moment of Truth. Presentation means that other people have to see you Pretending. You have to Pretend in a way which might convince them. You cannot be dreamy. On this I am ruminating – most dreamily – when I realise that Dr A and Dr Feldner have both now left and Adolf has found me.

I know what he wants. He is still worrying about his essay. *He doesn't have time to do it. Why can I not do it for him?* We have been through this argument before. Now Adolf has a new Strategy. He produces Matchboxes. Some modern boxes with Matches still inside. But much more importantly, an envelope of most unusual specimens. Such as I have never seen.

These Matchboxes would impress even the Phillumeny Club. Where did Adolf get them? I suspect Herr Spellbinder. It is well known that he can lay his hands on almost anything – for the right price. I count thirty. That brings the total to 595. Only 405 to go until I reach 1,000. More importantly, these Matchboxes will make it easier to plan my Album.

Adolf and I have a deal between equals. I take the Matchboxes and tip the Matches themselves down the side of the plant pot as I have done with all the others before. I pick up Adolf's exercise book. Normally he would not allow anyone to look at his work but now he is happy enough for any solution to his difficulties.

I can see the work which Gottfried formerly completed. Gottfried is not as Clever as people think because he has done the work so tidily that the fraud will easily be detected. If I look back a few more pages I can see the work that Adolf did himself. The letters are upside down, the ink smudged, the spellings Wrong. No wonder he doesn't like people to see.

I get a History book down from the shelf. Surely one cannot get into trouble for copying out what is already printed? Adolf leaves me alone and goes back to the Ward because Sister Viktorine is calling. When he comes back, he is most impressed, saying: Matchbox, you are a bloody miracle. You are able to copy the neatness of my handwriting most exactly ~

Dr Feldner's words have certainly had an effect on me but also on Dr A. Formerly, he was a Man veering in an unstable manner between harsh words and tears. Now he is suddenly Authoritative. We are all learning many things and understanding how the World Works.

The only Person who does not do well out of all these many new approaches is Dr Feldner. Professor Hamburger corners Dr A: Hans, forgot to mention this morning. Feldner. The Man's clothes are dreadful. Only the other day he was wearing one green sock and one red. Also, there are stains on his tie. Breakfast I would say. Egg yolk.

Dr A is asked to suggest that Dr Feldner makes a little more effort.

Hamburger: With visitors coming to the Ward from all across the World, it is most important to present the Right Picture.

Dr A certainly understands this Point. Presenting the right picture is, indeed, all important. No Decadent Jewish Ideas. No throwing of ink bottles or poor handwriting. No egg on tie ~

3.d. All Waving Ribbons Now

Oma is coming to tea on Sunday. I brush my hair and polish my shoes. My blouse is not crumpled, my stockings do not sag. When Oma arrives, she is still clad all in black. She says good afternoon to me in a pinched and clipped voice. (Does this indicate some desire for Peace? Perhaps so, for when she spies me at Mass she merely Pretends I do not exist.)

Yet still my new-found courage falters. She is set against me and will not change. I wait for her to enter the School Room with the other parents but instead she bustles into the Meeting Room with Sister Viktorine, eyeing me most sourly as she closes the Door, saying: She has always snooped.

Certainly I would like to listen, yet unfortunately this is impossible as the Nurses are striding back and forth most often, bringing tea for the parents. I do not know What To Do and must begin to count the Floor Tiles or press my fingers together ~

Then Frau Schreiber does rescue me. She is Adolf's mother and I recognise her because I have registered her in the photo which Adolf keeps next to his bed. She says – *Adelheid, my dear, why don't you come and join us.* I am most humiliated and hesitate but she beckons with such Warm Enthusiasm that I must move closer.

This gives me a chance to Observe her (Unconscious and Uninhibited Responses) most precisely. Her blonde hair is piled up on the top of her head and her lipstick is scarlet and forms a ring around her flashing smile. Her voice sounds like the twittering song of a bird, golden and fluttering. She seems ready to burst into tinkling laughter at any moment.

Adolf is now carrying a cup of tea towards her with Utmost Attention. Crowded around her like pecking and nodding sparrows are many Small Children who pull at her skirt. Or push each other over or stamp on shoes or pull plaits. Yet Frau Schreiber says most cheerfully: Oh Too Many Children. Too Many Children.

She lets three of them sit on her knee all together. Adolf also plays with the Children, which I had not expected as he never plays with the Cabbages. He has a coloured spinning top and he kneels on the floor, sets it rotating at eye-blurring speed so that its many jewel-like colours merge and buzz.

As the Children gasp and giggle, Frau Schreiber leans down and kisses the top of Adolf's head. He is red to the tips of his ears but also proud. When Frau Schreiber calls me to come into closer proximity, I am pleased to stand beside her. She says: Adelheid. Such a beautiful girl. Adolf has told me how clever you are. How proud your family must be of you.

She kisses the crown of Adolf's head again: Just like me with Adolf.

I continue to position myself next to Frau Schreiber for a full twenty minutes, before that Lady has to leave. When she departs, Adolf gives her a scarf as a Gift and she is Exceedingly Pleased. When Oma departs, she inclines her head in my direction, but does not speak. If only Frau Schreiber would give me a home, but she has Too Many Children ~

Clearly, my Strategy in relation to Oma is not working yet but I am not entirely discouraged. At least the Papers were not signed. I am Out of the Bath and Reasonably Warm for Another Day. I lie shifting and shuffling that night and thinkthinkthink. What I know is that Oma is not inclined to be impressed by *an Unusual Mind* or *Brilliance*.

Suggestions of Cleverness will only render Oma more than normally Annoyed. Oddly, it is Dr Jekelius who unlocks this Conundrum. *Undoubtedly capable of Domestic Work*. The next morning I am up at first light and I do Domestic Work. Wash, dry, everything, wipe all the cupboards, the floor, the table. I do this with Great Precision as Oma has taught me.

The kitchen is Exceptionally Clean as it has never been before. For the Truth is that the standard of Domestic Work in this Ward is most low. Although everyone talks all the time of High Standards, and although the Corridors and the Ward are kept mopped and dusted, often the Disorder behind the scenes is shocking.

Sister Viktorine is good at looking at people's toes but Less Organised in other ways. At least the Bath in which I shall drown will be Extremely Clean. Mops are always needed. Maths less reliably required. Sister Viktorine is amazed by my work and truly grateful. Such a Good Girl. So very helpful ~

October shuffles into view, dreary and predictable. Yet still there comes a Cheerful Moment when all the appointments are finished and the Doctors are briefly congregated in the Meeting Room. (I am sitting in the Velvet Chair.) Dr Frankl says: I feel we owe a collective thank you to Adelheid. Is it not wonderful how hard she has worked over the last few days?

Fräulein Weiss does then say: Yes, Adelheid. We must offer our thanks.

Sister Viktorine indicates that I must sit down at the table saying: You are trying so hard. Wonderful. Wonderful.

I sit there feeling swollen and radish-like, staring at the table.

Dr Frankl produces a package: I also used to collect Matchboxes. I asked my Mother to look them out.

He flourishes a brown envelope from his jacket pocket and tips Matchboxes onto the table. A shower of them, a fountain. Falling like slow rain, like autumn leaves. I stretch out my hands to caress them. Not just modern boring ones. Matchboxes from long ago with intricate pictures. My Collection will soon be the best in all Vienna.

As my hands investigate them, I see Fräulein Weiss smiling so much that her face is wide open. I glide my hands through the pile, welcoming these new friends. How many are there? Fifty or even one hundred. I am suddenly so much closer to 1,000. I am now well over halfway to my target of 1,000 Matchboxes. So many, so many.

Dr Frankl has located himself beside me and is helping to turn the Matchboxes the right way up so that we can see them clearly. Images of the Imperial Eagle, a drawing of an overfed cow in an Alpine meadow, an advert for a Johann Strauss Walzer Konzert, unknown people fighting with pikes. Ladies in bustles dancing in a room of mirrors and chandeliers.

THE MATCHBOX GIRL

One Matchbox has a Bear on the cover. Like the one I already have but older. Dr Frankl moves it closer to the light. The Bear on this one is extremely fierce and it stretches out a clawed paw to eat us up. I Observe Dr Frankl's face. He is peering at me searchingly. His eyes are smoke-grey and behind them are long tunnels of light.

His neat fingers pick out the Bear Matchbox. He moves it towards me and bares his teeth, growls at me. Fräulein Weiss laughs. Ggggrh, grrrgh, grrgh, grrgh. I take the Matchbox from him and now the Bear is threatening him. It will soon eat him up and Fräulein Weiss will be all savaged as well. Grrrgh, grrrgh, grrrgh. His hands are thrown up in Pretend terror ~

That was the Most Happy of Evenings. Later we all proceed up onto the Roof Terrace. I am given a ribbon and I wave it. Dr A is watching us and making Notes. I think then of the many evenings we have spent here with the Maps, the compass, the diagrams of the Streets and how he has often remembered which shops exist, and in which place, even when I do not.

Like me, he has now become skillful at such questions as relay races, Schwarzer Peter, ribbon waving. Wavewavewave. Adelheid – Hop around on one foot looking as though this is fun. We are both doing well at this. Until Dr A turns and perceives what no one else has seen – except me – which is that Professor Hamburger is watching him.

Dr A ceases ribbon waving immediately, looks awkward. I carry on most enthusiastically. If you are going to Pretend then you have to do it well and you have to Present what you are doing. I keep going onandonandon until Sister Viktorine says: Enough. Now. Remember what I have told you, dear. Always important to know when to stop.

We are moving on to skittles. I roll skittles as well. Many skittles. Then a moment when all is finished. We have stopped and the City breathes a sigh of relief and is briefly still. Peaceful, settled with everything just where it should be. Sister Viktorine waves at me and I return her signal. This makes her know that I am here. It makes me know as well ~

3.e. Fräulein Weiss at the Tram Stop

That was our Moment. The Matchboxes given by Dr Frankl. The Roof Terrace and the waving. I should have known. For that night I did dream of Matchboxes and they were blowing everywhere, carried by a capricious wind, dashing across the Meeting Room and the Corridor, blown against the curtains, coming to rest on the floor or the tables.

Because of that dream I could not sleep and hence got up as the day was waking. It was true that the window in the Meeting Room had been left hanging open and the room was most chilled. Sister Viktorine arriving soon to instruct me that we must get the stove lit for it was now quite glacial in the City. The winter on us as suddenly as the fall of an axe ~

I am in the Meeting Room at break time.
 Fräulein Eder enters: Fräulein Weiss, Professor Hamburger would like to see you.
 Fräulein Weiss: What, now?
 Fräulein Eder: Yes, right now. Although you might want to arrange your hair.
 Fräulein Weiss remarks that she *sees no need* and will attend immediately. Sister Viktorine is making her eyes into alarm bells. Dr Frankl hovers with Papers dangling from his hand. The pipes are rattling, the floorboards squeaking. Someone is bashing a drum. A child keens. It seems I can hear Professor Hamburger's gramophone playing but this is Incorrect.
 I do Washing Up then clear up some errant toys which have been abandoned in the Nursery. Ten minutes, twenty minutes. In the

Corridor a gasp, a flutter of feet and of constricted breath. Cheeks are flushed and tempers throb in the tips of fingers. Fräulein Weiss strides into the Meeting Room. Sister Viktorine pulls her aside: What's happened?

Fräulein Weiss: I've been sacked.

Sister Viktorine gasping: No. Surely not. Why? How?

Fräulein Weiss: Hamburger, of course. Although he is not the only one.

Sister Viktorine: They can't just sack you.

Fräulein Weiss: Yes. They can. Easily.

Sister Viktorine is crying. She takes hold of Fräulein Weiss's arm but Fräulein Weiss breaks away and walks one way, and then the other, raises a hand to her head. Dr Feldner appears, prevaricates, moves away. Fräulein Weiss stares up at the ceiling and shakes her head. Then she picks up her briefcase, begins to gather some Files from the Meeting Room table.

Sister Viktorine: You are not going now?

Yes, right now. I won't work for Hamburger one day longer. Not for Dr A either. This must be partly his doing.

Sister Viktorine: Oh no. No. I don't think so. No.

Fräulein Weiss: For God's sake. Wake up. Can't you see?

Sister Viktorine looks tearful and offended but soon recovers saying: Dr A would not be involved in such a matter. He is a good Man. Anyway, you are needed here.

Fräulein Weiss: Apparently not. It seems I am Overly Emotional and Unscientific.

Sister Viktorine is weeping: You can't just go.

Fräulein Weiss desists from pacing, stands still: You are right. There is much that needs to be put in Order. I must hand over what I am doing. I will be taking copies of all my work. Dr A may have a PhD to write but so do I.

Sister Viktorine: Surely?

Fräulein Weiss: Sssh. You may be right about Dr A but Jekelius ~

If I could throw an inkwell then I certainly would. Instead, I take my Maths book and tear it up. Pull out one page after the other, rip each page up into many pieces, watch them drop into the bin. No one tries to prevent me because the Ward has turned into a Zoo and

Otto-Heinrich-Johannes-Kaspar or Liesl-Anna-Maria-Helene are weeping, drooling, pinching.

Adolf remarks: Ah well, what can you expect? No jobs for the Jews.

I go into the Dormitory and conceal myself under the bed, pressing myself tight against the wall. Opa, Opa. Where are you? Please, please. I need you. I see him now, walking away from me, waving his hand. Ahead is the Karl-Marx-Hof, which is a modern apartment building as big as a fortress, the walls orange. Opa is going in that building and I am to wait outside.

I am not to say anything at all. I stand in the allotment gardens, just outside the gates. Waiting, waiting. I crouch down beside a shed, hug myself to keep warm. Soldiers arrive, gun carriages are pushed through the gates. Wait, wait. The air is split by a terrible crash. My eardrums are bashed into the centre of my head.

Windows blow out, showering glass. The roof rises and then falls, the walls begin to come down, flowing like waterfalls, brick upon brick. The sky above still indigo and serene. A screaming echoes back and forth. Dust is coating everything. Where is Opa? He died on his way back from Russia. He is buried in the Central Cemetery ~

Adelheid – Stay calm. Do not panic. Focus on the Floor Tiles. Your own fingers. Press them tight together. Hiding under a bed is not a Strategy. I am scurrying up to the Roof Terrace when I hear Dr A's voice – low and uncertain – sounding from his Office: Ahem. Ahem. Fräulein Weiss. I am extremely sorry. Really. Please sit down.

Fräulein Weiss: No, thank you.

Dr A: Please. Ahem. I would like you to understand. I was not a party to this decision. Your work has been very much valued. You have made a great contribution. You personally have taught me a great deal. I don't think that anyone doubts—

Fräulein Weiss: Clearly, they do.

Dr A: Well, I do not. From a professional standpoint.

Fräulein Weiss: I am Jewish and a woman.

Dr A: Come, come. I do hope you would not attribute such motives.

Fräulein Weiss: What is happening in Germany—

Dr A: Fräulein Weiss, I am most certainly aware. I myself was in Germany not one year ago and I saw things there which were. Ahem, very Distressing. I do know that not everything we hear is an Unpleasant Rumour. When I last saw Professor Hamburger, I specifically discussed the need to maintain the staff.

Fräulein Weiss: Clearly your Point was not understood.

Dr A: I do not have Final Authority in this Matter.

The Door of Dr A's Office closes ~

Later Fräulein Weiss sends for me. A decision has been made that I am now ready to return to my home. Oma is happy for me to reside again at the Café. Things will be different now. Arrangements have been made. Discussions have taken place. However, my behaviour this morning has been Most Disappointing.

I never thought that I should be pleased to return to Oma but I am. Even though this also means that I must go back to School. Yet the Café and School are Worlds I know. All of this is better than the Freezing Bath. (This I think while fixing my eyes on the watery green vase and the watercolours of the Wienerwald.)

Fräulein Weiss: Are you listening to me, Adelheid? You are moving on and so am I. Change can be hard but it offers great opportunities. We must not cling rigidly to our routines. We must try to be capable of Independent Thought and be ready to Improvise when the need arises.

She also saying: We need not be Reckless but we must Embrace Adventure. Do not involve yourself in Adult Affairs. Know when an activity or a game is finished and stop at that moment. Do you understand? You have shown everyone how useful you can be in the Domestic Sphere. But you can do more than that. You are a clever girl.

Fräulein Weiss goes on to explain much la-la-la-la-la. Not to leave the Café. Good behaviour at school. Return to the Clinic every two weeks etcetcetc. We could have done more to help you. We are all subject to forces beyond our control. The people around us do not always understand us etcetcetc.

Plus: As I have told you before – you must not get involved with Adolf. I will also be leaving tomorrow and will be sure to say a proper goodbye. Now I must take these Papers to Dr Frankl. In fact, you could do that task for me. She hands me a pile of Papers with a Note on top – *Complete and ready for Filing.*

I go to look for Dr Frankl but he is missing.

Sister Viktorine: Dr Frankl? You'll have to leave those Notes on his desk. Fell down the stairs, hit his head. What a day. I fear he is slightly concussed but Dr Feldner has patched him up.

Adolf shrugs: Frankl. No Strategy. Should have gone on a Hiking Holiday.

He also is being despatched to his home tomorrow. I expect he'll be installed back here soon enough. Sister Viktorine always ensures that he gets what he wants. Others are departing also. Adolf says: A regular clearout. Women, Jews, Bedwetters, Cabbages. The ribbon wavers are in retreat. No more soppy Red Vienna. Place is going to the dogs ~

The next morning, I am sitting in the Reception Area with my Suitcase packed. (Suitcase, journey etcetcetc.) Sister Viktorine has identified a small box for Franz Joseph so I may carry him easily. She also has much advice to offer, saying: Consider the effects of your behaviour on other people. Understand the signals which are being given.

Dr A tells me that I am not to worry. Saying: You are a Scribe now and you must go out into the World to Report. Your powers of Observation are needed.

Dr Feldner comes and thanks me for all the many interesting conversations that we have shared. Says: You have made such progress with your schoolwork – and Adolf's.

He suggests that when I visit in two weeks I could write down a Matchbox or two that I particularly covet. Then he could make enquiries as to where those Matchboxes might be found? Says: You know Hansi and Herbert? You've met them? The lads I sometimes bring to the Café? We head out to the park on Sundays. Maybe Oma might allow you to come?

I am Pretending to ignore Adolf because that is what Fräulein Weiss has told me. Adolf knows this is only Pretending and says: I know where you are, Matchbox. I'll be sure to find you. See you at school. Remember. We are friends, aren't we ~

Soon Fräulein Weiss herself appears. She is wearing a new blue and green dress. Sister Viktorine is Pretending to be Cheerful but the

THE MATCHBOX GIRL

Truth is that she and Fräulein Weiss have always been like the two twins stuck together. *Three legs and three arms and they can walk along the road of Life most Happily.* How will they survive apart?

Everyone saying: You must write to us.

Where is Fräulein Weiss going? No one knows. Surely she will not find it easy to get another job? Fräulein Weiss says that I can accompany her to the tram stop on Alser Straße. Everyone cheers as she leaves and slaps her on the back. They are only behaving so riotously because Professor Hamburger is not here.

Dr A makes sure that I have got my Maps and Notebooks. It is certain I will need them. He shakes my hand and says: Adelheid, I never give up hope that one day I will hear you speak ~

Fräulein Weiss and I stride out together. She puts out her hand. I do not take it but I am pleased to walk beside her. She might want to cry but she smiles instead. We go to the news kiosk and she allows me to choose two Matchboxes saying: Remember the advice that I have given you. In particular, Adolf.

At the tram stop many people are gathered about.

A Man behind a newspaper spits: Tram broken down.

Fräulein Weiss stares along the rails, sighs: Ah well. I shall have to wait. You must go on, Adelheid. God knows how long we might be here.

She shakes her head, turns to me. I am still holding the Matchboxes she has given me. Numbers 646 and 647. She seems to suddenly focus on the Matchboxes and says that she should not have given those to me. It is Dangerous. A Child should not have Matches. Then she takes the Matches from me and tips them all into her bag.

I am horrified. Does she not know that Safety Matches are not Safe? She peers along the tram rails again. She is stepping out in hope, in determination, trying to see opportunity, not loss. I am Doubtful. After all, she is too old to get married and where will she get another job? I walk to the beginning of Lederergasse.

When I turn back, Fräulein Weiss is still glancing in frustration along the rails at the Tram that doesn't come. In her bag, she is carrying many highly inflammable Safety Matches plus some Paperwork which could change the Future of many — and yet will not. She doesn't know. The Tram will never come ~

3.f. Embracing Adventure

How I love to walk through my City once again. I have enjoyed watching it from the Roof Terrace but now I want to be inside the Streets. What joy it gives me to join with the narrow strip of sky above the tall and close-gathered Streets, to feel the breeze on my cheeks, to see the colours ripe and russet with autumn, on that morning of my doubtful freedom.

Glad now to get away from the suffocation of the Hospital. For over two months I have not seen my home and now I feel its nudging, magnetic pull. When I arrive at the Café, I step under the green awning and stare through the Window. Everything is just as it has always been. Palms in pots, red plush seats and green velvet curtain.

Gold-striped wallpaper and patisserie in a glass case. I raise my hand to touch the gilt lettering on the glass. Café Stadler. Of course I know that I must never use the main Door. Adelheid – *Make sure the customers don't see you.* So I step through the once grand Doorway which is to the side of the Café.

This Doorway leads through a tiled tunnel with a vast chandelier (no longer working) which nevertheless glitters darkly, ready to drop on your head and shower the passage with ebony diamonds. To one side is the Office where Frau Vogt the Caretaker lives, watching everything that happens in the building with viper eyes.

She is half concealed behind a curtain of faded red velvet, like a miniature cabaret. As I pass, she nods her bulbous head. One knows that she is, in fact, a snake because she has no lips and a forked tongue. Her eyes appear like holes that someone gouged with a knife ~

THE MATCHBOX GIRL

Standing in the Courtyard, I Consider our building. Although the exterior is heavy with pediments and dirty-white busty ladies and curly arches and bunches of grapes, this inner Courtyard is non-stucco and the walls are plain. Oma's family once owned this whole building, and she lived in one of the grand front apartments. Before *the Times*.

I turn away from those many stacked and stained Courtyard windows and walk in through the Door of our Storeroom apartment. Stop then and breathe in the smell of Opa. The sting of his tobacco still hangs in the air. Oma has placed a black cross beside his photo which stands propped on the hall table. How dare she?

Adelheid – Please remember. Do not involve yourself in Adult Matters. I stand in the Hall, trying to remain calm. So many memories. I edge open the kitchen Door to where there is light, steam, warmth. Oma nudges her hip through the swinging Doors to the Café, shrugs, says: Ah. There you are. Back again.

I use my Suitcase as a shield, gripping it tightly to my chest. Smile. Smile. Oma: Put your possessions in your room. I have placed a Cabinet For You.

She indicates to me then a locked box residing in the depths of the Wardrobe. A box sufficiently capacious for many Notebooks. Arrangements have been made. For this I am indeed most Grateful. (Other than the locked box, my room is unchanged. Narrow as a coffin but the ceiling neck-stretchingly high. The Window peering out onto the Courtyard.)

Everything is just as I left it – the stringy carpet, the iron bed and the towering Wardrobe squeezed in tight against each other. The Crucifix, the picture of Franz Joseph (Emperor). A grainy light enters through the lace which obscures the Window. I must rescue Franz Joseph (Rat) from his box. He can inhabit the bottom drawer just as he always did.

I creep then to the Door of Oma's room. Opa's shoes still against the wall, his trousers hanging over the back of a chair, his cap on the bedpost. I return to the hall, remove my coat and hang it up. Then arrive in the kitchen where the Chef is chopping the heads off chickens. His knife falls with a smash which cracks my bones.

Feathers flutter, blood gathers on Chef's knuckles. The kitchen is all bustle, steam and grease. Lukas comes to shake my hands most warmly. He is a Man I have never liked yet now I am strangely glad to see his drooping moustache and plaintive eyes. He stands crooked because of his damaged leg and rubs his dainty hands together.

He might like to regale me with complaints about something-somethingsomething but Oma crashes in carrying plates with the remains of Tafelspitz (boiled beef), sauerkraut and dumplings. A chicken squawks. The Chef turns and gives me a horrifying grin. Oma: Adelheid, start cleaning the pans, then the glasses. We'll need some coal.

Later Oma inspects my work and she wants to say – *Hurry up, stand still, fetch this, clean that*. But she can't find anything to criticise. I have made sure of that. For once, Oma is uncertain. She clears her throat: Well, Dr A – didn't think much of the Man – but maybe he has had some Success ~

At six o'clock Oma says: You may stop work now, Adelheid. Until eight o'clock you are free to do – well, whatever you want. So this is what the New Arrangements are to be. I must give credit to Sister Viktorine and Fräulein Weiss. I cease work and fetch my Notebooks. Even my Matchbox Envelopes and Albums. Initially, I am nervous.

When might Oma leap upon my Notebooks, rip out the pages, start to set them alight? This does not happen and instead Oma tells me that I will have this time every day to do as I want. This she says in a most affectionatereasonableindulgent voice as though this was her own extremely Sensible and Excellent Idea ~

The next day – School. I am quivering as I step through those Dreaded Gates. *Simpleton, Idiot, deaf-mute*. I try to smile but the other Girls only laugh. Yet Adolf keeps his promises. During the break, when Hildegarde tries to purloin my Satchel, he drags her around to the hidden entrance to the coal cellar. There he slams her head against the wall and spits in her face.

Problem solved. Later Adolf hands me his schoolbooks and I place them in my bag. I know how this Deal works and I can perform my part most easily. I return the books to him the next morning. The teacher tells him that he has clearly tried incredibly hard. She does not say the work is good. It is not. I have made sure of that.

He can't write and I do not speak. *Yet we walk along the road of Life together.* This is how it works but I always know there will be more ~

So it happens that some months later – or maybe a year – I hear a knock on my bedroom Window at night. I raise the lace curtain to perceive Adolf in the Courtyard wearing an extremely smart suit with his hair slicked flat. He comes with a silk dress, velvet shoes. Mercifully, Oma is a sound sleeper. Adolf says: Bring the Rat. We need the Rat.

Do not get involved with Adolf. A Bad Influence. So said that admirable Fräulein Weiss. Yet I do wonder. Fräulein Weiss had unpopular opinions and lost her job. So should one rely on her advice? I am capable of Independent Thought and do not want to wait for a Tram which will never arrive. One does not need to make a Fuss about every Small Thing.

So in this way, Adolf and I become Herr and Frau Schmidt, a smart young couple in Vienna who go out many nights in their most glamorous clothes. Even though I am thirteen (fourteen, fifteen) yet I am the Married Woman Frau Schmidt with her husband in his dapper suit with the pleated trousers, the turn ups deep and neatly pressed.

Just like the Play we made at the Hospital, we Pretend what Herr and Frau Schmidt might do. Together we go to a bar in the jewel-box Centre of our City. Some obscure place, dark and crowded. Adelheid savours all that there is to Observe in this New World. A jukebox jigs, men play billiards. Waitresses bend low, their dresses revealing much bosom.

Adolf says: Get out the Rat when I tell you.

So many coat pockets. I am breathless at the possibilities. Matchboxes are positioned on tables, abandoned on the bar. They are suspended from the light fittings and dodging between our feet, under the tables. Like magpies, we collect bright and shining things. I put my hand in my bag and my fingers close tenderly around Franz Joseph.

Adelheid — Wait until no one is looking, put Franz Joseph on the table adjacent to ours. A woman in a jadesatindress screams, her mouth a roaring red tunnel. The Man beside her leaps up. The table wobbles, tips over. *No fighting in here. There's a rat. A rat. For God's sake.* Wine is spilt all down the woman's precious dress.

A punch is thrown, the Man's hand moving back most slowly and then coming in hard.

People are screaming. Everyone is stumbling, fighting to get out. The bar is raining Matchboxes. I'm stretching out my hands and they are cascading all around me. Adolf is operating by the coat rack. Wallets, cash, a crystal evening bag.

He catches my wrist: Come along, darling. Rough sort of bar. Best cut out of here.

Sometimes we do not bother with the Rat. Instead, I Pretend to faint most dramatically. Adolf teaches me well. *Identify where the washrooms are. Meet you at the tram stop.* Sometimes I must climb onto sinks or cupboards, squeeze out of high windows. I come to know the intestines of many buildings.

I open Cellar Doors onto clandestine Meetings. Socialists? Fascists? I do not know. Once I am chased by a midget. Another time I hide under a bed where half a Dead Pig is being stored. I encounter a Man with a feather headdress wearing women's underwear. Often, I do not find the Rat but do not worry. Rats know how to Embrace Adventure ~

3.g. The Matchbox Empire

Years collapse one into the other. My Life is mainly – Rats and Bars and School. Even the girls at school start to appreciate me because I have money, lipstick, cigarettes. I do not understand Fashion but it turns out being a Golf Club is not such a bad thing. Other girls of my age are most interested in committing sex acts and they talk about *what is love?*

How boring. Surely that is when you have severely overestimated the qualities of another Person? Yet I am overjoyed merely to be included. I return to the Clinic less and less. It is not necessary now to give Instructions to Adelheid as I am all one Person now. I keep in mind the advice of Sister Viktorine but I no longer need to concentrate hard.

Oma now does not mention that I was ever at the Hospital. Yet I always continue to see Dr Feldner because he comes to the Café with Hansi and Herbert and I accompany them to the Votiv Kino cinema. Herbert, who is the younger brother, is a pleasing small boy but Hansi has a Bad Reputation and a sneering face (saying See If I Care). Oma dislikes him heartily.

Sister Viktorine also appears occasionally to chat with Oma who offers her a free coffee or a late-night brandy. Sister Viktorine relays news of the Ward: Sadly, Dr Jekelius has departed but the Good Dr A continues to promote the work of the Ward tirelessly. Cares so deeply for staff and Children. Did you hear he has scaled the Matterhorn? Such courage ~

During these years, I come into the possession of many new Matchboxes and the Truth is that I could arrive at 1,000 Matchboxes without much trouble. Particularly as many customers in the Café now bring me Matchboxes to add to my Collection. But I am growing up and become discriminating. I never was a Socialist. Matchboxes are not all created equal.

I do not want just any ordinary Matchbox but a Collection which spreads across the World. Matchboxes from Africa, or India or even South America. This being possible as people from many countries visit our City. Even when I can only find boring Viennese Matchboxes yet I can swap them with the Phillumeny Club.

I love to imagine all the countries of my Collection. I feel as though I am taking possession of the Whole World. A great Empire, arranged just as Dr A suggested. Sometimes Adolf and I go to the railway stations in the south and west of the city, the Südbahnhof or the Westbahnhof. Stare at the departure boards. Graz, Linz, Salzburg, Klagenfurt. Munich, Paris, Venice.

This is our City and our Futures lie ahead like so many open Windows and Doors.

Occasionally someone says that I am Adolf's girlfriend.

He says: Dirty rotters. No understanding of Business ~

Time flows on and the Rat Business ends. Adolf has departed school (I may stay on two years). He has become involved with groups of young men who wear baggy, pinstriped suits and do not cut their hair. Also playing American jazz and swing music and committing sex acts. Fights often break out in the Streets between this group and the HJ, the Hitler Youth.

The HJ is officially illegal but you would not think so. Many boys have given up their Karl May adventure books (set in America) and are wearing black corduroy shorts, black raincoats and Tyrolean hats. Some even wear belts with massive buckles emblazoned with the words Blut und Ehre, Blood and Honour.

Some adults also are known to wear a Nazi badge under the collar of their coat. Yet no action is commenced against them because as Opa would say – *in Vienna despotism is always mellowed by indolence.* Those adolescents who are less bold wear long white socks which signals allegiance but cannot lead to arrest.

Sister Viktorine shakes her head dolefully when she speaks of Adolf. Surely he will soon be in trouble with the Police again?

His poor mother is most worried. The Winkler sisters and I know that most Schlurfs have already been shoved in the Green Henrys (police vans) repeatedly, their curly locks forcibly sheared or castor oil poured down their throats.

Frau Schreiber comes to the Café and bemoans her son's behaviour. Oma is polite and offers Pretend Concern. Yet the Truth is that she never liked Adolf and she considers his mother Cheap. I do not care if she is Cheap. She is an Elegant Lady and always most charming to me.

Mercifully, it soon turns out that Adolf is not the only Person who needs schoolwork completing. Hildegarde also has need (not surprising as she was always dim). Fortunately for her, I am ready to help. Most unexpectedly we become friends – or make a Deal. Hildegarde is going to secretarial college as soon as she is sixteen and I want to go as well.

If I learn to type, then I will be able to present my Writing and my Notebooks more tidily. This is Important as I now have a Proper Job (not just as a silly Scribe but a Real Journalist). I write for the school magazine. Hildegarde (who is appointed Editor) tells me the articles she wants me to write. Usually, it is dresses and hats. Her sister Gerda creates the drawings.

Many of the Girls in my class join the Bund Deutscher Mädel (League of German Girls, BDM, also illegal). The lads let them ride on the back of their motorbikes, which Oma says is *Common*. I yearn to join but Oma will not allow me. Nevertheless, I am able to help Hildegarde with diverse tasks. I write out Reports most precisely and clearly.

(Making sure that everything is expressed in most sober and formal language, no longer writing as though everything is a silly Adventure Story.) Also, Hildegarde must design posters for winter fundraising and so I do the letters, measuring carefully and straight. Everyone believes Hildegarde does the posters ~

In that time there was talktalktalk of Politics. Old people are obsessed by the idea of an Independent Austria. Yet they also say that our Country is not economically viable (such failure of Logic). Why is it not a good solution that we should join with the new and powerful Reich, our neighbour with whom we share our language and culture?

Germany is forging ahead. The New Order. The Will to Reconstruction. However, our Chancellor Schuschnigg has made clear that he will never agree to a Union. Yet we all know that Germany is now a Properly Organised Country with jobs and high wages. Meanwhile in Vienna people continue to wear clothes in which several people have already Died.

I peruse many Leaflets and newspapers in order to be Properly Informed. The majority are simply relying on Gossip and Rumour even though everyone has been told againagainagain that they must not repeat idle speculation. Do they not understand that Facts and Evidence are important? I have always known this yet increasingly I comprehend it even More Fully.

The whole reason why I was sent to the Curative Education Ward was because people were not Clear in what they said. They did not tell the Truth. Everyone was always Pretending and Steering. This was regrettably necessary as the System was not explicit in its ideas and demands. Befuddlement was Inevitable.

Now when I read Information about the Reich, I see what it can mean to have a System based on Truth-Clarity-Logic. My Past Problems were perhaps not caused entirely by my own failings, but by the inadequacies of a System riddled with Uncertainty and Hypocrisy. So many people are involved in ridiculous Performances involving Bears and hearth rugs.

This was a Problem of Old-fashioned and Complaining People.

Happily, one knew they would soon have to step aside ~

I go to the Votiv Kino with Hildegarde and Gerda. We see films of the rally at Nuremberg. The air in the auditorium crackles and fizzes in amazement as we see the torches, spotlights, unending rows of troops. What might Fräulein Weiss think? I do not suppose I will ever know but then Sister Viktorine comes to the Café with a letter from that same Fräulein Weiss herself.

Where has Fräulein Weiss been all this time? Sister Viktorine speaks to Oma in such a muffled voice that I cannot hear. I attempt to slide the letter off the bar so I may take a glance but Oma sees what I am doing and Sister Viktorine says — *Best not to involve yourself in adult affairs.* Yet happily *the Alchemy of Circumstance* is in my favour.

Oma must serve a customer and Sister Viktorine is required to help an elderly Man get up from his chair and move (with his shuddering and poking walking stick) out into the Evening Street. All this Fuss takes considerable time meaning that it is possible for me to look at the letter at my leisure. Sadly, I view little which is of Interest.

Just an address in New York. Fräulein Weiss writing. *Please, please, try to persuade Georg. He needs to leave now. Tell him this. He can come here. He must not delay any longer.* How Very Strange. What is she doing in New York? And why is she asking that Dr Frankl should come? She had been pleased enough to leave him behind ~

After My Death: Boston, USA, November 1937

I Answer for you now that Question in relation to the career of Fräulein Weiss. This I may do since here in my Posthumous Life I know all that did Unfold. For this Purpose, we travel now to the City of Boston in the USA in the year of 1937 and together we enter a square concrete Hall at the Docks. Here we find Fräulein Weiss who has been waiting there now some hours.

A Question of the Paperwork. She hoped when she left Vienna she would leave the Paperwork behind but it is the same everywhere. Waitingwaitingwaiting. She has travelled from New York to meet Dr Frankl. The telegram had arrived after she had given up all hope. *Leaving Liverpool on the RMS* Laconia *on 7th November. Arrival Boston 15th November.*

She doesn't know why he changed his mind. *Pogroms come and go. Emigration is dishonourable.* She had heard those arguments many times. Perhaps his mother had died? He might not have written to Fräulein Weiss about that Matter as she had never been fond of his Mother. An hour ago an announcement had confirmed that the ship had docked.

Waitingwaitingwaiting. Georg was never good at Paperwork. Will he be sent back? Fräulein Weiss herself was sent back the first time. It is important not to look at other people in the Hall. Most are men on their own, hoping that they might see their wives and Children soon. Fräulein Weiss does not want to encounter anyone she might know.

Back in New York, at the end of the street where she resides, there is a Man selling Matchboxes and she knows him from Vienna. He was a rabbi there. Often one sees whole families, red-eyed and creased, standing in one queue or another, devoid of hope. She is different, lucky, guilty. She has money, a place to live and she has Work ~

Initially Fräulein Weiss had attended at East Boston Immigration Station but then it had become apparent that the Ship would not arrive at that point. She had spent some long time walking through low brown buildings, past wharfs and warehouses. Above her towered the funnels and masts of massive ships. Is she now in the Right Place? She is still Uncertain.

People are appearing now, rushing through the gates. Tearful reunions are taking place. She looks away, embarrassed. There he is – right there. Older, smaller and, yes, he still has that irritating uncertainty. Why is he not looking up? Looking forward? Looking for her. She wonders if it is too late to simply disappear. He has her address in New York.

The Receiving Hall is crowded but, when he raises his eyes, he seems to know exactly where she is. He steps towards her. Neat, precise, mild. Good-looking. Quietly stylish, some might think. She steps forward to greet him. They must embrace, of course.

However, she reminds herself that you don't have to marry a Man just because he is now living in the same Country, and you don't have to marry a Man just because you have no one else to marry, and you don't have to marry a Man just because you used to be lovers ~

Fräulein Weiss steps forward, wonders for a gasping moment if she might cry. She reaches up to embrace him. They shuffle like dancers who have lost the rhythm and both laugh awkwardly. Then she is holdinghimandholdinghimandholdinghim because he smells of Vienna. Except he doesn't, of course, but everything about him retains the essence of that City.

He says: Thank you. Thank you for coming to meet me.

She feels embarrassed in relation to her sudden enthusiasm. Around her other women are weeping and crying but she is not like them. They must get away from here. *Is there a bag which she can carry? They can take a cab into the City.* They are walking together. In America. Focus on the cab, the hotel.

Will it be possible to find a cab in this area. Might they have to take the tram. And then there is the hotel. She had booked a quality hotel called the Langham in Franklin Street. She wanted him to have a good impression of this New World but now she sincerely wishes she had not come. Oh God, the hotel ~

Miraculously, they locate a cab immediately. The windows are steamed up. Evening – brown and damp – is descending on the City. The cab smells of cigar smoke and the seats are creaky beneath them. The driver addresses them cheerfully in a language they do not understand. She has booked just one room at the hotel. She can explain – an administrative oversight.

Together they look out through the steamed-up window at the looming shadows of cranes. She experiences a horrible excitement, like a child being taken on a thrilling journey. He is too close to her on the seat. She considers herself to be pathetic. She is not a teenager and neither is he. They are no longer the young people who kissed outside his mother's apartment.

They cannot hold hands as they did once while walking in the Wienerwald. He can be made to understand that this is a practical arrangement. When she first came to America, Fräulein Weiss had expected to meet a New Man. The Fräulein Weiss of Vienna was considered clever, prickly, serious, old. Her name had been linked to rather too many men. She was a liberated woman, she was used goods.

Americans were surely more liberated, broad-minded? At first, everything had progressed as she had hoped. She had learnt to smile as often as the Americans do. She no longer winced when people laid an over-familiar hand on her arm. She went to bars, smoked and laughed, but she has to form whole sentences in her mind before speaking and she knows her voice sounds heavy. It is not coming from the same part of her body as before.

One weekend she went out of the City to the suburbs to visit a university professor, one of her new colleagues. His house was full of fabulously functional appliances and he was most interested in his closely shaved lawn. All here is marketing. He shows her what she wants him to be, not who he is – yet still she had tried to believe that she could love him.

Vienna was stuck to her, clinging. The letters, the Fear. What could she say? How could she explain to him how she had become dislocated not just from her own World, but from her own self? Gradually a chill had set in, an awful isolation. Some part of her longs to be welcomed, another part rejects everything she sees.

In dreams she walks the Streets of Vienna trying to find her way home. What place is there for all this longing – and now Georg? She is glad that he is safe, of course, but what more? The cab is delayed in traffic. Around them the City, seen through the failing light, is all low brown buildings, fire escapes, streetcars, the glittering facades of cinemas and bars.

Georg tells her that he made sure to bring letters of recommendation, and he has already booked the exams he needs to qualify. He has also conveyed a copy of his Paper. *Language and Affective Contact.* If he Translates it, then perhaps it might be published in America? He recounts news of former colleagues.

Sister Viktorine. Dr Feldner. Everyone has missed you. She asks: Hans?

Yes, of course. Of course. Just the same.

She says: Still using your work – and mine?

Ah, come now, Anni. Be fair. It is not about my work or his. I wish you'd been there over the last three years. He's really made something of that job. He is clever. It took me time to see it. I thought he was just meticulous, enthusiastic, but I was mistaken. He has figured out how to steer the dreaded Hamburger. He absolutely pleaded with me to stay.

Fräulein Weiss: Was that helpful?

Georg: I shall miss the Children. I will miss them badly ~

The cab is pulling up at the hotel. Georg takes out his Suitcases and offers to pay. He has dollars. She understands that he wishes to reveal himself as not quite helpless but he is helpless – for all his cash and his first-class ticket and his Research, for all his letters of recommendation, academic Papers and exams already booked.

Together they walk into the hotel Reception which is as long as a tennis court. The floor divided by marble chequered Floor Tiles, the Ceiling lofty, the walls lined by blue velvet benches enclosed in circles of soft light. Fräulein Weiss speaks briskly: So the thing is. I accidentally only booked the one room but there is bound to be space.

However, the Liveried Young Man at Reception is unhelpful.

No, ma'am. I'm very sorry. We have nothing available.

Wretched Man. Is he withholding all those other empty rooms as some kind of joke?

Georg says: No problem. I can find another hotel.

Fräulein Weiss says: No. No. Absolutely not. I booked the room for you. I can find another place. I can even take a late train back to New York.

Georg says: Well, look, look. Let's not argue about it. Not now. Let's go up to the room and get ourselves a drink. Don't you think?

The Man on the Reception hands Georg a pen so that he may sign the register. He writes his name and then stares at it for a moment as though he has forgotten who he is. He looks at Fräulein Weiss, raises his eyebrows, adds an E to his name. Georg. George. He shrugs and they both laugh ~

Together they are carried swiftly upwards in the muffled lift. Georg opens the Door. The room is all bed. Long silk curtains are held back by elegant twisted ropes. A shiny chest of drawers with three arched mirrors, a low and brittle occasional chair. But mainly the room is The Bed. George puts his bags down on The Bed.

A knock comes at the Door. A waiter with a tray and a bottle of wine appears. Georg has the tip ready. He opens his Suitcase. It is crammed with books and Paperwork. Fräulein Weiss already knows that he will find it harder than he thinks to Translate that work, to get it published. How do you Translate when the words don't exist?

Fräulein Weiss considers again that American who visited Vienna. What was his name? He talked about plumbing and bed bugs. She saw it then and she has seen it so often since. You try to communicate with the people in this Country and they smile but then, at some point, you realise that they are not interested at all. Or perhaps they don't understand.

She herself has made no progress on her PhD – although that is partly her own fault.

Georg suggests that she sits down but she is uncertain. In order to get to the chair, she would have to move past him in the narrow space. She will leave, get the last train, arrange to see him in New

York. She sits on The Bed, feels the chenille bedspread stick to her skirt. He passes her a glass of wine, disappears into the bathroom. She gulps the wine down ~

A Sudden Startling Truth comes to her – there will be no other hotel room. There never was going to be any other room. Georg is a Practical Man. He will not make this Difficult. He was once in love with her – embarrassingly in love. They are both older. She pours herself another glass of wine, tips it down. Through smeared glass, she sees the lights of the City moving.

Looking out, she vainly hopes that there might be something out there other than an American street with those ugly, plain buildings. Why does America have to be so ugly? So basic? So utilitarian? She thirsts for Vienna. Why can't they return home? Georg has removed his jacket and holds a glass of wine in his hand. She moves to the chair.

Cigarette? His cigarettes will taste of Vienna so she declines.

She remembers all the brisk advice she has given to Children over time. *Don't whistle or stare at the ceiling. Look people in the eye. Be clear in asking for what you need or want.* Best to get it said: Listen, Georg. I decided that we should. I got a licence. You have to get a licence. I did that in New York. We need that.

The wine is back in her throat. She coughs and splutters, worries that she might be sick. She hacks again and again, relinquishes her glass of wine so that she can locate a handkerchief. Why isn't he doing anything? At least in this situation he must be able to respond with certainty.

Finally he says: Listen, Anni. Thank you. Thank you.

She wants to kill him now. She wants to punch him or kick his shins.

He is looking at her too intensely: Look, this is important. You absolutely must not feel any obligation. Our situation is Difficult. You should not feel in any way that—

Oh shut up, Georg. Please. Can't you just?

She drinks more wine, sneezes and wheezes repeatedly, fails to find Words. Georg is rummaging in his Suitcase. Anni thinks – I am too old for this, too old. Yet at the same time she is instructing herself – *In these new circumstances everyone must scale down their expectations.* She is also hearing how he said – *I shall miss the Children.*

Does it always have to be Other People's Children?

Is it too late for them ~

He is approaching, offering something. A ring. A heavy ring, old, bulbous and intricate with labyrinthine green stones. He takes hold of her reluctant hand. She has always had stumpy, tree-trunk fingers. Of course, the ring won't fit. She is sure of that. But the treacherous ring slides spitefully into place.

Georg says: The ring belonged to Mother and she sent it for you.

Oh God, his Mother. His Ghastly Mother. Georg is holding her hand, looking down at the ring. Yet his mother has now entered the room – or they are in her Sitting Room. On the Esteplatz. An apartment at the top of that cliff-like neo-classical building. An affluent world of stained glass and marble foyers. Everything so stiff and correct but stagnant, dying.

So many photographs in twisty silver frames, china dogs, pots of dusty dried flowers. All Dead and flaking away. Enough to suffocate. One's eyes drawn hungrily to the tree tops waving in the breeze, poking cheerily above the solid stone balcony. Longing to fly away like the birds chattering in those waving branches.

Old Frau Frankl watches as the grubby maid pours tea with shaking hands. *You study at the University? You modern girls, really.* What she wants to say is – *Don't you dare mess around with my Georg. With your messy hair and ridiculous job. So many lovely young girls who would make proper wives.*

Anni whispers: Georg, I am sorry. Did she die?

Georg is silent for a moment. Then says: She has aged, she is ill. She was brave, made me promise to go. She shouted at me, told me I must. Not just the ring. She gave me all her jewellery. She wanted to give me more cash also but I wouldn't. She knew I would come to find you. She wanted you to have the ring.

Georg swallows several times then speaks again.

She sends you all her Love and her Best Wishes for the Future.

The Future.

Anni gasps: Oh Georg. I'm sorry. We can do the Paperwork. It will be possible for her to come. We can start straightaway.

He says: Maybe. Don't worry now, Anni. Dear Sister Vik will look after Mother. We'll be on our way back before too long.

Fräulein Weiss feels a sudden flush of hope. Go back. Of course.

Georg says: Britain and France will stand firm. There isn't the support in Austria.

Suddenly he is decisive, drains a glass of wine: Don't marry me out of pity.

I'm not. I'm not ~

4.a. Where is Monsieur J'Aime Berlin?

We return to Vienna now. The date is that Momentous Moment of 15 March 1938. (I am sixteen years old now and I firmly intend to write in a Sober and Informative Fashion, reporting only the Evidence. Yet in reality the Events of that Time were so Chaotic that the Words themselves are disorientated.) How can I explain?

For so long everything was the samesamesame. Until it was all changechangechange. One Eternal Day it was – *We stand by the Chancellor. Red-white-red until we are Dead. Austria is a Sovereign State and will permit no interference in our Internal Affairs.* Schuschnigg's referendum will prove our wish to continue as an Independent Nation.

During those frenzied days, even at night, the City was bright as broad daylight. Lorries drove past piled with propaganda posters which were plastered across every wall. *If you want freedom, peace and bread – support the flag that's red-white-red. With Schuschnigg for Austria.*

The Inner City appeared covered in snow so many were the Leaflets dropped by planes. Then it was RumourRumourRumour. Hitler will never allow a ballot. Oh nonono. Loudspeakers in the Streets and squares announcing thisthisthis and thatthatthat. Flags up, flags down. The Austrofascist Kruckenkreuz (Austrian Cross) or the Nazi Swastika?

In that Brief Instant, it seemed that the Nazis were Outmanned and Outgunned. Everywhere one saw the Socialist sign of the three arrows and the clenchedfistsalute of Freedom. Megaphones blared. *We shall lay to rest the humiliations of 1866.* Ballots happening, ballots cancelled. Nazis outoutout or ininin. You could not keep abreast of Happenings.

Then all becomes Clear and Brilliant because the Führer is coming. Every stone is speaking, every tree is cheering.
The sky itself is loud with praise.
A New World is coming.
Everything, forever, changed ~

Today there will be a Fantastical Parade which starts at one thirty. In the Café, Lukas has the Radio tuned and we grasp every word. Across the road, at the Amtshaus, the Fatherland Front flags have been torn down and swastikas unfurled all along the white facades. The City is a sea of conker-coloured uniforms. *No more bunting or brown can be purchased anywhere.*

If Opa were with us, he would certainly be telephoning to London to see if they might pay him for an account. A special Matchbox has been created with the stern face of a German soldier and a Swastika. Of course, I am too old now for such Childish pastimes yet still I am thrilled when the Stationer Herr Wächter brings a Matchbox for me.

Youngsters in Hitler Youth uniforms are bustling through the Streets selling metal swastika lapel badges and handing out free flags. *We are part of seven million young people who belong to Adolf Hitler and will share in his joy.* My flag is already positioned in a vase on the windowsill and I also have a most shiny tin badge.

Only three days ago Oma might not have allowed this but now she is making herself ready for the Parade. Frau Winkler from upstairs has asked Oma to accompany her and they will be able to stand right at the Door of the Rathaus as Herr Winkler is an important Man in the World of National Socialism and has even met Herr Hitler himself once.

So hard to know what to wear because although the sun shines with a violent springtime light yet the temperature is not much above freezing. Oma pinned her hair in Papers last night, now applies powder and lipstick. She stands at the mirror adjusting her fox fur, which she has hastily taken out of the box on the top of the Wardrobe.

Lukas and I are nodding and ducking like chickens for the Café is crowded with so many people we may hardly find a way through the crush. I need to be out in the Streets. How can I report on what is going on if I cannot see? Hildegarde appears at the Café Door in her brown uniform. She has come to ask whether I can go with her to the Parade.

She salutes and I salute back. Oma gives Hildegarde a smile which is both a welcome and a warning. I check that I have got my Notebook in my pocket. Hildegarde explains that I cannot march in the procession as sadly I am not a member of the BDM. I could soon become a member. Everyone is welcome.

Hildegarde continues: One may not be aware that there are different types of Hitler Youth. Bann G for deaf. Bann K for the cripples and Bann B for the Blind.

Oma spikes a pin through her hat: Adelheid is neither Deaf nor Dumb.

Hildegarde presses on, explaining the New Regulations even though her nerve is fading. *No one should have any Fear. The Führer has come to prevent Civil War.* Oma smiles warmly once more, shuffles Hildegarde out of the Door. As she departs, Hildegarde mouths: Stupid old goat ~

A party of ten tumbles through the Door and we are rushing. Soon Frau Winkler sweeps in through the Café Door: Are you ready, Gabriele?

Oma is more than ready: Now Lukas. I am leaving you in charge. On a great day such as this, many customers may come in. It may even be the case that Herr Winkler and some of his colleagues, who are all close associates of our Führer, will want to eat here today. Please ensure that everything is done to the Highest Possible Standard.

She stares haughtily into the mirror and tilts her hat: Adelheid, Do Not Leave Here. Do you understand me? Stay In The Kitchen. Do Not Even Go To The Door.

This she says then nods her head to indicate that I am to step through into the Corridor of our Apartment. She snakes her head towards me, hisses: Are you listening? The Situation here is changing at speed. If you are ever going to find your tongue, now might be The Moment. Do You Understand ~

No sooner has Oma stepped out of the Door than the members of the Phillumeny Club arrive. In Truth, they have probably been hanging around in the street waiting for her to leave. Today there are four. Among them is the Stationer Herr Wächter. Immediately they order beers, lay out their Matchbox Collections. I fetch the beers.

They say to Lukas: Come, come. Sit yourself down. While the old trout is out.

Lukas raises a hand to curl his drooping moustache and then posits himself most comfortably which he should not properly do. I am instructed to pour him a beer. Usually, I would never do that because we all know what the result will be. But I do not care. I just want to listen to the Radio.

The old men saying: Nonono. Hitler will never be accepted. There is not the support for him. Never has been. Have you not heard the news from Café Meteor? The Socialists are arming. If Schuschnigg had held the Referendum. At least sixty per cent would have voted to keep Independence. Are all those people just going accept this scandalous intrusion?

The Radio reports that the Parade is starting. I go to the Door. People now are hustling past the window. Columns of juveniles in brown uniforms march down the Streets in unison. *The Legitimists are planning to take control. The extreme Nazis are gathering at Café Central. You may expect nothing from the Police as most are Nazis now.*

The Phillumeny Club call for more beer. Lukas glares at me. He can get the drinks himself. Doubtless the Führer will be much concerned by this Collection of walking sticks and dentures who are going to oppose him. Yet still the Old Men say: The Socialists could take him down. What do wages matter? We will not be bought. It is freedom that is needed.

Herr Wächter adding: Schuschnigg did not want the Nazis and he didn't want the Socialists. But the only people who can keep Hitler out are the Socialists. Instead, he chucks us all in Wöllersdorf, won't let us organise. Now look. The support for the Nazis is strong in Graz, Klagenfurt, Salzburg. If they carry the Provinces, Vienna cannot hold.

Others adding: We need have no Fear. The new generation. They will rise. No more imperialist War. Seize the means of production. Lukas, you must know the plans. Why are you not at Café Meteor? It may only be a choice between the Black Terror and the Brown but I prefer our own independent Austrian Fascists. Lukas? A Young Man like you. (Lukas is not young at all.)

A Man stands up from the table of ten, waves his hand grandly: Have you seen the rows of tanks, the planes? The organisation. You think the Austrian home guard are going to stop him? It would be a bloodbath.

Another Phillumenist saying: Grillparzer has said – *They shall not have them, the green banks of the Danube.* Many are prepared to die. People such as myself are prepared to spill their own Blood for the Freedom of this Country. Lukas, are you not going with them? Pass my walking stick. Get me another beer.

They should keep their voices down. The Winklers are absent but still Caretaker Frau Vogt is in her Office and she is as much a Nazi as even the Winklers. The Club Men say – *Come sit down with us.* I do not want their greasy hands caressing me. *More beer, more beer.* Why can they not get it themselves?

Herr Wächter saying: Schuschnigg was never going to stand firm. Hitler has always had him in his pocket. Where are the French? Where are the English? Hitler is a Hungry Dog and must be fed. Poor little Austria, she is a morsel small enough to give.

Herr Wächter rising to a climax now: I have spoken to Mr Gedye. Asked him what we may expect from Mr Chamberlain. He is wagging his head most sorrowfully. Mr Chamberlain? Or is it Monsieur J'Aime Berlin ~

The laughter is riotous. I press my ear to the Radio. The Führer is coming. From the buildings all around we hear the cheers going up. Even the drunk old men fall silent now. I hurry back to the Door. The Café is a small vessel rocked in the great tempest of the City. People are perched on rooftops, hanging out of windows, dangling on doorsteps, waving.

Radios and gramophones play. Mobs are pushing and crowding down the street.

Herr Wächter spits on the floor: I'll bomb the Man to hell.

Others saying: You are going, Lukas? About time too.

Lukas stands up, his face the colour of raspberries, his skin shiny with sweat. Drink has made him bold: Yes, I am going. Going to cheer – and going to join the party. Because actually. You look at Germany. Employment, high wages, economic boom? You want

Uncle Jo, you want Hitler? What is the difference? I am welcoming the Führer and whatever he can bring.

He performs a wobbly salute while the others yell abuse at him.

Trembling Lukas is twisting his scarf round his neck. I grab my coat also.

Lukas: Don't you dare. You'll get me in trouble.

Herr Wächter adding: Oh no. Not you. Not safe.

Yet the Old Men themselves are upright now: Just go to the Door. Perhaps see.

Only Herr Wächter is still sitting at the table. Suddenly he is weeping, shuddering, shaking his head. Is it right to leave him? He is an old friend of Opa's but I am ashamed of him. I go and fetch a beer. He ignores the beer, says: Your Grandfather would be horrified. Appalled. The people of this Country. All just run after a rabbit.

He stands up, wavers, pulls at my coat but I push him away. He staggers backwards and collapses onto a thin-legged chair which groans under his weight. What does it matter what Opa thinks? Lukas is right. This is Socialism. A new form of Socialism but really just the same.

Herr Wächter is sobbing: Miklas. A true Austrian. A real President. A Man who stood firm. *Gott schütze Österreich.* God Protect Austria –

I hurry out into the street, heading down towards the Inner City. I ascertain once again that my Notebook is secure in my pocket. I look back at our building which now seems pathetically reduced. On the middle floor, the Winklers have rolled banners down from the window. At the top, where the Altmanns live, the shutters are all firmly closed. Are they not going to the Parade?

Loudspeakers are on every lamp post. Bells ring from every Church. The pavement pulses beneath our feet, throbbing with drums and marching and cheers. Sap rises in every bud, blood rushes in every heart. I must get to Heldenplatz but how will I ever achieve that? How can I inscribe a Report if I cannot see?

All around a storm of cheering rises, falls, rises again. Rumour sweeps in on the wind. All the German peoples will be reunited in one great Reich. The Ostmark has come home. Time for us to stop bowing down to the British, the French, their miserable Peace treaties. They must know that this is a Family Affair, a matter between Germans.

My feet skim across the ground as I am carried forward. I will never get to the Heldenplatz. *Wherever the road leads we will follow.* The shouts, cheers, roars beat on our eardrums, grip us tight by the collar so we cannot breathe. *National boundaries will no longer exist. Blood calls to blood.*

Our Führer leads his people out of the darkness into the blazing sun. All around thousands of Swastikas are caught in the breeze. A great tide is rising which carries the voice, the hope, the prayers of our land. The salutes go up, HeilHitlerHeilHitler. The noise is battering me. I need to get To Some Quieter Place. The pavement ahead is giddy, swooning.

A hand catches hold of my coat. I turn to see Adolf. I grab hold of him and he pulls me behind him. He indicates a tree which is just a few steps away. Surely it will be ripped up by its roots? Washed away in the crowd? But no. HeilHitlerHeilHitlerHeilHitler. Adolf shins up towards the branches of the tree, catches hold of me ~

We are above the crowd, sailing a sea of millions of heads. The Catholic Church is marching and the Unions and the marching bands and long lines of soldiers and Children and elderly women. All with their flags. All welcoming the Prodigal son of Austria home. Lines of troops, hundreds and thousands of them, and then the military vehicles.

HeilHitlerHeilHitler. Marching in straight rows. Thumpthumpthump. Cars coming down the Ring with SS men on the running boards. Everyone pressed up against the barricades. The Tragedy of our Country is at an end. No more people wearing Dead People's clothes. The Führer will bring jobs, a canal to connect us to the East.

We are now the second Capital of the Reich. No longer Austria now but Ostmark. A sudden, splintered silence. A roar which rips the air. He is an Austrian and he is coming home. HeilHitlerHeilHitler. Arms are flung up againagainagain. Bang, bang, bang. The buildings shake. Even the sky is juddering and jolting.

Multitudes are attempting to climb the tree. Pushing and shoving, reaching higher. Planes are thundering overhead, their wings nearly brushing against the upper branches. Adolf pulls me higher. The cheers are raging, tearing, shattering. We see the Führer's car and he is standing up, saluting, greeting the enraptured masses.

Tiny, tiny in the distance. My feet wedged in a forked branch. People pushing in front of me, shunting. HeilHitlerHeilHitlerHeilHitler. The tree jumping, creaking. The sky buckling, twisting, unsteady and dizzy, suddenly nauseous, bewildered. I mustmustmust. Think of Matchboxes, put them into an Organised Plan. I cannot. The whole World is swaying.

Closer, closer. We do not hear the crack but feel. I catch a branch above. I can flyflyfly.

Bashing against heads and shoulders, my feet twist and cartwheel, my hands bash and grip. Nonono. The crack comes as the pavement rises. The shouting cuts into silence. I only know. I only know. The World will never be as Young again as it was on that Day ~

4.b. Finding a Role for Every Person

A Mistake has been made. Things have been Misunderstood. I am in the Curative Education Ward at the Children's Hospital. I am Extremely Large and everything else Extremely Small. I might crack my head against the ceiling or smash a leg against a miniature window. A bandage has been wrapped around my head.

Sister Maria is beside me and she is still Exactly The Same. Gabbling all the time, her spider-hair still sticking out of her cap. Yet now I am as tall as her so why am I lying cramped in a Child's bed? She says: No need to worry. Sister Vik called Grandmother. They moved you from the main Ward. Better etcetcetc.

The jumble of arms, legs, branches. The smack of my head on the kerb stones. My stomach lurches, I drop my swollen head back onto the pillow. Sleep sucks me down. The Chaos of the street is still pounding, vibrating. Are these remembered sounds or is the City still Alive with celebration? I pull the sheets over my head.

When I wake again it is night and a Nurse moves up and down the Ward, holding high a lamp which bobs, wavers, dances. She was not here in those Earlier Times. I would remember because she is most charming with doll-like skin and her flaxen hair brushed most smoothly under her cap. Just as the dawn is breaking, she brings me a glass of water.

Says: I am Sister Clara. Don't worry now. Sleep.

I might like to stretch out my hand and touch her. She lifts the glass away from me, her hand cool and firm on mine ~

I wake again, stand on fickle legs, move to the Door of the Ward. In the Corridor, everything is buzzing. Sister Maria says that I must return to bed. She tells me that *the Ward is Absolute Chaos. So many Children arriving in the Reception. They must all be Assessed and Documented. Many are Hysterical and what can be done?*

Dr A appears but he is no longer the Young Man I remember. He is now most absolutely the Director of this World-Renowned Ward and he is not pleased: Why are there so many Children?

Sister Maria: Well. Obviously. Well. I couldn't really say.

Sister Viktorine appears carrying a pile of Files.

Dr A: Why has the dining room not been cleared?

Sister Viktorine: I am very sorry. Three Nurses are Missing.

Dr A: Missing? What do you mean?

Sister Viktorine: Not here. I don't know. I really can't say. I suppose it is what one expects. Obviously, for certain families the situation is most worrying.

Dr A looks puzzled: Is it? Why?

He shakes his head, shrugs, sighs, returns to his Office.

We have nothing to do with Politics here ~

I must get out of the Hospital. I am not a Child and I will not be put in a Ward for Cabbages. I will never be allowed to join the BDM if anyone should find out that I am here. This is a Question of Categorisation. Even when I was young, I should never have been in this place. I go out into the Corridor to find where my clothes are being stored.

I can only hope my Notebook is safe in my coat pocket. Fräulein Eder has put a ladder up against the wall and her hand reaches up to take the cracked and dusty old crucifix down. Propped against the wall is a picture of the Führer.

Sister Viktorine: Cardinal Innitzer has made his views clear. Love of God and Love of the Fatherland go hand in hand. I see no reason why the crucifix should be removed.

Dr A confirms the crucifix must stay. The picture of the Führer can go next to the Cloak Room: Ah. Ah. Yes. Please get a mop and stop that child from doing that ~

I pass into the kitchen, pour myself a glass of water. So strong are my memories of this place that I automatically fill the glass againagainagain. From the Meeting Room, Sister Maria's laughter. Then Dr Feldner.

No more Grüß Gott (Good Day). Apparently, the Casualty Department is Absolutely Heaving. All the saluting. The Heil Hitler salute while on a bicycle.

Other Nurses are giggling. *Difficult on a crowded bus. I'm amazed someone didn't lose their eye.* People should not engage in such disrespectful talk. I hurry from the kitchen but find no escape, for Sister Maria and Dr Feldner are now goose-stepping in a manner most silly. Do they not see that the Ward really is in Chaos now?

Apparently, Herr Spellbinder has not arrived. Of course, he is a known black marketeer hence it would not be surprising if he has been arrested. Dr Feldner is saying that he will go to the police station and enquire. Sister Viktorine objects that this would be most unwise but he will not listen (having always been most impulsive and unpredictable).

Some of the Cabbage Children are wailing and gobbling because they have lost marbles under the Door of the Office which once belonged to Dr Frankl. I remember how that used to happen when I was here. They jibber by the Door looking distressed because they do not know whether they can enter.

I push open the Door. Although I know that Dr Frankl has left for America and is now married to Fräulein Weiss yet still I expect to see him. And Fräulein Weiss also. (The watery green vase on the mantelpiece and the paintings of the hikers in the Wienerwald.) A Man is sitting at the desk. A Man dressed in a full Nazi uniform ~

The Children scamper away. I am left clinging to the Door frame. A Devil's Eye marble has rolled close to the Man's black leather boots. Adelheid – Stand up straight and salute. I am part of the new regime. I mustmustmust. The Man stares fiercely: Has no one ever told you to knock before opening a Door?

I am reversing back across the Corridor. Where are Dr Frankl's pictures? The vase?

Sister Viktorine is behind me: Oh. Oh.

For a moment, she is flustered but then Pretends most energetically. She is the Head of Nursing and salutes enthusiastically: Good morning, sir. Can I help you?

The Man says: Perhaps you were not told of my arrival? I am Dr Böckler and I will be working in this Ward from now on. I have come from Berlin.

Sister Viktorine says: Oh I see. I am indeed very sorry. I was not aware of your arrival. Otherwise Appropriate Arrangements would have been made. But no matter. Welcome to the Curative Education Ward. We are extremely pleased to have you with us.

And this Person?

Sister Viktorine is smiling in a charming manner but she does not speak. She clears her throat, nods. Where is Dr Frankl? Where are the vases and pictures? Who took them away? I feel tightly strangled and plaster is cracking from the walls, the bookshelves are tipping forward, ready to fall. Time goes missing.

Dr A appears and begins explaining the work of the Ward to Dr Böckler. Mercifully, the Tram is soon rattling forward at high velocity. *Our work here is, of course, entirely compatible with the ideas of the Reich. I am aware that the Führer wishes every citizen to find a place in this New Society. This has always been exactly our Approach* ~

4.c. A Challenging Period of Transition

I am awake but not awake. Voices are bashing against each other. I get out of bed on seasick legs. What time is it? What day? Looking towards the Reception, I identify Sister Viktorine and she is extremely small, almost a child. Next to her two SS men are toweringly large and inflated, filling up all of the space. The SS men are questioning Sister Viktorine.

She explaining, trying to talk. I hope they see that we have a picture of the Führer on the wall. I pray they see me shoot up my hand. Yet despite the picture, they are going to sweep her away. She is standing straight and firm but shrinking all the time. The light fittings are intent on murder. The curtains have become prison Doors.

The whole Ward has turned solid. Sister Viktorine's mouth is controlled by a pulley, flaps openshutopenshut. A Child dashes out of the Ward, smashes straight into a bench, falls to the floor, turns stiff and shudders. Sister Maria appears and kneels beside the jerking child. Everyone turns to stare at this diminuative, writhing Person.

Sister Viktorine speaks in a pacific voice: Why I am needed? We are already extremely short-staffed.

Dr A emerges: Ah, Gentlemen, good morning. Some Problem?

Are you the Director of the Ward?

Dr A: Yes. Can I help you? Do come into the Meeting Room.

Now we will be Safe, now all will be Laid out Straight. I should like to go and position myself in the kitchen and hear what is said but I am so petrified that I cannot shift my feet. Things have been Misunderstood. Sister Viktorine is saying: I am not on the lease of the building. I only live there because of my Friend.

Dr A saying: What questions? Why must she go?

Talkingtalkingtalking. I cannot hear. Then Dr A's most precisely: I really cannot run this Ward without my staff. It is not safe for there to be no Head of Nursing on this Ward and I have no one who has sufficient experience to replace her.

Voices: These are my Orders etcetcetc.

Dr A: You must return to your superiors and say that Sister Viktorine cannot make herself available. Professor Hamburger, Director of the Hospital, will be making a speech to all staff. Everyone should go the Lecture Theatre in ten minutes. After that I will be able ~

Sister Clara ushers me back to bed. The SS men are retreating. Dr A huffs: Really. Do these people think that no one has any work to do? Please, everyone. Do not stand around gaping. Sister Viktorine, who is available to stay in the Ward while we attend the speech? Joachim, please put that back in your Trousers immediately.

Dr A fetches a File from his Office and expounds to Sister Clara that all the staff are required to sign this Paperwork. This is a mere administrative formality but it must be completed without delay. The File will be left on the table in the Meeting Room. Everyone hurries to sign. The Paperwork must be in Order.

Sister Clara says: I am joining the Party. After work. If anyone wants to come.

Sister Maria: Quite right. I shall come with you.

Sister Anna: What about the Doctors. Are they going to sign?

Sister Viktorine has now emerged from the Filing Cabinet: Don't be impertinent. We are simply being asked to state our loyalty to the Government of this Country ~

Sister Clara is gathering everyone together in preparation to move down to the Lecture Theatre on the ground floor. Soon all the Nurses, except Sister Anna, have evaporated (or so I think) and Dr A with them. No one has locked the Door of the Ward. This is what I was hoping. Yet I do not have a moment to search for my clothes before Dr Feldner returns.

He strides down the Ward still wearing his hat and coat and then Sister Maria manifests herself (she should have gone downstairs). They huddle by the Filing Cabinet. Sister Maria is gasping, telling Dr Feldner what has happened. Yet also saying: The speech. We must go.

Dr Feldner whispers: I know. I have spoken to Hans. He will manage Hamburger. Hamburger is powerful now – very. We need to keep him happy at any cost. At the Police Station. Not just Fräulein Eder. The goose-stepping in the Corridor. Everything. They knew.

Sister Maria: How? Who?

Dr Feldner: I don't know. But don't trust anyone. And listen. Be careful of Hans. I fear he is inclined to do something heroic and that's the last thing we need ~

All the Adults have departed now and only Sister Anna is occupied in the Nursery. I discover my clothes on the shelves near the lockers. Happily, my Notebook is still encased in my coat pocket. I slide away without glancing back. Yet as I come to the bottom of the stairs, the Door to the Lecture Theatre is open.

All the staff of the Children's Hospital – not just the Curative Education Ward – are crammed in. Many now wearing uniforms. This vast and streamlined white chamber has tiers of wooden benches rising high up the walls. Sunlight pokes in through towering windows which stretch from the floor to the ceiling.

The moulded benches – and the smooth white writing desks – spin out from the centre like the shell of a snail. Giant palms are gathered near the lectern. Just near the Door, there is a gap beside these rising seats. I slip into this gap, hearing the low voices of Dr Feldner and Sister Maria above me until silence is called.

Professor Hamburger speaks with great passion: The medical profession is at the heart of this new Vision of the World. The Führer cares deeply about the Health of his People. Disease will become a thing of the past. Resources will now be available to research diseases which for too long have blighted our society.

Professor Hamburger continues: The Genetic Purity of the population will be assured through the Eradication of Hereditary Conditions. The population will need to increase to drive this great era of change and therefore women will be prioritised. Mothers will be given the highest level of support possible.

Dr Feldner whispers to Sister Maria: So tiresome but it will all blow over. Our dear Prussian friends. A talent for mass hysteria. Compensates them for all that Personal Gloom.

All nod in unison as Professor Hamburger says: The Curative Education Ward is at the centre of these changes. Manpower is essential to the success of the Reich. Those Children of a constitutionally weak type will need the best levels of support. The Worldwide reputation of this Hospital can only be increased.

Saying moremoremore: Austria has returned to her true home as part of the wider family of German-speaking nations. The coming period of transition may bring challenge and difficulties but all can be confident etcetcetc. HeilHitlerHeilHitlerHeilHitler. The arms fire like arrows all around.

Professor Hamburger's words cause us to grow to seven foot tall. I feel myself ascending, lifted by all those yearning hands. This is how the World was always meant to be. I want to stand in that crowd and Participate ~

As I hurry through the Streets many shutters are padlocked and restaurants are either battened down or empty. The windows of our local barber are shattered. Leaflets remain thrown about and swastika banners hang limp in the drizzle. I take account of what Professor Hamburger has said regarding a Transition Period. Ahead, the road is blocked by a Green Henry and an ambulance.

Women stand at the cordons with their heads nodding together, speaking in hushed voices. *Fallen from a Window.* Two stretchers are being carried. The women scurry away when they see that the police are moving towards them. I find my way home via several shadowed Backstreets.

Before I enter the Café, I brace myself for Oma's criticisms but it soon becomes apparent that Oma is too distracted to chastise me. Lukas has not been seen since the day of the Führer's arrival. How can she manage the Café without him? Thank goodness the Café is calm as the University is closed but that will not last. Where can the Man be?

Usually, one would know where to look but apparently he is not at his home. I am sent down to the Cellar for beers. Dust and ash all about and also tiny fragments of Paper. Someone has been burning documents in the Furnace. Perhaps the Leaflets and other documents which once lived under the hall rug?

In the Café itself, I check the Atlas and find no Papers there. I am content for I have never wished to be associated with Socialists.

Oma shouts then to *stop dawdling*. The sink is piled with Washing Up. The floor slick with grease. I start the geyser and string up damp tea towels. After that I do not have time to think until the lunch is finished ~

After lunch Oma says that she must converse with me. She makes her Point most clearly. Our City is going through great changes and it is not Safe at present. She has spoken to the school and *under the circumstances* there is no Point in me going back there. I would have been leaving in the summer anyway.

No. No. It will not be possible for you to go to Secretarial College. You understand why that would not be Appropriate. I do not understand. I am as clever as any other girl in my class. Everyone can Serve, everyone can Make a Contribution. Of course, she needs me to substitute for Lukas but I want to go to College so I can type up my Reports.

For the next hour I am full of condensed Anger. Then I realise that maybe I can solve this Problem myself. Why did I not consider this idea sooner? Opa's typewriter is in the bottom of his Wardrobe. I find that the ribbon has dried out but I can buy a ribbon from Herr Wächter. I have no book to learn from but it cannot be difficult ~

Later that evening, Dr Feldner arrives at the Café. He has stopped on his way back from the Hospital to ascertain that I got home safely. Oma offers him a Schnapps and he drinks it, standing at the bar. The Café is empty and Dr Feldner and Oma talk, their heads close. Oma mentions *certain provisions and precautions.*

Dr Feldner leans forward, whispers, nods. *Issues of Paperwork. Ariernachweis. It is now clear. Yes, yes. At the Hospital today. Sister Viktorine. Her birth certificate.* I listen most carefully. This explains why Sister Viktorine was in trouble. Everyone now must have Paperwork inscribing details of their parents. Sister Viktorine does not have such Paperwork.

Although this Information is new, it also feels familiar. I have always seen how Sister Viktorine rushes to defend certain Children, particularly the Children whose families are poor. Particularly, the Children with no fathers. Yet this is not a Proper Problem. It is merely an administrative difficulty which can be regularised quite simply.

Yet as he is going, Dr Feldner speaks to Oma again most secretly. *Also. You are aware? Certain Rumours from Germany.* I decide not to listen. We have been told most specifically. We have been told that no-one must listen to Gossip and Rumour. I have seen this emphasised in Leaflets and books from the BDM. It is disappointing that Dr Feldner does not know this.

After he has gone, calling goodnight to me through the kitchen Door, I pass through to our Apartment and I discover that the key to the back Door has gone from the nail. I hurry into my bedroom and discern that a padlock has been put in place to hold the window closed. I hate Oma for this but she may do as she likes. I will find a way to Serve ~

4.d. Oma's Paperwork is Poorly Organised

During that year of 1938 we lived on the brink of Transformation. What would it be like to be part of Germany? In Vienna we have always considered Germany to signify weak coffee, ugly clothes and thriftorderthrift. Equally, it is well known that the Germans have always scorned their frivolous neighbours on the banks of the Danube.

Surely now we will see an end to Schlamperei (Viennese slovenly behaviour). The Reich will not tolerate the lazy and fanciful, the politically and economically backward. Surely now all will be the Will to Reconstruction? Lorries do arrive full of supplies (clothes, food, building materials) from Germany and are warmly welcomed.

Also, plans for the new canal which would make us into *the Hamburg of the South East* are taking shape. However, after those early days of Marching and Banners, things generally continued the samesamesame. Of course, for me that was partly because I was stuck at the Café and could not go out anywhere.

But Hildegarde also confided in me of similar frustrations. The BDM might tell her *every young woman carries with her the dignity of the Reich* but what has actually changed? Despite the cruel limitations imposed on me, I continue to ensure that I am Properly Informed. I listen to the Radio, read the newspapers, listen to all that is said in the Café.

All this I transcribe in my Notebooks. Hildegarde finds a job that I can perform while staying at the Café, which is painting tinnies (metal badges) for the Nazis' Winter Relief Donation Fund. Herr Wächter finds a ribbon for the typewriter (and tries to fix the keys which stick). Hildegarde lends me an Instruction book. She is also learning but her fingers soon tire.

As a result, I type Reports for the BDM and put her name on the bottom. Sometimes I then retype the Reports and put my name. (This for a reminder that I am a Person who understands the Proper Ordering of the World.) Oma says she will *boil her head in a bucket if I do not stop clattering on that typewriter* ~

Soon the University reopens and customers return to the Café. Yet the conversations are muted. No one may trust the maid within their own house let alone a stranger. Oma reports *how many have blackened the reputations of their neighbours to our new Masters*. One careless word and we may all end up in Dachau.

All now use the German glance (look over your shoulder before you speak). When the Winkler girls come into the Café with their Mother they order Sachertorte (chocolate cake) and boast of their new skills. No more pretty dresses and hair in curls. Voice and dance lessons – out. Gymnastics and swimming – in. Hair must be worn in plaits hanging at the front, no lipstick, proficient in all Domestic Tasks.

After one month a ballot is Organised. Tick *yes* or *no*. Some excellent Matchboxes are produced which show an image of the ballot Paper and indicate where to mark your cross. Oma obtains one for me and I am grateful. Yet I am troubled by my Collection now. Is it a truly Patriotic Collection which reflects fully the glory of the Reich?

At the plebiscite Cardinal Innitzer advises voting Ja. Why would you vote against something which has already happened? The vote is won by 102 per cent. I have little time to consider this anomaly because Lukas is still absent. When his name is mentioned, people dance their eyebrows, or wag their heads, communicating in a silent language I cannot fathom.

One day Adolf's mother alights at the Café. The bell at the Door jangles, the curtain sweeps aside. She strides in with a lightning smile, manoeuvring a ship-like pram. She sports a shimmering green silk dress and a shapely coat which sticks out stiffly from her waist. She takes a seat, scoops a tiny baby from the pram, bounces it on her knee Saying: Too many Children. Too many Children.

I remember that singing voice like a bird song, golden and fluttering. She wonders whether I might know where Adolf can be found? Oma makes clear that I know Nothing. Personally, I wonder whether the police have perhaps found lodgings for Adolf. Oma is hoping that Frau Schreiber will depart soon but I enjoy looking at the baby.

Usually, I do not like babies but this one is pleasing. Her tiny toothless face crumpled by laughter, her tendril fingers reaching out like new shoots. She is waving her hands at the shadows which fall through the window. I once liked to wave my hands like that. How I long for a time when Life was all sensation ~

Frau Winkler and Oma are obsessed by comingsandgoings within our Building. The Altmanns from upstairs have gone, simply vanished. Frau Winkler says: Good riddance. Bled our Country dry. Oma has put her sign outside the Café. *No Jews Here.* One must do this because otherwise customers are apprehensive of Trouble.

Yet privately Oma does swivel her eyes across the ceiling: All very bad for business.

Oma soon bustles off to the City Housing Office to enquire about the Altmanns' apartment. However, that apartment is given to a family called the Mosers. They are coming soon from Berlin. Frau Winkler must be careful of what she says. It's not for her to criticise the decisions being made.

Yet late at night, once the Café has closed, and the Schnapps has been poured, Frau Winkler, Oma and Caretaker Frau Vogt all give vent to their Frustrations. (In our Country this is known as Raunzen – which is a particular Viennese whininggripinggrouching much enjoyed in our City.)

Frau Winkler: Some people in this Country have always been Loyal.

By this Frau Winkler means people such as herself. *Even when those Fools from the Fatherland Front made it illegal, many saw the Future, took the risk and offered their support. But where now is their reward?* The apartments go to the stuck-up Berliners. Oma can certainly agree on that Point.

She has never liked the Piefkes (Krauts) – those vulgar women with their hair twisted on their heads in plaits. Flat shoes on their big feet, clumping along the pavement like camels. The men with a roll of bristly fat round the back of their necks. *Why should those people have everything? Many of them seem to have mistaken this City for a holiday camp* ~

One Sunday afternoon Oma has stepped out to a tea party and Herr Wächter is assisting in the Café. This should not be a Problem as no one comes in much at this time of day. The tea drinkers are all gone but the evening drinkers have not arrived. Herr Wächter tells me a joke. *Have you heard? Strawberries have been banned. Why? Because they are red.*

I do not want to hear such talk so I get out my Maps. If I cannot walk through the City, I can at least draw pictures in my head. Yet Herr Wächter is jovial and garrulous, determined to interrupt my work, saying: Heard about Lukas? Happened while you were in the Hospital. She wouldn't tell you. Too proud.

He slaps his hands together and chortles: Got another job. Working in the Hotel Sacher and being paid nearly twice what your Grandmother paid him. Boasted a lot about all the experience that he had *in one of Vienna's finest Cafés.* Shame you didn't see your Grandmother's face.

Herr Wächter is creaking back and forwards, jibbering with laughter. I am indeed sorry that I was not here to see these Adventures. Yet I am also Angry because Lukas is able now to get himself a better job and yet I cannot ~

Just as I am considering this Manifest Injustice, the Door of the Café opens and a young SS Officer walks in. He is a member of the Medical Corps (one knows this as he wears the Rod Asclepius and sleeve diamonds). Herr Wächter and I stand up straight, smile, shoot our hands. Once someone would have run to remove any Socialist Paperwork from the Atlas. The mat on the hall floor would also have been pulled straight.

Happily, Herr Wächter and I do not now need to consider these Questions. Also, everyone knows that Oma herself was never a Socialist and has now properly become a Member of the Party. *At least now we have got some discipline in this City.* Yet I am agitated that some of my Matchbox Plans and Envelopes are on the table.

Perhaps my Collection will show me to be not properly Loyal? Things can easily be Misunderstood. Surely this Man will not notice the Album? But he does – reaches out his hand, turns the pages. He has a thick silver ring with two lightning bolts and one notes also a strange bald patch on his nearly shaved head.

Herr Wächter tosses his head sideways in a gesture which indicates to me – *Keep out of the way.* I step aside, move behind the bar. Herr Wächter fetches a beer, begins to show the SS Man my Collection. Herr Wächter will surely concentrate only on the first few pages. Soon he is talking most largely of the wonders of this Collection.

But it is not his Collection, it is mine. Samesamesame. Again, Herr Wächter looks up at me and flicks his head sideways. Apparently, it is not enough to hide in the shadows of the bar. I move into the kitchen, hunch on a stool near the sinks and buzz with Rage. If I could show my Reports to our visitor then perhaps he would understand.

He would see how Useful I am. Just like Opa.

Watch. Keep out of the way. Say nothing at all ~

After the SS Doctor has drunk his beer and gone, Herr Wächter appears in the kitchen. He then does apologise, saying: Listen. You think you can trust people but this is not your Opa's World. The worst is not an uncomfortable interview at the police station. You understand?

Says then: Look. Let me say it direct. You know what the Problem is? I mean, not the obvious Problem. You understand? What is worrying your Oma? Your Father's name is not on your birth certificate. Ariernachweis? You know what that is?

I do know. It means Aryan Certificate. But my Father? I did not even know I had a Father. Is this what Dr Feldner was talking about? Sister Viktorine and the Paperwork? I was condemning how Disorganised Sister Viktorine is. Yet now I am being told ~

The Stationer saying now: It shouldn't be a Problem. I knew your Father. He may have been a Reckless Idiot but I can assure you that he was one of our Homegrown Reckless Idiots. All this racial purity. Bunkum. All mongrels here. But the Paperwork. You understand?

I do not. Why is there no name on my birth certificate? I do not care who my Father was. But why did Oma not ensure that the details were recorded Properly? She is presenting herself ohsocorrect but she does not get basic things right.

Herr Wächter now saying: The important thing is. Your Oma has hidden the Papers and they need to stay hidden. She doesn't want you out in the street because you will be asked. If you find yourself in that situation, you need to scram, create a distraction. You see?

I do understand but I also know that this Situation can be easily resolved ~

When Oma comes back, I am dismissed to the kitchen again and harsh words are exchanged. Herr Wächter saying – *You cannot keep such Information from her. Dangerous for her not to know. She may make a Mistake etcetcetc.* Oma is most displeased. *What right have you? Interfering in my Family Affairs. Stirring up Trouble.*

It is not uncommon for Oma and Herr Wächter to have a Lively Examination of their Differences. Oma really cares nothing for me in this Matter and is only Furious that her poor quality of organisation has been exposed. So I think. Yet in this I may be Wrong for soon Oma says to me slyly that she has something for me.

Would I like a new pair of shoes? She does then produce a most stylish pair of shoes in burgundy-coloured leather with solid heels and laces with miniature tassels. Plus, a cut-out leather design across the toes. The shoes are brand new and the size is just right for my rather large feet. They are the shoes of Frau Altmann who has vanished from the top floor.

That lady has given me shoes before because I am the only Person with the same size feet. Always before they have been thoroughly worn, not smart and newly made like this fine pair. Oma and Frau Winkler would have taken the shoes themselves if they were the right size. They have already taken many things from that apartment, before it was sealed off.

Over the weeks that follow I also discern our Chef wearing Herr Altmann's winter coat although it is much too small for him and creaks at the seams. Also, Oma with a new feathered hat and Frau Winkler with a shimmering fur coat. Yet still Oma complains about the disappointment of the shoes. Jews have such big feet ~

4.e. A Dog with a Bucket on Its Head

The revelations of the Stationer Herr Wächter led to a decision in relation to my Matchbox Collection. It will not be a World Collection now but will show only the countries of the Reich. This is a Great Sacrifice as I lose half the Collection. Also, since I cannot leave the Café, how will I find new Matchboxes?

Yet this is a Properly Patriotic Approach. Of course, I should destroy the American and British Matchboxes in the Furnace. A New World cannot be birthed unless everyone lays aside their Childish desires. Why should I cling to pieces of Paper? Yet I cannot discard these Old Friends. Finally, I lift the rug in the hall and conceal them under the Floorboards ~

The summer comes and the days are slow as syrup. What can I write in my Notebook? We riseworksleep riseworksleep riseworksleep. The days have no beginning and no end. The hours, the minutes, the days have become beclouded and vague. The Winkler sisters are going away to a summer camp with the BDM. I yearn to accompany them.

Lukas is going on a Strength Through Joy excursion to the Sudetenland and other parts of Germany. Such free trips are now open to many rough people from Ottakring, Simmering, Floridsdorf and other lower-class Districts. (*Flattering the Reds.* Oma says this with a dismissive sniff.)

In August, the air is solid and unmoving, sticks like wet fabric. I lie awake dreaming of Opa, of the days when we would travel on the tram to the public lido at the Gänsehäufel, an island on the Danube. Now I can't even lever open my bedroom window. In our Storeroom flat, the flies invade, the drains stink, dust rasps in my throat.

The only moment when I may breathe now is late in the evening when the Door of the Café is left open. Oma sits there then with either Upstairs Frau Winkler or Frau Vogt. Frau Winkler saying: All these adolescents together, no proper supervision. I'm sure that is not the intention of the Führer but he can't be there to supervise every Meeting.

Oma nods most sympathetically. She understands *supervision*.

Frau Winkler saying: Of course, young women of Good Catholic Austrian families should be encouraged to have Children or we'll soon be overrun by that mob from the East. Breeding like rabbits. Yet after Nuremberg, four hundred unmarried young women fell with Unwanted Pregnancy. Four hundred.

Oma is keen to stress her own part in preventing such Horrors: Of course, I am most careful with Adelheid. All that blonde hair. Wearing red lipstick if I let her. No more Brain than a duck. Anyone can see where that will end ~

Oma also talks about The Race Laws even though she has not Properly Informed herself. Whispering: I just hope Hitler has understood that here in Vienna we have always been free to decide who is a Jew and who is not.

Frau Vogt then listing all the people who are said to have either left the City or committed suicide. Dr Geller from the kidney Ward. He did not turn up to work. Now they have been to his flat. He and his wife. Poison. Dr Bensaïd found hanged in his Cellar. Dr Haussman, arrested. Also, Socialists, journalists. Where will it end?

No one should repeat Gossip and Rumour. I open up my Maps and dream of the places I might go to if I could leave the Café. We have found out that Adolf is in a camp near Salzburg. He is being re-educated and trained. In that area of my Country are many lakes hence he may at least be able to swim and experience the breeze ~

Just at the Moment when I think that I can't endure being incarcerated for one day more, Dr Feldner comes to the Café. He brings Hansi and Herbert with him. These youths I do know well because I used to go with them to the park and the Votiv Kino. Herbert, as I have said, being gentle and polite and his older brother most truculent and stubborn-faced.

He having coarse thick hair which sticks up in a quiff and a belligerent chin. He was at School with me and had an even worse Reputation than Adolf for unruly and disruptive behaviour. Once he was found swimming in the outdoor pool at Franz-Josefs-Kai after it was closed for the day and was sent to Court.

Yet he is always friendly to me and now, when Dr Feldner comes to suggest that I might go out with the boys for the day, I am pleading in my head that Oma might say yes. Dr Feldner saying – *It will be much cooler on the Danube.* Oma immediately says *yes* but not out of any desire to please me. Oh no.

The Truth being she is Truculent with Dr Feldner for bringing the lads into the Café. Has he not read her notice? Perhaps she is also agitated for me? I do not think so. She probably considers that if Dr Feldner wants to take such risks then that is his business ~

I am expecting that Dr Feldner will direct us to that public lido at the Gänsehäufel which Opa did favour. Yet instead we take the 31 Tram from the Ring to Floridsdorf and to another part of the Danube which is called Angelibad. Compared to the Gänsehäufel this is a low-down corner of our City. Why have we come here?

Soon I understand. A new law has just been announced which bans Jews from public parks. Probably a beach is the same as a park yet this area we now traverse is not Properly Organised. A main gate does exist through which one would usually pass yet Dr Feldner says: No need to bother. I know another way. Used to come here as a boy. Hole in the fence.

This is Incorrect Behaviour but I do not think of this as I desperately want to swim. We walk along a sandy path into pine woodland. This area is a Bretteldorf, a village of wooden cabins, and also the Wagons of Gypsies may be seen among the trees. Pedal boats are stored under canvas. The echoing sounds of the water are close.

We arrive at a fence, and just as Dr Feldner said, a huge hole has been cut. Herbert, Hansi and I scramble through the hole, but Dr Feldner's long legs scissor over the top. The boys strip off their clothes as they have their swimming suits underneath. I only have an old swimsuit of Oma's which is far too big but what do I care?

Here the river is wide and lazy but still the water is sharp and icy and the delicious cold chills my grateful bones. I dip my face into the water againagainagain. After we have swum, we sit on the sand amidst frilled deck chairs, umbrellas and prams. It is then that Herbert says he has got a present for me, pulls Matchboxes out of his bag. A fat envelope.

Conveniently all are from the Reich. My bag is not spacious enough to contain them therefore he says that he will guard them in his rucksack until we return to the Café. Soon the lads start to whack a tennis ball back and forth. Then Dr Feldner suggests we should all head towards the gate and get an ice cream. We pull on our clothes and commence to walk.

The beach is edged by a long promenade-like path which is really just a cracked concrete track. Just as we come towards the gate, we see Dr A ahead of us. To my great surprise, he is pushing a pram. Of course, I knew that he was married but I did not know about the children. Also, what is he doing in such a place? I recollect now that he has relatives in this lowly yet verdant area of the City.

Dr Feldner waves to him: Have you met my Nephews?

Nephews? Ahem. No. No. I haven't.

Dr A shakes hands with the two lads.

Dr A says: Ah yes. And Adelheid. Of course. Still doing your writing, I hope?

Dr A nods his head and bounces awkwardly on his toes. Two SS men have come through the turnstile and are striding towards a vagrant-looking Man who wears trousers and braces but no shirt. Soon they are checking his Papers. Everyone appears to continue just as they were but an Electric Current is pulsing through the air.

The beach is tipping, the sky blue as blood. People are performing a Play. Sitting up straight in their deck chairs, searching for their Papers. Children and dogs are called to Heel. Young men are ambling away, Pretending nonchalance but hurriedly losing themselves among the Cabins and Wagons. I remember what Herr Wächter said ~

A Dog rushes through the families on the beach, barking and snapping. Its head is caught in the handle of a Children's play bucket and that red tin bucket is now affixed to its head. The dog tears at the bucket with its paws, leaps, barks, tries to rip the bucket off. It is panicking now, running again. Picnics are scattered, sun umbrellas fall, a small child is mown down.

Everyone explodes in tight laughter. Dr Feldner smiles gaily, raises the tennis racket and whacks the ball over the fence, into the woodland. He turns to Herbert: For God's sake. What are you doing? That was stupid. Now we've lost the ball. You'll have to go and find it. Hansi, go with him. Hurry up now.

The lads hurry to the fence and crawl under it.

Dr Feldner shrugs: Those lads will never find that ball. Better help.

He climbs over the top of the fence. I scramble after him although my dress is catching in the wire. I do not want to leave the beach but what choice do I have? Maybe we will be able to go back when the Soldiers have gone? Dr Feldner is indicating into the woodland: Have you found it, boys? Hurry up. We want those ice creams ~

The Matchboxes. Where are they? I turn back towards the beach and see that Herbert has left the rucksack. It is lying on the sand. I turn to run and retrieve it. Dr Feldner catches hold of me. *No. No. You can't go back.* I don't care what he says. All this is stupid. *It is just a rucksack with swimming clothes.* I want the Matchboxes.

I pull away but he has got me pinched tightly. I thought him a weak old Man but his fingers are sunk deep into my arm and he will not release me. I struggle and kick and fight but Dr Feldner continues to pin me. I grasp at his fingers and try to lever them off my arm. I twist and writhe, stare up into his eyes, see them wide with Fear ~

4.f. I Am a Useful Girl

The theory of Causation is once again proven to be inaccurate. That day at the beach may have appeared as a bitter disappointment. Yet at that time *the Alchemy of Circumstance* did come to save me. First, the struggles of that day were scrubbed out. The bag on the beach was discovered, delivered back to me by Sister Maria. Dr A must have retrieved it.

In addition, Lukas returns. He has been dismissed from the job at the Hotel Sacher. Just as Oma had predicted, the Hotel had soon discerned his True Nature. Happily, Oma is a Christian lady and she can Forgive. Lukas can reinstall himself and begin to labour for her again. On the same *very reasonable* salary that he received when he quit.

The Problem being that he then occupied my job. Which I had never desired but still, it was better than nothing. Of course, Oma only recompensed me pocket money but now I'd lost even that. *Still plenty of work to do.* This she said but it was not True. I still replicated Information out of the Newspapers but there was nothing else to Write ~

Then changechangechange. I am to have a new job. Sister Viktorine visits the Café just three days after the beach, the dog, the bucket. She and Oma have their heads bent down in long and subtle conversation. From what I can discern, this discussion involves much Misunderstanding and Spaghetti Thinking. Politicspregnancysupervision etcetcetc.

Heads nodded sagely. *One can Serve the Reich in many ways.* On Wednesday, Thursday and Friday evenings, I am to help Sister Viktorine at the Hospital or assist a needy Person in our neighbourhood such as is recommended by Father Gärtner at our Piaristenkirche Maria Treu. This is my fresh and exciting job.

Elderly ladies in wheelchairs, house cleaning, making soup for those with no teeth etcetcetc. Washing the stained and smelly clothes of poor people. Sister Viktorine takes me to the relevant kitchen, or the washroom, of such needy types and I must promise Not To Leave. This I do enjoy for I am Out in the City. I Observe details. I inscribe with care.

People thank me most kindly for my work. I *follow Instructions carefully and consider what the effects of my behaviour might be on other people.* One such is elderly Frau Frankl, who is the mother of that Dr Frankl who used to work at the Hospital and is now married to Fräulein Weiss. (The two of them living together in Baltimore in the USA, as Sister Viktorine has reported to me.)

This Frau Frankl (this mother) lives at Esteplatz number 4 in the Third District. Her flat perched at the top of a majestic building, crammed with many photographs in twisty silver frames, china dogs, pots of dusty dried flowers etcetcetc. I dust all precisely, replace exactly. Frau Frankl gives me warm milk though she has not food herself.

Also, a glass bead bracelet which I do love most thoroughly ~

September comes but the heat still kindles bright. One evening, Sister Viktorine requests may I assist Frau Schreiber? This unfortunate lady has not been well. The Children are such a blessing but, sigh-sigh, they do bring work. I am most delighted. I recall her from when she came to the Café with the baby just a few months ago.

Frau Schreiber lives under the railway arches in the direction of Ottakring. Why does she reside in such a collapsing region when she is most smartly dressed? The plaster on the building is stained and much flaked. The Schreiber Apartment is half underground. Yet in truth, although Oma and I are above ground, our circumstances are not much brighter.

Is Frau Schreiber a victim of the Times? Is she paying the price for the Mistakes of her Youth? Has she been *cheated out of her birthright*? She does not appear a distressed Person for she wears a satin dress and her hair is twisted into a shining arrangement high on her head. She embraces me which is most Embarrassing yet I let her fold me in her perfumed arms.

She saying: What a treat. What a treat. I'm so glad you've come ~

All around are Children. Toothy, grinning Children with knotted hair and clothes not darned. They are as besmeared as she is sparkling. The flat also sordid (broken boards, bulging walls, smell of mildew, a window filled by a board). Yet I am pleased by this New Adventure three nights a week from four until ten o'clock when Sister Viktorine accompanies me home.

Sister Viktorine saying how essential it is for Frau Schreiber to rest. Yet she never does relax herself. Instead, dresses herself with the utmost care, trying on one captivating dress after another, asking me *redbluelongershort what do you think?* Saying: A woman must keep herself looking well. Hard when I'm no longer young.

Often, she seems to surmise exactly what I am pondering.

Sighing and shaking her head as she fixes a hair pin: All the girls your age want to be good National Socialists. Why not? I am all for Hitler. Used to be nervous in the Streets late at night. Not any more. But telling these young girls how to be housewives for the Reich? Me, I don't believe it. All men want the same and why not ~

She may be referring to a Hiking Holiday but I do not *involve myself in Adult Matters.* Cut up bread for supper. Also, providing sometimes a slice to Herr Spellbinder who lives upstairs and often visits to see the Children and play Schwarzer Peter with them etcetcetc. Pour whisky in the Children's milk as Frau Schreiber has demonstrated. *Helps to get them off.*

Wrap baby Herta up warm and lay her in the pram. Frau Schreiber has a friend visiting: We girls need a bit of fun. I reckon we can keep each other's secrets?

That is how I escape again into my much-loved City. Walkingwatchingnoticing. Idling happily on street corners or at the Doors of bars. Has a New World come? Not that I can see. Some of the drinking has ceased but other than that, it is not much changed. I was hoping to write a Report on many interesting things in my Notebooks.

In the past, I was with Adolf or Hildegarde and so then I knew What To Do. Now I am alone with the cumbersome pram. Some evenings I watch girls in brown uniforms standing out in the Schlesingerplatz outside the Amtshaus or at HQ in Albertgasse. A banner is being painted, girls are piling up firewood. The poster on the railing is one I made for Hildegarde ~

When I return to Frau Schreiber's apartment. There, there. My eyes do stretch most poppingly large. Hanging on the back of a chair is a cap and a grey-green jacket. This garment has shoulder straps and a braid on the pocket. On the collar are three pips and a stripe. From this I know that this jacket belongs to an Obersturmführer.

I hurry Herta into the bedroom and wait for Frau Schreiber there. This soon becomes the new pattern of our evenings. Yet the problem being that the autumn that year is short. Even in the middle of September, heavy rain thrashes the City, the drains overflow, the gutters cast water from the roofs. Wind yanking hats from heads, carrying away branches and signs.

For this reason, I do not desire to walk too long and navigate the Pram back to the apartment which Frau Schreiber does understand: Will you be all right in the bedroom? I hope Herta will not cry. I have a visitor and I would not wish him to be disturbed.

Initially, this is easy enough for Herta sleeps quite soundly and the other Children are Quiet as well. I am contented in the bedroom. Sit in a comfortable chair (like in the Meeting Room) situated by the Window. Outside a storm twisting. In the back yard washing which should surely have been fetched in? It waltzes in the wind ~

Then comes a night when Herta wakes. Her nose is obstructed and she has a cough therefore she snuffles and whines and cannot settle. I do not know What To Do. It occurs to me then that Frau Schreiber's friend does perhaps not know of Herta's existence – or mine. Surely Frau Schreiber would explain but would that be enough?

I am not Jewish or a Socialist or a Troublemaker so why does it matter? Yet I must find a way of keeping Herta quiet. I do not want to pick her up. Her face crumples now and soon she will be wailing. I should like to put a pillow over her head. Why does she have to make so much Fuss? I hate her with a passion. Maybe I could lift her? I must.

I lean down and grip her but her fists wave and she is most Angry. I should like to bash her into silence. What is Wrong with her? What can I do? Maybe it is my face which is upsetting her. People do find me upsetting. I position her on my knee and turn her around, jiggling her up and down. This is what Sister Viktorine does.

Herta becomes calm. Yet this has nothing to do with me holding her or with the jiggling. I know what has happened. She is looking at the washing. Because the wind is whipping, that washing is jigging up and down on the line, casting bizarre shadows as it flaps. Herta's little fists now wave in furious Joy.

After that I have no Trouble with her. Even when it is so dark that she cannot see the washing yet still I hold up my fingers in front of her face and wave them around. This she enjoys. (I also do relish this old game.) One night she stretches out her tender fist to take hold of my finger and pulls it in her gummy mouth, biting on it most happily.

Usually, I would consider this Disgusting but such is her pleasure that I am contented for her to do as she wants. Such games we play most delightedly together ~

4.g. The Most Successful Speech of Dr A

October blows in bringing capricious days. Sister Viktorine instructs that I must come with her to the University Buildings. I am to help with making refreshments. I have done this before in the Lecture Theatre of the Children's Hospital but never in the University Buildings. Sister Viktorine tells me that Dr A is making an Important Speech and the Nurses will attend.

In this University Building, the banked seats are crowded. Many attendees are attired in uniform. The floor of the hall is polished to a shine. The windows are perilously high above and the sky beyond inky and infinite. Professor Hamburger is prominently positioned. (Sister Viktorine, Sister Maria, the other Nurses – at the back.)

Sister Maria: Let's hope he's got the right script.

Sister Viktorine tells her to stop being disrespectful. Dr A begins with great confidence and enthusiasm. He lays out most clearly all the many benefits of National Socialism. All of this I knowknowknow from my own reading. He then moves on to talk about the Work of the Curative Education Ward.

This he explains in exhaustive detail, saying much about the brilliant Dr Erwin Lazar etcetcetc. This I do not think is right to say in these new Times. *We must never give up on the education of abnormal individuals who seem hopeless from the outset.* Dr A may be going off on a Tram Track and failing to consider *how his words might be received*.

In the front row an Old Man nods, start to snore. Dr Feldner elbows him in the ribs. He wakes with an unfortunate snort ~

Dr A shuffles his Papers. He has perhaps not Organised them adequately. Silence descends and much fidgeting is heard while people stare intently at their shoes. From outside the hall a siren blares and a drunk is singing loudly. Now Dr A seems to find his route again and says most loudly and clearly: *But difference is not always inferior.*

Sister Maria sticks her elbow into Sister Anna's ribs. Eyeballs swivel along the rows, legs are crossed and uncrossed. The feeling seems to be that Dr A is wandering into Error. No one wants to look at Professor Hamburger too directly but equally they need a lead. Is this a statement with which one should agree? More huffing, scratching, scraping.

Then Professor Hamburger nods most vigorously and others affirm as well. Dr A has steered around a tight corner most successfully.

Now he continues: Sterilisation is to be treated with care. In this new society, we need a full range of different skills.

Professor Hamburger nods again in sincere agreement. The speech tramlines onwards but I neglect to listen. Dr A is explaining about the Little Professors now and his Research. How every Child must receive the Best Sovereign Care. All effort must be focused on the Individual Child and the particular needs and abilities etcetcetc. ~

I had wanted to write a Report about this Speech but it is not enrapturing. I have heard all this Rigmarole before and I do not see the Point. Perhaps I should write about this hall instead and all that I can see here. The whispers and echoes, the long curtain standing to stiff attention. The intricate patterns of the parquet floor and shabby gilt lining the wooden wall panels.

The speech puffs and squeals, comes to rest on the buffers. The towering silver urn is wheeled into position and I start to dispense tea and coffee. All agree that the ideas that Dr A has contributed are indeed interesting. The Troubled Child can be assisted to make a contribution to the Reich. Dr A is close to me as Professor Hamburger takes a glass of wine.

A senior Nazi (one knows from badges and pips on the uniform) strides forward and salutes Dr A who also salutes although rather awkwardly. Professor Hamburger says: Vital work. Most important. Dr A and my other staff are achieving wonderful results in helping those who do not conform to understand how to participate fully and offer their services to the Reich.

Dr A says: Ah. Ahem. No. Actually, that isn't quite ~

The senior Nazi has already moved on and the Nurses come to help to clear up the glasses and cups. Everything is washed, dried, put away, tea towels hung up to dry, kitchen floor swept. I follow the Nurses out of the building. Outside the air smells of damp leaves and a hazy rain sparkles around the streetlights. A soldier is positioned at a gun nest surveying the whole Street.

Sister Viktorine is thrilled by the events of the evening, says to the Nurses: Wonderful speech. Wonderful. He explained our work with absolute clarity. We are so lucky to have him at the helm. The new Research that he is doing encapsulates the essence of what the Ward has been trying to develop over the years.

Sister Clara says: But what about sterilisation?

Sister Viktorine: That has no relevance to our work.

Surely it does.

No. No. It most certainly does not. I would have thought you would have understood this by now, Clara. We do discuss certain problems as Constitutional, or Inborn. However, neither of those words imply that a problem is Inherited.

Clara shrugs her shoulders, which she should not do. She obviously has not read the relevant documents and is not Properly Informed. This I find disappointing as I am generally enamoured of her, due to her being so neat and tidy and also a Party Member. Perhaps she does not have enough time to read?

We reach the corner of Alser Straße (where the Nurses' Home is situated). Sister Viktorine will continue now to her own building which is further up the street. Usually, she would walk me home but now she delegates to Sister Clara and Sister Maria. I could walk on my own but she will not allow that ~

The Nurses stop to light cigarettes now that Sister Viktorine can't Observe. The fiery tips dance through the dark as their hands move. First, they speak of the hazardous situation in the Sudetenland where our Führer declares that these German lands must become part of the Reich. Once all are united, Bolshevism will be defeated forever. The Germans must have security.

Then the conversation takes a new route. Sister Clara whispering: What actually does it mean – sterilisation?

I also have heard this word uttered in hushed tones. Sister Maria says now in a tooloudvoice: You know, in Germany? Getting your private bits snipped.

Sister Clara blenches, flicks cigarette ash, says: Oh. That. Really? Gosh. Well, why not? I mean, why do we have so many Children with problems? We've all seen. It's the Parents. One has to halt the spread of Hereditary Diseases. Look at the money being wasted. Everyone knows that *excessive care of the inferior allows inferior genetic material to circulate.*

Sister Maria is unsure: The Point is that you cannot see immediately. That's what we do, isn't it? We look deeper. Sometimes people appear most Simple-Minded but then we discover that they have more abilities than we supposed.

I do not agree with Sister Maria. I have read about this. Apparently, Doctors will soon be obliged to report Inherited Conditions. It makes sense. Why tolerate people in Society who can make no contribution? Useless Eaters. Why cause suffering by bringing Children into the World with Incurable Diseases? Sister Clara and Sister Maria start to talk about Dr A.

Sister Clara says: Does he not realise? Shouldn't he be more careful?

Sister Maria: Well, obviously, he is a fruit cake. Everyone knows that. But there seemed to be broad approval, didn't there?

Sister Clara huffs, rolls her eyes upwards: I don't know how long he's going to be in that job. He should join the Party.

Sister Maria: He is a Party member.

Sister Clara: No. Didn't you know?

(I did not know and am deeply shocked. Why does he not join?)

Sister Clare continuing: In fact, he's being investigated. I was told. Plenty of people would want his job. Dr Jekelius for one. He would come back from the Public Health Office straightaway for that job. If that happened, I myself would think of staying. As it is, I am looking for other work. Who wants to be stuck in a backwater ~

Indeed, many questions must be considered. This I do confront again only four days later when Oma is thrown into Distress and Confusion. This being caused by the news that the Bishop's Palace (next door to the Stephansdom) has been sacked and partially destroyed. Cardinal Innitzer himself has been hit by flying glass or stones. Oma weeps at the thought of carbines, revolvers and sabres in such Holy places.

Many people have gone to Mass at our Piaristenkirche to show their support. Oma continues lachrymose, Sister Viktorine also. I may go with Sister Viktorine to light a candle. I am pleased by this decision as this is an opportunity to record what I see in my Notebook. Although I do not care what has unfolded. Nazism and Catholicism can walk hand in hand. Why make a Fuss?

Yet when we come to the Bishop's Palace the situation is indeed disquieting. The windows of the ground floor are all shattered. Books, papers and furniture have been thrown from the windows and lie scattered about. Everything charred and coated in ash. I stand beside Sister Viktorine as she lights a candle and says a prayer.

As she turns away, she sees Father Gärtner and falls into conversation with him. I turn aside and gasp at the stacks of rubbish which lie all about. HJ boys and BDM girls are sweeping up rubble and dust, piling up what remains of tables and chairs which have been blown apart. The air is thick with smoke and grit and now rain is dripping down, forming puddles amidst the debris.

Soon I discover Matchboxes amidst the swept-up rubble. Two regular Austrian Matchboxes but then also four Matchboxes which come from Berlin, two of which have the swastika on them. I pick up these Matchboxes and stand staring at them for some long Moments as Sister Viktorine recites another prayer.

When she comes to find me, she agrees I may take possession of the Matchboxes as they are placed with the rubbish. I am glad even though I am really too old now for such Childish Hobbies. It is silly to believe that Matchboxes may tell you how the World Works ~

This damage to the Bishop's Palace being only the commencement of the disruption of this Time for only two nights later huge Chaos is done in the Second District. This we do hear from Lukas. The man who resides in the room opposite him tried to drive a Fruit and Vegetable lorry through that area and was turned back. Of this Lukas does inform us in a tooloudvoice.

Members of the Phillumeny Club also presenting themselves now for a morning coffee. *Glass all over the Streets. Several of the synagogues burnt down.* Many people having to escape from their apartments and houses due to the ravaging fires. The responsibility for all this being not exactly clear. This the Phillumeny Club do say, nodding their heads.

Oma says: Appalling. Is there no end to the disruption in this City?

All are agreed that our Führer himself would never support such disorder ~

4.h. Some Failures of Fancy Dress

Now arrives December and snow eiderdowns the City. All is indistinct but also sharply present. The streets are both muffled and full of echoes which ricochet all about. The trees droop under their heavy shrouds of white. The water in the drains and gutters lies stationary. Even the taps in the washroom freeze.

I sleep in my coat. As I walk to the Hospital, many are out with shovels and brushes, scarves wrapped around their blistering lips. The van which brings food for the Café is not able to get up the street. Oma is most worried but the paucity of food does not matter as who will walk to the Café, slippingslidingwobbling like a Music Hall Act on the tight-packed ice?

Yet still on Sunday Dr Feldner asks if I might go sledging (the streets now mainly swept and shovelled). He is accompanied by Hansi and Herbert and both are bundled up in fur caps, wool socks up to their knees and scarfs tightly wrapped. They have propped their sledge up outside the Café.

Dr Feldner: Come now, Fräulein Brunner. Everyone must enjoy the snow.

I pull on extra wool stockings, two vests, a stiff old sheepskin which Oma no longer wears. Soon we are out in the Glory of the Street with the air biting our cheeks and snow blown up in sudden gusts. We walk down to where Professor Freud used to live. He has gone from the City now. *Good riddance. Him and his dirty ideas.*

His street has a stomach-dropping slope. Many Children are gathered already and one sees that the road has turned to packed ice. Children are pushing snow down the backs of each other's shirts.

Hansi and Herbert let me take a turn on the sledge, standing behind me to push me down the street. I feel the sledge move away and gasp as the speed gathers.

They have instructed me that, as the road turns, I must jump off. I see the kaleidoscope whizzing of the building facades, the sledge racingwobblingtwisting. Someone throws a snowball but I am moving so fast no one can hit me. Jumpjumpjump. I fall, laughing, into a pile of snow. Hansi hauls me out, his lips are bloodless, his eyelids thick with ice.

We remain out in the Frolicking Street until the light is blue and spectral and Mothers are calling and scolding. Then we go back to the Café. I expect that Dr Feldner might suggest that we all sit down for tea but he doesn't and I note that Oma is pleased. Yet even she can see how much I have relished the sledging and thanks him for his kindness ~

Two days before Christmas the snow is still on the ground but it has lost all its virgin purity. Salt is spread on the pavements and the roads. Grey slush congregates mournfully in the gutters and occasionally drops in clumps from roofs. Sister Viktorine will take me to the Christmas Party at the Clinic but first I must do my Work for Frau Schreiber.

The Party at the Clinic is *fancy dress* but I have no costume to wear. When I arrive at the dreary apartment of Frau Schreiber, she is highly ecstatic. Adolf will be home for Christmas. He has not given an exact date but surely tomorrow or perhaps the day after? Frau Schreiber has missed Adolf so badly.

The small Children are celebrating as well. The little ones barely know who Adolf is but they join in the sparse yet fevered preparations. The Party. I am Nervous. I will not know What To Do. As so often before, Frau Schreiber divines my thoughts. *You could be a Film Star.* (She would once have said *American Film Star* but no one talks about America now.)

I am hesitant. I did enjoy dressing up for the Rat Business but I am older now. However, Frau Schreiber is a wound-up toy doll and you cannot unwind her. Here – a silk dress, a jaunty hat, high-heeled shoes. I will not be able to wear the shoes to walk to the Clinic but I can transport them in a bag. Hair, lipstick. I am Frau Schreiber's captive.

Sister Viktorine arrives and Frau Schreiber says: Doesn't she look beautiful?

Oh wonderful. Yes. Wonderful.

That is not what she thinks. Like Oma, she believes Young Girls should not dress up too stylishly or they will get Unwanted Pregnancy. Does she not understand that this is different? It is Pretending, it is Fancy Dress. Sister Viktorine herself is dressed as a rabbit: A neighbour lent me this fur coat. It does have a few holes but since I am an animal.

She has manufactured rabbit ears out of fur gloves and a piece of wire rolled up in a headscarf. Frau Schreiber places on me a sticky kiss, hands me a present wrapped in coloured Paper and tied with string. I know that Sister Viktorine considers that I must wait until Christmas Eve to enjoy this present. Yet Frau Schreiber says: Of course. Open it now.

I remove the tissue Paper to find most alluring earrings. Bold discs with a circle of blue glass which sits against the ear, then a disc of bright red hanging below. I have never been bestowed such a present. Frau Schreiber squeezes me and says she will send Adolf to find me. Just as soon as he is home. After Christmas he'll be back at the engineering works ~

I traverse the Streets with Sister Viktorine in a state of some Agitation. A Christmas Party with Cabbage Children? I would rather not encounter such Types but the staff at the Clinic will want to include allallall. A Christmas tree in the Reception Area is decorated with streamers and tiny Clay figures painted Extremely Poorly. Sister Maria is playing the piano.

Dr Feldner is wearing a voluminous and furry Bear suit which covers even his head and face. Dr Jekelius has returned for this celebration and is costumed as a Ruthless Pirate. Herr Spellbinder is also a Pirate, which in his case does not require much Pretence. Soon he is staging a mock fight with a cardboard sword against Dr Jekelius in the Reception Area.

Professor Hamburger is sporting reindeer horns and has thrown open the Door of his Office so that we can hear his gramophone. All the Cabbages are decked out in costumes, tidy and neat. Oddly, none of the proper dribblers are Present. (Soon I find out why. They are hidden away in the Nursery with the Door shut.)

Are the Nurses not aware of the benefits of whisky for calming children? I would certainly recommend it. Sister Clara arrives hoping to make an impressive entrance and indeed she does appear most elegant with her blonde hair elaborately styled. She is Eliza Dolittle and has a full-length, waist-pinching dress and wide-brimmed hat atop her hair. I don't know who Eliza Dolittle is.

Dr A shakes his head: No, no. You have not understood, Sister Clara. You can't just dress up as Eliza Dolittle, you have to *become* Eliza Dolittle.

Sister Clara looks offended, which is perhaps not surprising since Dr A and his wife are dressed in ghastly traditional Austrian peasant clothes – with Dirndl and Lederhosen etcetcetc. They probably wear such clothes when they are on holiday in the mountains normally. You can't dress up as the Person you are. Does he not understand ~

Such a shame that Herr Böckler could not be here. A prior engagement. Such a Busy Man. On the long dining room table food is laid out. Dr Jekelius helps everyone to make Paper hats. Someone has brought in greenery from the garden. Fräulein Eder, dressed as a milk maid, sits in a corner smoking and adjusting her curled hair.

Sister Viktorine takes me aside. She has forgotten to show me. Would I like to see? A letter from dear Fräulein Weiss. Now Frau Weiss-Frankl. She is now in Baltimore. A white clapboard house with a porch all along the front. Wide branches spread across the photo. *Wonderfully homely and comfortable.*

A Young Man enters and he is wearing a HJ uniform. Everyone turns to look at him. I am aware that this is a Person I should recognise but I don't. And then. I look again. Adolf. Really? He makes his Heil Hitler salute. Everyone returns the salute. Dr Feldner steps forward and puts out his hand – or paw.

Says: How very good that you came, Adolf. Are you just back?

Adolf says: Just half an hour ago.

He decided that he might take the opportunity to pass by on his way home. Professor Hamburger comes forward and pumps Adolf's hand. I do not know why I am shocked. Does he really look so different? Not entirely. It is just that the Adolf I knew spent his whole Life working out what you shouldn't do – and then doing it.

Now I am surprised that he should portray himself *as tough as leather, as hard as Krupp steel and as swift as a greyhound*. Also, I am jealous. As I well know, he cannot read or write. Yet he can join the HJ. Saying also: Joining the army after Christmas. Garrisoned in Linz.

Frau Schreiber will be disappointed. I am deflated also. What is *Appropriate Behaviour* in this situation? What am I meant To Do? The clothes his mother lent to me feel itchy and tight. Too bright, too shiny. Sister Viktorine says: Your mother thought you would return to the engineering works.

Adolf: Actually a friend of hers helped me. Obersturmführer Teichmann?

The brushed wool jacket on the back of the chair, the braided cap on the table. Professor Hamburger talks about how the Curative Education Ward is contributing to the aims of National Socialism. *Service rather than Self.* Adolf is an example of how the Reich is willing to offer employment even to those who may have experienced difficulties in the past.

Sister Viktorine: Adelheid. Have you said hello to Adolf?

Ah, Matchbox. Sorry. Adelheid. Look at you. Wherever did you get those clothes? I bet I can guess. My mother did mention. Fancy dress, I suppose. You've got to be careful. Wouldn't want to give the Wrong impression. Things can be Misunderstood ~

He thinks I am one of the Sluts. How dare he? In the Reception Area, the gramophone is singing and piratical Dr Jekelius is trying to do sex acts with Sister Clara. All are joining in a grotesque waltz. Dr Feldner in his Bear suit swinging Sister Maria (Gretel from the Fairy Tale). Sister Viktorine manoeuvres through the dancers, rabbit ears nodding.

Help with the Children. I have assisted enough. I'll do some Washing Up. I overhear Professor Hamburger speaking to Adolf. *Hitler is a Man of Peace but the Reich must secure its territories. If the integrity of the German lands is threatened, then the Reich must be ready to act in defence.* I try not to listen but his voice is Insistent.

There will not be War. One can rely on our Führer. In Austria there is no appetite for it. The memories are still too raw. Adolf departs and I do not say farewell. Dr A says: What a pleasure to see him looking so well.

Sister Viktorine: National Socialism has achieved what we could not ~

I do not like this Party but I cannot depart without Sister Viktorine. Even when the clearing up is done, I must wait while she disciplines two children wearing crocodile masks. One has shot the other with a button from a cardboard-and-elastic-band gun (what can one expect?). The Door to Dr A's Office is open hence I enter that room. A terrible mess. Books and Papers toppling.

I slide towards the desk, thinking to sit down on the chair by the window, as my shoes are pinching. The light is extinguished but brightness from the Corridor shines through so that I can see enough to find the Chair. Yet it is for this reason that I do not perceive that Dr A himself is also present, standing at the Window in the thickening shadows.

Beside him stands a boy. What can they be doing?

He does not turn around but speaks: Come and see.

I move towards the window and stand beside him. The boy does not look up but continues to stare through the Window. The glass is largely coated by ice so that the Street beyond appears only as a smudge of lustrous lights, the distant rooftops merely veiled edges, layers of soot against soot. Dr A says: Don't look through. Look on the glass. Can you see?

I comprehend now. The ice on the Window creates a miniature glacial landscape of churning sea and frozen craggy rock. Forests of Stalactite and stalagmite. So many cathedral pinnacles supported by intricate webs of tracery. Above a swirling sky of stars, so many patterns which are Perfect – circles, arrows, chevrons. They overlap and repeat.

Each one different. Unique. Standing together we are falling into the World of the Snowflakes. A whole universe of minuscule Galaxies crowded with Icy Wonders. The small or the large? Dr A says: How I miss our friend Dr Frankl ~

The boy stretches out his hands towards the glass as though he might reach right through it and touch the icebound window landscape. For a moment, his gawping, pale face is illuminated, iridescent. I know the type of boy. A Penguin. Like Gottfried and Bruno and

Thomas. He stands as I once stood, Observing. Just as I formerly studied Maps, Matchboxes, Notebooks.

The Velvet Chair in the Meeting Room. Herta and the washing waving on the line. Dr A wants to draw me back into that World of Perfect Small Things. Stars and Poetry. Yet none of that does comfort now. I am too Angry with Adolf. Also Angry with Dr A. He is a Grown Man and outside – in the Realms of a Blessed Reality – a New World is being forged ~

After My Death: Unhappy Christmas, USA 1938

In that Vienna Christmas of 1938 we saw the photograph of the house in Baltimore where Dr Frankl and Fräulein Weiss are now living. That lady now takes the name Frau Weiss-Frankl yet I shall always call her by the name I remember. A white clapboard house, porch along the front. Wide branches spreading. *Wonderfully homely and comfortable.*

Yet what is the Reality of her Life? I shall tell you using the Techniques of Improvisation which she did teach. So You see Fräulein Weiss now and she is stamping towards that cheerful, white front gate. She opens it wide, slams it behind her. She should wait and hold the gate open for Dr Frankl.

Instead, she might well slam the front Door on him. She does not actually live in this house. Her work is in Chicago and she has travelled across America to spend Christmas with Dr Frankl. The journey takes two days by train. She was only able to get a week off work. She asks herself – *Why not just be kind for a few days? Can we not decide to be happy* ~

She does not slam the Door, she waits for Georg. At least, he will know not to attempt a conciliatory conversation. Isn't he also bored with the endless gratitude? The Georg she knows (without an e) might have admitted boredom but George the Enthusiastic American will not. She and Georg (always plain Georg for her) are so lucky, are they not?

She holds the Door for him, is aware of him hanging his hat and coat on the hall stand. Is he moving even more quietly than usual in an attempt to calm her? If he is, then she hates that, hates him, hates the whole thing. The house is chilly. The fire they lit earlier has gone out. She should perhaps relight it but she hasn't the energy.

She could have spent the day tidying and cleaning the house, decorating it for Christmas. She thinks of childhood Christmases in Germany — the smell of marzipan, cloves, cinnamon, the candles lighted on the mantelpiece, the ringing of bells and the home-made models of angels. Glühwein, Christstollen and Lebkuchen.

What is the Point of making any effort with this house? She does not live here and Georg himself is only camping. He has applied for several jobs. Why bother to play at homes? Instead, she has spent the day catching up on work. Georg asks her now if she would like a drink, offers to stoke up the fire. *No. Thanks. I think I'll head up.*

Georg nods, settles himself in an armchair. Everything about him irritates her. They spent the evening at a party Organised for his colleagues at the Harriet Lane Children's Home which is part of the Baltimore Hospital. When they were leaving the party, he had said, as he put on his hat: Lovely party, wasn't it?

No. Dreadful. Dull and fake. Like everything in this Country.

Maybe she had gone too far but what she had said was true. Everything here feels thin and insubstantial. The frantic simulations of spontaneous sincerity are exhausting. The women are inhibited, insistently feminine. They speak softly, do not open their mouths. Their make-up is perfect, and they are permanently sheathed in shift dresses and matching accessories.

Yet one is uncertain whether they have been to the beauty parlour or the taxidermist. She wants to ask — *What good is freedom if everyone is so incessantly conformist?* But she also feels pity. For if you have so much that your Life must be good, then what do you do if it is not? You have only yourself to blame. How can one live with such guilt?

At least no one else at the party had heard her comment. She wishes now that Georg would chastise her for behaving badly, for being Awkward and Inappropriate, for failing to be charming to his colleagues. Why doesn't he get Angry about anything? In particular, she had most definitely decided that she does not like Georg's boss. A Man called Kanner ~

In the bedroom, she doesn't switch on the lights. Instead, she throws off her shoes and wraps herself in a cardigan, pulls the eiderdown over her. A pack of cigarettes lies on the bedside table and she lights one, sits up on her pillow so that she can see out of the window. Shingled houses, picket fences, post boxes. It should be easy to be happy in this World.

She should probably not have taken the job in Chicago. The Truth is that she is lonely there. Her apartment is quite comfortable but she has no energy to use it as a base for a new life. Instead, she just sits at the window, long into the night, staring out at the lights on the lake. Hearing from below brief snatches of jazz, drunken shouts, car Doors slamming.

She should have stayed here in Baltimore with Georg. After all, she is married to him. When she and Georg were first together, there had been hope of a child but now she is forty. Too late. She had hated the waiting, the hope. Perhaps she went to Chicago to kill that hope – to assert career over marriage. Both for herself and for Georg. They had not talked of it.

He had supported her decision. He does take her work seriously, he always has done. He had applied for a job in Chicago also when one was advertised but he had not been interviewed. So many Doctors from Europe are looking for work. The ideas here are different. She tries to Translate but sometimes the words just don't exist.

A Psychologist, Mrs Weiss-Frankl? I see you don't have a PhD? A specialist in Intelligence Tests? Why is this approach relevant? The type of child we are looking at here is clearly Not Intelligent. She stubs out her cigarette. Pulls on warm socks and heads back downstairs.

Georg looks up: Can't sleep? I'll do the fire.

He adds kindling, strikes a Match.

Fräulein Weiss says: I'm sorry that I was rude to Kanner.

Georg turns slowly, the Matches still in his hand.

Yes. Yes. It was unhelpful. And unnecessary, I thought. Really.

This is the closest that one can get to having a row with Georg. *Unhelpful. Unnecessary.* Why won't he scream? This is the dance of their marriage. She is Angry, uncooperative, critical. He is pleasant. She calms down, cries, he offers comfort. Despite her constant irritation, she does find something touching in him. His humility, compassion, slow kindness.

She says: I'm just Angry with Kanner. I don't like him.

Yes. You did make that plain.

He starts to laugh and she laughs as well. It had been rather obvious.

She says: So self-satisfied. So entirely sure that America is the centre of everything. He himself central as well. Friendly to you but actually patronising. The Little Man recently arrived from Europe who carries his bags. Georg, you are older than him, more senior. You have twice his Brain, twice his talent.

Georg is shaking his head: Anni, Anni, come on. You know that he has helped us. Really, he has been generous. We can't afford to argue with him. He is our best hope. I need a reference and we get on fine. I can steer the Man.

I know. But when I mentioned our work in Vienna, he just wasn't interested. I mentioned the Curative Education Ward and he behaves as though he has never even heard those Words. He does know. He must.

Yes, I know. But that's what we are doing here. Explaining, Informing. I am going to Translate the Affective Contact article. You need to get back to your PhD. In these conversations I am having about Donald. You know about Donald? I sent you the Notes ~

Of course, she knows about the boy they call Donald (Triplett). Georg talks of him often. Donald had first come to the Harriet Lane Children's Home over a year ago and everyone at the Clinic had observed, discussed, shrugged. All of the American staff admit to being mystified. How can they explain Donald T?

A boy who constantly shakes his head from side to side, whispers or hums the same three-note tune. A boy who is determined that everything must be done in the same way in which he first saw it done and is obsessed by anything that spins. This boy reads well but cannot tolerate the Fact that *bite* is not spelt the same way as *light*.

This boy is not lacking in Intelligence. Aged two he could count to one hundred, repeat the alphabet backwards and forwards, say the Lord's Prayer and name the American Presidents and Vice Presidents. Yet he has no friends and continually repeats meaningless phrases. When painting he mumbles again and again *Annette and Cecile make purple*.

Yet this is not as meaningless as it appears. (Georg had realised that Annette is the name of the red tube of paint and Cecile is blue.) As soon as Georg met Donald he knew. When Anni saw the Notes she also knew. Georg had explained to Kanner, talked to him about his ideas about Affective Contact.

Georg says now: Kanner is interested. I am going to start going back through the Files. It won't be the first time that they have seen this kind of Child but they haven't made the links. I said to Kanner – this is rare but it is not unique. That's why I am translating the article. You could give me a hand, if you wouldn't mind?

Anni thinks – *Translate? If the word doesn't exist, then the idea isn't there. And how do you Translate a whole culture? Here all they want to talk about is psychoanalysis.*

Now she says: Of course I will help. You will find others. But what I have said about this before is Correct, isn't it? They are looking in the Wrong places. It is not the institutions. If they had more Children coming in from the schools and the Courts. They would see.

Yes, of course, but it is a different system here.

Anni knows that there is no Point in discussing the situation further. She won't change Georg. It isn't that he isn't ambitious. He is – but he isn't competitive, that's the difference. He is finding a way to carry on the work that he has always done and that's all that matters to him. Why does it have to be such a struggle?

Georg answers that question which she hasn't asked: Come on. You know. It is always like this. The Hospital, the Clinic, the School. The institutions which are meant to enable our work are actually placing obstacles in our paths. We are always in Enemy territory. I am not talking about being Jewish. I'm talking values, approaches, ideas.

Fräulein Weiss knows but she is happy for him to say it again. These well-worn words are a comfort. As they head up to bed, she tells him that she regrets going to Chicago, but he will not allow this. New Worlds and cultures are certain to be challenging. But the experience, the opportunities, the conversations are all valuable.

Soon they will go back to Vienna. He will see his Mother again. She is too tired to write but dear Sister Vik has sent a long letter with all the news. She will keep his Mother safe until the Papers come through. The British and French will not tolerate the situation much longer ~

When Fräulein Weiss boards the train three days later, she stands for long minutes pressed against Georg's shoulder. They did have a Happy Christmas, after all. Georg is right. Chicago is an adventure. But now that she is back in that City, she stands again at the window, staring out at the lake, trapped within her own minimally furnished cell of the American Dream.

Neon displays flash even in the daytime. Endless Streets criss-cross each other in eerie quietness. Big houses with yards and cars and so many shoesshoesshoes. One understands how hard it must be to have such good lives. How can one explain an abundance that fails to sustain? Everyone is behaving well for someone's benefit – but whose?

She must work on her PhD. She must at least read or write up Case Notes. She doesn't have the energy, cannot even find the will to cook supper. Just sits in a chair by the window watching the lights go out, the City still electrically charged and buzzing, falling asleep there and only moving into the solitary bedroom at three or four in the morning ~

She is at that window one evening in the spring when the Doorbell rings. An Elderly Man she does not know is standing there. She prepares to be professional. No doubt this Man is seeking someone who will help out with a family difficulty. She can easily do that. Of course, the family will be Jewish therefore she will not insist that they make an appointment.

She'll agree to meet them privately, to see what advice she can give. Yet the Man is not mentioning a Child. Instead, he is explaining that he is from the local Jewish Welfare Organisation. What support might she need? Initially, she finds the question marginally offensive. She *provides* support, she does not *receive* support.

Things have been Misunderstood. She has money and an apartment, even a distant husband. Yet the old Man is querulous, placid, solicitous. She cannot brush him aside. She says politely that *really* she does not need anything. Yet still he presses. He and his wife live just two Streets away. *Join us for our Shabbat Dinner?*

Now? Right now? She can hardly claim to have other things to do. Yet she is not dressed Appropriately. He waves this objection aside. She walks with him along the streets to the dilapidated

Chicago brownstone. Lights shine at every window. His apartment is on the third floor. It is like home. Silly, silly. It is nothing like her Family Home in Germany.

Yet this apartment is a proper home. Filled with limp furniture and dwindling photographs and the Evidence of lives which continue. She recognises the smells – chicken soup with matzo balls, some other spice she cannot name. The table is already laid with the challah, wine and silverware. The elderly Man's wife asks if she would help to light the candles.

She starts upon this familiar task but is seized with Fear. Soon they will start to sing. Those Words from so long ago that she never understood. She finds herself weeping uncontrollably. Why? She never thinks of herself as Jewish. Yet she cannot stop weeping. The Old Man sits beside her, takes her shaking hands in his ~

5.a. The Flying Coffee Tray

How can we live in a World where we are always imprisoned in the Present Moment, knowing nothing, seeing nothing? Certainly, on that soontobedeclared Momentous Day in September 1939, I was merely doing all the usual things. Cups lined up for coffee, bread sliced, butter cut into the thinnest curls (even though it isn't really butter now).

By 8 a.m. customers are arriving. I pour and slice and fry. The Stationer Herr Wächter enters and I pour him coffee. Frau Vogt takes up her customary position. Lukas is not with us as he has an ulcerous foot. The kitchen runs with condensation, the geyser coughs and splutters. *Come on, girl. Get those napkins shaken out. Empty the crumbs from the baskets.*

The bell at the Door tingles most discreetly. The shoulders of the Man who enters have a familiar slant. Tall, uncertain, a Young Man who also appears Old. I know his battered brown leather briefcase. For a Moment his eyes meet mine and his eyebrows ascend. I take him a coffee and he soon settles down to work on his Papers ~

The Door swings open with a bang, the bell ringing hysterically. A group of SS men stride in. (Someone whispers – chimney sweeps, which appellation is given due to their black uniforms.) One of the tables near the Window is already taken but the couple there hastily decamp. Someone places a record on the gramophone which only Oma should properly do.

The SS are full of hearty talk about Poland. *The unruly Poles have long caused problems. The Führer will bring those insubordinate Slavs into the Reich now. Poland has always been part of the German lands. Land was* taken from Germany at the end of the First World War. Bolshies in the East etcetcetc.

Oma smooths her hair and steps across to the table. She takes the Order without delay. A couple of other tables hurriedly empty, people gathering up their coats and umbrellas, nodding a polite acknowledgement, sliding out into the street. I clear hastily, stacking plates and gathering glasses, then wipe, lay the cutlery out again with military precision.

Oma nudges her hips through the swing Door carrying a tray. *Good morning. Good morning. Yes. Not bad for the time of the year. Yes. Yes. Hot milk as well? The bread is fresh this morning.* The men are joshing and joking. Perhaps they were out late last night and are still flying high on the beer and the dancing.

One of the men turns the gramophone off and switches on the Radio. He has sabre scars on his cheeks and teeth which slope inward. As he moves back to his table, he nearly sends Frau Vogt's Semmel and boiled egg into her lap. Her face is sour as a green apple. The Man begins to conduct, waving his arms while the others laugh. When he stops, I move towards the table. The music starts up again and his arms swing.

I step aside but I am not fast enough. Clumsyclumsyclumsy. The tray leaps out of my hands, rises, hovers, trembles, gasps in the openness of the air, realises that nothing now lies underneath. Downdowndown. It throws itself onto the floor with a terrible clatter. Men laugh uproariously. Frau Vogt fixes me with a satisfied and evil smile.

Oma dashes out of the kitchen, her face slapped and gaping as she sees the crockery spread all over the floor. A lady from another table starts to pick up teacups and spoons. Oma cannot get down to the floor because of her knee. The men at the table are certainly not going to help. Frau Vogt is relishing the Chaos and Disorder.

The Man says: For God's sake. What were you doing?

How dare he? Everyone in the Café saw. I was doing my job. Doing my job rather well, in fact. He was the one *Behaving Inappropriately*. Everyone is peering down into their coffee or reaching for their coats. Time to go but I cannot ~

Dr A is looking directly at me, his eyes narrow, his mind calculating. His hand trembles as he raises his coffee cup to his lips. He knows, he knows. The playground, the worm down your shirt, the scuffed new shoes. The dog with the bucket on its head. *Don't show your Papers.* I hurry to help, collecting the bread and pots with the jam half spilling out.

When I get back to the kitchen, Oma is standing with her hands clasped to her head. Trays do not get dropped in the Café Stadler. She did not see what happened so now she will think this is my fault. That Man is like Adolf. He wears a uniform, tells others what they may or may not do, even though he is playing around like a Child.

What To Do? I quickly pour more coffees, salvage the bread that is not damaged. I step out into the Café and the tray whirls gracefully through the air and lands like a dove. The Man is watching me as I turn to go, his eyes skimming across my apron. Oma is on her feet now, filling the geyser again: Here. For God's sake, at least tidy your hair.

My hair was neat but scrabbling around on the floor has made me look messy. She pushes my hair into my cap and pulls the cap straight. My hip edges against the swinging Door as I carry another tray. Loud guffaws of laughter come from the tables near the Window. The Café is steamed up now, the air damp and stifling.

I slide this last tray down onto the table. Some crusts have fallen onto the floor. I'll have to come with the dustpan and brush. I know that everyone in the Café is observing me. Frau Vogt is loading me onto a train. The air itself is speaking, saying that This Is Not About A Tray, A Cap. Everyone is seeing me and not seeing me.

They want to reach up and catch the tray, to bring it safely to rest, to run the film backwards so that the teapot lands back on the tray, the eggs in their cups, the toast lying straight on the plates. A hand hovers and then reaches out, snatches the cap from my head: Why did you decide to cover up all that pretty hair?

I did not think that they would speak to me.

What is your name, girl ~

The Stationer Herr Wächter is choking. He staggers upright, coughs, wheezes, presses his hand to his chest. Someone is calling for water. Frau Vogt is assisting him although she knows, doesn't she? My feet have grown roots deep down into the floor and they will not come up no matter how hard I pull. I tug and tug and finally they unstick.

I turn away, heading back towards the kitchen. The Man saying: You. Come back here. Didn't anyone ever tell you that you must speak when you are spoken to?

He's going to ask for my Papers and I must not show him. I must run. He's tugging my mouth open with his bare hands, he's shining a light down my throat. I would like to bite his hand off, straight through to the bone. Sister Viktorine. That morning in the Ward. Voices are questioning fiercely. Sister Viktorine is extremely small, almost a child.

The men filling the whole space. She standing straight and firm but shrinking all the time. The plant pot is jabbering. The light fittings are intent on murder. The whole Ward solid.

What if they take me away? Sister Viktorine had people who explained about her Paperwork. Oma appears: Quick, Adelheid. Don't hang around, please.

The Café is rotating fast as a spinning top. I am so tired that I feel myself close to Death. What can I do and where can I go? I am meant to be a Useful Girl. None of this is my fault. So deep is my Distress that I have failed to notice. The Café is now crowded with people who are piling in from the street. Even out on the pavement they are affixing their ears to our Radio.

All these people are silent. The expressions on their faces are stunned, strained, serious. When the Deutschland anthem begins, many salute. We hear a ponderous, crackly, booming voice. The British have issued an ultimatum. The Führer will not bow to their requests. The British have declared War on the Reich ~

5.b. A Person of Great Social Utility

How did it happen? *The Alchemy of Circumstance?* I do not know. Next morning, I was up at six just as I always am. I am tying on my apron when Oma dashes into the kitchen: No, no. Not today, Adelheid. Pack your Suitcase. You will be working at the Hospital now and living in the Nurses' Home on Alser Straße.

Suitcases? Journeys? I can't understand but I dash to pack my things. Oma says: Hurry up, hurry up. Sister Viktorine will be coming at seven. Make sure that you do exactly what she says. Exactly What She Says ~

I wait at the Door of the Café for Sister Viktorine. Finally, finally, I am going to walk through the Streets of my City again and I will have a job. A real job? I do not know but that is what Oma seems to say. What does it matter? All this is beyond my imagining. How glad I am also to get away from Oma who starts to weep at every Radio announcement.

Like all the Old Jeremiahs, she can talk only of the Horror of the last War. Famine, Spanish flu, lack of coal, hyperinflation, benches chopped up for firewood etcetcetc. All this I have heard many times before. When Sister Viktorine arrives, I want to skip along the street with her. Instead, I am careful to *Behave Appropriately* and not to draw attention to myself.

The Streets are astir even at this premature hour. Instructions have been proclaimed. Doors and windows to be blacked out when night falls. Rationing will soon start hence all must buy food before it begins. Why is there no meat on sale? One must start on the canning of vegetables. Fuel will soon not be available for private cars. No defeatist talk must be allowed.

When I arrive at the Hospital, Sister Maria gives me a proper uniform. Tight-fitting cap, long white gown, new job. I am not an actual Nurse, of course, but a Ward Assistant. At the end of the day, Sister Maria links her arm in mine and we walk to the Nurses' Home together. I am not to walk on my own. At the Nurses' Home I live in a room with Sister Maria.

I am delighted because although Sister Maria is Silly and talks too much (Radio Maria), yet she is also Kind. I soon discover that I can continue to engage in my Notebooks and Matchboxes at night as she sleeps most soundly. Or she goes out, just as Adolf did, in the time of my Childhood. I Pretend that I have not noticed. *Do not involve yourself in Adult Affairs.*

Although Sister Maria is kind, yet Sister Clara is a better Person for me to copy. She is a Member of the Party. I wish that I also could be a Member. When Sister Clara sees how Useful I can be, then maybe that will be possible. When I go back to the Café next Sunday, I wear my Nurse's uniform and Oma prepares a coffee. I sit at a table like a proper customer.

If only your Grandfather could see you now. Lukas is still limping with his ulcerous foot and is not pleased to see me elevated. When Hildegarde, Gerda and Frau Winkler come in, they say how impressed they are but this is Not True. A Nurse at the Hospital is much better than collecting firewood and making soup for the BDM ~

Now I am as Happy as I will ever be. This I think – yet it turns out I am Wrong. I will explain how this comes to be. As part of my job, I am to clean the Office of Dr A. I saw how Disordered his Office was when I came to the Christmas party. Now the situation is even worse because Dr A is also now working for the Public Health Office in addition to his normal work.

He has difficulty finding time for his Research – which is probably beneficial since those ideas are all finished with now. The silly old Gift of the Child has turned into a modern idea called a Person of Great Social Utility. Also, Dr A is now responsible for the administration of a new service called the Motorisierte Mütterberatung (Motorised Mothering Advice Service).

The Motorised Mothering Advice Service is the first of its kind anywhere in the World. Cars go out from the Hospital all across the many provinces of our Country. Doctors and Nurses travel in these vehicles, also a Welfare Officer. Their job is to assist Mothers by giving them advice – for being a Mother is the most Important Job in our new Reich.

This is the succour that Frau Schreiber should perhaps have received. Also, maybe my own Mother would not have gone to Berlin *leaving no forwarding address* if she had had such aid. Dr A initially suggests that I could bring benefit by organising the Papers in accordance with the different regions of our Country. Styria, Carinthia, Vorarlberg etcetcetc.

An Office at the end of the Corridor is empty and all the Paperwork relating to the new service is to be moved into that space. Dr A remembers well how I enjoyed our Maps of the City back in the Distant Days of my Youth. I arrange all the Paperwork as best I can. Soon I realise that an Actual Map is most necessary.

Happily, I have such a Map in my bag at the Nurses' Home and so I convey it to the Ward and pin it on the wall. When Dr A sees this, he is extremely gratified. *Excellent. Excellent.* The lists also must be typed up rather than inscribed by hand. All forms to be typed with three carbons. I can use the typewriter in the Reception Area at the end of the day.

Much easier to use a typewriter where the keys do not jam. I am glad I taught myself. Dr A suggests I might be given the whole job of organising the Service. Sister Viktorine is doubtful but Dr A is certain. *Maps, Files, Reports, Observations.* This is exactly the kind of job that Adelheid can do. *Look, she can type perfectly well.*

So it is that within a week I am promoted from a Ward Assistant who only mops up vomit, changes soiled bed sheets, serves food etcetcetc. Instead, I have my own job which is so specialised it has no name. The Office at the end of the Corridor is All Mine ~

Soon all the cars which are part of this service are allocated numbers and the routes are all marked. I am given my own typewriter to work on. I put pins in the Map to identify villages already visited. I can locate all the cars exactly in my mind. I travel with them through parts of Austria I have never visited. Places perhaps like Hausbrunn where the family of Dr A resides.

Empty emerald fields, a cream-coloured church with a russet spire, low white houses. Stations and garages, lakes, woodland tracks, cornfields and meadows. Also, Alpine villages of wooden houses nestled at the foot of eternal peaks. I make calculations about how long a journey will take. Must accommodation be booked in a local inn?

I supply the list of such necessary bookings to Fräulein Eder. I also ensure that the Doctors and Nurses have all the Records they require before they depart. All their Reports come back to this Office. Unfortunately, the Notes are sometimes unclear or incomplete. I copy out the sections which are poorly written and tidy everything away in the right File.

There being a File for every Village, the Mothers listed in alphabetical Order with details of all their Children. These Children have been checked by the Doctors and Nurses. Mainly the problems are the samesamesame – rickets, diarrhoea, lice. In a special column at the end the Doctors note down Children who have particular difficulties.

Everything is transported in special envelopes from the Front Desk. It becomes known among some of the Doctors and Nurses that I enjoy collecting Matchboxes and so quite often in the envelopes are Matchboxes from the places where they have travelled. This I do much enjoy particularly as I am focusing my Collection now on the Reich.

I am also responsible for making sure that Dr A signs all the completed Reports. I place them in the Correct Order and note in pencil where he must sign. This is most helpful as he is often busy and has no time to verify the Paperwork himself. I make sure to take it to his Office for him and stand with him while he quickly puts his – most untidy – signature in place.

Dr A is impressed by my work. I am keeping his Office exceptionally Orderly. I remain late at night because he stays late. Even at ten or eleven he is here working on his Research. Sometimes when he has a few moments to spare he visits my Office to monitor my work and I know he enjoys the arrangements of the Maps and the Files and the Notes.

In the evenings we also stand at the window to look down into the street, just as we once stared down from the Roof Terrace. One evening, a column of soldiers is marching down the street. Of course, our hearts stir, for these men will go the Front. Dr A tells me that his Brother will depart soon. *How proud one is of all these men who are defending their Country.*

We write Heil Hitler at the end of every document ~

5.c. The Attending of Tea Parties

As part of my New Position, I am also required to go to the Records Room. You may remember that I have told you that this Room is situated just across the landing. I have had Many Dreams – both Sleeping and Waking – of that Room. When I may finally enter that place, I am giddy with excitement. Such a Magical Adventure.

A long Attic room with compact Windows. Perhaps not so appealing in itself. Yet everything in that room neatly Organised and every piece of Information carefully placed in Files. All the Paperwork I am marshalling in relation to the Motorised Mothering Advice Service will eventually be housed in this room. I should like to reside in that place forever ~

Initially, I am instructed to transport Paperwork to the Records Room directly. However, soon the Procedures change and all Paperwork must be passed via Fräulein Eder. She will then Instruct me what must be taken to the Records Room. Some instead remaining in our own Filing. In fact, I know these Instructions myself so her interference is not needed.

Nevertheless, I obey. In the lengthy hours of the night (also in the Day) I dream of Matchboxes and Files all put away most neatly. If I get fatigued when I am labouring, I say to myself – what if the Führer should come? Are we properly prepared? This could indeed happen as on three occasions two SS Officers come to the Ward.

They enter Professor Hamburger's Office. One day I am asked to attend with some Files for them to consider. Five Files. I remember that most exactly. I would not make a Mistake. I signed them out. The Files travel into Professor Hamburger's Office. Yet I note that when Fräulein Eder returns the Files to me only Four are Present.

I check the sign-out list. Could I have made a Mistake? What then is most strange is that the list is not there. It is usually on a clipboard by the Filing Cabinet and yet the front page is Missing. This is most Incorrect and so I take the clipboard to Fräulein Eder in order that she can see the Mistake. She snatches it from me.

There is no need for you to look at that. Sister Viktorine also tells me – *Go back to the Motorised Mothering Advice Office and get on with your Work.* So that I do. The page of the list never returns to its Proper Home. I check later and it is still not there. My work is Correct and Fräulein Eder's is not. Not surprising because she is a slovenly woman and not Intelligent.

I do not doubt that over time it will become clear who does their work Properly and who does not. At least Dr A certainly appreciates my efforts. On Monday morning he gathers the Nurses together to review the tasks for the week. Even though I have only been working in the Hospital for a month, yet he says what an excellent contribution I make ~

At the Nurses' Home that evening, we all crowd onto Sister Maria's bed. We often do that in our few free hours and I am Embarrassed and Uncomfortable but glad to be included. Sister Maria tells me how well I have done, saying: Pretty difficult to get much praise out of Coat Rack Dr A. Never notices what anyone is doing – not even himself.

Sister Clara is with us but she does not sit crowded on the bed. Instead, she perches most upright on a prim and pretty miniature Armchair and wafts her hands in front of her nose because of the smoke. When brandy is passed around, she doesn't take the bottle because the Rules of the Nurses' Home say No Alcohol.

She is right in this Matter and I hope she notices that I do not drink. Now Sister Clara says she will soon be moving on to a much better job. She had the good fortune to bump into our former colleague, Dr Jekelius. He told her extremely privately, in total confidence, that he will soon be appointed as Director of a new Clinic.

Sister Clara will lodge her application immediately. No doubt the Curative Education Ward will be closed down. What is the need for it? Behind Sister Clara's back, Sister Maria is being Rude and Childish, waving her head from side to side, lolling her tongue, moving her hands like the winding of a handle ~

That soon-arriving Sunday, all the Nurses are invited to tea at the home of Dr A. Sister Viktorine decrees that I can walk there with Sister Maria. The Streets are without most cars as the sale of petrol to private Persons is forbidden. Mercifully, it transpires that for us the distance is most short. Dr A only lives in Berggasse, two Streets away from the Nurses' Home.

This I had not understood. In fact, I had never considered that Dr A has a Home. This is Silly as I know that he has a Wife and Children. Yet still when I arrive at the Apartment I find myself shocked and unsettled by the Fact of this other Life. Yet the apartment being most comfortable. His wife is expecting another baby.

She is making a most strenuous effort to welcome us all most kindly, although burdened with toddlers Gertrud and Little Hans climbing on her lap. So strange is this Domestic World that I don't know What To Do hence I order Matters in the kitchen and carry away the dirty pots and plates. Noticing only that Dr A does not seem at home in his own house.

First, going off on a Tram Track in relation to Great Mountains I Have Climbed. Then disappearing from his own party Yet I Observe him at a certain moment. The noise is too painful for me therefore I wander down a Corridor, lose my bearings, find myself at a half-open Door. Dr A is with Little Hans who is now laid in a cot to sleep.

The light curtains are half drawn so the light is vaporous and drifting. His hand reaches to stroke the Child's head. The Moment still and calm. What comfort it must be for that tiny Child. His caressing hand expansive, the child's head precious. Which makes me consider how he must enjoy his own Children being usually responsible for so many Cabbages ~

Quite unexpectedly, a letter comes to the Nurses' Home addressed to me. I have never had a letter before, only postcards which I sometimes received from travelling Opa in my Childhood. The letter is from Adolf. He is at the Rennweg Barracks in the south of the City. Would I engage to meet him for tea on Sunday afternoon?

The other Nurses are all crammed onto Sister Maria's bed, leaning over her shoulder so that they can glimpse the letter. *Adelheid is going out to tea with a soldier. Maybe he will even write letters to her from the Front.* The next day Sister Maria reveals the letter to Sister Viktorine and that lady says that I may be excused to go. Usually such is never possible.

I have on no occasion had such Excitement in my Life. I find my Street Map and look at where I am to travel. Sister Maria lends me her most prized dress. This dress is not a dressshowingbosoms worn by a Slut. Still rather wide for me since Sister Maria is not so Golf Club. The material of the dress is a most soft silk, which I do savour against my skin.

I also polish Frau Altmann's shoes, which still appear quite pristine. Plus, I wear the earrings which were given to me by Frau Schreiber. Sister Maria saying how the red and blue of these small ornaments complement the gown precisely. Even Sister Clara is flattering to me. I am nervous of behaving Inappropriately. Adelheid – Concentrate Exceedingly Hard.

The dress does aid me, also the earrings and my hair being curled neatly behind my ears. Adolf is most pleased to see me and I him. Of course, I do remember his behaviour to me at the Christmas party but I have Forgiven him. He may be a soldier but I am now a Ward Assistant. However, I do also find myself puzzling why he has invited me.

Soon this does become most clear. The tearoom where we meet is just outside the gates of the barracks and is clearly visited by many soldiers and so he wishes to show himself a Man with a lady friend. (When in reality, he is not handsome and not Clever and has only his considerable cunning on which he may rely.)

Yet I do not object to this Pretending. It is like the Rat Business. One knows how to wave a toasting fork. I am both stared at and ignored. Adolf is most swollen with pride. The Café where we are situated considers itself a most high-class institution yet rims of dirt can be perceived at the bottom of the cups. Adolf now offers to take me back to the Hospital ~

Just as we are approaching that august building, we apprehend Herr Spellbinder walking towards us. I assume that Adolf will stop to say good afternoon but he strides straight past. I also keep my eyes firmly fixed ahead. Herr Spellbinder gleefully saying such things as — *The Engländer may be an Almighty Fool but he has never lost a War yet.*

When we come to the Door of the Hospital, it happens that Sister Viktorine is departing. Again, I expect that Adolf will engage with her but he only raises his hand distantly. At the Hospital Door, he says that he will not be seeing me for some time. Still he seems to hesitate. He says goodbye yet again, promises to write.

Also, he presents me with a Matchbox which he has purloined from the Café which we have just visited. I decide that I will keep it in my pocket while I wait for his letters to come. Just as I am thinking that I suddenly realise. I understand. I may not see him again. He might die. As I apprehend this his faces changes as though he also now more fully realises.

Yet, nevertheless, he gives me a brassy grin and turns away briskly. He thinks in this way to express his bravery. Yet I have known Adolf many years and I see. Distractions involving Rats are sadly not a recognised currency in the World he now inhabits ~

5.d. The Paperwork of Aurel Iselstöger

A boy called Aurel Iselstöger comes to the Clinic. The November day is glacial, the stoves lit. I note the coming of this Boy because I recollect him from School. He is four years younger than me and he is Most Eccentric but also excellent at drawing. Also, he always used to stare at me profoundly. I know him as that certain type who is of interest to Dr A.

What Adolf and I would have called a Penguin but which Dr A does call a Little Professor. When he arrives, he is as I remember him from School. Except fourteen now and attired in tank top, shorts, long socks and embarrassing sandals of a type only worn by small children. His hair slightly wet from the comb and his school bag full of sketchbooks.

He has been despatched to the Clinic by the School who do not wish to keep him since he causes disruption. I do not remember any such disturbance and one knows that the Reports from Schools cannot be relied upon. In the reception area, he gets out a sketchbook. When he sees me, he staresstaresstares just as he did at School.

He is accompanied by his Mother, a youthful lady and most prepossessing. Clearly an affluent and cultured person besuited in an orderly wool dress and a trim jacket with braided edges. All this I see before Aurel and his mother are called into Dr A's Office. I am occupied with the Files of the Ward that day as Sister Clara is sick with a stomach situation.

The Point being that I expect Aurel and his mother to be in that Office some long time as Dr A always takes hourshourshours to ask all his questions. His appointments always running behind time as he is most meticulous. Usually Dr A will begin by asking the child – *Do you know the meaning of your name?*

Often Children do not know but some go off on some digressive Tram Track about the sixteenth century. *Some people believe that it means Wise One but that cannot really be the case. Instead it is perhaps more likely that it means gentle one etcetcetc.* Yet Aurel and his mother have not been positioned in that room ten minutes when Dr A appears at the Door.

He asks me to bring the School Form. This Form is used to instruct that Children should be exempt from school. This Form Dr A does use most often as *School is not the right place for many youngsters.* He no doubt remembers Gottfried – or perhaps his own experience? I carry the Form into his Office and see Dr A, as expected, has written a page of Notes.

Yet surely he is not finished? I have also presented a copy of the Admission Form. I do that because it is clear to me that Aurel will be admitted to the Hospital. Frau Iselstöger is sniffing delicately and wiping her eyes with her handkerchief. Dr A takes the School Form but then hands the Admission Form back.

Saying: No, no. We don't need that.

I am most surprised by these unexpected developments.

Dr A says: Please copy the details onto the School Form.

I sit down at a side table and copy out the name and address. Dr A often requests me to enact this due to his bad handwriting. Frau Iselstöger dabs her glistening tears again and throttles her handkerchief while saying: What can I do? If Aurel is not at School then where is he to go? I know, Dr A, that you are aware that he is not without ability.

Here she parades Aurel's sketchbook: He draws most beautifully. I had hoped, as I said, that you might keep him here. With just a little help I do feel that he can achieve so much.

Dr A makes his eyes evasive and is most firm: I am sorry, Frau Iselstöger. I do see your Point and I am aware that Aurel has abilities. But the policy of the Clinic is changing. We are adapting our approach in the light of the new Regime. I'm sure you understand.

But Aurel can make a contribution. I'm sure he can.

Dr A: Frau Iselstöger. Aurel is indeed a boy of considerable artistic abilities. It is only a question of the School. Best not to attend. I'm sure that you wouldn't wish to put me in a difficult situation? You are aware that new legislation is being introduced?

That wouldn't apply to Aurel?

No. No. Certainly not. Particularly given that some of his difficulties were doubtless caused by a childhood accident. A blow to the head? Is that not the Case?

Frau Iselstöger appears bemused. Then her eyes click wide. She has understood a Sudden Startling Truth.

Oh yes. Maybe. Yes. Absolutely. I see your Point ~

Dr A clearly does not want to discuss this situation further and so says: I feel that Aurel will do much better at home where he can pursue his artistic interests. I am sending notification to the School. You did mention relatives in the Country?

Dr A has cornered Frau Iselstöger and is edging her towards the Door. He has always been a Man who can be attentive and sympathetic yet on other occasions extremely frosty and distant. Regrettably, Frau Iselstöger (despite understanding a Startling Truth) stands her ground. Even though Dr A is advancing decisively, yet she is affixed firmly to the floor.

Dr A is curt, decisive: Our time is really at an end. Did you say – the Tyrol?

Well, yes. My sister does live—

Splendid, splendid. The mountain air can be of inestimable benefit.

But I thought—

Dr A moves to the Door and swings it open with a flourish.

Frau Iselstöger is failing to *understand the signals which are being given.*

Says: Well, really. I had hoped—

Dr A looks at me narrowly and then advances again, peers out of the Door into the Reception Area. Then takes a pincer hold of Frau Iselstöger's arm and navigates her into the space behind the Door, skewers her into that circumscribed area. This I have never seen.

Get the Child out of Vienna. Do it now.

It isn't true. What they say?

Don't wait to find out. A Childhood Accident. Remember.

Surely?

Now. Today. Don't delay.

Nimbly Dr A steps back and holds the Door from the other side. It is as though the last minute has never happened. All is normal, polite, official. Dr A saying most cheerfully: Good day to you and to Aurel. The best of luck. Fresh Country air. The mountains. One should never underestimate the virtues of these simple cures ~

The Door is slammed shut. Dr A shudders, takes a deep breath, grabs his Notes from the desk and pushes them into the stove. With a sudden crackle and a flash of gasping flame they are gone. This is not Correct Behaviour. Even if he makes a mistake in his writing – which he often does – then he simply crosses it out.
 I will try to pull the Papers out of the stove. I must.
 Yet they are already conclusively burnt up.
 He twists back to me: Have you written in the details?
 I have indeed written in most neatly the name and address etcetcetc. What should ensue now is that Dr A should attach his Notes to the rear of that Form also adding that supplementary Form which is for the School. The School Form he does attach but the Notes have gone. He takes the page I have supplied him and writes – *No further investigation needed.*
 This would be the Correct Procedure to be followed if no Notes had been made but they were made. I saw them. He goes to the window and, with fidgeting hands, pulls it open. Frigid air gusts in. We hear the slamming of doors as ambulances arrive at the Main Hospital, the distant ringing of an alarm bell. Sister Viktorine now ventures into the Room.
 She registers the smoking stove but immediately turns away. Dr A instructs me: Thank you. See that the School Form is sent. Then put that File away in the front of the bottom drawer of the Filing Cabinet.
 These Instructions are not right. That is where a File goes when we will not see the Child again. Such Files are then soon taken up to the Records Room. Yet that is most definitely not the Instruction I have been given. All Files must first go to Fräulein Eder. This is the Correct Procedure. Does he not understand ~

Sister Viktorine is now speaking to Dr A. Could he come to the Ward? The Child Eva is having a tantrum. Or perhaps a fit? I am situated in front of Fräulein Eder's desk. What action should I undertake? I did hear Dr A's Instructions but he was mistaken. I will be severely reprimanded by Fräulein Eder if I do not do as she has said.

Fräulein Eder's Instructions come straight from Professor Hamburger and his Instructions come from the Führer himself. I must show *Breadth of Vision and Independent Thought*. I reach to situate the File on Fräulein Eder's desk but Sister Viktorine is behind me: Adelheid. What are you doing? Dr A told you to put that in the Filing Cabinet.

I am obliged now to do what she is telling me even though it is Wrong. The Files are not really her concern and she is not a Person with a Logical mind. She is now following me as though she means to verify what I am doing. I place the File where I am told.

Sister Viktorine then says: Come with me.

I follow her into the Meeting Room and she fixes me with Angry eyes, saying: Adelheid, I am most disappointed. You are not concentrating. You must listen to what is said. These are not minor matters. Mistakes can have serious consequences ~

5.e. A Flock of White Birds

We are enslaved by the thickening winter which gathers all around and I am not so contented at the Hospital as I once was. I cannot sleep therefore I sit up long into the night copying newspaper Reports. My mind is troubled by Waking Dreams. The laughing clown of the Matchboxes has jagged teeth and is pointing an accusing finger at me.

I weep for the wobbly American with the drooping moustache on his unicycle who is riding away into the far distance and will never return. The white Czech lion with gold claws stalks the Corridors of the Ward (and my Mind). A mistake will be made, I will be blamed. I am worried that someone is investigating my locked box and disturbing my Notebooks.

The key of my locked box is hidden in my pocket all the time and sometimes I hold it tight in my fist. News rises up through the Hospital via various Filing Cabinets. Via the pipework and the stairwells, the cracks in the ceilings. Children have been transferred to another Hospital and post-mortem Instructions have been transported with them.

How can that be? Is it an administrative mistake? A Nurse has been reprimanded. She has written pneumonia on a Death certificate. That must be rewritten. The child cannot have died of pneumonia becausebecausebecause. Professor Hamburger asks repeatedly to examine the lists of the Children who are present in the Ward. Files are missing.

Dr A used to habitually leave the Door of his Office open. Yet now that Door is often definitively sealed and Dr A is occupied on the phone most frequently. The SS breach our threshold and are in

Professor Hamburger's Office some long time. Dr A must expound the Cases of certain Children againagainagain ~

When I am accomplishing Night Duty, I hear noises which frighten me. Voices burble and chatter. These sounds arise from the Meeting Room. This only happens when Dr Feldner is in the Hospital and I fear that he is listening to the Feindsender (Enemy Radio Station). At the beginning of the War all Radios had to be checked and labelled and the law was quite Clear.

It is a serious offence to listen to Radio Stations originating outside the Reich. Yet in our City there exists no shortage of youths who are obsessed by Radios and comprehend all their internal workings. One simply builds a small bridge into the back of any Radio and one may hear all over the World. This is treacherous and a Major Risk ~

Christmas comes into view and I return to the Café to help Oma. A week later deep snow pillows the City and the furnace is also broken in the Nurses' Home. Chilblains blossom on our hands and feet. In order to keep warm, three must curl up in the same bed. Sister Maria has cherry brandy left over from Christmas. The Rules of the Nurses' Home (as I have said before) say No Alcohol.

Yet the drink is welcome because of the extreme cold and the scent reminds me of the Rat Nights with Adolf and makes me wonder where he now resides. I have had two letters but both concise and neither, of course, written by him. The Person writing the letters being most correct (and therefore incorrect) in their handwriting.

One such night Sister Maria is present – which often she is not – and Sister Clara has stepped out for the evening with Fräulein Eder. They are conjoined friends now and Fräulein Eder has a sleek new fur coat which leads to certain Rumour and Gossip. *Apparently, you need a fur coat now for a Hiking Holiday. Fancy that.*

The three Russian Doll Nurses begin to tell Fantastical Stories ~

People are going missing. Not just the Jews. Everyone knows about them and most are gone now to Madagascar which must be done for reasons of racial purity. However, they are not the only ones. Sister Maria reports about Germany. People are having their private bits snipped. Others are disappearing, simply evaporating.

THE MATCHBOX GIRL

They vanish from the City at first light. Taken away on buses or trains, the windows blacked out. You arrive at a Hospital and find that the relative you are intending to visit is not there. He has been transferred. You do not know where. You receive a letter. Ashes can be claimed after the payment of a fee of 150 marks.

Apparently, a Grandmother opened the ashes of her husband and found a hair clip. Another elderly man is recorded as dying of appendicitis – except his appendix was removed when he was a child. This is like the Fantastical Stories when I was a child. Freezing baths, drownings, the soap and the sponge lying beside him in the coffin etcetcetc.

I desire to be Sister Maria's friend and she is compassionate to me but she doesn't understand the New World. This is what I think but the drink has got into my head and the City has become unstable and everything is swirling away, disappearing down drains, parts of buildings breaking off and being blown away. The Paperwork also. Where is the Fifth File ~

I wake. Is it morning yet? Is there light at the window? Or is that eerie pallor caused by a further fall of snow? Before I fell asleep, I had pulled my coat over me. Now it has dropped to the floor and I am numb from the biting cold. I reach down to recover my coat and I wriggle it on. My socked feet carry me to the window.

The City is swaddled, spectral, rapturously quiet. All around me the air is bleached but this is not the white of the snow. Snowflakes like great white birds? Nonono. I am still dreaming. White birds, pieces of Paper, scattered Files. Why are they coming down towards our City, twisting and twirling through the stunned air?

Who can have been responsible for this? The sheets of Paper are printed with Information. Two or three have landed on the sill and, if I open the window, I could reach out and take them but I will not. I retreat to my bed and swathe my coat around me but I do not sleep. Where is my key? Who has opened my Notebook box?

When I wake later, I am sure that the sheets of Paper were a dream. When I look out of the window, white is layered on white. More snow has fallen. Was it just snow I saw? Nonono. The sheets of Paper actually exist. As we are hurrying to the Hospital – at least the heating is on there and we may get a hot cup of coffee – those Papers are scattered in the Streets.

My Fear then is great because the Nurses will pick up those Papers and ask Inappropriate Questions. We have been warned about Enemy Propaganda, about how attempts will be made to poison our minds. We scurry past, blind to all. But then the wind suddenly gusts and brings down many Papers from the trees and the rooftops.

Sister Maria picks one up. She should know not to do this. She is a Party member so why is she behaving Wrongly? We are close to the Hospital. Workmen hurriedly sweep the Papers away. Sister Clara is hissing at Sister Maria ~

I arrive at the Hospital with my breath rattling in my frozen lungs and my eyes stinging. What if Sister Maria has been seen? Also, Herr Spellbinder is asking people if they have seen the Information on those sheets. Both he and Sister Maria are putting us all in Danger. Sister Clara is now rebuking Sister Maria most vigorously.

We can hear their argument all along the Corridor. Yet Sister Maria will not apologise. She says it is *none of Sister Clara's business*. Sister Clara has no Authority over anyone hence she can *keep her mouth shut*. I start work immediately, trying not to listen, trying not to think. All morning I am shivering and I long to hide, to sleep ~

5.f. The Tragedy of Therese

Summer does soon roll in and two female patients called Margarete and Lotte are admitted to the Ward. Margarete is a tall and heavy girl with a bouncing walk and stringy plaits. Her bottom lip sags but her face is sunny and she glances around most cheerful, as though all the world is glittering and perfect. Lotte is similarly both pleasing and vacant.

Of course, Sluts come and go from the Ward every day, week, month. Usually, I take no notice. Yet these two girls are rather different for, although dumb as Door nails, they are tender and smiling. Occasionally they draw pictures for me or bring flowers from the garden. Often, they want me to play marbles with them.

Occasionally, I do play – but only in the evenings when my work is completed. Yet even when I am working, I do watch them, swirling and spinning in the Corridor with their skipping ropes and Paper hats and games of Pretending to be Film Stars. They are Feeble-minded, their faces flat and vacant. Yet I like to watch them Play.

In the evenings, Sister Maria takes me with her to the Votiv Kino to watch the newsreels. The Reich has conquered Denmark, Norway, Luxembourg, Belgium, the Netherlands. The Bully Boy British are driven back. Gott strafe England (May God Punish England). The cowardly French do not defend Paris.

We see our troops marching on the Champs-Élysées. The Church bells in Vienna ring for many hours and we know the War will soon be at an end. The British and the French are demoralised and powerless. The Reich holds the air bases and ports of Northern France from where they will begin the attack on the British ~

Then unpredictably. In the midst of this joy. No warning. I am told that the Motorised Mothering Advice Service is to be discontinued. Why? Surely the work being done was Useful? Will I now be sacked from my job? Sister Viktorine says that one has no need to worry. The Ward is understaffed. Plenty of cleaning is still required and also managing the Files.

Now I do not have an Office to myself and must participate in the bustle of the Ward. Sister Viktorine does kindly offer me Advice in how one might Approach this challenge. Adopt a stance of entirely Neutral Receptivity. *Feel all the emotions that a Mentally Afflicted Child might cause in you but then also detach from those emotions.*

I try to do what she says but still it is all too clamorous ~

During this fidgeting summer the laws change. Sister Clara gives me Leaflets and articles so that I might understand. Regrettably, some other people are not able to understand the details of this new legislation. This becomes evident in the circumstance of a young woman called Therese. Sister Maria remembers her from an earlier time when she had been in the Ward.

Usually, Sister Maria is most patient and compassionate with all the Children yet even she does say Therese was *most difficult and disruptive*. Even Sister Viktorine found her *patience sorely tested*. Sister Maria informs me that in that earlier time it had finally been agreed that Therese's problems were beyond the scope of the Ward.

That meaning the Ward does only deal with minor Cabbages of the type of Margarete and Lotte and also occasionally penguins etcetcetc. Yet despite this earlier decision, now Therese's father does return to see Dr A, coming without an appointment and waiting some long time before Dr A is finished for the day.

Dr A keeps him at the table in the Corridor. This is what the staff do when they do not want the parents to get their feet too far under the desk. Yet the father of Therese (smallneat with tweed suit, rawredface and clipped moustache) is not to be easily shifted. He shakes his head mournfully, holds his feathered green hat tightly in chafed purple hands.

Says most mournfully: Was it not clear to you? You saw when she was here. A Danger to herself and others. Since her illness, she has no rational mind. Yet she has the urges that others have. Do you not see where this will lead? (This Man does make me think of Oma in the way he makes his Point.)

Dr A is most patient, listening to this tirade for some time before saying: Yes, yes. I entirely see your difficulty. New laws, indeed. But they do not apply to your daughter.

The father saying: Why not? What is the Point of these laws if they cannot protect her and others around her? Is she a Person who should be bringing Children into our World?

Dr A explaining most carefully: Herr Ballhausen, these new laws are designed to prevent the spread of hereditary disease. Now therein lies a difficulty as we do not, in my opinion, have the knowledge necessary to know which diseases are, in fact, inherited. However, what I can certainly say is. Ahem. Ahem. Your daughter does not have a hereditary disease.

Here Dr A does stress his Point saying: You yourself told me, when you first came to see me, that her development was entirely normal until she contracted Encephalitis.

The disease he mentions here has been common in our City for many years and no one understands the cause. It is a disease which makes people sleep for many hours, days, weeks. After waking they are most often Dangerously Mentally Afflicted, finishing up at Steinhof.

Herr Ballhausen: What law can help me then? What can I do?

Indeed. Indeed. It is a most difficult situation ~

Of course, no one may speak of this matter in the hearing of Dr A. Yet later when the Nurses gather for their tea, and Fräulein Eder is also present, a dispute breaks out. Once again Sister Maria is at the core of this conflict. She insists that Dr A is quite right in this matter. However, Sister Clara and Fräulein Eder are not in accordance.

It all depends on how the Paperwork is filled out. Dr A could do more to assist. The legislation should have been phrased more widely in order that more people might be included. Is it acceptable for the Father of Therese to suffer in this way? Is it right for Therese herself? I wait for Sister Viktorine to reprimand everyone but she remains silent, only watches closely.

Personally, I consider Sister Clara's Point is Correct ~

In September Professor Hamburger and Dr A are having one of their Little Chats. Usually, these Chats take place in Professor Hamburger's Office with the Door closed but today they unfold in the Meeting Room because that gentleman has complained of an odorous smell. As a result, the whole Office is being meticulously cleaned.

Everyone says that the bad vapours must be the result of damp but why does one have a problem of damp in the summer and at the top of a building? Sister Clara suspects Herr Spellbinder. He is meant to deal with the maintenance. The lavatories are always blocked, the telephone lines down, the window near Fräulein Eder's desk broken once more.

I wash the same plate againagainagain. Professor Hamburger is talking of the new Opera that he saw last night at the Wiener Staatsoper. The Reich is succeeding in its mission to ensure that Vienna remains at the centre of culture. Professor Hamburger saying: You, of course, Hans. I know. Poetry is your interest. And mountains.

Dr A agrees: Ahem. Yes, mountains.

Professor Hamburger: Good, good. I was most gratified, you know, when I attended the Conference for Child Health. I think I told you. The new German Society for Child Psychiatry and Curative Education. I would have wanted you to speak but the programme was full. Nevertheless, our work was much praised and discussed.

Dr A: Yes, I had heard. Obviously, that is very much a result of your promotion of our skills. I can only thank you for that.

Professor Hamburger: Yes. Yes. And your recent speech. That was also well received. In particular, your willingness to admit that Curative Education can only ever be one aspect of our approach. That, as you know, improves your position greatly.

Dr A: Well, thank you. I'm glad the speech was well received.

Yes, of course. But we must continue to ensure that this Ward remains at the centre of the Curative Education approach within the Reich. That position is not assured. You will have heard perhaps that a new Clinic is being established? It is to be based at Steinhof.

Dr A says he is not aware. (Yet how did he not know?) Everyone has heard ~

Professor Hamburger elaborates: Yes. Yes. The announcement will be made in a few days. This new Clinic is also to be engaged in the work of Curative Education. Our friend Dr Jekelius is to be in charge. An excellent promotion and much deserved.

Dr A: But why a new Clinic? We have the capacity here.

Yes, yes, Hans. I know. But this Facility will be slightly different. The work we do here is excellent for the Child with relatively minor problems. We deal here with those who are Educable, obviously. The Reich is very keen to Categorise Children Correctly, to sort those who can be Educated from those who regrettably cannot.

Yes, of course. I have read this in many Reports.

Professor Hamburger: Those Children who cannot receive such help. The Severely Troubled, those for whom recovery is tragically unlikely. The institutions to which we refer such Children are often already full.

Dr A: Well, yes. I am simply puzzled by the use of the name Curative Education?

Hans, Hans. The name hardly matters, does it? The Clinic will be known as Am Spiegelgrund, located within the grounds of Steinhof. The Point is that we must not allow this Facility to overshadow our work. We must cooperate closely with Dr Jekelius. I recommended him precisely because he will forge ahead.

Dr A: Well, I most certainly hope that everyone is aware of the new Research that we are doing. Ahem. In particular, my Research on Autistic Psychopaths. Certain types of Child. Extreme difficulties and yet ~

Professor Hamburger is now searching for a Strategy to run Dr A into the buffers. Saying: Yes, you made that Point in your speech. What I am saying is we must maintain the lead. I should have put you forward for this new Position but the Powers That Be do not see you as I do. If you wish to rise to a higher level—

Dr A sounds most prickly: I hope that my Loyalty has not been placed in question. I have made clear. In my recent speech. Curative Education is only one approach. But this Research that I am doing. Ahem. If I could explain.

Hans. Please. Research is not enough. What is required is decision-making. We are under pressure from the very top, from the Office of the Führer himself. Take this recent case. The Child. What was his name – Viktor Stelzer. Repeated convulsions, muscle cramps, almost certainly blind. We simply waste resources. It is in his best interests that we should transfer him to Am Spiegelgrund. You see my Point?

Dr A: Yes, I do.

Well, I'm glad because the Fact is that, what with the Motorised Mothering Advice Service ending, you will have some time available to become involved in new initiatives.

Well. Yes. Maybe. Although in reality. We are quite short-staffed. With my appointments and management and the Research—

Professor Hamburger: I have just said. Research must be laid aside. Hans, please. I know your talents. You can rise to the highest level. I have recommended you to work with Dr Jekelius at the Vienna Public Health Office on the assessment of certain Children.

Thank you. I really feel—

Hans, Hans. For God's sake. Do I have to spell this out for you? Step back from this Research and look around you. Are you not aware that I find myself in a difficult position? You are not a member of the Party and that is your business ~

I nearly drop the plate which has been dried several times. So it is True. I knew this but I did not know. Why is Dr A not a member of the Party? This puts everyone in our Ward at risk. Professor Hamburger is explaining: A Doctor at your level of seniority is really expected to progress through the political hierarchy, not just the medical hierarchy.

Adding: I am putting my neck out for you here. It is not for me to place you under pressure to join the Party. But the Fact that you have not done so is remarked upon.

Dr A: People doubt me because I am a Catholic?

No. No. But questions are asked. You must be aware, surely, that you have been investigated? Now you will be investigated again.

Investigated?

I can hear the shock in Dr A's voice. I lay the plate down to make sure that I do not drop it. Of course, Sister Clara had reported this Information but I never thought. Is this why men from the SS do come to the Ward? I wait to hear Dr A's voice but it does not come.

Professor Hamburger: Yes, of course. That is why this new position is important. If you follow Dr Jekelius's lead, you will progress.

Take clear decisions about those Children who need to be transferred without delay to his care at Am Spiegelgrund. Then I shall be able to report to my superiors that they need have no concerns.

Dr A: Thank you. Thank you. I had not quite understood.

I'm glad we have discussed this frankly.

Dr A: This investigation is now closed?

No. That is the Point I am making. A Report was written on you and now another is being written. There will be no Problem, of course. I shall make sure of that. You will start your work at the Public Health Office at the beginning of next month?

Dr A's voice now sounds enthusiastic, squeakily cheerful.

Yes, of course. I am truly most excited about this new opportunity ~

5.g. A Friend Does Not Say Goodbye

How I wish now that I could writewritewrite. Not just copying out Reports but writing all my diverse Questions. I am back in my Youth and my thoughts are Too Big for my Brain. I long for someone who might keep me steady. For Fräulein Weiss who is far away in America and no one may communicate there. I think again of my Opa. Where is he? I need him now.

I can only hope that Dr A will be more careful in his approach and try to keep us all Safe. I think he has understood. This I conclude because, just one month after the events which I have just recreated, he is in the Meeting Room late at night and Dr Feldner stops by to bid goodnight. Dr A has been working on a speech which he must give at a Conference.

Dr Feldner now says: I read your speech, Hans.

Oh yes. Really. Well, thank you for that.

Very good. Except the beginning. All that National Socialism stuff – perhaps a bit too Nazistic for your reputation?

Dr A is most frosty: What do you mean?

Well, you know. The health of the Reich. Racial hygiene. All that stuff. The importance of improving the Blood Line. Never thought that was your thing. I mean, you've got to be careful. It's important to show enthusiasm but best not to lay it on with a shovel.

Dr A is Angry: I don't like the tone of this conversation. This is not a joking matter.

Oh, come on. How else will we get through? I did think the speech very good. It encapsulated much of what we have recently been realising.

Thank you.

Yes. They'll make a good Nazi of you yet, Hans. Me as well – quite possibly.

Dr A stares at his desk stonily. Dr Feldner has always been most provoking and he does not give sufficient consideration *to how what he is saying is being received*. Now he continues: Come on, old chap. No need to be so down. All this will pass. Fashions come and go. We'll hold things together. At least what we are doing is being recognised.

Let's hope so.

Dr Feldner: Of course. Anyway, we've got our friend Dr Jekelius. He's certainly keeping his end up. No worries for him about straying too far into National Socialism. Wagner with Hamburger last week. A night out at the Burgtheater tonight.

Dr Feldner has always talked in this disrespectful way and Dr A used to allow it. Now he is curt: Thank you, Josef. However, I must make clear. I am disappointed by your attitude. This new institution, these new policy directions. This is the way ahead. I need your support.

Of course, Hans. You know that I can be relied upon.

Dr A: Thank you. And, while we are talking of these matters, I would also ask you to keep a close eye on Herr Spellbinder. I strongly suspect that he is using the Radio in the Meeting Room for improper purposes ~

A month later Herr Spellbinder must go away for a few days as he requires a minor operation. No one is surprised because in addition to looking smeary and stained, he has also become thin. His flesh sags on his great frame and his face is craggy and ashen. Yet when he returns, he does not appear in any way improved.

Perhaps it will take time for him to recover? On the day when he returns, Sister Viktorine makes a hot drink for him, talks to him in a voice so low that I cannot hear. Later she is crying by the Filing Cabinet. When she sees me looking, she closes the Door on me.

Later Dr Feldner says to Herr Spellbinder: You have our full support. You know that?

Herr Spellbinder replying: I know you told them. Why didn't they listen?

Just spite dressed up as science.

Again, the Door shuts and the voices evaporate. Together Dr Feldner and Herr Spellbinder have gone into the Meeting Room and I become aware of Foreign voices on the Radio. I thought that Dr Feldner was meant to be preventing these Activities. Later he says: Bloody Radio. Problem with the knob ~

The next evening we go to the Votiv Kino and celebrate the planes of the Reich preparing to fly to London to carry out the bombing raids. Many men of our Country are risking their lives in the defence of the Reich. We are showing the Bully Boy British that they can't threaten us. They think to bring the Reich to its knees but they will not succeed.

The French are already thoroughly humbled. The U-boats of the Reich are ruling the seas. Our Führer announces an emergency programme for the building of air raid bunkers all across the cities of Germany. But in Vienna we have no need of any such protection as it is not possible to fly with heavy bombs so far across Europe.

The year turns yet again and unwelcome October visits again, the winter not cold but infinitely burdensome and dejected. I go back to the Café one weekend where the Phillumeny Club gather because Oma has gone out to the Catholic Lady's Guild (now National Socialist Lady's League). Lukas reporting that, outside the gates of Steinhof, crowds are gathering.

Herr Wächter then arrives with further news. *Not surprising there are protests. People want Answers. Where are their relatives? Where have they been taken, why were they not informed?* The SS broke up the protests. A Man was pulled into bushes and his head was smashed by a soldier's boot. Others were arrested later.

At the Hospital this disorderly behaviour is derided. Then Reports appear in the newspaper which correct these seditious Rumours. Sister Clara parades them to us. It is not the case that patients have gone missing from Steinhof. It says this in the *Völkischer Beobachter* newspaper hence it must be True ~

Yet Sister Maria persists. Does she not know that she puts us all in Danger? *If one of your relatives had gone missing then you would know, wouldn't you? I mean, how likely is it that these people are just inventing these stories? What do you think, Sister Clara?* Sister Maria is a Fool and I wish she would shut up.

Soon I am deeply sorry for my thoughts. For when I go back to the Nurses' Home that evening with Sister Clara, I open the Door of our room and find that everything has gone. Where is Sister Maria's hairbrush? Her lipstick? Where are her stockings which hang on the back of the chair? What has happened to her photographs which were taped on the wall ~

Come on. No need to go on like that. Sit down. It is all right. Sister Anna and Sister Elena tell me that Sister Maria had to go home urgently as her mother is ill and so she can't look after the Children. I do not understand. This is not Logical. We must look at the Evidence. Why have all her things been put away when she will be back soon?

I must not sleep or the dreams will commence. Yet even during the day, terrible images are plaguing my mind. I am running through my beloved City and am so full of joy yet soon I look up and see that all the road signs have been changed, all the names of shops. They read now Traitor, Liar, Moral Degenerate, Racially Unclean.

I must not allow these disreputable images. Yet why did Sister Maria not say goodbye? The other Nurses say – *A letter will come and then we will find out.* I try not to be unreasonably distressed, one must not make a fuss. I meditate on Opa and Fräulein Weiss. Neither has come back. Also, Dr Feldner is away now for a few days and no one clarifies where he is. I know without doubt that this departure of Sister Maria will bring Trouble for me ~

5.h. Dust on the Washing Line

Trouble wastes no time in descending upon me. Sister Viktorine says I must share a room with Sister Clara because Nurses from another part of the Hospital need the room Sister Maria and I formerly shared. Sister Clara is Angry because she has not been appointed to a new position. This is due to excessive time off work because of her stomach troubles.

One might deduce that the Gossip might stop now that Sister Maria (Radio Maria) is not with us but that is not the Case. All the blabberblabberblabber that once did issue from her mouth now spouts from the two other Russian Doll Nurses (Radios Anna and Elena). Everyone feels their nerves stretched on the rack but nobody speaks.

Sister Viktorine's eyes are often waterlogged, her voice gravelly, and she shouts at us for the least Mistake. There is much Filing Cabinet talk which I do not hear. Sister Clara is promoted. Usually there is no Person who is second in command but now Sister Clara is raised to Assistant Head of Nursing. Every day I wait for a letter ~

One month passes and then two. I am writing in my Notebook. Copying out Reports and Leaflets, drawing Maps to show the progress of the armies of the Reich. It is hard to keep control of my pen, to stop it writing otherotherother things. I am a Loyal Person and will not write anything which could place myself and others in Danger.

Yet too often my mind is ambushed by these poisonous Waking Dreams. One day I hear quite clear an announcement on the Radio which tells of a Regulation for the Suppression of Wordless Children.

On another occasion, I enter my room at the Nurses' Home and find Herr Hitler himself rifling through my Notebooks. (Of course, not true.)

We slouch towards Christmas but it brings little joy. Sister Elena organises a celebration in the Nurses' Home. Sister Clara has departed for the evening with Fräulein Eder. Sister Elena says – *Good riddance.* Cherry brandy is passed around. Sister Elena tells a Story. She heard it from her mother who has a cousin who lives near the Hartheim Castle.

That cousin came to visit. Something clandestine is unfolding at the Castle. The buses which leave Steinhof with the windows blacked out? That's where they are going. Smoke pours out of the chimneys. The cousin, Fräulein Reiter, was hanging out her washing and it was a windy day. The washing didn't seem to have become clean.

What had caused such stains? Was it smoke or perhaps ash? Fräulein Reiter tugs the washing off the line, strides back into the house. She spreads the sheets out on the table and examines them carefully. They are speckled brown but what are those tiny threads? Fräulein Reiter picks two or three off the fabric.

She goes back to the Door, stares out towards the castle.

The specks are tiny particles of human hair ~

These Stories. Fantastical and Not True. I am less and less able to sleep. I hear again the voices of my Childhood. *Idiot, Simpleton, deaf-mute.* The ceiling above me rustles and whispers. *Why is she working in this Hospital? Not a Person who is Educable. She should not be writing in Notebooks.* (But where then may I put all the thoughts too Big for my Brain?)

Yet still these voices tell me that what I am writing is Seditious and that I am not loyal to the Reich. Also, an idea forms in my head that a machine of many wires has been connected to my brain. This machine exists to enable others to listen to my thoughts. It also suggests vicious and untrue ideas to me.

Can you think of a word which links to the Reich? The machine is saying – the devil, the devil. Wrongwrongwrong. I hold onto my key tightly. Soon Sister Clara says that she cannot sleep as I am moving around in the night. What am I doing? Why am I always writing and drawing Maps? Why can I not sleep like Normal People?

Soon Sister Viktorine suggests that I should sleep in the Bunk Room. This is the room in the Ward where the Nurses who are doing the night shift sleep. The room is small and cramped, not like the rooms in the Nurses' Home. I am happy enough to relocate but what no one is saying is that I will effectively be doing the night shift every night now.

When I move my case, my bag, my locked box from the Nurses' Home, Sister Viktorine opens the lofty cupboard in the Bunk Room. I can put my possessions here. The cupboard is already full and Sister Viktorine has to lift up a box and put my Albums underneath. *Are you listening? Be sure not to touch anything else in this cupboard ~*

In the Dining Room a small boy is whispering about his younger sister. She finished up in the Murder Box. *You know about the Murder Box? They said she died of pneumonia but my father said she never did. The Murder Box is where they put all the bodies. It is like a cart which goes through the Streets. It is where they put all the Children who behave badly.*

Sister Viktorine is extremely Angry. *This is not True. Hurry up and eat your lunch.*

Later Sister Elena says it is True. She is a Fool. I wish she would not say such words. Once they are said, then they do not disappear. Instead, they hide behind the curtains and seep under Doors, or slip through windows. I hear them all the time, whether I am awake or asleep. Sister Viktorine lines us up in the Corridor and speaks in a fierce voice. *No one is to repeat any Gossip or Rumour ~*

In the Bunk Room I can hear every noise. A different Nurse is with me each night, as the rota dictates. The only Person who, like me, is in the Hospital every night is Herr Spellbinder. Late at night he is often in the Meeting Room. He puts some coal in the stove and tells me that I can listen to the Radio with him but I will not.

Also, Dr A is in his Office doing that Research which he has been told is not now needed, yet still he continues, working even into the lean hours. One evening in January, I am helping Sister Viktorine to take an inventory of the Medicine Store when we hear Herr Spellbinder calling. *A lady is here. She says that her name is Anni Wodl.*

A woman appears, her eyes are like running sores, her hair matted and jagged as leaping flames. For a moment, Sister Viktorine looks as though she might run. Then she steps forward and smiles most professionally. The woman is chatteringchatteringchattering. *Berlin, Albert. My son, Albert. Dr Jekelius.*

Sister Viktorine instructs me that I must go into the Bunk Room and stay there. I go gladly enough. Sit on the bed, then move to the Door to listen. The machine in my brain would like me to listen but I knowknowknow that I must not know anything about this woman ~

A week later, the Terror which follows me steps out of the shadows and into my waking Life. My key is safely in my pocket. But thenthenthen. Where is my Notebook? I remember. I left it on the Meeting Room table. I must never leave it where anyone may see. I rush to the Meeting Room but my book is not there. I am certain I left it on the table.

Things shift around. The Papers are not in Order. Wherewherewhere? In the Corridor, Sister Clara is waiting for me. Also, Fräulein Eder who is situated at her desk. A lighted cigarette is in her hand. Only the lamp on Fräulein Eder's desk is on. That lamp throws a circular shadow, lights up the side of Sister Clara's face, Fräulein Eder's smoking hand.

Sister Clara holds up my Notebook. How could I have been so stupid? Sister Clara is flicking through the pages. She should not. My book is private. Sister Viktorine is nowhere to be seen. Everyone else has gone home. The World is tipsy and slippery. I am alarmed and yet also strangely not alarmed. I can read *the signals which are being given*.

Sister Clara and Fräulein Eder would like to accuse me of writing Seditious Words. They want to convince me that they can read inside my head. But they cannot and I have not done any incorrect thing. It is not possible that I have drawn the Wrong Conclusion as I have taken care to draw no Conclusion at all. Soon I see that Sister Clara does know these facts.

She swings the Notebook in her gentle fingers, shakes her head. Looks over at Fräulein Eder. Both of them shrug. Sister Clara saying: You need not worry, Adelheid. Fräulein Eder and myself. We know. You are a Loyal Person. Sadly, not everyone in this Ward is.

You may have been a friend of Sister Maria but you are not like her. That is True, is it not?

Fräulein Eder then says: No need to look so worried. You know that Clara and I care for you, don't you? You know we are your friends. You will be protected. We will make sure of it. But it would be better not to write things down. Things can be Misunderstood.

Sister Clara then steps forward and hands the Notebook to me. I take it and I turn away. In the Bunk Room, I sit on my bed, hugging my Notebook against me. Opa, Opa, where are you? Sister Maria, Adolf. Fräulein Weiss. I need you. Please, please. How may I reach you in that faraway America ~

After My Death: Avoiding Blitzmas in Baltimore

Of course, in my actual life I knew nothing of Fräulein Weiss and her life in America. Yet I tell you now some details of how she has now given up her job in Chicago and come back to live in Baltimore. *Homely and comfortable* – except it still isn't. She has just attended once again the Christmas party for the Harriet Lane Children's Home where Georg is still employed.

This time she said nothing, *behaved Appropriately*. Yet now they are back from the Party, she cannot stop herself from complaining to Georg about his boss, Kanner. Georg will not allow these criticisms: Leave it, Anni. Don't you see? Increasingly, Kanner understands. He always has. Ever since Donald. The Point is that he promotes our work.

Fräulein Weiss: While making his name.

Georg: Yes, probably. His main interest does seem to be in finding the right name to describe some Children who can't really be grouped together in the way he wants.

Yes, exactly. He's looking for a great new idea which he can discover and develop. All the work you have done. Don't you see how it will be? Kanner's Syndrome. Written in neon lights. He will use the Donalds of this world for his own purposes. You know that?

Georg sighs: Look. I don't care what name is given to anything. I just want to understand these Children better so we can help. I'm not interested in some artificially constructed pattern. However, Kanner is – and it's my job to help him.

Fräulein Weiss: You need to get your Paper published. The Affective Contact Paper. We need to finish the translation and send it out.

That's what I am doing. Kanner is supporting me. He will send it out.

Whose name will be on the cover?

Anni, can we just not talk about this ~

They sit in silence. What is there to say? Fräulein Weiss came back to Baltimore four months ago just as the War in Europe was beginning. She insists that War was not the reason for her decision but perhaps it was? What has she been doing since returning? Nothing. She no longer even thinks of the PhD she once planned. What is the Point?

It is the language she finds difficult, the breaking of the relationship between words and things. This desiccating alchemy drains the World of its colour. All living connection has gone. None of the people here say what they really think. This country, these people are drowning in things. One is crushed by the sheer meaningless *thingness* of all these objects.

Two months ago she got her Papers so she can stay in America. She thought that would make it easier to find a position but nothing has happened. Even Kanner has tried to help but so many from Europe are looking for work. The only thing that has kept her sane has been going to lectures at the University.

In particular, she attends the lectures given by Dr Meyer. The aged Swiss doctor has lived in this Country for many years and understands how it works. He invites Georg and her around for drinks, offers Anni tea after his lectures. She understands Meyer. He also writes references for her, helps with applications ~

Now she finally has a job – at the Wrong time and in the Wrong place. For Georg and her, the situation has become like some humorous farce with people popping in and out of various Doors, a series of ridiculous coincidences. Or a mystery tour of this vast Country? She had waited and waited for the right job to come up.

Then she had accepted a job in Washington. A job which is not at her level but geographically close. She can take the train. It will only take half an hour. But only two days after she sent her acceptance letter, Georg was offered a job in Nebraska and they both know that he must take it.

His salary at the Harriet Lane Children's Home is half what he was being paid in Austria. He's been trying to get a new job for three years now. Everyone says that it should be easy, given his experience, his qualifications. The Truth is Doctors from all across Germany and Austria are begging for work.

It seemed as though he would be offered something in San Francisco and then in Chicago but neither of those positions materialised. So one must be thankful for Nebraska. Of course, his career must always be the priority. He can earn more than three times what she is offered. It had taken a long time even to find Nebraska on the map.

She imagines it now as a place of polar Bears, Arctic explorers, lone huts lit by quivering lamps. If she is in Washington and he is in Nebraska, it will take days by train. It is further than Paris to Vienna. She is tired now, kisses him and goes up to bed ~

From downstairs she hears the Radio. Georg often listens at night. She used to listen as well but not now. She avoids newspapers which might have pictures. Instead, she waits for letters and enjoys their bracing tone. Her sister sends cheery news from London about Blitzmas. *No longer studying but joined a team of Jewish volunteers running a soup kitchen.*

The Italians in the next-door flat are reporting that, in Italy, pasta is being rationed. Mussolini's regime will soon collapse. It is harder for Georg, much harder. Anni wishes that he wouldn't listen to the Radio. It worries her that he's moving from station to station, fiddling with the knob, tuning in to one programme after another.

What he wants is news from Vienna but nothing comes. He also waits for *The Jewish Advocate*. When it arrives, he might like to hurry to the Door and tear open the packaging but instead he lays it aside on the hall table as though it doesn't matter. Then he opens it secretively after she has gone to bed. She has warned him. That Newspaper isn't accurate.

However, the Warsaw Ghetto is not a scare Story. Everyone has heard that on American Radio. Parts of the City must be shut off due to a typhus epidemic. One third of the City sealed up and unable to get out. Is the same happening in Vienna? Georg still writes to the lawyers in Vienna but the letters are returned ~

Now he comes up to bed and curls up close to Anni, wrapping an arm around her saying: Anni, Anni. There's no need to worry. America will come into the War soon. Didn't you hear that at the party? Everyone was saying it. Roosevelt will change his mind. I just heard that on the Radio as well.

She pushes herself closer to him as he says: You know I'll come and see you. I can travel from Nebraska. It isn't so far.

She lies awake, listening to his breathing. She thinks now of Meyer. Thank God for Meyer. She has spoken to him about Georg. He shrugs and agrees: Yes, Georg is genuinely original and brilliant. Also under-appreciated but the cream rises to the top over time.

Fräulein Weiss says: Does it? Does it?

Meyer laughs merrily: Probably not. No.

Then he raises his palms in that gesture which is so typically European. Sister Viktorine always used to do the same. Fräulein Weiss has to choke back tears. She yearns for the Curative Education Ward. She longs for Sister Viktorine. Sometimes for Hans. How odd to feel a sudden aching for a Man that you never liked ~

6.a. What I Did Not See

Adelheid. You are needed for a special job. You must accompany Margarete as she is attending an Assessment. Her father cannot take her. Surely this is not Correct. I have been told – *You must never leave the Hospital.* Yet now I am being ordered – *You must meet them at the tram stop on Alser Straße at two o'clock.*

Yes. An Assessment at Am Spiegelgrund. Sister Clara gives me some money for the tram for both Margarete and myself. *You better take your Notebooks with you. You might need them. Hurry up.* I am not to leave Margarete at the Door. I must wait until all the Paperwork has been completed. These instructions must be followed exactly.

Events are piling up on top of each other, too many circumstances all at once. I never predicted that I might hunger to retreat home to Oma but now I do. Margarete is a child who is most restless, always skipping, fiddling, touching. You cannot tell her anything. She must hold my hand. I do not want to touch her but I must. I am at least glad of the tram journey ~

At the Bellaria tram stop Margarete is there with a maid servant who immediately walks away, saying nothing. Margarete is pleased to see me and waves a straggly plait at me. I hold tight to her hand. As we wait, she chatters in a most loud voice. She is excited but she *will not be at this new Hospital long*. Her father has told her that she can come home soon.

We board the tram together (number 46) and Margarete is quite calm. She must be tired because usually she would not sit still. Now she sucks her fingers and lolls her head. Change to tram 47 and then travel some distance as Steinhof is at the outskirts of the City. I have visited this place before and I am joyful to return as it is more like a Palace than a Hospital.

Many separate buildings are set on a green bank, each one with wide terraces and high windows, all looking out across verdant fields. A most elegant and calming place. How I love open skies and birds merrily conversing. We find our route most easily and walk up through pine trees to the building which is now the new Facility.

This place is like our own Hospital but far more delightful because of all the trees and shrubs gathered about and also, at the top of the hill, a bleached white church with a twinkling golden dome. Arriving now at an imposing front entrance, a broad terrace – but we discover the entrance is actually at the rear. A Door with a number and a small porch overhead.

A pleasant breeze blows, the air rich with the dusty smells of high summer. The Door is open and so we step inside. What a gracious and noble place – no wonder Sister Clara wants to work here. The Reception Area is stately and spacious. A Nurse opens a Door into a Ward and inside are iron beds. Much like our Ward but spotless and Properly Organised ~

I lay out the Papers on the Reception Desk. In order to perform this, I must open my bag and take out my Notebook. When the Nurse comes, she spies my Notebook and smiles cheerily saying: Ah yes, Sister Clara told me. The Writing Girl.

We are to sit on a bench and wait. I should like to leave because Margarete has rediscovered her energy and will not sit still. Although I try to hold her hand, she rises and wanders back and forwards through the Reception Area, bouncing up and down, singing a tune and waving her head from side to side. Now she is heading for the Reception Desk.

I have left my Bag on the bench and I must retrieve it. Despite the glory of the day and the architecture of this fine place, I wish I could slide away unnoticed. This is not a suitable job for me. People here might ask me Questions. As I turn back from picking up my bag, I see that Margarete is shuffling through the Papers on the desk.

She is pointing at something. I stand beside her and look. This is the File which I myself put on the desk when we arrived. Here is the heading showing the Paperwork of the Curative Education Ward. I see Margarete's name. She is showing me her name ~

Nonono. She is showing me. Adelheid Brunner. It is I. Me. Adelheid. My name. Written down. If it is in the Paperwork, then it is Correct. It must be Correct. The handwriting belongs to Fräulein Eder. *They have come for me.* Am I a Nurse or a Simpleton? This was intended all the time. *Ah yes, the Writing Girl. So many Notebooks.*

Sister Viktorine or Dr A must have agreed because of the unacceptable way I have behaved. I put Files in the wrong place. How can I explain? I must make a Report explaining the Facts of this Case. Yet what would I write? I am a Cabbage Child, unreliable and not to be trusted. Margarete has disappeared out of the Door.

I speed after her and find her heading along the side of the building. I must persuade her to desist. She is staring at something on the ground. The place where the rubbish is collected for the furnace. Here there are bags on the ground and several large carts which contain sheets for the laundry. I see now what has caught her magpie-like attention.

A Matchbox on the ground which she wishes to give to me. If I pick it up, smile, then I might be able to get her back inside. I move closer to the sacks, look up at the laundry carts. See. See. A Thing sticking out. Nonono. I am mistaken. Not a child's arm. Margarete is pushing the Matchbox at me. Small, grey, bent at the elbow, trapped under the lid of the cart ~

How can I write this? I do not clearly remember. I cannot say. Only frozen images remain, like blurred photographs. I am back in the Childhood where I must give myself instructions and consider my every action with care. I snatch the Matchbox from Margarete, pull her inside.

Keep my mind locked down. Many things have been Misunderstood. I am a Cabbage Child, I draw the Wrong Conclusions. Name on the Paperwork. And now. People die in Hospital and their bodies must be stored somewhere. Of course. The Murder Box? No such Box exists. Opa, Opa, will you not help me?

I sit down on the bench. Too weak now. Improvise, Improvise. What does that mean? Margarete is spinning round and round, giggling and shrieking. Everything else is also swirling and turning. They will push me down and steal my Notebooks. I am clinging to my bag. Opa. Fräulein Weiss. Adolf. Sister Viktorine. Dr Feldner. Please.

Margarete is still frolicking on the stairs, pretending to be a Film Star, swinging from the stair rail and singing and now the letters of my name are huge, filling half of the Reception Area and I call out inside my head and I am pleadingpleadingpleading. What would the Bear-baby-fairy do in this situation? Wilhelm-Freezing Bath-sponge. In the coffin.

This is not a Children's Game.

Margarete produces marbles ~

I open my eyes and he is there. Opa. Sitting on the bench. Not Opa in his Actual Life but yet also not Definitely Dead. Here. My mind is full of confused images. The Karl-Marx-Hof, the guns. The hours spent standing in the shed on the allotment. *Stay here, do not move. I will come back. Do not say anything to anyone. Say nothing. Nothing.*

Opa, tellmetellmetellme. What should I do? He looks me in the eye, his shaggy white head shaking wildly, his head goes back. He is assessing the Evidence, finding the Truth. Coming to save me. To take me away from here. *You know that they are lying. They are all lying. You know, don't you* ~

I stride up to the desk. Everything now is Clear and Simple. Everything Large and Grand and Swollen with Truth. I take up the pen on the desk and cross out my name, the ink dribbles, my hand shakes, so that the erasure is most untidy with not just one line through but scribbling, digging into the Paper and my name has gone.

You can do that. You can just cross something off a sheet of Paper and then it is gone. It is only Paper, it is not necessarily Correct, yet what am I to do with Margarete? She is still pirouetting and gyrating, her head nodding, her tongue lolling, and I must get away and I cannot delay. I cannot take her with me but she will follow. How can I prevent that?

Her bag is on the bench and beside it the tin with the marbles. I hold them out to her and she stops swivelling and giggles, her eyes full of pleasure. What she likes more than anything is to play marbles and I know how this works and I know that I will go to Hell for this and be Damned Forever. Under a nearby Door is a gap just large enough. I aim with care.

It must go through that gap and it must fit. It must. I watch it spin away and it is gone and luck is now on my side. Margarete skips towards the Door, grabs the handle, disappears into the room beyond. She has an extremely short memory, she probably will not even notice that I have gone. I give ear to a voice above on the stairs.

I cannot go out of the front Door because that Person will glimpse me. Another Door is behind the desk and I step towards it still gripping my bag and push it open and it leads into a small Corridor, a back kitchen with sinksbucketbrushes, move on past that, push open another Door where steps are leading down and, Adolf, I know this will be the right way.

Doorsdoorsdoors and washrooms why am I always running? Another way out, this is how they transport the coal into the building and I plunge down the steps. I am in a room where there is no light only a grey gleam which comes from a Door and I hurry on through the long room and I should not look and I must not look.

I am a Person who imagines things which are not there. Plant pots do not speak neither do teaspoons or cups butbutbut all around me are bottles and what is in those bottles, take a deep breath and stagger and stumble, my hands fumbling forward. I must get to that Door and now my fingers reach and the Door is locked but the key now scrabblestruggleforce.

Grass trees sky all of it tilting and tipping, but there here definitely I could touch each one and name it, hurry down the tumblingstumblingdropping bank, for a moment stare back, another sapling arm the same arm waving arm on a balcony. A Heinrich-Wilhelm-Dietrich-Otto the head barely at the level of the balcony rail waving arm grey and bent ~

6.b. Mistakes Can Have Consequences

I am a person often confused by Waking Dreams. Nothing happened. I really can't remember. I did not see anything. I was instructed to perform a task and I did my duty. Back now in the Curative Education Ward, I turn my eyes away from Sister Clara or Fräulein Eder. I *do not concern myself with Adult Affairs*. I draw no Conclusion.

Yet I am aware. I cannot fail to see. It is Clear. Sister Viktorine is most Angry. Sister Clara should have been aware. Adelheid is not to go out of the Hospital. That is the Rule, that is Quite Clear. How could she have made such a Stupid Mistake? How can she act as Sister Viktorine's Deputy when she makes such Errors?

I feel the eyes of Sister Clara and Fräulein Eder on me.

Is it only hate that they feel? Perhaps also Fear?

I am not as easy to erase as they hoped ~

The days peel away, one layer from another. The fabric of our building has become Breathless, Flaking and Dry. You look down at the floorboards and see the many Wards of the Hospital that are down below. Everything like a Skeleton. Veins, bones, muscles. The flesh all scraped away like an anatomical drawing.

Yet how strange that everything also continues just the same. The weather continues to be mellow and breezy. The Ward is less busy. Once again, Sister Viktorine must go away for a day to help to look after her Aunt who lives in the Countryside. Fräulein Eder is also absent with a stomach complaint and therefore Sister Elena is working on the Reception Desk.

I am asked to order the Files as Sister Elena hates that. Everything must be finished off today because Dr A will also depart this evening. He is speaking at a Conference and won't be back until next week. Just after I have laid out a biscuit and milk at eleven o'clock, I hear a voice. A voice with a bird song twitter, golden and fluttering.

Frau Schreiber enters the Ward, pushing a familiar weighty pram. Her blonde hair is smoothed down and her mouth painted luscious red. She wears a green silk dress with a pattern of flying birds. When she sees me, she smiles: Adelheid. There you are, sweetheart. How lovely to see you. So long, so long. What a good girl you were. Helping me out.

Despite her elegant dress, Frau Schreiber is not the same. No one is the same now. She is brittle, desiccated, her smile suggesting mild hysteria. She must have given birth to yet another baby and she is probably finding the work burdensome. Although she must have a proper maid servant now since she has risen in society. I position myself in order that I can see the new baby ~

No new baby. The child lying in the pram is Herta but not the same Herta. She must be three years old and her body is too long for the pram. Her legs are pushed up to one side so that she can fit. Her sleeping face is cramped against the side. Frau Schreiber starts to cry: Ah yes. Poor dear Herta. Perhaps no one told you?

Frau Schreiber pushes a sweaty curl away from Herta's closed eyes: So ill. So very ill. That's why I have come today. The staff here have always been good to me.

She raises her eyes to the ceiling, shakes her head. What has happened to the real Herta? Where is the little girl who sat on my knee in those long winter evenings? Was that almost two years ago? Why would a child of that age sleep in the morning? Here, now. A monster child, a changeling. I go to fetch a glass of water for Frau Schreiber.

She says: Thank you, Adelheid. Thank you.

Then she informs me about Adolf: Going away again at the end of the week. They all are now. It is all being kept very quiet. We will know more soon. One must be careful.

Now Dr A has advanced out of his Office and Frau Schreiber also informs him about Adolf and his success, saying: That's something that this Hospital achieved. I don't say much about that now, of course. You have to be careful – but I was so grateful.

Dr A says: Adolf is indeed a credit to us.

Dr A takes Frau Schreiber into his Office but, due to the heat, he leaves the Door open. I go to fetch polish and a duster.

Yes. Yes. So I see. Difficult, very difficult.

She was doing fine. She was perfectly healthy before. With Adolf it was different.

Ah, yes. Completely different ~

Encephalitis. The word is not said loudly but it drops with a muted crash and its echoes spread all around. This is surely not what has happened to Herta? In this Ward, that word is feared beyond all other phrases for we always know it can never be good. I think of Therese.

Frau Schreiber says: Dr A, I came to you because I didn't know who else I might ask. She is most often in pain. She's sleeping now but when she wakes.

Dr A: Yes. I do understand. Ahem. Most difficult. The War places great pressures on many people and for Mothers the conditions are often particularly challenging.

Frau Schreiber: Dr A. Please. I will be frank with you. I have nine Children. Nine. Even before the War it was not easy. But now, really. What with Adolf going away. I know I am lucky. I have a good place to live. I have received assistance. But still.

Frau Schreiber is starting to weep: This isn't an easy decision but I've got to think of her. What kind of Life can she have? I need to consider the others. I hope you understand.

I do, Frau Schreiber. I do. I could admit her for Assessment? We don't like to give up on any Child. It may be that the case is not quite so severe as the Notes suggest.

Then you would return her to me?

That would depend.

That's what I'm saying. I can't, I just can't. Do you not understand?

Dr A is most calm and clear: Frau Schreiber. I am sorry. The best I can do is to make an Assessment and we will then consider the possibilities.

Sister Elena is summoned and she lifts Herta from Frau Schreiber's arms, gathering the blanket around her tightly. Frau Schreiber gives a small but strangled cry, kisses Herta's sleeping cheek. Says: I only want the poor little soul to have some Peace.

She leans towards Herta, strokes her sleeping face ~

Frau Schreiber exits and the afternoon gallops past. One need not fear. Dr A will know What To Do. Herta is not so sick as they are saying. He might need to find a place for her in the Country but some of those places are good. Sister Viktorine has told me so. I expect that Therese has gone to such a place. This is the best in such situations.

Sister Sophia has settled Herta down in a cot in the corner of the Ward where the shutters are closed. It is cool there and she will sleep soundly. As evening comes, we hear a rustling in the Corridor, a suppressed gasp. Everything is still and sweating and pulled tight as a violin string. News has come that the Reich has invaded the Soviet Union.

That was what Frau Schreiber meant. *We will know more soon.* Adolf is going to the East. As the Nurses leave for the evening, many are hurrying to the cinemas. *Having crushed our enemies to the West, we will subdue the violent masses to the East. War is being fought now on every front, yet we have full confidence in our Führer.*

After this announcement I am fully occupied for several hours – bathing, changing, organising medication, helping with the supper, clearing up after a Child who is vomiting repeatedly, then putting some Files away. It is not until ten o'clock, when the Ward is dark, lit only by the low lamps from the Corridor, that I look into Herta's cot ~

She is not there. Not there at all. Evil witches, changeling babies. One must not believe Fantastical Stories. I stare at the space where she should be. Nonono. Sister Viktorine? I must find her. Yet immediately I remember that she is not here. I see Sister Elena further down the Ward, assisting a child who has dropped a crutch.

Does she know that Herta is gone? I speed then into the Meeting Room and I locate the Files. My hands stumble through piles and piles of Paper. The File has gone. *The Fifth File.* Has Professor Hamburger taken it? I turn to Dr A's Office and find that he has left for the evening. I remember then the Conference.

Fräulein Eder's desk. I must not be seen looking through her Files but I have to know. What has happened? Where is Herta? The Instructions that Dr A gave have surely not been followed. It was said Herta must be kept here for Assessment. A Mistake has been made. I find the File – *Transfer to Am Spiegelgrund*.

Now I understand. This is the newest Facility and the treatment she receives will surely be Excellent. But the point is that the instructions of Dr A have not been followed. These words are surely not inscribed in his handwriting? Professor Hamburger must have written this. Sister Clara? Fräulein Eder? Did Dr A change his mind? I have never known it to happen ~

6.c. The Wrong Conclusion

The Correct Procedure has not been followed. This is not what was agreed. Sister Clara is still present because she is responsible for the night shift. I always dread the nights when she is on duty. Now I feel my nerve failing. As I clear up toys in the Nursery, the eyes of the dancing peasants on the frieze are following me and they gossip and whisper.

I hear chatter and laughter rattling through the rooms of the doll's house. *Oh the writing girl. Yes, the writing girl. Just sign your name here. No need to look in the laundry cart.* The rocking horse tosses his mane and stamps restlessly. I am tired, so tired. Those voices. The Meeting Room. Dr Feldner and Herr Spellbinder are listening to the Radio.

Raging voices which I have heard before. *Hitler has let everyone down. Hitler is too weak, he has not gone far enough. He is tolerating Jews and gypsies and other foreigners.* This voice also rants about Churchill. *That flat-footed bastard of a drunken old cigar-smoking Jew.* Who is the Man and why is he criticising the Führer?

Plus, speaking about hose pipes and feather dusters. Strangely I am reminded of the Rat Business and the Cellars of the Cities. The things I saw there. All gone now, the sewers and Cellars rinsed clean. Why are Herr Spellbinder and Dr Feldner listening? I must not directly consider this question. The wires in my head are reporting on my thoughts.

Yet I know – Herr Spellbinder and Dr Feldner are not properly Loyal. So why do they listen to a Man who states that our Führer is not sufficiently Disciplined? I need Matchboxes. I hurry to the cupboard in the Bunk Room. The Albums under another box.

A corner of fabric hanging down. I lift the lid, see the dress that Sister Maria lent – that flower pattern in red and blue. The electric touch of the flowing silk.

Are you listening? Be sure not to touch anything else in this cupboard.

Sister Maria particularly enjoyed this dress so why has she not reclaimed it? Nearly eight months now. I lift the dress out of the box. Underneath, a pair of shoes. It is not right to look at other people's things. Yet still I push the shoes aside. Papers, purse ~

I flounder into the Corridor, moving like a Person who has been smashed on the head. Herr Spellbinder is there in the half-light, observing me. He knows about the Papers, the purse. I am sure of it. He knows about Herta too. This I can be sure of because he is holding those same Papers which were written, and then changed, only a few hours ago.

I need Adolf. I need him now. He is a Person I can trust. He will clarify all this mystification, make sure that the proper Procedures are followed. I remember him on Sundays with the coloured spinning top which spun and glittered with so many kaleidoscope colours. I need Adolf and I know exactly how he can be found.

Herr Spellbinder is still watchingwatchingwatching, his ebony eyes smouldering, his ravaged face rigid and stripped naked. It is as though we have thrown a bouncing ball and we expect it to return. We listen for it againagainagain but the silence is absolute. I pull Adolf's crumpled letter from my pocket. It has the address of the Rennweg Barracks.

Herr Spellbinder apprehends what we must do but now Sister Clara is summoning me. A scream breaks from the Dormitory. I must follow Instructions. Sister Clara is enjoining me to present myself in the Dormitory without delay. She herself heads into the Medicine Store, shutting the Door behind her. Herr Spellbinder moves then with the speed of a leopard.

Strides to the Door of the Medicine Store, whips a small screwdriver from his coat pocket. The Door handle clatters to the floor. He moves towards the phone on Fräulein Eder's desk. My mind is suddenly clearcalmcertain. I hold out the Matchbox which has been in my pocket all these months. The Matchbox from the Café near the barracks.

You can trust Matchboxes. They are always Correct. Herr Spellbinder understands.

Together we are like clockwork toys. He dials the number, asks to be connected to the barracks. *The mother of Herr Adolf Schreiber has an important package to deliver. She will be in the Café until eleven o'clock.* I take the Papers, the Matchbox, pull open the Door of the Ward. *Wait here. Do not move.* But now I am running ~

I know exactly how one arrives at the barracks. It is that same 71 Tram (I do not forget that it signifies Death). Yet when I reach the Schwarzenbergplatz I must alight due to some event taking place involving many police and troops yet mercifully no one checking papers. Still I resolve that I will walk from there. It is not so far.

Darkness is now descending. The night is mellow but, once I am past that clamorous event, the Streets are strangely empty. A light wind worries through the laden summer trees. I walk to the side of the street, with my head down, merging into the shadows. The route I must take is circuitous since I do not want to encounter any official Person.

Near here is the Aspangbahnhof and I see the outline of trains, people standing in lines. This will be the Jews who they are sending away. Although only those who have not departed already, those who did not organise their Papers and leave. The lights are not put on at that station. I look at my oncebrandnew shoes ~

I identify where the Café is situated but I hesitate to enter. I wait across the street where I will see if he appears. What if the message is not passed on? I reach the great wall of the barracks. It occupies a whole block – a cliff-like wall nearly a mile in length. Along the road, flashlight beams and army vehicles, gates where one might enter but sentries posted at every point.

I cross the road to the Café and try to peer in. The windows are too high. The Door is not on the street but in a vast archway leading to a Courtyard. The Door is half glass. Soldiers are crowded at the bar. A gramophone plays. Adolf is not in evidence. I head back across the road, crossing the Tram Tracks and sit down to wait. In my pocket, the Paper crinkles ~

The Door of the Café is thrown wide open and three soldiers tumble out, fooling and prodding. Adolf is not among them. I hear laughter and see the lighted tips of cigarettes dip and swoop through the air. A group of girls are heading towards a distant gate, moving close together. Do they work in the barracks? Could I have clandestinely walked in with them?

But then if Adolf comes here, I will miss him. I cross the road to the Café again, glance up and down the street. No one is coming. I can wedge my foot in a panel in the stonework. I hoist myself up and stare inside. The room is dark wood and smeared mirrors, all is smoky, bodies pushed together, heads tossed back. The stones are pulsing with music.

I am grabbed from behind. Hands dig into my hair, into the collar of my dress. My beret is pulled from my head. I fall backwards but the hands keep hold of me. *Caught you, thief. What is she doing here? Who is she?* The Door of the Café crashes open. Soldiers are hurrying out. I am pulled into the archway, towards the Door of the Café.

Tell us who you are. You'll be arrested as a spy.

The light flashes into my face again, blinding me. What can I do? *Do not ever show anyone those Papers.* I raise my hands to shield my face from the exploding lights. Beneath me the cobbles are entrapping my feet. A figure pushes through the crowd. A familiar voice – *Here. Leave her alone.*

Adolf's hand stretches out and I sense his familiar fingers lock on mine. *Know her? How do you know her? Mind your own business. No. Get away from her. You come here. Who is she? Your girlfriend?* Adolf pulls me further away from the street, the Door, towards the Courtyard. Beams of light now stare down from the windows above. Adolf turns around and shouts: Leave us alone and mind your own business. Get out of here.

Gradually the others withdraw and we are alone ~

My throat is lined with sandpaper. I'm struggling for breath. I slide my hand into my coat pocket and pull out the Paper. I must focus on why I am here. Adolf stares at me and then takes the Paper. He walks towards a falling streak of light so that he can read. It will be difficult for him to accomplish this but he will manage. Sister Viktorine made sure of that.

He refolds the paper and approaches me. I know that he will now accompany me to the Hospital and enquire about Herta. He will comprehend that a Mistake has been made, that the Paperwork is not Correct. But when he returns his face is shattering with Anger. I think he might strike me, but instead takes the Paper and shoves it back into my pocket.

Says: What in God's name are you doing? Taking official Papers out of the Hospital?

I stare down at the obscured cobbles which sway in a nauseous dance.

His voice is rasping: You Stupid Interfering Fool. All this has been discussed. Obersturmführer Teichmann has communicated with my mother and they have decided. Herta has been very ill – very. She needs the best possible care. So why bring this Paper?

He wags his head, sighs. He needs to ring his mother. She will know that this Is Not What Was Agreed. Yet even as I repeat this inside my mind, I begin to see my Spaghetti Confusions. What exactly was it that his mother said? She could not cope, she would not take Herta back. I press the Paper on him again.

He says: For God's sake. Why don't you understand? Herta is a Useless Eater.

Above us, jeering from a window. The shadows of arms and heads. Adolf's face is flushed deep red, his eyes bulge. Once he was the boy who saved me, now he is one of the bullies. You must be one or the other. He will slam my hand in a Door, burn me with a cigarette, report me to the Police.

Yet even in this moment of Terror I knowknowknow. His Wolf Performance is exaggerated, unconvincing. This is not a World of threats with inkwells and foot stamping. He could be in my position and he knows it. Yet saying: You are a Cabbage also. Always were. Merely one of Dr A's curiosities. The Murder Box. *They will come for you* ~

Soldiers are spilling out of the Café again. They surround us and one of them catches hold of my coat. The window above is flung open. A voice says: Is she your girlfriend, Adolf? Come to say goodbye, has she? Going to marry her, are you?

Another voice: For God's sake, look at this.

A hand catches hold of both of my plaits. Lucky Man, Adolf. Going to give her one before you go. Better get on with it. I will if you don't.

Adolf's face is briefly illuminated by a torch beam. He is white, hollow, teeth clenched. Appalled by the soldiers but also scared of me and of that Paper. *Going to give her one, Adolf? Not scared, are you?* A beam of light far brighter than any other, dazzling. Blocking everything. A voice growling. Adolf saying: I have never seen her before. I have no idea who she is.

Adolf catches hold of me and forces his mouth against mine. His hands are grappling at my dress. I feel something hard pressed against my leg. *Ad-olf. Ad-olf. Ad-olf.* His hand is grappling at my knee, pulling up my dress ~

Yells and the snapping and howling of dogs. The young men are dashing back to the Café. Adolf pushes me and I tumble back but then leap up, run. I cannot go back through the archway. Still thronged with soldiers. Yet Adolf taught me well. Look for the washroom. Small Door. Push it open and find myself in a Corridor.

In the murky shadows, I push forward, my feet shuffling, scared that the floor may drop. A dull gleam of bruised light. Another Door ahead, nudge it open. Here more light – blurred glass, a streetlight beyond. Calmer now, calmer. No one is following. Climb onto the sink, lever open the window. I push myself through and find myself in another Courtyard ~

So I escape – and yet I am Undone. Why go back to the Hospital? However, I can only walk where habit tells me that I must walk. I am gulping each breath but no air is enough. Inside my pocket that Matchbox of Happier Days is weeping. When I finally come to the Hospital the Door is closed because it is now most late.

A sound is swelling above me. The rattling, groaning noise of a plane. I look up at the low sky, cloudy and starless, shades of tar and gunmetal grey. This cannot be an enemy plane. It is well known. This City will never be bombed. We are the bunker of the Reich. Too far to fly, too difficult to attack because of the hills all around.

Yet nownownow. Too late to run. The plane is skimming the top of my skull. The roar of the engine assaulting my eardrums. White birds all around me, swirling down. Just like those others I saw. Enemy Propaganda, one must not touch it. One must not even admit to having seen it. I start to run back towards Lazarettgasse but then turn again.

I must get into the Hospital by some means. I know there are ways. Herr Spellbinder and Adolf once used those hidden routes. Cellars, back stairs. Still those white birds descend, twisting gracefully down from the heavens. Some catch in trees or land on roofs but others flutter down to alight on pavements or gutters.

Paper the size of a school Notebook. Printed in black and white. An evil silhouette hovers over a Hospital bed, brandishing a needle. Dr Jekelius. *The overlord of the syringe. Haunts the Corridors of Steinhof in a white doctor's coat. Does not bring new Life to the ill but Death.*

Why would anyone drop these Leaflets? My feet are still running back towards the Hospital and yet I do not move. I am chased now by Paper. Blowing, flapping, sticking. The main Door opens. A figure steps out. Dr Feldner. He is staring at the Leaflets but also notices me. He is holding the Door open, I dash towards it, dive inside.

I wait for Dr Feldner to shut the Door but he does not. Instead he turns to me most deliberately and puts out his hand. I know what he wants. I hand him the Herta Papers. He shakes his head slowly, pushes them in his pocket. Then I must catch hold of the Door as he steps out into the blizzard of Leaflets where he should not go.

What is he doing? He bends, picks up a Leaflet, holds it under the light. This is not Correct. Yet most strangely I know that I must stay close to him. In this most Unsafe of situations, I am Safe. Thus, I remain at the Door making sure that it does not slam. Around him the Leaflets still fall.

He turns to me and lifts his hat, peers at me searchingly, nods. Opposite are the windows of the General Hospital. Above the lights of our own building. So many can look out, so many are observing, prying. Yet Dr Feldner still peers up at the sky, trying to see the plane even though it is long gone.

He smiles then, laughs madly, raises his hand, punches the sky.

Keep it up, lads ~

After My Death: Fog in Bedfordshire, 1941

Who would drop these Leaflets? And whywhywhy? For many years, I did not have an Answer. Yet lost Information is found and becomes available, new History is written, ever more documents are released. A day comes when I do understand and so I tell you now. This you may think is a Small part of the Story yet who may say what is Small and what is Large?

For what appears insignificant may later be judged to be the whisper that caused the avalanche. That voice on the Black Radio. I hated to hear it. I knew. Something was uncanny, skewed, deceptive, and it was that which led to the Matchboxes, which led to the dress. Which. Then. After. Like a run of dominos, when one falls then anotheranotheranother.

We must now travel to a distant place being most obscure. I hope you are following this narrative closely. Please concentrate. This place being a village in the middle of England called Aspley Guise and a House called the Rookery which before the War was an average, square, prosperous, stained-glass family home ~

In that House we find a Man called Maurice who on this russet-tinged September afternoon of 1941 is proceeding to the front Door to collect the post. This movement being difficult for him because, although a Young Man, he has only one leg so that he must ease his weight onto his crutch and steady himself before opening the front Door.

He doesn't turn the porch light on. The blackout has not been put in place yet but this will unfold in an hour. The postman gives him a nod, attempts to hand him a thick package. Maurice cannot grasp the package therefore the postman obligingly pushes it onto a shelf just inside the Door.

Maurice manages, now that the postman has departed, to gather the package under his arm. Briefly he surveys the Garden. In this part of England, the fog always hangs thick as smoke and settles heavy in the lungs. Maurice manoeuvres himself back to the drawing room, sits at his desk, opens the post.

German newspapers, Reports from the interrogation of Prisoners of War. Useful. Maurice's job is Research, Checking Papers and Filing. He knows what information he must seek and how it must be ordered. They want the names of certain Streets, usually in Berlin. Also, the names of certain Blockleiters and Reports of local scandals.

Particularly anything involving hose pipes, feather dusters. When Tom and Peter write the Radio scripts, they use authentic details. The Germans are sadistic by nature and sexual perversion appeals to them. *The aim is to turn German against German and thereby weaken the German War Machine. One must ignite the inherent sadism in the German nature.*

This particular package contains the usual newspapers and Reports but it also contains Leaflets. These are not from Germany. They have been made, designed and printed by somebody in London. Careful use of the Fraktur script. Maurice knows the style and when he sees them, he feels a sharp chill spreading into his hands, his chest.

White bombs. Leaflets designed to be dropped over Enemy territory. That was his job before he came to Aspley Guise, before he lost his leg. He flew in the first white bomb raid to Vienna in January 1940, flying out of Villeneuve in France, before that country was humbled. He had been eager to go.

He was needed because he knew the City of Vienna. He had relatives there and spent four years residing there, while studying at the University. He had been young at the time of that first flight. Very young. It was a year ago ~

He hears Tom's voice booming from the Dining Room. Tom is his boss and used to work at the *Daily Express*. He has a journalist's confidence. He is with Peter and they are writing, rehearsing. That is what they do all day. Then they head over to Wavendon Tower to record. Soon they will not be required to do that as studios are being built in the grounds of this house.

When Maurice first arrived at Aspley Guise, he had feared that they might try and make him speak in one of the Radio programmes. His German is good enough but it was soon clear that he couldn't do it. He had always hated being in plays at school. Now he hears the raging voice of Peter performing Der Chef.

Churchill. That flat-footed bastard of a drunken old cigar-smoking Jew. A rattle of laughter, a Door shutting. It is only five o'clock but Tom and Peter start on the drink early. Tom likes to keep himself well. Here at the Rookery the food is generous, the drink plentiful. No Wartime shortages here.

Yet Tom also works all hours and expects everyone else to do the same. His litany is – *dirt, cover, cover, dirt, cover, cover.* Maurice considers the Leaflet in front of him. Dr Jekelius. The figure is cartoon-like, ridiculously sinister. Would anyone believe such a thing? Like the fictional Der Chef himself.

Black Propaganda. Pretending to be more Nazi than the Nazis in order to bring them down. Sowing doubt and Confusion. Could this Strategy work? Is anybody actually listening? Maurice cannot believe that these broadcasts have any effect. Too extreme. Ranting and raging. One would have to be a fool not to recognise it as a hoax.

Maurice lays the Leaflet aside, hears the maids putting up the blackout in the hall. Dinner will soon be served. After that, some of the girls or the lads will ask him to come out with them. They are instructed that they must not even walk into the village but the master of this house is slack. People in other houses are not so fortunate.

Maurice knows little about the other houses but he does hear mention of the French House, the Italian House. It seems that everyone is situated in this same village but Maurice barely even knows where in England this village is located. He was brought here in a blacked-out van, all the signposts taken down.

When the typists go into the local town, they talk about Glenn Miller's band. Wouldn't he like to step out for the evening? *Up with the lark and to bed with the wren?* When the lads have had a drink they slap him on the back – *What does a leg or two matter between old friends?* They are right. What does it matter ~

THE MATCHBOX GIRL

Tom appears now, his vast frame filling the Doorway, a glass of whisky swinging in his hand. He gives Instructions about Research and filing of scripts. Peter is sorting through those Reports which have just arrived. His hands flick over the Leaflet about the Viennese doctor: *Did a good job on that one, didn't they? Could use that.*

   Maurice says: I don't think so. Vienna. Not Der Chef's patch.
   Shame. Can't you find a Berlin child murderer?
   They smile and nod pleasantly, worried that he is offended.
   You all right? Coming for dinner?
   Yes. Yes. I will.
   Still Peter says: That Leaflet. High quality piece of work. Could you do some digging? It is a good Story. Cheer up, old chap. Rather too salty for you, is it? I know you have moral objections to a Wrongo ~

Wrongo. It sounds better than Lie. They always tease him. He made a mistake when he first came here, raised tiresome Moral Questions. Peter is open in his polite contempt but Tom is more careful. Peter starts again now: *Undermine them. Play to the darker side of their nature. I love a good Wrongo myself.*

   The gramophone goes on. A maid appears with a tray of drinks. Maurice considers them all to be ridiculous. Do they really think that what they are doing can make any difference? Before the War, Maurice had travelled to Berlin. He saw the rallies, felt the power. He had even hoped that a similar unity and focus might spread to England.

   How could he have been so Wrong? One of the Radio technicians says now – *Come out with us? Tom doesn't mind. I'll take you on the back of my bike.* He does sometimes join them, bumping on the back of the bike over the potholes, through the moonlight, seeing the bombers taking off from Tempsford and wishing that he was still flying ~

After supper he goes to his ground-floor room. Usually he reads or writes letters. Now he thinks often of his Viennese cousin who is interned on the Isle of Man. That was possibly the only advantage of his injury. At least no one could suspect his political loyalties. He too could have finished up on the Isle of Man.

But after the Hospital, a job in the Political Warfare Executive had been offered. Mother-tongue German speakers were urgently needed. *Work on translation.* No mention of Propaganda by Pornography then. Still there were worse places to spend the War. Here he could even light a fire because no one here seems to mind how much coal you use.

Instead, he takes a blanket from the bed, sits himself down in front of the empty grate. He loosens the straps, takes off his wooden leg, rubs the stump. Strange that he never thinks of the flight when his leg was crushed, when the fire started, the plane came down. Instead, he always thinks of that earlier flight to Vienna, the Leaflet drop.

The intense, jarring cold, the shaking and juddering of the Whitley. Three planes had set off around five o'clock from Villeneuve. The cockpit heating was no use at all. In the training sessions it was stressed that this was extremely good practice – night flying, navigation, endurance.

What you are doing requires even greater skill than bombing. They would need to think hard about height and the direction of the wind. The Leaflets could potentially be carried away over long distances if it was a night of gales. He was to be the navigator. It all made sense but still he was disappointed. This was a pansy mission ~

No one had flown so far into enemy territory before but that did not ease the disappointment. Why take the risk of covering such immense distances and then drop only Leaflets? Plus, Vienna was the worst possible target, sitting in a bowl, surrounded by hills. Minus twenty, and although their leather flying suits were padded with layers of sheepskin, still the cold gnawed.

He would not be needed until they were over the City therefore he had no occupation for six long hours. He remembers the Bavarian Alps. He had stood up at the ice-caked window to see those snow-capped peaks showing up magnificently in the starry night. He had been on a walking holiday there.

By the time they came to the City, the ice was a serious worry. The oxygen would surely fail. He tried to get through to the rear gunner but no one could hear him. Had the Man become unconscious due to the cold? They circled. Wind, height, the direction of the slipstream. He had the Leaflets prepared.

No Nazi Doctors then but Leaflets about the Personal fortunes hidden away by the Nazi leaders. Where? Where should they drop? The City below, a mass of burning embers, the tarry waters of the Danube. He remembers swimming in the summers. The Stephansdom. This is what he needs. He tries to identify other landmarks. The University? The Hospital?

Where are the places that he knows? The cold is melting his flesh, crumbling his bones. He cannot breathe or see or hear. His mouth is frozen, his teeth smacking together. Here. Now. No more delay. The flare chute is stiff and he must fight to get it to open. Caked in ice. He cuts the strings, gets the first two piles of Leaflets through the chute. No problem.

The last ones. His mind is rambling, drifting and he can barely raise his arm. The Leaflets are dashing everywhere, swooping, battering, muffling. The pilot shouting – *Clear the Leaflets*. Why can't he get through to the rear gunner? Maurice forces his lifeless arms to gather the Leaflets, pulling all the flesh from his hands but feeling nothing.

He stuffs Leaflets down the chute. Cuts the strings on the last bundles. The Leaflets are blown back into the plane, flapping everywhere. They bash into his face, blow through to the cockpit. Maurice cannot grasp them. The pilot is shouting. *For Christ's sake, you Idiot. Clear the Leaflets. Clear the bloody Leaflets* ~

7.a. No More Tin Soldiers

The problem is this. We do not know what we know at the time when we know it. Do You understand? I am living in a World which has become detached from the Words which explained it. Of course, I always knew that Words are treacherous. That is why I do not speak, but I was, nevertheless, certain that writing can tether the ever-shifting rivers of life.

Now I tell You. The morning after the Wrong Conclusions. Significant news is being communicated. Sister Clara has been promoted. She will now work for Dr Jekelius at Am Spiegelgrund. This is a major new opportunity and demonstrates the value of her work. She will be leaving immediately as the need for staff at the new Hospital is urgent.

I do not know. I do not understand. All day I have been waiting for the axe to fall. Three people know that I left the Hospital last night. Herr Spellbinder, Dr Feldner, Sister Clara. Others must also know. Except that *the Alchemy of Circumstance* has acted to remove the Person most likely to tell. Perhaps if we all Pretend with growling Bears and toasting forks.

Everyone indeed Performs this Spectacle with great enthusiasm. Sister Viktorine offers her congratulations and so also do Dr Feldner and Dr A. We must all line up in the Corridor to say goodbye. Everyone wishes Sister Clara the very best of luck and thanks her warmly. She is most charming and gracious. I also must shake hands with her.

Of course, no choice. I mustmustmust. I even look her in the eye and smile most widely as I have been taught. Yet when I feel her hand in mine, a strangling blackness descends. A writhing Fear, a desire to destroy, even to kill. For this hand in mine. So tender and warm and sly. This was the hand. How can she be promoted? How can ~

Adelheid – You know what you must do. I wait until later when the Ward is tranquil. I kindle the stove in the Meeting Room even though the night is warm. I make sure that the flames are blazing well. Then I go to the Bunk Room and take the key to my locked box. I lift out the Notebooks and carry them all into the Meeting Room.

I open the stove, tear out a page. Sister Viktorine appears and grabs hold of my arm. She tells me – *No, no, no. You cannot. You mustn't.* I pull my hand away, she pulls back. We are wrestling. She has gripped one of the Notebooks, tugs it from my hand. I let go of that Notebook, pick up another, push the whole of it into the stove.

Sister Viktorine is weeping saying – *You cannot.* Calling also for Dr Feldner to prevent me, continuing to wrench the box of Notebooks away from me. Yet Dr Feldner appears at the Door, watches, does not move. He knows, he understands. Sister Viktorine saying – *Nothing in there. Nothing.* Her mouth hangs open like a tunnel and tears spout.

Dr Feldner only shakes his head: Let her do it. She knows what she is about. It was never safe. Those books can be used against her – against us. We can no longer take the risk.

I burn the books and I burn them and I burn them. It takes too long to rip out every page so I shove them in whole and attack them with the toasting fork while flames rise and rush from the front of the stove, rage in the chimney. A voice inside my head is screaming. I do not listen, I do not weaken, or bend. I have no Mercy.

Sister Viktorine is sitting at the Meeting Room table, her head dropped down on her arms, sobbing. Yet I continue to rip and burn and poke and bash. All the while the words are screaming and screaming, pleading with me to rescue them, to raise them out of the flames. Each letter protesting, each syllable shrieking in terror ~

I do not care. I am glad to see them suffer and crackle and explode and turn to nothingnothingnothing but ash. I destroy them not because they contain Lies but because they are the Evidence of how

I Lied to myself. All my Life I have been lookinglookinglooking. A Person so interested in Observation and Evidence and Truth and yet I was blind.

What is the Point of Words if they do not tell you the Truth? The Third Reich was Truth and it was Independent Thought. Everything I wrote was entirely and completely Correct but yet I must ask whether any Word of it is True? How can this be? Sister Viktorine is Distressed for she thinks I have lost my mind – but I am returning to myself.

Back to the beginning. To the Child who I once was. The Child who existed before the Performance began. That Child who did not know What To Do and yet was able to see a Sudden Startling Truth. *Know when an activity or a game is finished and stop.* Dr Feldner lays a hand on Sister Viktorine's arm.

She is repeating again and again: How can we live in such times?

Then she is calmer and she comes to me in compassion and speaks gently: Adelheid, how can I explain? I do not understand myself.

I am not listening but she puts her hand out and catches hold of my chin. I try to pull her hand away but she is holding me tight, insisting that I look into her eyes. Saying in a voice which is quiet but fierce: Let me tell you this. Listen. It is all that I know. There is only one Führer and that is Jesus Christ ~

What You must understand is this. The problem is not that I discovered new Information. No. What I discovered is Information which I always knew. *You know that they are lying. They are all lying.* I did know. I did. We are all stuffed full of feathers. The British are so stupid and yet they fly to Vienna to warn us of what we can already see.

Why was I given Frau Altmann's shoes when they were brand new? *Someone has fallen from a window.* Why two stretchers? The Stationer Herr Wächter saying – *You know what the problem is? Not the obvious problem.* Adolf saying that Herta will get *the best possible care*, then saying that she is a Useless Eater. Where is the Fifth File?

What is the difference between Lying and Pretending?

There is no difference ~

Of course, I have always known that there are Lies. Individual Lies. What I cannot comprehend is a whole World built on Massive

Lies. Everything you touch is a Lie. What other Information do I know and yet fail to see? How might I rely upon my own mind? Yet this thinking does come later, slowly, in creeping stages.

In this early moment, my mind is a pack of cards. Put all of the cards of the same suit together. Here are three jacks. Group them next to each other. But invisible hands take hold of the cards again and again. Shuffle, deal, cut. I never manage to order the cards before they are pulled out of my hands. Shuffle, deal, cut. One Truth reveals another.

All my brooding is thisthenthat and so also and thereforewemustconclude. One idea tumbling into another. One Truth falling and taking it all. All. You build your toy Fort or your Farm with your wooden building blocks. You want your Fort or your Farm to stand up. You want to keep your toy soldiers safe.

But now? Now? You take out one brick. The building is trembling and teetering. You might as well pull it all down because there is no brick on which you can rely. These are not Children's toys. This is not about tin soldiers. This I know yet the human mind does not have the capacity to dismantle one World and construct another at some extreme speed ~

In the hours of daylight, I can continue. I can. We must all press on undaunted. Yet the hours of darkness are longlonglong. The nights unending. No sleep. No Peace. The rustling sounds of the Ward. The Black Radio whispering. Foreign voices. Should we listen or not listen? I long for Peace. I put a pillow over my head but the voices still gabble.

That voice I did not want to hear. The woman who came to speak to Sister Viktorine. I hear her now. Is she a Ghost or is she actually present in this Ward? So many dead are strangely alive yet also so many Alive who are strangely Dead. Anni Wodl is one such Person. She walks the Wards of the Hospital and she will not be silenced.

She wails and pulls at her own flesh. You can hear the sharp rasp of her breath, like a cornered animal, stinking of fear. Anger also rises from her like smoke from a fire. She sizzles like a burning coal, fiery and sharp. She is going to tell her Story whether anyone wants to hear or not. Albert, Albert. He was my child.

I insisted that I should see Albert. But That One. You know who I mean? He used to work here. I said to him – please, please. Albert does not deserve to die but he would not listen. He must die. He said I was cruel to want to keep Albert Alive. He told me I am Weak.

The progress of the Reich is being limited because we spend too much money on this cruel process of keeping people Alive when there is no hope. I'm not a Fool. I know that Albert was never going to grow up to be normal. Yet he smiled and was happy. He was starting to say some words. I told all that to him, that Man, but he would not hear me.

I was putting my own personal feelings before the needs of the Fatherland and I should stop being so selfish. So he said therefore what could I do? I said this isn't good enough. I don't believe this is what the Führer wants. I went then to Berlin. Everyone told me. *You must not go. You put yourself and others in Peril.*

I did not care. Albert is my son. I am his mother. Who else is there to speak for him? I took the train to Berlin. I supposed they would slam the Door in my face but they did allow a meeting – at which they said exactly the same. It is for the good of the Fatherland. In this time, we are all called upon to make sacrifices.

They did not deny it, they did not deny any of it. Finally, I considered it all in dark and agonising detail. I looked in my heart and I knew that I was entirely defeated. So I went back to him again. I said to him finally – *Please, please. I understand that Albert must die. I will make that sacrifice. But I beg you. I do not want him to die in pain.*

I told them that he is such a little boy with such a sunny smile. He is so Peaceful. A boy like him can never harm anyone. He must at least be taken into God's arms gently in order that his suffering can end. I asked him this. He said that yes, of course, this must be the case. All would be done in the gentlest and most humane way possible.

I went back again. I said that I wanted to see his body. His dear, dear body. I must say goodbye to him one last time. They would not permit me. They would not allow me this one request. Except one Nurse. Poor woman. Her eyes were like deep pits. God save her. She did not want to be in that place but what is her choice?

I know her. Her mother is in that same facility. In Steinhof. They only allow her mother to stay in there because her daughter is a loyal and long-serving nurse in that same Hospital. She is trying to protect her own mother. Bless her soul. She said that she would take me secretly to visit Albert. I went into a room, such a room.

So many, so many. Tiny and shrivelled. Lined up under white sheets. There is Albert. His face. His body. He was half starved, dried out, and you could tell, you could absolutely tell. I could see. The suffering, the suffering. He died a violent Death. My son, my son. He died a violent Death. They say that there are no lethal injections. There are no gas chambers.

I asked them directly and it was not denied ~

7.b. Raised Eyebrows and Small Nods

In those days after that great conflagration of Notebooks, I saw a multitude of Sudden Startling Truths. Yet soon I became less certain. I could not live with the endless reshuffling of the pack of cards. Like the sun, the Truth burnt and dazzled and blinded. One might not look at it directly. I also could not rely upon the faces of the people around me.

This I had always known but now I find myself again watching-watchingwatching. *It is not just Fräulein Eder. It could be anyone.* However, I also know that some others do share my questions. Who are they and what do they know? Again, like the Child I was, I am looking for a code, a key. Yet no matter how much I observe, I know less and less.

The only positive development is that, without Sister Clara, the atmosphere of the Ward is less tight. Fräulein Eder is also less bold in her unpleasantness. She has always been a nasty Person but also timorous and, without Sister Clara, she returns to the petty and narrow nastiness which has always been her specialisation.

Sister Elena assures me that Fräulein Eder will not cause trouble now. Saying: When you went missing, Dr Feldner made Fräulein Eder confess that she wrote down your name on that list. He said many times – *in the light of our former connections.* Sister Elena does not comprehend that phrase but Fräulein Eder is keeping her mouth shut now ~

I want Peace, I want to hear Nothing but the Gossip starts again. Radio Anna sets the brushes and mops in the broom cupboard talking. *Sister Clara is indeed very lucky because Dr Jekelius will soon be promoted. He will surely soon be going to work in Berlin for the Führer himself. But why is he so elevated and honoured? Why?*

Have you not heard? He is in love with the Führer's sister. Don't be so stupid. The Führer doesn't have a sister. Yes, he does. Everyone knows he does. The Rumours are shaken out in the bed sheet. The Nurses shake, scrub, scour. Children are checked for lice. Leg braces are strapped in place and inkwells filled.

The Führer does have a sister called Paula but no one likes to say. She met Dr Jekelius because one of the Führer's relatives used to be a patient at Steinhof. You mean, she is a Nurse at Steinhof? No. No. A patient. Aloisia Veit. Aged 49. A schizophrenic. The mops are excited now, dancing up and down the Ward in ecstasy at this most scandalous suggestion.

This patient at Steinhof was the distant cousin of the Führer. She was chained to her bed and raved about a grinning skull. She often didn't even know her own name. Pillows are plumped up and windows flung open. The birds are shrieking, the clouds riotous. *So Dr Jekelius wants to marry a woman who is Hitler's sister? Marry the Führer's sister?*

Since Dr Jekelius is such a clever doctor, he has cured the mad Aloisia and made her well and now he wishes to marry Paula. So this explains why he will surely be promoted to the highest level? Sister Clara also. She will become most senior and important ~

This is the Gossip while we workworkwork. Sister Viktorine being ever more vigorous and exacting in her many demands. Everything must be Correct. Everything hygienicsprucedupscrubbed. We cannot allow the Children to play in the Corridor. Shelves and skirting board are scoured. We must be readyreadyready. The Ward may be inspected at any time. Do you understand?

Dr A is also now most particular about every minute detail. At night I hear the Black Radio. I do not listen. Yet still I cannot fully ignore that raging voice. The strange shouting and ranting. I cannot understand. Who is this Man? Why are Dr Feldner and Herr Spellbinder listening? The dawn brings no relief, as Lotte is always pestering me.

She is ripping out her hair and digging holes in her arms with the point of a pencil. She is missing her friend Margarete. Where is Margarete? Where is she? Lotte cannot play her Film Star games without Margarete. That arm I saw was only the sleeve of a shirt. I feel so giddy that I must sit down and hold my head ~

Dr Feldner is the only Person who understands. One night he discovers me listening at the Door, trying to fathom that Radio voice. He sits me down in the Meeting Room and converses with me most kindly. He tells me that the current situation is most Troubling for a Person such as myself. We are in Enemy territory? Have I understood?

He whispers then these words. The voice on the Radio, the Man is called Der Chef, and he is not a German at all. Instead, this is an Enemy Radio Station. Der Chef exaggerates. He Pretends too hard. One must not do that. Yet that is why he is comic and some enjoy listening. It is hard for a Person such as myself to understand.

Dr Feldner shrugging: We are now in a World where you have to do the Wrong Thing in order to do the Right Thing but everyone must also Pretend that they have not seen you doing the Wrong Thing. Should they happen to see you doing the Right Thing then they must tell you that you are doing the Wrong Thing. Are you clear?

This he seems to find most amusing although I cannot understand why. As I have done manymanymany times before, I ask myself what kind of man Dr Feldner is. Apparently, an inveterate gambler. A man who mocks authority (any authority) and a failed Catholic priest. Now an atheist and yet the good friend of Sister Viktorine. How to explain?

Yet now he does give me advice which is most significant. He says that everyone is lying all of the time and we must do the same for to do otherwise is unsafe. Yet what we Must Not Do Is To Lie To Ourselves. *This is important. Have you understood, Adelheid? Hold your nerve. Be truthful in your own mind. No one can take that from you* ~

Dr Feldner then proposes that I should perhaps attend to my Matchbox collection again. I do not feel inclined. So many of my Matchboxes are now hidden under the hall floorboard at the Café and I cannot get them back. Yet Dr Feldner is most insistent and gets out the various envelopes and the Album and my plans.

How comforting these old friends feel in my fingers. What a pleasure it is to lay them out on the Meeting Room table. Yet the old Questions of Categorisation Trouble me with a new force. If I see a Matchbox only as belonging to Hungary then what else might I Not See About This Matchbox? The colour, or the design, or the date.

Yet even in the considering of these Questions, I increase my grasp of my own mind. Adolf may have said – *I have never seen her before. I have no idea who she is.* Yet I know. In that moment when I crossed out my name, I became a Real Person. I fix my mind on this fact and count the wooden blocks on the parquet floor againagainagain.

I press one finger hard against my palm. The next finger, the next. The Girl with the strange Waking Dreams. The Girl who liked to look at every blade of grass. I am finding my way back to her. The many leaves which blow on the trees in the garden. The evening light at the window, some flowers from the garden, a child singing a tuneless song. The velvet fabric on the chair in the Meeting Room.

This is what saves me ~

One does not need a Notebook to write things down. I can still record all my thoughts insidemyhead. I must do this. In thinking of this Question, I consider also Dr A who is always ahead of me on the mountain path, waving a pole to indicate the route. He is working later and later, and often conversing with Sister Viktorine, just as he always has.

In these deepest night times, they both stop being Pretend People and, like me, they return to their original selves. Their heads nodding slightly, their words quiet and thoughtful as they puzzle over those many Interesting Questions which are part of Dr A's Research (even though that research is supposedly laid aside).

Sister Viktorine raising her hands in that strange gesture, as though she may draw the Whole World into her embrace. One night I hear them investigating how they are both quite similar, in that they do not originate from Vienna. They both come from small towns in agricultural areas. Dr A feels that urbanisation is one of the causes of the new intolerance.

He is not talking here of our current moment but of changes which happened at the beginning of our century. *What strikes me is how, as people move to the Cities, the range of what is considered Normal* has narrowed. Dr A also shows Sister Viktorine Information about the families of these Children he studies. *See how strands of genius and difficulty are so intertwined.*

Sister Viktorine also talks to Dr A of more private things. Speaking then of the deep shame that she felt when she was a Child because she has never known the identity of her father. The Children at school did not speak to her because of this. Yet mercifully God has redeemed her and lifted her above this pall of sin.

When she was at the Front, she saw such Horrors but she also realised that she could Serve. What a mercy it was that she came to this Clinic. It is her home, her family. *God believes in me and I believe in the Children. I do his work. In Serving the Children, I Serve Jesus Christ. I value His creation. This is how I have lived* ~

As I listen to this conversation, I am drawing up plans of how I might rearrange my Albums. Yet also I am reflecting about how I might assist Sister Viktorine and Dr Feldner. Even though I cannot read clearly the language of Raised Eyebrows and Small Nods yet I am sure both know the Truth. Dr A also – although his Performance is more polished than theirs.

That long-departed Dr Frankl felt that there are different kinds of language. Maybe we must all now learn the language of dogs. Certainly, a way must be found to *steer* this situation. Everything must be kept to the highest standard all the time. Visitors may come to the Ward at any minute. One cannot approach this directly but perhaps there are ways?

You need a new Strategy, Matchbox. A Person such as myself can be useful in Enemy territory. I also think of Fräulein Weiss. *At some point you might be faced with a situation where you would need to stand up for the Truth.* Yet she did finish up dismissed and now we all know that the worst is far, far beyond mere expulsion.

An Answer comes to me. It is always best to go back to the beginning, to what has proved to be a good Strategy in the past. What matters is the quality of your Pretending. There is one way I can Pretend most well. In the silent hours just before dawn, I work. I make sure everything is ready, just as Sister Viktorine instructs me ~

7.c. A Fire in the Laundry Room

The Moment falls upon us with a gruesome force. Yet initially I do not apprehend it with clarity. I have worked too hard and do not sleep. I have put my mind in a bottle and screwed the lid on tight. So that when two SS men enter the Ward, I think that I am back in that other time when Sister Viktorine had to defend her position.

Or perhaps I am inhabiting that World of Dreams where I try again and again to salute but my hand is stuck down and will not move. More men in uniform are now arriving. This is real. For a moment, Sister Viktorine seems to crumple but then she quickly unfolds herself and remembers What To Do.

Nothing to fear because we are ready, we are all ready. Sister Elena hisses at me. I step into the Store cupboard where I can see but not be seen. Professor Hamburger hurries forward to welcome the visitors. Dr A steps out of his Office in a most sprightly and efficient manner. Dr Jekelius is full of good cheer.

I remember then the figure on the Leaflets and I know that it was merely Enemy Propaganda. Dr Jekelius is just as he has always been – exceptional sleek and smooth with his black slick of hair neatly oiled in place and his smile most engaging. He slaps Dr A on the shoulder and calls him Hans. They often work together now at the Public Health Office.

Dr Jekelius recounts his own Happy Years working in this most excellent Ward. The quality of Dr A's work is known widely and his commitment to improving the racial hygiene of the Reich is much praised. Dr A is introduced to Dr Heinrich Gross who will take a tour of the Ward before discussing some specific issues with Professor Hamburger.

Dr Gross is close to where I stand. His back to me. He is barely more than a teenager and has a weeping spot above his collar, his hand is raised now to worry at that spot. His hair is cut extremely short but even then one can see that he has a bald patch above his ear. The visitors move towards the School Room ~

Sister Elena has opened the Door to the Roof Terrace and some Children are being hurried up the stairs. Nods, raised eyebrows. Other Children are ushered away to the Nursery. I find a cloth and set about burnishing the benches in the reception area. Sister Viktorine plays the piano until Professor Hamburger tells her to stop.

Dr A waves his arms with enthusiasm in the direction of Theodor – a boy who has been the cause of many lengthy discussions and the writing of copious notes: This is why we reserve judgement, try every possible method of support.

The Tram is departing: This boy is most interesting to me. Valuable to our Research etcetcetc. The Autistic Psychopaths. Entirely unsuited to the usual school environment. Anti-social, Inappropriate Behaviour, no community spirit, violent outbursts. However, if you look at his skill with Radios and his interest in electrical circuits.

Professor Hamburger: Yes, yes. Hans. Thank you.

Dr A is gathering speed: We jokingly call these Children the Little Professors. Exceptionally good at code-breaking-type exercises. Social utility etcetcetc. What we think of as disease may simply be difference – and also opportunity.

Dr Gross: His language abilities? His written work?

Here Dr A stumbles. Everyone knows that Theodor can neither read nor write. The exercise books are located. Dr A is a Man swinging wildly on a cliff edge. Yet Dr Gross is most impressed by those school books. (Clutch the hearth rug, wave the toasting fork, but the Bear cannot growl as his mouth is cruelly held by a muzzle.)

Dr A is saying only: Yes, yes. Ahem. As you see. When he first arrived, it appeared he was unable to read or write. Note how the handwriting improves. Even over the last few days. Sister Viktorine must be congratulated. Sister Viktorine casts her eyes down modestly, then sneaks a swift and questioning glance in my direction ~

We think we have won. What Fools, what Fools. A War cannot be won with a pen. Where is Dr Jekelius? He is fetched from Dr Böckler's Office. Fräulein Eder is following him. She looks flushed and rumpled. Have they been committing sex acts? Of course, this cannot be the case since we already know about the Führer's sister etcetcetc.

    The Point being that Dr Gross says: Some Files we have identified. The Fifth File. But not just one File. A pile of Files.

    Dr Gross says: I have asked Dr Jekelius. Where is Lotte?

    Sister Viktorine draws breath, briefly shuts her eyes. No one here is going to ride away on a bicycle or fly off on a rocket. Lotte greets the room with a preening grin. She wants us all to join in her Moment of Glory. She is asked to stand in front of Heinrich Gross. He considers her carefully, stretches out his gentle hand. Lotte shakes that hand, curtsies unsteadily.

    Professor Hamburger says: One recognises the type. Romany undoubtably. The sallow, the big ears, the misshapen mouth. The Files confirm. Mendacious, hysterical.

    For a moment a Stupid thought passes through my mind. *Does this concern identifying big ears? Then that is most of the Children and also the staff.* Yet this thought only comes because of all the other notions I am trying to suppress. Cannot now be stopped. Margarete, spinning and titivating, descending the stairs Pretending to be a Film Star ~

I screwed the lid on tight but my mind has broken out of the bottle. That Information which I have always knownandnotknown. That last Sudden Startling Truth. It attacks me now with Vicious Force. I am not thinking about Lotte or about Margarete, I am considering only myself. Yet we are all the same. They are Cabbage Children and so am I. *The obvious problem.*

    This New World. So goodtruecorrect. But not for Margarete and not for Lotte. Not for a Cabbage Child like me. I thought I was different, better. I am only working in this Hospital because they find a use for me here. Merely one of Dr A's curiosities. I could be swirling on the stairs or having the Wrong Skin, the Wrong Ears, the Wrong-shaped head.

The room around me is roaring and swooping. Dr A is speaking again with enthusiasm but he is a Man staring at a burning building and the hose is nowhere to be found. Foolish to hope that a Child's Trick might make us Safe. Dr A now dissolves into uncertainty, prevarication. Returning to the Young Man who I knew when I first came here.

Yet the toy cupboard is not quite empty. The tin soldiers will defend their wobbling Fort until their last breath. Dr Jekelius has mentioned Lotte's Schoolwork. I am already moving to fetch her exercise books. Everyone might wish to stop me. Yet they let me go because I will find the books most quickly. I keep them in alphabetical order by class.

Dr Gross is moving on to other Files. I am most hasty in fetching the books but also have time to pass by the Bunk Room. I hurry then towards Dr Gross. Sister Viktorine and Dr A have both seen the Matchbox envelopes underneath the exercise books. Sister Viktorine is mouthing the words – *No, no, no.*

She is saying silently – *Always important to know when to stop.* But I won't, I won't. Dr A steps forward to head me off but I have already moved past him. Dr Gross considers me briefly as I position the exercise books on the table. He opens a book, turns the pages, raises a questioning eyebrow. Says: Surprising. An adequate standard.

I am still standing close. Others would like to push me to the back but I am not going to permit that and they cannot challenge me without *drawing attention*. The work is adequate. Not more. Not like Der Chef. One must not exaggerate. Lotte smacks her lips together, pushes her hands between her legs. Sister Viktorine grabs hold of her hands and slaps them.

Dr Gross says: As I see in the Notes. Problems of sexual promiscuity.

Dr A says: Yes. Undoubtedly. Weak moral character. But she has improved greatly. I am fully confident that with absolutely the best Sovereign Support and Assistance—

Sister Viktorine stops Lotte before she can begin to unbutton her blouse. Jekelius is saying that Am Spiegelgrund would be the most Appropriate place. Sister Viktorine mentions the problems of Lotte's home life. Unfortunately, she has a difficult relationship with her stepfather. It might be better if she could live apart from him. There might be others in the family who could offer an alternative? No one listens to her.

THE MATCHBOX GIRL

Dr A is saying that there is nothing that they can do at Am Spiegelgrund which cannot be done in this Ward. Our Curative Education Ward clearly being the centre of this work. Most esteemed in the World etcetcetc. Yet Dr Gross is inclined to agree with Professor Hamburger. Yes, yes. One sees it all in the shape of the skull.

Just spite dressed up as science. Strangely it is Dr Jekelius who questions, seems inclined to disagree with Dr Gross. Are the Rumours about him true? Has he become soft and pliable because of Paula? Like Grandmother (who in her Youth married the Wrong Man), he may be a Victim of Romance. It no longer matters if this might be True or not.

A black silhouetted figure crouches. They will stab stick a needle in her. She'll go up the chimneys at Hartheim and finish up hung on the washing line. Or get taken away in the Murder Box. No one will save her because she isn't a Little Professor. She is a Cabbage Child and there is no hidden mystery to her. She is like me.

Now she is leering at the men again, rubbing herself, licking her lips. Dr Gross takes up his pen, looks for the forms. Once her name is written, then who will cross it out? Margarete, Margarete, I may have murdered you with a marble but I will not. I will not. Sister Anna grips me tightly by the hand but I shake her off. I step forward.

Do not let the cattle get in the way. Around me the walls grind and shudder, begin to crack. The high windows shine down in vicious disapproval. The faces all around have the teeth of wolves. I open the envelopes which lie on the desk. *Create a Distraction.* Matchboxes are always your best hope. Dr A: No, no. Put those away. (He would like to slap me, strangle me, hide me on the Roof Terrace.)

Dr Gross: So what is this?

No. No. Adelheid. Dr Gross doesn't have time for that. Adelheid, what are you doing? The temperature in the room coming to the boil, the Nurses bob and hiss like snakes. The walls are pillows which suffocate, the ceiling descending like a vast eagle claw. Sister Viktorine is smiling at me most warmly while treading forcefully on my foot ~

I knew it. Dr Gross has caught the scent. He feels the yearning, the tugging, deep inside. *No, no. Do let me see.* I know that feeling when you must see, when you long to touch, when you are drawn into that World. He is looking at the Envelopes, spreading their contents on the desk. I think he will be so distracted that he will not look at me. I am Wrong.

He asks: Who is this young woman?

Dr Jekelius will remember me. He already does. I know it. Everything freezes now. Eyeballs are fixed on the floor. Someone is edging Lotte to the back of the room. A terrible train crash is about to take place and no one can stop it. The Murder Box. *Misshapen head, Life unworthy of Life.* I look around at the witchandwizard faces which circle all about.

In that moment, we all know. The Bear is only a hearth rug and a toasting fork. The arm is hanging from the laundry cart. Anni Wodl is walking the Corridors, weeping. Blown away, washed down a drain. Soon all that will be left of me is my shoes, or my purse. *Unfortunately, she had to return home to help her Grandmother* ~

Amazing. What a Collection. I smile and point out the Indian Matchbox (Canary Yellow Elephant) and a Czech Matchbox (two-tailed white lion with crown and gold claws). Now Dr Gross floats gracefully above his chair and smiles most Cheerily: Carefully Organised. Quite a Collector. I should like to contribute something. Only the regular thing, I am afraid.

He fishes in his pocket, holds up a Matchbox with a swastika and asks: From where?

He must think I am Stupid. It is the sign of the Reich and indicates the purity and supremacy of the Aryan Race. I look up at Dr Jekelius. Dr Gross is asking his question again. Dr Jekelius is speaking. *Yes, Adelheid. Yes. I remember. She has been here.* Here. Here. The word drums in our ears ~

The fire alarm rings, clattering through the building, bashing against every eardrum, making our teeth shake. Plant pots and tables are jumping up and down. Theodor-Heinrich-Johannes-Kaspar start to hide under the desks. Liesl-Anna-Maria-Helene moan and bang their hands on their heads. Dr Gross is looking at his watch.

Professor Hamburger is talking about Dr A: Most reliable. A Man who can certainly be useful in our new initiatives. In particular, the Gugging Hospital.

THE MATCHBOX GIRL

Sister Viktorine is marshalling the Children. Everyone knows the Correct Procedures. Line up at the Door. Do not take anything with you. We will assemble at the bottom of the hill where the road comes down to Lazarettgasse. *No one is to push or shove. No running on the stairs. Hurry up, please. No, no. Stop doing that.*

We stumbleslipgasp down the stairs. Crowded close, breath too hot. Piling into each other. Then we are told to stop. *Stop. Stop now.* Herr Spellbinder is talking to Dr A. *Go back upstairs please. Go back.* Dr Gross and Dr Jekelius have looked at their watches, consulted their diaries. They really cannot wait while this matter is resolved.

Dr A: A fire in the laundry room. Electrical wiring. Herr Spellbinder deeply regrets.

Theodor and his interest in electrical circuits? Dr Gross and Dr Jekelius are now leaving (taking some Files with them). We mightmightmight. Safety. Everyone sucks in sudden breaths, feels their bones begin to harden once again. Yet what I see most clearly is the way in which Professor Hamburger looks at Dr A. Observing him down to the tips of his toes ~

7.d. The Confusions of Dr Jekelius

In those watchful and anxious days which followed the visit of Dr Gross, I am waiting to be reprimanded for my Foolish Behaviour but no one speaks. On the evening of that day, Dr A passes me in the Corridor and his eyes hold mine. This has not happened often before. Dr A rarely looks directly at me or anyone else.

Now his look jolts through me, like electricity. Maybe I am a *great savant*? (Should I calculate Christmas Day in the year 1800?) Yet surely he knows? We are all *savants*. Sometimes we just know a certain thing and we cannot say how. Yet that is not what transpired in this Case. The clue was the bald patch above Dr Gross's left ear.

I saw him all those months ago when he visited our Café. One phillumenist always recognises another. Opa believed in *Breadth of Vision*. By contrast, I have always observed how the Small Things often transform into the Big. Am I a Cabbage Child or a Little Professor? Dr A and Sister Viktorine know that the Answer might be less than straightforward ~

Will there be more visitors to the Ward? We cannot know but autumn surrenders to winter and no one appears. Everyone waits for news from the Front. Lists are posted up of the Dead. Our spectacular Operation Barbarossa shows the World that the Reich can never be defeated. Red pins fan across the map undefeated by snow, ice, blizzards. (Plus bears, Bolsheviks.)

The severity of the Russian winter grows ever more extreme, yet still we learn that the soldiers of the Reich are so close to Moscow that they may see the towers of the Kremlin ahead. The Reich will now stretch across Europe and beyond. Yet when I go to the Café on Sundays Oma is complaining that no potatoes are available, also no flour.

I am increasingly pleading for sleep. My head is colonised by all the people who have gone. They board a bus or a train to go for a walk in the country but they are lost in the forests and never return. They are ripped away by high winds or fall into deep holes in the Streets. The cobbles closing back over the holes so that no one even knows they are taken ~

Dr A continues with his many appointments and Notes and conferences. Yet he does also find time for his Research. He requires Sister Viktorine to check the Case Studies. How should these boys (Fritz, Harro, Ernst, Hellmuth) best be described? He says again and again that he wishes that Dr Frankl was still working in the Ward.

Dr A possesses a draft Paper which Dr Frankl was writing when he departed. It is about Affective Contact but Dr A is unable to untangle what exactly that means. Something about dogs? About language? How we cannot Translate? No doubt Georg is continuing this work in America. Perhaps he has finished that Paper by now. Dr A longs to read it.

Dr Frankl is also in our minds for other reasons. At the Filing Cabinet, Sister Viktorine and Dr Feldner talk of his mother. Her health is poor but friends are making sure she gets food. Sister Viktorine says: Pray that she will not be deported. She will not survive that. Poor Georg, I cannot even write to tell him. How has it come to this?

Sister Viktorine and Dr Feldner also talk of Hansi, Herbert, their parents. How much longer before they receive the yellow postcard ~

Those late days of November are pale, stagnant, fragile. One day I hear raised voices from Dr A's Office. The woman's voice is shrill: I have four other Children. There simply isn't room in the apartment. You have agreed, have you not? Encephalitis. Elisabeth is violent. She attacks the other Children. I cannot cope.

Dr A murmurs his sympathies: Ahem. Indeed most difficult.

(I remember the Files which Dr Gross took from our Ward.)

The voice says: What am I to do? An institution. In these days there are more possibilities. This is something that the new Regime has achieved. Women are not to be burdened.

I hurry out of the kitchen. I do not want to know. Yet I cannot prevent myself from examining the list of the day's appointments. Elisabeth Schreiber. That name. Nonono. It cannot be. Time has become pleated and I am back. Encephalitis. The same name, the same condition.

It is not. The voice is not the same. The woman who emerges from the Office has a clamped mouth and a turkey neck. Not the same Frau Schreiber who is Adolf's mother. I forget about that conversation immediately and do not consider it. How quickly such circumstances have come to seem Normal ~

Three days later I hear Professor Hamburger calling for Dr A. His voice frustrated, bad-tempered. All know that he is having problems with his stomach. An ulcer is suspected. Now he says: Why have my Instructions not been followed? I wrote on the Notes. Where is the name? Yes, Elisabeth Schreiber. My Instructions?

Dr A is tipping over, pulling at his tie: I cannot say, sir. I handed the Notes over.

Sister Viktorine is hurrying down the Corridor, running her hands over her gown to make sure it is not crumpled: Yes, sir. Yes. Your Instructions were quite plain but I could not carry them out. It was not possible.

Not possible? Why?

Am Spiegelgrund is full. We were told that Information by letter recently. Even then, sir, I made sure to telephone. I even asked to talk to Dr Jekelius. He was not available and under no circumstances could the child be admitted. She has been sent to St Josef's Children's Home instead.

Professor Hamburger says: Oh. Full? Really? Yes, they do seem busy. Very well.

With that he is gone, shutting the Door of his Office decisively.

Dr A says: Thank you, Sister Viktorine.

Sister Viktorine comments: At Am Spiegelgrund they do appear to have a large number of cases of pneumonia. I suppose one expects that in a new organisation where Procedures are only now being established. We are so fortunate that we do not have those problems here.

Lips are pressed together, heads wisely nodded ~

In December the Japanese strike with a stealthy offensive at Pearl Harbour. Two days later, Professor Hamburger is once again searching most urgently for Dr A. Eight o'clock at night yet everyone still works. Dr A and Professor Hamburger must speak in the Meeting Room as the light in Professor Hamburger's Office is not working. (What does Otto know of this?)

Professor Hamburger says: Your work at the Public Health Office? A review is currently being carried out into the Children's Homes. Many are not managed in accordance with the New Order. Concern has been expressed about Gugging. Know much about it?

No, sir. No. I do not.

Professor Hamburger saying: A large number of Children within this Hospital are not in school. That is unacceptable. Either the Children must be in school or some other solution must be found. This is the New Policy.

Yes. I am aware – obviously.

Good. Good. A Commission is being set up to investigate. I want you to be part of it. You will be working with our friend Erwin Jekelius, of course. The work needs to move ahead swiftly now. You will be contacted about a Meeting.

Dr A's voice is croaky. He says resources, priorities etcetcetc.

He is willing but if there is anyone else.

No. There is not. There is no one else I can rely upon.

Yes, sir. Yes. I am sorry. Of course, I do understand.

Thank you, Hans. I am extremely grateful for your loyalty. You know I have offered you many opportunities. As I have said before, if you wish to be promoted then you should not hold back from initiatives of this kind.

No. No. I quite understand. A most interesting possibility.

Good. Good. I will explain that you are willing and available. The work involved should not be that great. Not more than a day or two.

Surely we must assess?

No. No. It will all be quite straightforward. A Wartime situation. One must not fall into the temptation of goodness ~

As Christmas comes, the Filing Cabinet becomes most garrulous. Sister Anna has heard things about Am Spiegelgrund. I must listen even if I do not understand. I need to be Properly Informed. *Why is it that if you call Dr Jekelius at Am Spiegelgrund he is not available? Not available later in the day or next week. Not available for some time.*

Sister Anna says that Dr Jekelius has asked the Führer if he can be married to his sister Paula. One assumes he did that only in order that he might be promoted yet further? He has miscalculated. The Führer is displeased. He does not wish to be reminded of his Youth in Vienna. Dr Jekelius is asked to sign an agreement that he will forget the whole matter.

Of course, he will sign the letter. He is loyal to the Reich, as we all are. What does it matter to him for surely he does not care for Paula? He only wanted to be brother-in-law to the Führer as that would surely lead to power and prestige. Now his bid for promotion has failed. He did not understand the mind of the Führer.

Yet now the Story becomes ever stranger. Surely it is not true? It seems that Dr Jekelius has really fallen in love with Paula and he will not forsake her. He has defied the Führer and says that he still wishes to marry her. He will not sign the Paperwork. Has he become mad or is he in love? He was always a Man with a sentimental streak, a liking for the ladies.

Now he has been arrested and is being sent away to the Eastern Front. Dr Feldner says how sad it is that he is gone. *He was a wonderful colleague. He will be much missed.* But the Filing Cabinet says: Better the Devil you know. At least he was easy to steer ~

7.e. The Lights Go Out

That shadowed night in February begins with snow and the Children performing a parrot-house concert with Sister Viktorine playing the piano. Everyone settled down for the night, all put in Order. Dr A has been out all day at a Meeting. He comes to the Ward briefly at five and then goes home for supper. Often, he comes back later in the evening to work on his Research.

Yet now it is already gone eight and he is not back therefore perhaps he will not come tonight? His Father is ill and so he goes to visit with him. He even takes his Files to his Father's apartment in order that he can work there. He often discusses his worries about his Father's health with Sister Viktorine.

I hear the bell ring at the Reception and I see that a messenger is delivering Paperwork. He leaves this Paperwork on Fräulein Eder's desk. I wonder if I should take it to Dr Feldner but then I see Herr Spellbinder gliding silently towards it. I don't wish to be seen observing therefore I go back into the Meeting Room.

Ten minutes later Sister Anna comes in with a File: If Dr A comes back, he must sign these Papers. It must be tonight. The Papers need to be taken to the Public Health Office.

Sister Anna departs for the night. I put the Papers to one side and return to my Matchbox plans, working with pencil and ruler to draw up the exact positions where they must be placed. Adelheid – Keep calm. I am concerned as I do not think that Dr A will return tonight. Should I go and find Sister Viktorine?

My fingers turn the pages of the File. The Papers are headed Gugging Commission. Is that the Meeting that Dr A attended today? A list of Children's names, comments, ticks, crosses. At the foot of the document, I see where Dr A must sign his name. I lay the Papers aside but my itching fingers take them up again. I count the Children on the list. Two hundred and twenty names. Thirty-five crosses.

Taking up a pencil, I write down these figures. Of course, I know that I should never mark any Papers, not even in pencil, yet I perceive powerfully that my life now depends on the inscribing of these numbers. Only this minor act of Writing can keep me tethered, can ensure that I do not wash away entirely or become detached and carried in the wind.

My hands are starting to shiver. I push the Papers away but once again I find myself reaching for them. Adelheid – Do not look. I stand erect, grip my fingers to my throat. *I should not involve myself in matters which I do not understand.* Where is Sister Viktorine? I walk out into the corridor, try not to Think ~

Get out of here. Run. It is not safe. I am back again at the Karl-Marx-Hof. I stand in the allotment gardens, just outside the gates. Soldiers, gun carriages. Wait, wait. The air is split by a terrible crash. Windows blow out, showering glass. The roof rises and then falls, the walls begin to come down, flowing like waterfalls, brick upon brick.

Yet I must not leave the Ward. I must never leave the Ward. Dr Feldner appears and enters the Meeting Room. Then we are in darkness. Darkness as black and heavy as treacle. The fall of this black curtain hits me in the chest and knocks all the breath out of me. Children are screaming.

Dr Feldner: Adelheid. Adelheid. God knows. Fuse. Get the candles.

Dr Feldner's hand pincers my arm. Usually, I would pull away, but now I am glad. Is this the work of Otto the Electrician? *Get the lamps. The cupboard in the kitchen.* I must not think of the File lying on the table. I pull open the Meeting Room Door and smudges of light gleam from the long kitchen windows ~

Calmer now. I know exactly where the lamps will be. My fingers reach and touch, I run my hands along the shelves to find a box of matches. So many Matchboxes and no matches. I have put many-manymany down the side of the plant pot over the years but I cannot get them out of there now.

In the Ward a child is keening. Eventually I manage to light a lamp, then another. I carry one such lamp out into the Corridor as I know that Sister Viktorine will need some illumination in the Ward. A tall figure wavers, suddenly looms close. I know his shape and the way he moves. Dr A says: What in God's name?

I hurry past him with the lamp as the screaming gets louder. Sister Viktorine is comforting a child. A boy called Billy states: We are all going to die.

Sister Viktorine tells him to stop being silly, instructs me to light more lamps. I head back to the kitchen, light another lamp. Dr Feldner: Bloody Spellbinder. Orderly? Disorderly more like. Can't somebody find a railway line for him to blow up ~

Dr Feldner remains in the Meeting Room and I hand him a lamp. Those papers are still on the table. I have not forgotten them. The Papers must be signed. I push them towards Dr Feldner. He puts his lamp down on the table, reads the Note on the front. Turns the pages, lowering his head. Looking and looking. He sees where I pencilled the numbers.

Surely he will lay them aside for he is needed in the Ward? Yet he keeps staring, pulls the lamp closer. The wailing from the Ward is increasing and although his name is called, he does not move. I leave him and go to the Ward, hold the lamp for Sister Viktorine while she instructs Cabbages to climb down from windowsill, talking in a firm and soothing voice.

When Herr Spellbinder is finally discovered he must face the wrath of Dr A: One thing after another in this Ward. How can we do our work when we have broken windows, blocked drains, water pouring through the ceiling? Not to mention the constant stomach complaints which beset some members of staff. How can anyone work with this level of Disorder ~

Dr A stamps back to his Office and organises the Papers for his Research. This he must do employing a lamp since the lights are still not operational. In the Meeting Room, Dr Feldner pushes the Papers towards Sister Viktorine. She is conveying some clean towels through to the Ward. He moves the lamp so that she can read. Dr Feldner saying: The Meeting he was at today.

Really? Sister Viktorine is determined to take no interest.

He points down at the File but she is still focused on the towels. Look, look. Here.

She turns her head away: I must go back to the Ward.

Am Spiegelgrund? Do you know of any who have returned from that place?

Many cases of pneumonia.

She is trying now to leave the room but he has blocked her way.

Sister Viktorine, you are an honest woman. Do you believe?

Sister Viktorine trembles and flaps: All that is finished. There were protests but it has finished. Please, move aside. It is not for us to look at those Papers or question the decisions made. Dr A is a good Man and a Catholic. This is a Catholic Country. It is not the right of Man to decide who lives and dies.

She moves on towards the Door but still he is blocking her way.

Her voice is rising to a shriek as she tries to elbow past Dr Feldner: Dr A Does Not Know. He does not understand. He has always been a Man who misses the obvious Point.

Dr Feldner hastily: How lucky he is. What a luxury not to know ~

Footsteps. That familiar cautious tread. Dr Feldner lays the Papers, straightens them precisely. Sister Viktorine steps through into the kitchen even though she is still taking those well-travelled towels to the Ward. Dr A appears at the Door: Ah Josef, how are you? I hope the power will be restored soon. Is Sister Vik here? I was worrying about Billy.

Sister Viktorine appears from the kitchen, heads with Dr A to the Ward. Otto-Heinrich-Johannes-Kaspar are still lined up on the windowsill as there one finds some gleam of light. Liesl-Anna-Maria-Helene are playing at smackthebaby and bashing the head of a toy bear on the floor. Still the Papers are lying on the desk in the Meeting Room ~

Finally, the Children are pacified. In the Meeting Room, Sister Viktorine and I take care not to acknowledge each other. I grip one Matchbox after another. Plead with the Man on the bike. Balance on a unicycle. Imagine many blades of grass, count each one. Dr Feldner comes in and whispers: We must take these Papers to him.

THE MATCHBOX GIRL

Sister Viktorine: He will not sign.

He will. As you remarked, helpfully he does suffer from Tunnel Vision.

Sister Viktorine: He will not knowingly.

He will. Blind, yes, but never a Fool. Thirty-five out of 220. 185 Children who are not going to Am Spiegelgrund. A small victory perhaps?

Sister Viktorine fixes him with buzzing-wasp fury.

He is determinedly calm: Come, come. You know. If he loses his job someone worse will come. We save lives by being here. I thank God that I have not been called upon to decide.

Sister Viktorine sobs: Josef, Josef. Please. I know nothing of this.

Dr Feldner touches her shoulder tenderly: Of course. You know nothing ~

I step forward and take the Papers. Dr Feldner reacts as though he will prevent me, lifts the Papers out of my hands, then halts, stares at me. Slowly he returns the Papers to my expectant hands. I am the Person for this job because I will not be called upon to discuss anything. It is *an adult matter* and I am too stupid to understand such things.

It is late at night, we are all so fatigued, exhausted. Yet it is my responsibility to manage the Paperwork and I must not fail in my duty. I always take to him the many Papers which must be signed. I keep everything Neat and Correct and show him where to sign. Now Dr A looks up as he perceives me with the File. He studies Sister Anna's Note pinned to the front.

As he does so his elbow pushes against the lamp and it trembles, totters. I catch it, put it back together, hold it in order that it cannot fall again. The glass of this lamp has been cracked and mended so now it does not fit. I hold it closer to ensure that he can see. Time stalls. I wait, wait. From somewhere a gentle dripdripdrip. A tap has not been properly closed.

Wait, wait. Quietly, quietly. Slowly, slowly, it will be done.

Dr A: Ah yes. Yes. He flicks through the Papers hurriedly, nods his head. He identifies his pen and raises it with his left hand. Moves his shoulders, adjusts the cuff of his shirt in order to ensure that no ink may be spilt upon it. Writes in that familiar way, constricted and cumbersome. I know how this is done. Aim a marble under a Door, then disappear.

No Dinosaur will arrive to save us. Those same fingers which so tenderly stroked the head of his own Child on that distant Sunday afternoon. I am most glad that Dr A understands what he must perform, knows that kindness can kill. The signature blotted, the scales tipping alarmingly. He Pretends to be the Bear with such force that he becomes the Bear.

Saying: Leave it here. I shall deliver it. I need the air. A long day.

He sighs then and removes his glasses, briefly holds the bridge of his nose. Here is the choice – do you want to be the bullied Child or the Bully? When I go back to the Meeting Room both Sister Viktorine and Dr Feldner want to verify if the Papers have been signed. They do not have long to wait.

Dr A has finished his work for the night. Dr Feldner moves to the Door of the Meeting Room, watches Dr A put the Papers into his briefcase. Dr A then calls goodnight, highlights some last-minute concerns in relation to the Children. Felix is clearly Distressed and confused. Lena also. Will Sister Viktorine be sure to check?

Also, Dr A is disappointed to note that a Child today was found to have lice. That Child has been dealt with but, of course, the infestation can spread. We must make sure that the whole Ward is disinfected. We cannot take the risk. Cases of typhus in the General Hospital. I stand at the Door of the Meeting Room and watch him go.

Might he stumble and fall, or appear slightly stooped, or disheartened? That is not what I detect. He is lively as ever in retrieving his coat and hat, steps out towards the Door, does not look back. Who are the saved? Heartless Children. What might they have to offer ~

After My Death: A Letter to Kanner

We return now to Dr Georg Frankl and Anni Weiss-Frankl in that same wartime winter but in a most different place. Their Mystery Tour of America now bringing them to Rochester which is recorded to be near New York but which is actually six hours from that City and even further from Washington. Yet still Fräulein Weiss comes to visit.

At least it is closer than Nebraska but still a rented apartment. Yet they are so lucky, very lucky. They have enjoyed the long weekend together. Despite the Incident at the rabbi's house. Before that they had both slept late and relished a long walk through this City. This rented apartment is warm, spacious and central.

They will not be staying, of course. The job isn't permanent. As always, Georg's colleagues are friendly, welcoming. But one grows tired of always being the recipients of sympathy, all the poor new arrivals driven out of Europe. *You get along well enough as long as you don't challenge or appear overly knowledgeable.*

That's what Anni thinks when she is feeling bitter, and she is increasingly bitter now. She misses the darkness of Vienna, its brutality and bitter humour. Life there was large. She paces through the apartment. What other domestic jobs will she need to complete before she leaves? Georg is in his study reading. After that Incident, she has tried not to disturb him ~

Yet there is still the question of that letter from Kanner, Georg's former boss in Baltimore. It came on Thursday and now it's Tuesday and she is departing tomorrow. It isn't the first letter, not by a long way. Also, there have been telegrams. It is not surprising that Kanner is now frustrated. How difficult can it be to answer a letter?

She calls: Georg. The letter? Have you written it?

She hears no response from Georg hence she goes into the study. He is sitting by the window. Outside she sees the edges of buildings, brightened by snow. Behind the sky is blue grey, the evening drawing down its blinds. She feels a pang for him then. He has aged. They do not talk about Europe, about the War. She should be solicitous, offer him coffee or cake.

She says: The letter. Have you done it?

He looks up, shakes his head, returns to his reading: There's time.

You need to do it before my train. We won't want to deal with it in the morning.

She doesn't like to nag but why does he create situations where she needs to nag?

He says: Yes. Yes. I'll get onto it in a minute.

What will you say?

Anni, please. Don't worry. I'll sort it out.

She leaves the room, clears up in the kitchen, clattering and stamping more than is necessary. She enters the study again, places herself at the desk and positions Paper in the typewriter. She is waiting for him to ask what she is doing but he doesn't look up.

She says: I'll write it for you. Wouldn't that be simplest?

He is still looking at his book: What will you say?

She stares out through the window, considers. There are a few things she would like to say to Kanner. More than a few.

She needs to keep this polite: Well. Obviously, you need to say that you are sending him your finished article for his Guest-Edited Edition of *The Nervous Child*. You could also tell him that you wrote this article about Affective Contact way back in Vienna, that you have been hoping to get it published now for quite a while.

Anni adjusts the Paper and carbon in the typewriter: Obviously, Kanner would not understand that difficulty. Because he publishes articles all the time – but still you should tell him. Then you could point out that Harms has had the article now for eighteen months and that you had specifically asked that it would be published last summer.

Anni's hands hover above the typewriter keys: After that you must say obsequious things about how grateful you are for the honour of having your Paper published in the edition that he is editing etcetcetc. You also note his assurances that *your* article will be published before *his* – meaning *towards the front of the journal*.

Georg is shaking his head: Anni, Anni. Come on. You know it isn't like that.

Georg is on his feet now and he moves to the desk, takes out Kanner's letter which he had put away when it first arrived. He also pulls out the File in which he keeps his correspondence with the journal and with Kanner. He placed the telegrams in there. Anni knows that he has done all of that with the genuine intention of making a response soon.

She says: It is like that.

No. Kanner has great respect for my work. He always takes great trouble to tell me so.

Yes, exactly. That's my Point and you know it. The moment he saw your work on Affective Contact, he wanted it for himself.

Anni, come on. That's a big accusation to make.

Then why has the publication been delayed so long? Your Paper was going to be published in its own right. That was the original deal. Now it is going to be published with his Paper, which strangely has more or less the same title. Your Paper – *Language and Affective Contact*. His Paper, which incidentally he has not yet written – *Autistic Disturbances of Affective Contact*. Can you spot a pattern?

Anni, Anni. Come on.

He isn't going to acknowledge the Fact that you led the Research. He is a Man on The Way Up and your ideas are useful to him. He wants a big discovery, something new and eye-catching and you are providing him with it. You won't even admit that you are Angry. If you weren't Angry, you would have replied to him by now. I know you.

Georg is stirred now: Well, maybe. Maybe not. What does it matter? You know the situation. I owe Kanner. He has been tireless in his efforts to find work for me – and for you. In this Country, people have to make their career. They sell their ideas. Make themselves popular. Yes, he is ambitious. But I'm in no position to complain.

You are just going to let this happen?

I'm going to return the edited version of the article with Appropriate comments.

Anni says: Let me do it. Otherwise, this is Vienna all over again. Like Dr A.

Anni, Anni.

Stop playing the humble Jew. It was always clear that He worked for You.

Well, maybe. Who cares? What I do know is that he was always a thorough Man, conscientious. I am sure that he is carrying that work on – and doing it well.

Yes. Probably hasn't even noticed there's a War ~

She has gone too far. Much too far. Even she can recognise that her accusations are not entirely fair. Georg is staring out of the window as though some Horror Story is unfolding out on the blue-blurred rooftops. For a moment, she wonders if he might cry. He puts the correspondence back in the File, turns away. Says: I need fresh air. I'm going for a walk.

Washing Up. She'll do that. She runs water and eases her engagement ring off, places it in a saucer on the counter. Usually, she does this without even thinking but now she looks at that ring. Georg's mother's ring. She doesn't keep it clean, the stones have no glitter. She picks up a dishcloth. The sobs break on her so suddenly that she has to catch hold of the sink.

She sits down, tries to remain composed. That Vienna apartment. The view of the tree tops above the stone balcony. The lace, the ornaments, the fading photographs, the dried flowers. She must not think of Georg bidding farewell. She must not reflect. That other woman. In the house of the rabbi. Her anguished wailing. *Where are they? Where are those people?*

In the basement Sitting Room of that shabby house the woman's hands are flailing, she is tearing at the skin on her wrists. Desperate screams are trapped in her clamped mouth. Georg has assured her he will help. Could she just answer a few questions? The rabbi hovers anxiously. He should perhaps have called for a regular Doctor but Anni understands why this has to be kept private.

The woman's husband is Angry: She needs to be locked away, she keeps saying these things. Crying and wailing. Talking garbage.

Georg is firm, comforting. Anni stays with him while he calms the woman. She admires him then. Admires him absolutely and completely. He is compassionate and gentle and listens deeply, watches, takes in every detail. Is the woman really in a Dangerous mental state? Is this a normal level of Distress? What now is a normal level of Distress?

The woman starts talking about the Reports she has read and again she is saying: Where are all these people? They cannot just disappear.

Anni desires to walk away and take Georg with her. So many people are waiting for news. What are they even doing in the house of the rabbi? They never went to a synagogue in Vienna. How have they accidentally become Jewish when they always despised all that backward-thinking superstition?

The woman says: They are all Dead. I won't see them again.

Georg stresses that no one can be sure. It is not clear. Anni wishes that the woman was mad, that they could call for an ambulance and have her taken away. All she needs is someone to Lie to her. Georg does it admirably. He also speaks compassionately to the husband: The times are most Distressing. Sources of Information which may be unreliable.

Soon the Man is holding his wife solicitously by the hand. Best to get home, a quiet afternoon. George suggests music or reading. Perhaps a walk. Things like that can help. Afterwards the rabbi is most grateful. How very lucky they are to have Georg in their community now. This too is for the good. One must press on, keep faith ~

What faith? That woman. She was the reason why Georg had now hurried out. Not the letter. For God's sake, what does the letter matter? How could she have decided to argue about a ridiculous Paper when she knew Georg was upset? She pushes the ring back onto her finger and struggles into her coat. She needs to find him.

Outside the snow falls in fine but insistent flakes, the wind is capricious and flecked with ice. She doesn't know this City. She attempts to take the route that they took that morning. She should have put on boots. Where is he? Where is he? As she heads down the Main Street, she peers into the windows of bars. He isn't the type of Man who frequents bars.

Would he have gone to his Office at the Hospital? If this was Vienna, then he might. But not here. He doesn't know the place or the people. Where then might he be? She wanders into a ramshackle, low-built part of town, a no-place thrown up randomly, with no particular Order or purpose. Everything obscured now by the relentless snow.

Sprawling parking lots, patches of narrow wooden houses, nameless one-storey cement structures. The city has become a junkyard in a rising blizzard and she no longer knows where she is. One street after another. Left, right, left. Eventually she finds her way back towards the apartment. She sees him, striding towards her: Anni, Anni, where have you been?

Looking for you.

I hope you've got the key.

Oh yes. She realises now that he had gone out without a key and has probably been standing on the doorstep waiting for the last half hour or more. She feels silly and suspects that he does too. They are too old for this kind of Performance. He takes the key from her and opens the downstairs Door to the apartment block.

She says: You are utterly soaked.

You're not much better.

How kind he is not to point out that he is drenched because he's been waiting. Instead, he puts out his hand, and she takes it, and they head up the stairs together. Once they are inside the flat, he walks over to the window.

She says: Georg, take off your coat. Now.

He doesn't move but remains by the window, still staring out.

Georg?

He looks at her with steady eyes: My mother is Dead ~

The keening woman is here. Her shrieking, seething voice is thrashing through the apartment, making the innocent carpets and bland floral curtains gasp. *Where are they? Where are they? Where are all those people?* No one can stop the shrieking woman now. Not just one woman. So many of them. All across Europe, all across America.

Howling and tearing their hair. Anni wants to scream as well. She wants to join her voice to all those others and never stop moaning and yelling and wailing. But nonono. She is not going to surrender to this. She grabs hold of the collar of Georg's sodden coat, shakes him. He seems like a Man in a trance. She needs to wake him.

Says: That woman. Just remember what you said to her.

Anni, Anni, please. Don't you understand? It is better. A seventy-year-old woman with a heart condition. What chance would she stand? I prefer to know. I prefer to be sure. I can't explain but I am totally sure. She is Dead. I felt it. In September one day. I should have told you. I knew. It is better. Better to know.

Georg is stable again now, says: Come on. You need a hot bath, some supper. Then we can deal with that letter.

She replying: The damn letter. I'm so sorry. How could I ~

Later he will send her a carbon copy of the letter. She is surprised to find that he admits that the publication of the Paper will mark *an official termination of a peculiar and rather difficult period of my Life*. He also records that the challenges of translating the Paper had been considerable. He doesn't desire to be part of that work now.

His interest in the Autistic Psychopaths is at an end ~

8.a. A Bowl of Soup

That night of obscurity and signed Paperwork. I never thought about it. Those thirty-five were Paper Children. We had never known them and one must not make a Fuss about every Small Thing. The only change was felt in our attitude to Dr A. We should have hated him yet secretly we were impressed. We knew to what extent he would sacrifice himself to protect us.

Sister Viktorine talked more about God. Dr Feldner seemed quite unchanged – although later I would revise this view. He did stress to Sister Viktorine that we must all show our support for Dr A. We must assist him with his Research. Sister Viktorine did nod in agreement. Although, in truth, I don't think that anyone now continued to be truly engaged by that Research.

After all, who could be interested in such obscure Questions during a time of War? Yet we all required that Dr A continue in his position. The Research matters to Dr A and hence it must matter to all in the Ward ~

Everyone is anxious of what news may arrive from the Front. I open the Atlas and look at the place names. We go to the Votiv Kino. Leningrad is still under siege. The Führer is bitterly Angry due to the destruction of Essen and Lübeck. Later there is muffled talk of the Baedeker Raids. Soon the British pigs will know what it is to have your most precious towns destroyed.

We walk to the Rathaus where they post the lists of the Missing and Dead. Every day I look for Adolf but I never see his name. In early September, bombs are dropped on the outskirts of our City by

Soviet planes. They have flown 2,000 miles to reach us. We are meant to be the air raid shelter of the Reich. But now?

If the Soviets can reach us then the Allies will do the same. Yet they would not bomb the Old Centre of the City. All agree on that. Sister Viktorine tells Dr Feldner that Frau Frankl has received the yellow postcard (deported). So many are dying at the Front that it is hard to keep having Appropriate reaction to such loss.

Sister Viktorine says that at least dear Georg and Anni are safe in America. Dr Feldner's briefcase is full of potatoes to give to any Jews he might meet. Sister Viktorine becomes spectral and skeletal. All like pencil drawings half rubbed out. Yet the Performance continues. What is Rumour and what is Real?

I am still plagued by those strange dreams of the day and night. White birds high above the city transform into enemy planes. Here are the lists and here is my name. Margarete is crunching marbles between her teeth. The wires in my head report on everything I think. We live in a Fairground Hall of Mirrors. I cannot see clearly because I stand too close ~

No one really cares any more if I wander through the City. Such joy to return to my old haunts. I see Adolf's mother once. She is dancing in a bar with Obersturmführer Teichmann in his immaculate braided uniform and his soft black leather boots. I watch her jubilant and ravishing under the flickering lights of a vast mirrored chandelier held by a gossamer thread.

When I am at the Café, Oma and Frau Winkler are locked together in suppressed outrage. Hildegarde is not married and yet has an Unwanted Pregnancy. The Father of her child is a most lower-class Prussian who works in the Office of the Blockleiter (now referred to as Blockwart, meaning snoop). Hildegarde has been reassured that she must have no Fear.

The Reich needs those of racially pure blood, such as the Winkler family, to have Children. This is a woman's duty. She will be paid and she will have a place to live. Fräulein Winkler is tearful and spits with condensed Anger, saying: *This* is what we have come to.

Oma fails to suppress her glee: Your husband. What does he say?

Fräulein Winkler sighs: Apparently, the senior men in the Reich often have more than one family. But we are Catholics. What Future is there for her now?

Oma pours the Schnapps, arranges her face into an Appropriate expression of regret: A young woman of such promise. What a Tragedy. Our Adelheid was never considered to be worth much. Yet she has always understood the Value of her Virtue ~

One late evening I am leaving the Hospital to perform a visit to Oma. I descend the short hill towards Lazarettgasse. Ahead of me I perceive a Man leaning against the stone parapet which edges the slope. It is not uncommon to see people who are struggling on this slope – perhaps on crutches or being wheeled awkwardly in cumbersome bath chairs.

Yet this Man is alone and he is leaning against the parapet with his back turned. Is he just resting or is he a sick Person who is trying to make his way to the Hospital? Since I am a person of some status, I must at least try to identify what this Man might need. I approach him but he does not turn. Perhaps he does not hear my footsteps.

I notice then blood on the stone flags. I am praying now that a group of Nurses might come past and apprehend the situation but this part of the slope is deserted. No ambulances are turning into the Hospital. The Man twists round. It is the light, surely, only a trick of the light. I can see his eyes quite precisely – bright and sharp and crying with pain.

The rest of his face. This cannot be. The lower part of his face is a metal mask. It is from under this mask that the blood is dripping. I back away. Why is half of his face made of metal? I have seen many diverse soldiers suffering with crutches, stumps, hollow spaces where eyes should be, hair cut away from head wounds, spit running from damaged mouths.

But this metal face. I cannot bear the sight. I turn and run down the slope and I am deeply ashamed of myself as I should have gone to the Hospital to find assistance. Yet I cannot, I cannot. All the time after I can see his face. It appears at night, hovers over me, the blood seeping through and dripping onto the paving stones ~

THE MATCHBOX GIRL

During all these long months, Dr A is still trying to complete his Research. *How can we find a psychological method that does full justice to the singularity of the living personality?* In trying to find Answers to such Questions, he has become faded and fragile. Like Lynceus in Faust. *Born to see, appointed to watch, sworn to the Tower.*

Perhaps he is similar to me with my Matchbox Collection? I want everything complete, perfect, beautifully Organised. Yet that is Not Really what I desire. That aim could have been achieved many years ago. What then would I do if my work was finished? Would the World really then be Perfect?

I know in my depths that the World will never arrive at this Point. However, I do not want to have those thoughts. I want to believe that all can be cleanorganisedlogical. I must keep rearrangingplanningpolishing. Is it the same for Dr A? Does he also delay finishing so that he avoids a Meeting with the patched and ragged reality of our World ~

Dr A pays particular attention to a boy called Fritz who is most annoying, grabbing everything, destroying, throwing water in the Corridors or tossing books out of the windows. Dr A does see all this and yet he remains certain that Fritz is Intelligent. He makes a special application to the Authorities for a Personal tutor for Fritz.

Fritz must perform everything to a strict timetable. The same activity at the same time every day. Soon Dr A is most pleased as Fritz is able to pass an examination which means that he could return to school. Yet this does not materialise, for without the Tutor to help him Fritz can do nothing (which Dr A does not record in his Notes).

Often Dr A calls Sister Viktorine to him and asks her questions about the other Children. *Stuttering, obsessive questioning, grinning all the time?* What does this reveal? What might Dr Frankl have thought? Often, as she ponders, Sister Viktorine turns her head slightly, as though trying to apprehend sounds from some Distant Place.

Sister Viktorine explains that Dr Frankl observed that there are different kinds of language. Dogs cannot speak and yet they read the emotional content of what is being said. Could it be that different people understand different languages? This is not a question of Empathy. No. That was not Georg Frankl's view.

Dr Frankl felt that some Children communicate in a different language. If only we could Translate, Interpret. Learn that Language. Also, these various conditions are the same but also different. There is a series perhaps, or a scale. Is this useful? Can Dr A see how this might relate to his own work?

Dr A says that this does indeed relate to his Little Professors. In particular to the four Children who appear in his Thesis (Fritz, Harro, Ernst, Hellmuth). He finds them both noble and ridiculous. Their gazes empty and yet they have a fullness of attention. Fritz's gaze is entirely peripheral. He seems absent from his own Life. Even his voice comes from afar.

Is that voice not haunting – with its strange lengthening and sing-song rhythms? Harro also. His conversation is almost ridiculously adult and he comments on himself with such accuracy. Such penetrating insight and self-observation. So incredibly well informed not despite his distance from society but Because Of It.

Questionsquestionsquestions. *Who is accepted into the Group and why? Are these Children simply existing in the Wrong Era? If we were living in the Enlightenment might they not be considered Normal?* Also, more mundane Questions. *Why does a Child flap his hands through the light or obsessively watch a leaf blowing in the wind* ~

One day I observe Dr A watching most closely a certain Child who is still at the lunch table long after the others have left. Sister Viktorine stands with Dr A and they examine together. The child (a most tiresome and lumpen boy) sits slumped at the table and runs his spoon through his soup again and again.

Sister Viktorine and Dr A conclude that he is watching the globules of fat which swim on the surface of the soup. As he moves the spoon, the globules break up and spread randomly across the bowl. Then, when the spoon has been removed, they organise themselves and gather again towards the centre of that receptacle.

Why would he watch this? Why does the Child become most exceedingly upset when they try to persuade him away? Later Sister Viktorine and Dr A discuss this at wearisome length. Is it the movement which attracts him? The patterns? Dr A says: He is also most interested in looking at the stars. Is there a link between these two different interests?

Sister Viktorine: Perhaps. Perhaps.

Dr A shakes his head: The boy clearly has considerable powers of concentration but his interests are quite useless. The stars, yes. Bowls of soup. No. Perhaps if he paid the same level of attention to insects he might become a biologist? Yet his attention is always caught and held by the entirely trivial.

Sister Viktorine tips her head to one side: Is the soup trivial?

Soup? Trivial? Yes, of course. Isn't it?

Except he is seeing *something*. Do you not notice? His pleasure and engagement? He might merely be enjoying the *soupness* of the soup. Yet I do not think so. I believe the globules of fat have some important Life and Meaning for him. Sadly, we are unable to follow him to the place where we might share that Fascination ~

One day in the September of that slyly turning year, I enter the Office of Dr A. The room has needed cleaning for some time but usually he forbids me to enter. *No one must disturb the Papers.* Now he sits at his Desk, looking like a Man whose mind has flown away. Eyes staring, hair electrocuted, shirt escaping. He must submit the first draft of his Thesis soon.

Says: I can't find the reference. I need to mention it in a footnote.

I apprehend Sister Viktorine behind me: You have worked too long. You cannot go on like this. Come, you need to rest for a while. Come through into the Meeting Room and let me make you some coffee. Meanwhile, Adelheid can clean in here.

(Coffee now only a dreadful brew of malt and chicory.)

He says: Oh nonono. Everything is in Order.

This is most clearly Not True. Sister Viktorine steers him out of the room, managing him as though he is one of the more difficult Children. I position Papers which are on the same subject all together and group them in Files. I organise books in alphabetical Order. Dr A returns and I think that he is about to launch into violent complaint.

Instead, he looks around him, nods, begins to smile, saying: Thank you, thank you. Maybe you could also type up a list of what I have here ~

Thus I become involved in the writing of his Thesis just as I once helped with the Maps and Plans for the Motorised Mothering Advice Service. Every reference in his Paper must be checked againagainagain. The book title in full, the page number, the exact sentence. Sister Viktorine also helps when Dr A says: This sentence? Does this express our experience accurately?

Sister Viktorine always takes this work extremely seriously and tells me repeatedly what a clever Man Dr A is, how his work is ground-breaking, pioneering, how it may change all current thinking about certain personality types. Dr Feldner is less flattering: Well, if all else fails, he could market it as a cure for insomnia.

Sister Viktorine is not pleased by such levity.

Dr Feldner also saying: Of course, he overstates the idea of Autistic Intelligence. But then one never gets anywhere by telling a simple Story, and in this current climate his certainty and enthusiasm might certainly be Useful. When a case has to be made. If only he could put it in a more engaging style ~

When I am alone, I read what Dr A writes. I find it hard to understand. He is on the top floor of a house but there are no stairs. He may not have *considered how his words are being received*. He seems to say that there are many different kinds of Cabbage Children. Also, in the process of Categorisation something is always lost.

Can one write a Thesis stating what is entirely obvious? Perhaps Sister Viktorine does partly agree for she says: Really what he is trying to do is impossible. I myself could never write it down. I can only help the Children.

Then she goes off on a (whispered) Tram Track about Herr Lazar: In his time one would never have used the Children in this way. Reducing them simply to examples which might prove a certain theory. However, in this New Order everything must be systematised. Surely the work still exists whether one can demonstrate it or not ~

8.b. A Thesis is Completed

Late autumn. (Is it always autumn now — a permanent sense of fading, ending? The smell of rot and the fiery leaves damp and piled up in the streets.) Yet this particular day I recall — fine and brisk, with the sky cobalt blue, the sun achingly high yet the wind blustery and nervous. Just after lunch, a call comes to Fräulein Eder's phone.

Usually, no private calls come to the telephone at the Hospital. Dr Feldner takes the receiver. His head is tilted, his spine is stooped as he speaks. Through the open window, the yelps of the Children playing catch in the garden below. Sister Viktorine's joyous laughter. Dr Feldner says: Yes, I see. Of course. I shall come now. At four. Yes.

Fräulein Eder is noting what he says, as she always does. Dr Feldner informs Fräulein Eder that he will be leaving early as he has a family visitor coming. He does not need to explain his personal arrangements to Fräulein Eder so why does he say that? Why also does he drink vodka from the kitchen cupboard. One hopes this is not a problem of gambling ~

Two weeks later, on Sunday after Mass, I walk down to the Rathaus to look at the lists of the fallen. Rain is coming down in waves of grey which fall like curtains across our City. A woman is shouting, hitting those who try to calm her. This is unseemly behaviour. People should not weep excessively. These soldiers have died for the Fatherland.

The woman is asking — *Where is he? My son, my son. Where is his body? Will he now be carried home? Where will he find his rest?* My eyes search for Adolf's name as they have done many times before. I like to remember him as he used to be, back in the Days of the Rat

Business. His mother also. As she was in that time. My eyes scan the list again.

Adolf's name is not there but there is a name I know. Right at the top. Karl A. That is the name of our Dr A's brother. Could there be two people with that name? I wonder if Dr A and his family have been informed. The list has only been here two or three hours. Does his Father know? Or his mother?

I think then of the weeping woman. *Where is his body? Where will he find his rest?* The words at the top of the list. *Died for the Fatherland.* Opa and Oma had said, *never again, never again.* I consider the Man whose face is a metal mask. What good is it to knit socks, raise funds, write letters? What can we know of the Horrors ~

I do not expect to see Dr A at work the next day. Surely he will stay at home with his aged parents who must be devastated by this news? Nevertheless, he is at his desk at eight o'clock, just as usual. On the Ward, everyone is aware of his brother's Death. I am not the only one who checks the lists. Yet he says nothing and therefore no one makes any comment.

All we know is that the first draft of his Thesis must be delivered by the end of the week. He also has all of his normal appointments and he will not cancel them, he never does. Increasingly I think of him as he was in the Days of the Maps and compasses. A lone Man high up a mountain, waving a pole but no one sees.

In reality, the Research would have been finished many weeks ago if he did not insist on repeatedly changing what he has written. He returns to me with pages where there is a mistake, or a smudge, so that I can retype. He says (yet again) that he regrets he has not been able to include a case study of a Girl. None fit the pattern he is trying to elaborate.

His Office has once again become piled high with Papers, on every surface and also on the floor are many books, transcripts of speeches, Files, Case Notes. Sometimes he loses a vital reference and I must search for it. All around there are people who should like to express their condolences but they dare not ~

We come to the day preceding that deadline when the Thesis must be delivered. It is eleven at night and I am yawning againagainagain.

The work must be submitted by nine tomorrow. I have retyped the last page for him, he is gathering all the sheets together. The Story of those Little Professors. The ones who are apparently going to become code breakers for the Reich.

All the Case Notes are typed up and added as appendices. I have checked it all numerous times. After the work has been submitted there may be comments and changes. Maybe one more year of effort still to go, but even now Dr A wants to ensure not the smallest mistake. Just as we are finishing, Dr Feldner enters.

We have not seen him for several days. He has been busy at the Military Hospital in Mariahilferstraße and occupied with family matters. His face is grey and saggy, his eyes also droop. His shirt looks dirty and has not been ironed, his shoes are scuffed. He was never a tidy Man but now increasingly resembles a haystack. Many people are similarly dishevelled.

Dr A: Finished. Finally. I never thought I should finish.

Dr Feldner shakes Dr A's hand so vigorously that they both bounce up and down.

Thank you. Thank you. You know that your support means a great deal to me. I am also glad that my Father has lived to see this moment. He never thought that I would achieve much. He found it hard to get over the Death of my younger brother. That brother died extremely young but it was already clear that he would have had far more ability than me.

Why is Dr A talking of his younger brother who died many years ago and not his brother who has just died? Yet still Dr Feldner does say most enthusiastically: Yes, excellent. Excellent. Brilliant work.

Dr A: Is it? I don't know. This work is no longer fashionable. The moment for it has long passed. I doubt anyone will read it. A waste of time, I fear.

Not a waste. Not at all. You are right that it may not reach the required audience at the present time. Doubtless the Americans— (Here Dr A looks worried for no one must mention the Americans.)

Dr Feldner continues: The Research is impeccable. You have documented so much of our thinking about what Autistic Psychopathy actually is. If we do not write these things down, then later some other poor soul will start this work from the beginning again.

Dr A says: Thank you. Of course, we none of us entirely believe in these Categories but we must move with the Times. Primarily I have written down what you and others have known for years. I wish I had been able to send it to our former colleagues. It would have been a better Paper. Yet I have dear Sister Viktorine and she is, of course, a genius ~

Sister Viktorine blushes deeply and offers her congratulations. Finally saying that she has heard of his brother's Death and that she is deeply sorry. All of the nursing staff offer their sincere condolences. Dr A looks at her as though he hasn't seen her. I realise then how tired he is. I know what it is like when your Brain stops working through having tried too long.

Eventually Dr A nods his head: Indeed, a great Tragedy. Ahem. A Brave Man.

Yet even as he does speak these words Dr A is peering down at the Papers on the desk, staring at something in a footnote: Adelheid. I am not sure. Here. Should it read *for in this particular case* or should it read *in the light of this particular case?*

I know I have checked. Yet I kneel on the floor, search through a pile of books, check the reference for him again. Once that is done, he goes into the Ward in order to ascertain that all is quiet there. Sister Viktorine congratulates him again and they discuss Dr A's Father. What a blessing it is that he has lived to see this moment.

It does not surprise me that Dr A should consider this so important. During a Filing Cabinet conversation, I once heard Sister Viktorine say — *Really one wonders if he is defending this Thesis to the University or to his Father.*

Dr Feldner also offers his congratulations once again: I suppose we all have our different forms of Resistance.

Dr A is puzzled: Sorry. I am not sure I understand your Point ~

8.c. A U-Boat You Can See

A Young Man strides into the Ward accompanying Dr Feldner. I know him immediately even though he is standing with his back to me. My stomach turns like a fairground wheel. Every muscle is plucked and vibrating. An Eagle is eating my heart. I go to the kitchen and sit down. Radio Anna tells me the news most merrily. *Dr Feldner's Nephew has come to stay.*

I suck in a breath, nod my head enthusiastically. Pretendpretend-pretend. I hear a voice summoning me. I must start to serve the breakfast. As I pass through the Corridor, carrying a tray, I am so busy trying not look at Hansi that I nearly stumble. Hansi looks straight through me, as though he has no idea who I am.

He still has that sideways look, that slight sneer, yet evasive now rather than combative. When I reach the Nursery, Sister Viktorine is impatient. *Where have you been, Adelheid? Please don't dawdle.* Sister Viktorine knows. Her eyes are straining and staring as she tries not to cry. *They will come for you.* How can Dr Feldner be such a Fool?

Why is he behaving as though this is all quite normal? (Yet, of course, he has always been a man who likes to gamble. Does he think this is all some foolish prank?) Pretending now far too hard, worse than Der Chef. He marches Hansi into the Nursery with extreme enthusiasm, talks him through some of the Case Notes.

He even uses the name. Hansi. How can he? So many people in this Hospital, in this District of Vienna, know. Sister Viktorine is grinding her jaw in silent fury. Her only hope is that Dr A will intervene. Of course, we all know multitudes are hidden in the Cellars and Attics of our City. The name for such people is U-boats.

Perhaps Dr Feldner has not understood.

The Point Of A U-Boat Is That You Cannot See It ~

When Dr A arrives, he seems not aware: Chap in the School Room? Nephew?

Dr Feldner: Yes. Hoping to study Medicine.

Hansi appears, heading towards the kitchen.

Ah. Here he is. Let me introduce you.

Hansi comes forward to shake hands with Dr A.

Dr Feldner: I'm trying to provide him with some experience so that he is fully ready to start his training. There is such a need for Doctors now. It is important that he qualifies as soon as possible so that he may Serve the Fatherland.

Ah yes. Quite right.

Many people at the Hospital have been most helpful.

Have they? Excellent. Excellent.

The Office Door of Professor Hamburger opens. Horrible-inevitabledesperate. That Man himself steps out followed by Dr Gross. No larger disaster can now occur. The Matchbox man on a unicycle has crashed into a wall. Outside the Ward, the staircase is swaying, shifting, the steps knocking against each other. Teeth rattling in a shaken head.

Professor Hamburger says: Ah, good morning, gentlemen. Good morning.

Dr A and Dr Feldner say Good Morning.

Professor Hamburger continuing: Ah yes. Heinrich and I have just been discussing certain matters. Yes. Yes. Such excellent work going on in this Ward, we are always agreed.

Dr Feldner: Thank you. Thank you.

The pot plants are gasping and trembling. I think of all the Matches I have pushed down the side of those pots. Often I imagine how they might ignite. Surely that must happen now? Everyone is on the point of telling, of saying the Wrong Thing. How can the energy of so much Pretending be contained?

May I introduce my Nephew?

Dr Feldner tells the Story again of his Nephew. Hansi nods and smiles enthusiastically. I look at my shoes and remember Frau

Altmann and Sister Maria. If one Person falls from a window, why do you need two stretchers? A grey arm is sticking out of a laundry basket. The cards are being cut, shuffled, dealt. I press one finger against another againagainagain.

Dr Feldner says that just yesterday Hansi attended Professor Hamburger's lecture and found it most interesting, extremely helpful. Professor Hamburger shakes Hansi warmly by the hand: Excellent. Excellent. Young Man, you are entering the finest profession in the World at a time when the possibilities are limitless.

Turning to Dr Gross: Do you not agree, Heinrich? Limitless ~

Later that night Hansi is explaining to Dr Feldner how he has sprinkled pepper into the false paybook he is carrying. Dr Feldner has given the paybook to Hansi so that he might use it as identification if he is apprehended. Clearly, this Strategy is quite mad. Who would be convinced? Yet Hansi considers the pepper an excellent trick. It will give him time to run away and he is now buoyed up with hope. Dr Feldner agrees that this is an Excellent Idea.

Soon the Filing Cabinet conversations smoulder and flare. Dr Feldner whispering as he Pretends to shuffle through various drawers: I am simply fulfilling a promise. The Bustins are my closest friends, Hansi is family to me. He is a boy with a true heart although that is not always clear to see. I wanted to take Herbert also but they decided against that. Might be safer with them.

Shuffling, hissing, Sister Viktorine's voice: I know that the camps are harsh but that family can have a Life there. Things will change. They will come back.

I am not sure. I have heard things.

Sister Viktorine's voice is pleading: Dr A will find out. You place him in Danger.

Not at all. He never sees what is going on. I am sure we are Safe.

This Dr Feldner says with great certainty. Yet is he Correct? How can we know? It certainly appears that Dr A has no understanding. This is the Problem now. His Performance has become so impeccable that one cannot be sure. Usually, one would see a nod or a raised eyebrow but one sees nothing at all. Like me he has become a blank.

Sister Viktorine: Let me speak to those I know. Something can be arranged.

The clank of a Filing Cabinet drawer slamming, another opens.

Sister Viktorine again: You do have Papers for him?

No. I did find a fake paybook for him. Sprinkled with pepper. Might do some good? But, anyway, I am beyond suspicion. The good Dr Feldner, veteran of the Italian campaign. Known by all in this part of Vienna, working at the Military Hospital. No one will Question.

Dr Feldner's voice is iron now. Sister Viktorine will not persuade him. Yet still she insists: It only takes one Person. So many know.

I will get him a gun. That might help.

Sister Viktorine: A gun? A gun? This is a Hospital.

Dr Feldner says most loudly: Ah, here. File put away in the Wrong place. Again.

Whispers: Boredom. That's the main Problem. Thank God for the Opera. At least my Aunt can always get tickets.

The Opera?

Yes. It is safe there. Perhaps even the Nazis know that you don't arrest people at the Opera? Dear Sister Vik. Do not Distress yourself. Come, come. I have been called upon to decide. I do not have a Cellar. Or an Attic ~

8.d. The Danger of Small Lies

I retreat to the Café as often as I can in these dormant winter days. It is perhaps safer than the Hospital. Oma continues to whisper – *Surely the situation cannot get worse*. She has been saying this since 1934 so no one listens now. Yet Oma is indeed in difficulties because a few months ago Lukas went on a Hiking Holiday with the Polish POW in the kitchen.

This is tainting the German Blood Line through fraternising with Foreign Enemies. Lukas has been taken away to a camp (lucky not to swing) and so also has the Pole. Therefore, Oma has lost two members of her staff and, although the Ministry of Labour have sent her two new POWs (both wearing P for Polish), neither speaks German, neither can cook.

As a result, Peter comes to the Café. He is the Nephew of Lukas and he should properly be at School but he has been cast out apparently due to his extreme stupidity. Thus, one cannot have much hope for his skills in becoming a Waiter. Yet it paradoxically turns out he is extremely deft and effective.

However, I also do observe that the Atlas is back on the shelf and the rug in the hall of the Apartment is kept most straight. This suggesting that the Café is once again a post box for the Socialists. How does this come to be since Oma is a member of the Party and *doesn't want any Trouble etcetcetc?* This Question being soon swept away in larger Confusions ~

Sunday in mid-December and all around me the City feels tense, itchy, liable to shatter. A crystalline frost coats the city and I imagine what I might see from the roof terrace – all of our palaces, tree-lined avenues, parks and ornamental gardens returned to some mysterious essence of themselves.

How beautiful this would be if I could see, but I am helping at the Café. Oma's knee is most swollen and agonising and consequently she buzzes in constant irritation. In particular, she lets us know that she has not Forgiven *that witch Frau Winkler*. She could have intervened to keep Lukas here, explained the essential nature of his work.

Herr Wächter, the Stationer, is also aiding Oma. (Once a most comfortably upholstered man, he is now nothing more than a bundle of kindling.) Despite his assistance, Oma remains collapsed on a chair in the kitchen saying: After all I have done for that woman. Dear Hildegarde only got what she deserves. Cheap little madam.

A Customer complains about the soup. (Indeed, much of our food now does taste as though it has had close relations with chemical laboratories.) No wine is served and the worst is the weak Unity Beer which only the most thirsty can stomach. All seems about as bad as it can ever be until that cursed moment when Dr Feldner enters with his Nephew.

They take a seat near the window and remove their coats. I had hoped to leave behind this problem at the Hospital. Oma bustles in from the kitchen, registers Dr Feldner and his Nephew, and her lips squeeze tight. As the Nephew has no ration cards, she should not serve him but she will.

No sooner has Oma taken the Order, than with a grim inevitability the bell at the Door clangs and three SS men walk in. FritzFritzFritz hang up their coats and holsters and seat themselves near the bar. More of their compatriots arrive. Oma hurries to serve them. Peter nods at one of the customers who hurriedly drains his coffee, stands up and makes for the Door.

I know how this goes. Peter needs to move the Atlas. He needs to straighten the rug in the hall. Yet he cannot do either because he will be too prominent. Herr Wächter has already gone through into the apartment to deal with the rug. Caretaker Frau Vogt moving towards the newspapers. She picks one up as though intending to read it.

Yet I perceive that the Atlas is concealed underneath it. What is she doing? She is a convinced Nazi. Now in some carefully choreographed but invisible dance routine, she is heading out through the

Door which leads to her Office. How many people exist in the land of Raised Eyebrows and Small Nods. I cannot understand ~

When I serve Dr Feldner, he greets me merrily and is most grateful. His Nephew nods obsequiously, thanks me as well. Soon I am back in the kitchen. The lunchtime rush is upon us and hence I stand at the bar, waiting to see if there are extra drinks needed, ready to clear the tables as the guests begin to leave. I do not have any time to think. Pourcarrywipeclear.

The grinding minutes pass. I urge them on. A table of ten prepares to leave. Soon Dr Feldner is signalling for his bill. He thanks me, pays, then he and his Nephew stand up ready to leave. I observe as they tarry by the Door, donning their outer garments and scarves. I recall the days when coat racks, pockets and Matchboxes were my obsession.

I notice how Dr Feldner moves so that his back is between the coat rack and FritzFritzFritz. He thinks to conceal what he is doing. Surely not stealing Matchboxes? As ever, he is Pretending with great enthusiasm but little credibility. Thus I see quite clearly as he lifts a gun from a holster and places it inside his own coat. *A gun. A gun.*

Dr Feldner turns theatrically, waves a fond farewell to us all. Then steers his Nephew out of the Door, both of them striding off down the misty street. Surely soon the fireworks will ignite. It is not possible one steals a gun and this will pass unnoticed. FritzFritzFritz are wiping our good pork gravy from their chins but soon they will leave and then ~

The furore begins. *My gun, my gun. I left it here.* Oma is spooning braised red cabbage onto a plate and peers across at me. She has no choice but to offer assistance. Fritz is searching the coat rack repeatedly in rising desperation. The holster is here but where is the gun? Someone in this Café must know. Herr Wächter is offering to play a part in the search.

Some of the customers have taken up books and newspapers and are beginning to read. Others are intently watching globules of fat swimming in their soup. Two young ladies are trundling towards the Door but Fritz is now blocking the exit. *A gun has been stolen. Do you know anything about it?* Another Fritz is speaking to Oma.

Oma saying: The coat rack is rather close to the Door. Lunch hour so busy. Maybe more than thirty people have passed through that Door. That large table. Left a few moments ago.

FritzFritzFritz continue to interrogate the ladies. No one may leave until the gun is found. The ladies protest that they are due back at work. One Fritz looks at them with naked dislike and some considerable lust. He would like to strip off their clothes but, although one has fulsome breasts, they are not so sizeable that you might squeeze a gun between them.

A gun is also far too bulky for anyone to conceal in their private parts. Therefore how can he detain them? Reluctantly, he allows them to depart. Oma and Herr Wächter investigate the coat rack once again and make a grand Performance of searching behind curtains and along the tops of the panelling where the gun could not possibly be.

Both saying: I am sorry to say. A Person could enter. Without being seen.

In her role of respectable Café owner, concerned by a grievous and dangerous theft, Oma is utterly convincing. Peter is searched most vigorously but as he is *clearly simple* therefore what could he know? I am instructed to remove my apron and this I hurriedly do. But what is the Point? Nothing will be discovered ~

Surely this painful difficulty will now be at an end. One need not worry, all will be well and we are safe. So I think. Yet, as so often before, I have reckoned without the highly erratic nature of Dr Feldner who appears now at the Door of the Café. Stares around at the Fritzes in apparent great surprise: Is there a problem? May I come in?

The Fritzes would like to say no but they have no right to bar him from entering. Speaking to Oma from his lofty and shambling height he says with a flamboyant display of amiable confidence: Came back for a coffee. Need one after that excellent lunch.

Oma has turned into a bundle of hair pins, teeth and spiky bones. Her lipstick-lined mouth is frozen in a deathly smile. She would like to draw a gun herself and shoot him Dead. Nevertheless, she waves him towards the table which he previously occupied. I am to serve the coffee. Dr Feldner is perhaps gambling to avoid the trap of telling a Small Lie.

THE MATCHBOX GIRL

Meanwhile, FritzFritzFritz are persisting in their search. They operate with vast and thorough seriousness but, in truth, there are not now so many crevices to probe. All the pockets of the coats at the Door have already been emptied. Two shopping bags are tipped out. A gentleman is commanded to remove a voluminous jacket.

FritzFritzFritz push behind the bar but no gun could be secreted behind the stacked plates and glasses. I serve Dr Feldner his coffee and he unfurls a newspaper, straightening the pages punctiliously. His coat hangs open and the hem is surely pulled down low. The gun? He can't. It isn't possible. FritzFritzFritz have now reached him in their search.

You were here earlier?

Yes. Of course. You saw me.

You were not alone?

No. I was with my Nephew who is a medical student. He is to attend a lecture this afternoon and, being relatively new to this City, he did not know the route. I walked with him to the end of the street so that I could point out the way.

Take off your coat. Turn out your pockets.

I watch in Horror as the coat comes off. Dr Feldner appears to be trying to keep the annoyance from his face. He will not produce the gun from his sagging pockets. I know that. Yet still I am assailed with exactly that ghastly image. He empties out all his pockets. No gun. He waves his hand as though a magic trick has been performed.

Says with serious concern: What is it you are looking for ~

Dr Feldner persists in displaying the contents of his pockets. He is not as convincing as Oma but perhaps enthusiasm can be as effective as skill? That lady is now rallying and has clearly determined that a more robust response is needed. Evidently the gun was taken by someone who sneaked in at the Door and vanished immediately.

Most unfortunate. Indeed. Indeed. Oma now will shift that offending coat rack further from the Door in order to ensure that common thieves cannot steal her customers' possessions. Herr Wächter insists that those who need to return to work must now be released. They have been questioned and searched and clearly know nothing.

Fritz turns back to Dr Feldner: What is the name of your Nephew?

Oma will not allow this: Please, please. I must protest. I have known Dr Feldner for many years. He served on the Italian Front and he works both at the Vienna Children's Hospital and at the Military Hospital in Mariahilferstraße tirelessly tending the War-wounded.

FritzFritzFritz do not seem to be the most Intelligent of men. They are now running out of steam and becoming disconcerted. Their searches have produced no evidence at all. Doubtless they will be in Trouble for, of course, Fritz should never have left the gun in such a vulnerable spot.

Shaking their heads, and insulting Oma for her *slack standards of security*, they prepare to move on. She must not allow any criminal element into her Café etcetcetc. Soon they are evaporating out of the Door looking decidedly cowed. Others also leave, no one speaks. Everyone is glad to be exiting unscathed ~

Dr Feldner is now one of the few customers remaining. I behold him most carefully as he drains his coffee, places his hat fastidiously on his head. I question myself again – how many people are acting against the Reich? (This I should not consider yet I cannot desist.) I had supposed that he and Sister Viktorine, Sisters Anna and Elena were part of this most select club.

The Evidence is clear. There are manymanymany. Otherwise, Hansi would have been arrested one hundred times already. Even the ghastly Frau Vogt who is surely an absolute Nazi. Adelheid – Do not ruminate. Dr Feldner requests the bill and Oma bangs it down on the table while giving him a piercing look as corrosive as a bucket of bleach ~

8.e. Professor Hamburger Considers His Legacy

Dr A and Professor Hamburger are ensconced in the Reception Corridor. Professor Hamburger has lent his Office to colleagues from the Public Health Office. Rooms are being repainted after a minor fire. Professor Hamburger stares at the piles of Paperwork, grimaces, shifts in his chair. His stomach ulcer is plaguing him again and yet he cannot rest.

So much to be done. How is the Children's Hospital to be reorganised now that there are so few staff available? Every day Doctors are being called to the Front. Dr A himself has been asked to attend training sessions in case he is called up. Of course, Professor Hamburger will ensure that does not happen.

Saying now: You've heard the news from the Front?

Yes, sir. I have. Wonderful.

Yes. Just the final push. Soon we may look forward to Peace and an opportunity for all people, right across Europe and beyond, to enjoy the many benefits of the Reich. A great Future awaits, do you not think?

Dr A: Oh yes. Undoubtedly.

Enjoy the Opera last night?

Oh yes. I did, sir. Very much. Excellent.

Yes. Truly patriotic. It was always the Führer's greatest wish that Vienna should remain the Cultural Capital of Europe. Once the War is over, there will be no end to what might be achieved. Excellent work at Steinhof and Am Spiegelgrund. A Collection of fascinating samples is being assembled which will provide many Answers. You know of this?

No. I had not heard.

Yes. Yes. One continues to look forward to a time when ill health will no longer exist. We have made great strides. Are we not lucky to have lived in such extraordinary Times?

Most certainly.

Professor Hamburger shakes his head regretfully: Sadly, not everyone is of the same view. Complaints are made, investigations threatened. We explain that medical experiments are only ever carried out on those Unworthy of Life. People understand nothing of how essential this is for our Research. In particular to my work in relation to rickets.

Professor Hamburger winces in ulcer pain again then continues: Many have no thought for people such as myself who must make the difficult decisions which enable our work to go forward. Do they not see the importance of our search for a tuberculosis vaccine?

I am sure, sir, that your work is much appreciated.

Thank you, Hans. I know your Goodness. I myself have always agreed with Goethe – *I prefer injustice to disorder*. It is a great comfort that a Person such as yourself understands. We were most appreciative of your work on the Gugging Commission. Sadly, that is hardly the end of such matters. I have mentioned your name ~

In addition to the threat of more special tasks for Professor Hamburger, Dr A soon faces two new difficulties. First, his Father has suffered a seizure and is unable to rise from his bed. The wife of Dr A nurses him and Sister Viktorine offers support. Yet Dr and Frau A have five Children and how can they also take care of an invalid?

Dr A makes no comment on these challenges. Much worse is the news of his Thesis. It has been returned with comments. This is the normal practice but the comments do not please Dr A. He is heard to be fizzing and steaming with much annoyance. *The work has been Misunderstood. The individuals who have commented are not serious People etcetcetc.*

Why do they continually emphasise Gemüt (soul and community spirit) and Empathy? Neither is his work describing some foreign process which attacks the patient. It is an outgrowth of the patient's disposition. An Autistic Psychopath is the Human Being who is most fundamentally himself. He cannot be anything but original and spontaneous. He is uninhibited by the collective social will.

THE MATCHBOX GIRL

We have never seen Dr A so unsettled and Dr Feldner and Sister Viktorine are obliged to conduct a significant reorganisation of the Files. Dr Feldner saying how *the situation must be managed*. Dr A must be kept in his job *at any cost*. All must offer their support in the matter of the Thesis so that *all continues just as it is* ~

Sister Viktorine is once again labouring with Dr A in his study late at night. Also, Dr Feldner. I am called upon to retype parts of the Thesis. Dr Feldner saying againagainagain. It is not the ideas themselves. Of course not. It is simply the way they are *presented and framed*. One needs perhaps to show more precisely how this work fits with the Will to Reconstruction.

While this rewriting is in progress, the news of Dr A's Father becomes increasingly dire. He surely cannot recover. Meanwhile Dr A continuing to Pretend that he is entirely unaffected by any of these matters. Yet his Performance becoming increasingly jittery, edged with hysteria, ragged and frayed. Veering between strict and tearful.

A night comes when he seems close to collapse. He speaks again of Georg Frankl. This being a theme to which he does often return yet only when he knows that he cannot be overheard. Sister Viktorine saying with great certainty: Georg will come back to our City. I know that he will. It is only a question of time ~

Sister Viktorine continues to offer her thoughts while also saying: Of course, I really cannot understand the Science. One must have a great respect for those who can. Yet I do sometimes have my doubts because Doctors are operating on the inside of the body, even on the Brain.

Dr A agrees that Doctors do perform such work.

Sister Viktorine continuing: Yet even those Doctors have never seen a soul. Also, they cannot say what is the difference between a Person who is Dead and one who is Alive. A Person dies, something has gone – but what? The idea of the soul is old-fashioned. Yet still the question remains. How does one study something which has no material existence ~

The tenor of the City remains hushed, subdued, watchful. The Streets run with water and low mists congregate over the roofs and spires. No one now is speaking. Everyone is waiting but we none of us know what it is we might expect. We go to the locations where they start now to construct flak towers which will be used to shoot down any who might try to bomb our City.

Our Children are edgy, excitable. They play at interrogation and slap each other in the face if no answer is given. They talk of the Murder Box and Dr Gross (The Scythe or The Grim Reaper). He might come at any time and therefore the Children spend many hours oiling their hair, positioning their ties correctly, ensuring no crease appears on their clothes.

Willy reads from a new textbook for the study of Maths. *An idiot in an institution costs around four Reichsmarks a year. How much would it cost if he had to be cared for in that place for forty years?* Meanwhile, all are hungry. The food we have is less and less. The Children complain of Danube Soup (so called because it is blue).

Willy jokes that the bread is sliced so thin you can see right through to Paris. Once I would have complained of gristly meat. Now even a brief suck on a hairy rind of bacon is a luxury we cannot imagine. Everything tastes of smoke and chemicals and when worms appear in the potato soup some Children are pleased to eat them.

These same tiresome striplings are endlessly jumping off the windowsills, imitating the screeching wail and vertiginous dive of a Stuka Attack. (*Bombs, bombs on Eng-e-land.*) One particular boy passes hours on the Roof Terrace (obsessed by planes, talks about them until our ears drop off). We cannot explain to him that if he sees an Enemy Plane then he must not shout or point ~

One night in February, I am in the Bunk Room. I am aware of the fact that Herr Spellbinder is listening to the Black Radio. I hear hissing, shuffling. Information is being whispered from one Person to another. Herr Spellbinder is talking excitedly. Everyone is telling him to keep his voice down. He repeats again and again: Stalingrad Has Fallen.

Everyone is gasping. *We will kill ourselves rather than submit to the Bolshevik Beasts. How can they hold them back? If only Hitler would sue for Peace. It was never our War. The Allies will come to our aid. Why would they? What mercy would they show? If it brings an end to War, then I'm happy to have the Communists here. We want Peace, any Peace.*

An official bulletin confirms this appalling news and a day of mourning is announced. An edict announces that all the bars and nightclubs in the Inner City must close. Many shops also close at this time and carry notices in the window which state that they are now shut for the duration. Our City is gripped by a deep grief and depression.

Still there are some that do not accept. They are certain that although the City of Stalingrad appears to have fallen, this is a tactical retreat. Our cunning generals are leading the Russians into a trap. I know this is not True and yet also (illogically) I do believe – because I must. Does anyone ever pray for the Defeat of their own Country ~

8.f. The Return of Our Führer

You may ask yourself – how did people continue with their everyday jobs and even find enjoyment in their Life when they knew, or they half knew, or they suspected? Perhaps my Opa provides the Answer. One of his many criticisms against the Viennese (who he loved dearly) was that they are, at heart, a split-minded race.

Yet my Conclusion is that this is not a disorder of the Viennese but an essential characteristic of all Human Life. This is how one stays Alive. Is it not the Case that finally, although we talk grandly of Truth, yet we find ourselves profoundly grateful for the Human Mind and all its slippery deceits, its ability to forget, confuse, befuddle?

I repeat again that I do not offer this explanation in the hope of Forgiveness, nor do I offer any Justification of all that unfolded. All I can do is marvel at the many crevices, crannies, nooks and byways of the Human Brain and the Confusion in which we live even though we Pretend this is not so ~

I hear Fräulein Eder in the Corridor: *Can I help you? Are you looking for someone?* Sister Viktorine laughs. A merry, gasping laugh. Adolf is here. Sister Viktorine is shaking him by the hand and Dr Feldner also appears to welcome him. Why is he in Vienna? He must be home on leave? Sister Viktorine calls me.

I step out of the kitchen. Adolf is less plump but his uniform is neatly ironed, his hair slicked down. All most Correct. Yet my eyes travel down to his foot and remark that his boot is undone. Sister Viktorine pulls out a chair and he sits down in the manner of one well satisfied by himself. I am told to make hot milk. While I am performing this task, I hear the talk.

Adolf was at Stalingrad and saw the great victory. The Russians may believe that they have achieved something but ohnonono. Soon the Soviets will see. Adolf tells Dr Feldner he is taking the train tonight at ten o'clock from the Südbahnhof. He only came home because his foot was damaged and he was in Hospital for several days.

Sister Viktorine says: Your Mother?

She is very well. She came to see me every day in the Hospital. Of course, she lives now on the Ringstraße. The apartment is magnificent.

This he says but Sister Viktorine and I know. Adolf always has a Story. Yet Sister Viktorine smiles and nods, for Adolf is no longer a naughty boy at the Clinic but a soldier who is fighting for the Fatherland. I carry the cup of hot milk to him. As I move close to him, his eyes search for mine but he moves awkwardly, as though frightened of some damage I might do.

I stare at that boot as I do not want to look at him. He brings the Eastern Front into the Ward. The Stories of soldiers eating rats, of rotting bodies, of men frozen in snow and ice, of piles of dead horses heaped up beside woodland tracks. His face is those snow fields, those blizzards. His eyes are tunnels. He moves like a puppet, both loose and jerky.

I feel his eyes searching for mine. I must look at him even if I do not desire to do that. Our eyes connect and he crumbles, shudders, starts to weep, his shoulders judder, his hands are knotted. The sound is terrible – a deep, strangulated, wrenching cry. Sister Viktorine and Dr Feldner glance at each other, wagging their heads.

Sister Viktorine sits down next to Adolf, attempts to capture his hand. (I hear a Door shutting extremely softly. Hansi leaving the Ward by the back stairs. He is right to get away. No one in uniform can be trusted. No one can be trusted at all, not even Adolf.) He now saying: No. No. Quite all right. Just my foot.

Dr Feldner becomes efficient: Your foot. Of course. I can imagine. Most painful. Let me take a look. The dressing may be too tight.

Sister Viktorine and Dr Feldner position his boot on a chair and ease it off. Their voices join together, repeating the words – *The Kaiser-Franz-Josef-Spital. Yes, of course. Yes. Were you in the Hospital long?* Dr Feldner suggests that the dressing is insufficiently robust and will chafe inside the boot.

Sister Viktorine: Should I go over to the General Hospital?

No need. We have a podiatrist here. Always said we might need one ~

Sister Viktorine argues that the Office of Dr Böckler is locked but Dr Feldner is not to be discouraged. He tells Fräulein Eder that she has been working for much too long. She appears most depleted and pallid, she really must retire for the day. Fräulein Eder knows that this is all a Performance but she will not dispute with Dr Feldner.

Soon she is bundled out of the Door, Sister Viktorine calling a cheerful goodnight. Dr Feldner then seizes the key and heads for Dr Böckler's Office, returns within minutes with specialist bandages and also with pills. Sister Viktorine goes out into the Corridor to meet him, saying: What will Dr Böckler say?

He won't realise. Those supplies haven't been touched in years. I'm not even sure the Man is a Doctor. Anyway, many drugs are going missing from Hospitals.

Dr Feldner sets out to remake the dressing on Adolf's foot but I have seen the wound and it appears mostly healed. Sister Viktorine and Dr Feldner are whispering in the Corridor again. Sister Viktorine saying: Surely they did not discharge him from Hospital?

Oh yes. They send them back. Men who don't even know their own names.

Sister Viktorine suggests more hot milk but Adolf declines.

Dr Feldner is brisk: Get yourself warm. Let the foot recover.

Adolf nods decisively but then sobs again.

Dr Feldner says: Your mother? Should we call her ~

This seems a most Logical suggestion. Yet Adolf is suddenly so fired with Anger that surely he will leap from the chair and hit someone, or break the Ward into pieces. Instead, he fixes Dr Feldner with Angry eyes: I don't want to see my mother again. Do you understand?

Once more, he starts to weep. Sister Viktorine retires into the Corridor with Dr Feldner saying: He can't board that train. He needs rest. Surely, Josef, if you make representations?

I have tried in many other cases. It never works.

THE MATCHBOX GIRL

Adolf has wiped his eyes and seems now to return to the World. He is pulling his boot back on and packing into his kit bag the bread which Sister Viktorine has cut for him. He speaks but his eyes wander: I cannot stay here. The train leaves at ten.

His voice croaks and his eyes roll again: I am very good at my job.

Again, he weeps uncontrollably. Dr Feldner commands me to get the vodka. He pours out a generous measure and places it in front of Adolf. Then he looks over at me and he pours three more glasses, drinks, passes a glass to me and also Sister Viktorine. Despite spending my early years in a world of drinkers, I have seldom tasted alcohol before but I relish the burn in my throat.

Dr Feldner says to Adolf most briskly: Now, come, come. Drink that down and you'll feel much better. Sister Viktorine, please go and get some morphine.

Sister Viktorine gives him a disapproving stare but he nods his head.

Adolf says: They killed them all. There were forty and they killed them all. Just blew them up. Limbs blown all about. I only got out because I was the end of the line. The last.

Dr Feldner says: No need to think of that now. You are a hero. The Fatherland needs you. You do an excellent job. Have they not told you so? Have another drink.

Sister Viktorine returns with an enamel dish. On it lies a syringe.

Surely not with drink? Dr Feldner takes hold of Adolf's arm and the needle goes in. He pours another glass: Come on now. Drink up. This is the cost of building a New World. We know that you will never give up. None of this defeatist talk.

The injection performs its task immediately. Adolf's cheeks are flushed, his spine straight. He adjusts his jacket, rubs his hands together.

Dr Feldner: We are all so proud of you. Foot better now?

Adolf is unsteady but determined to hold himself erect.

Time to be off. We are all relying on you.

Adolf looks as though he might weep again. Dr Feldner suddenly starts up singing the Horst-Wessel-song, his voice booming. (Flag high, ranks closed.) Saying then: Sing, sing.

Sister Viktorine sings. She cannot refuse. Adolf puts his cap on, smiles, starts to sing as well. Sister Viktorine is helping him with his coat. Dr Feldner continues to encourage him with a desperate performance of enthusiasm. (The streets free for the brown battalions etcetcetc.)

Dr Feldner pulls me aside: You must go to the station with him.

I try to pull away but he grips my arm tight, saying: Adolf, you will be seen off at the station by one of the most beautiful young girls in Vienna. (Singing: The streets free for the stormtroopers etcetcetc.)

Sister Viktorine says: An excellent idea. Adelheid, you can borrow Fräulein Eder's fur coat. That will look smart. If she was here, she would offer it to you. She is so fond of you.

Sister Viktorine has seized the coat and is offering it to me. I sense Adolf look up at me. I do not want to regard him but again his eyes pull at mine. For a moment he is the boy with the hair oil and the cologne, with the scarves and the Rats. The Führer of the Ward and the pride of his glamorous mother. He wants me to believe in him just as I always did.

He doesn't move his eyes from me but he reaches down to the kit bag on the floor and from there he takes out an envelope and says: Sorry. I forgot. I should have given these to you straightaway. I found them for you specially ~

This is the people we once were. The Questions of Life are simple, the pleasures easily had. Of course, the envelope contains Matchboxes. Twelve. All Matchboxes of the Reich. I am not so much interested in the Matchboxes themselves but in that silent Language which now returns, which we both speak. The moments in those long-ago Cafés when the whole space cleared.

Matchboxes falling from the sky like rain, dashing across the sky like shooting stars. Dr Feldner and Sister Viktorine are laughing merrily now. Dr Feldner has joined me in laying the Matchboxes out, saying: Even a professional phillumenist would surely envy this? Don't you think so, Adelheid?

So it is that Sister Viktorine ushers me into Fräulein Eder's coat. I will become one of those women at the station who waves goodbye to a husband or lover. Dr Feldner is singing the Horst-Wessel-song again. More drink is poured. Adolf isn't limping now. Dr Feldner pulls me close: Ten o'clock. Make sure he boards that train ~

THE MATCHBOX GIRL

The Südbahnhof is damp, crowded, filled by an electric hustle of collapsing umbrellas and hurrying feet. Steam rises from the breath of a hundred mouths. People jostle and push. Some are singing. This building is low, flat, newly built. Although one wall is all glass yet all is thick with smog. Voices echoing everywhere. Adolf steers me towards an Information board.

Luggage is pushed past us on trolleys. We hurry past cigarette kiosks and newspaper stands. Above us a flat-faced and utilitarian clock ticks away the relentless and inscrutable minutes. A Man with a loudhailer announces a platform change. A Young Man in uniform slaps Adolf on the back and Adolf greets him heartily.

I know that Adolf is becoming uncertain. Yet still, he smiles at the Young Man and introduces me. The Young Man gives Adolf an approving nod. A band is playing now, three young men with trombones. We stand on the platform where Adolf's train will depart. Kit bags are piled around us. The carriage stands ready but the Doors are closed.

I look at the other young women around me. Many are gripping handkerchiefs and looking as though they might cry. Mothers are here too. Also aunts. Swarms of them. Auntsgrandmotherssisters. Adolf should not take notice of these women. He must not look at them. I must *create a Distraction* – but how?

Adolf says: My mother was going to come to the station. You know she's very well. Very comfortably established.

He must not cry. No one must see. The train is starting now, the engine roaring, steam billowing, a whoosh of sooty air, people are pushing and shoving. Adolf says: That Nazi. He's fucking her and she's loving it. Bloody pregnant again. More dirty little bastards crawling around the floor.

Adelheid – Do not listen. Focus on the train.

He saying: Telling me she loves me when that bastard just wants me to return to the Front. Shaking my hand and telling me what a hero I am. Drinking and dining in Vienna. The train is on time. While he lives in comfort in a four-bedroom apartment on the Ringstraße.

What Adolf does not say. Herta. Herta ~

The crowds swirl around us. The trombones toot. People are weeping, cheering, waving, holding onto hats. The crowd carries us towards the Door of the train. The young men are scrambling aboard. People are swinging bags up the iron steps. This is the last carriage of the train. *The last one in the line.* I am his girlfriend in Distress because he is leaving.

None of this is True. I am Distressed but that is because I now perceive. I can see Death on him. He will not return. He will Die if he goes, he will Die if he does not go. Adolf understands this also. He is jabbering about America (huge cars, with fins like great fish) although he knows that other Sudden Startling Truth and yet what can we do? It is not possible.

His eyes roam up and down the platform. I have already assessed the opportunities. This part of the station is not as enclosed as I thought. Along the train lines. It is possible. Yet he must board the train. Without fail. He leans down towards me and whispers. I cannot hear but I know. He is close to me, just as he was in the Days of the Rat Business.

This is our station. Our City and our Futures lie ahead of us like so many open windows and Doors. Years ago we used to come to this station just to look at the Information boards. Dreaming of the places we would go. But now. Now. I know what Adolf wants and it is easily done. I take a few steps away from him and then I stagger.

Back now in those Café Days with the jazz playing, Pretending I am feeling faint so that hands reach out now to support me and I am carried to a bench which is only a few steps away. Sliding away. Lost. My head swimmingswimmingswimming. I Pretend so hard that it is True. Through the knot of my fingers, a glimpse of his bag dropping from his hand.

He dodges, disappears. Around the back of the train. Across to the far platform or out along the tracks. Into the obscuring night. One hundred voices start shouting. Gun shots are fired. Everyone is standing stock still with eyes wide, mouths gaping. Doors of the train are slamming. Shots are fired. Againagainagain.

A woman is sitting beside me, a hand on my shoulder. I gasp as though I am struggling to breathe and this is not all Pretending. The train pulls out, hands waving, fingers outstretched for one last touch. Women weeping, screaming. I'm cold in every corner of my body. Have they shot him? Is he Dead? For a moment steam obscures everything. The train is gone.

The unknown woman beside me leans into me and whispers: Get out of here, run. People will know you were with him. I do not look at her, stand up, stagger away. Then walk most straight and Correct towards the crowd near the station exit. Soldiers are moving through the crowd. The way ahead is narrow as the barrel of a gun.

A soldier is searching a woman's handbag. Another woman tries to dodge through but the collar of her coat is grasped. They will ask me for my Papers. I must not show them. I must not. Adelheid – Get out. Keep your eyes down, push and hurry. Look at no one. I am at the gates and the soldiers are all busy checking other Papers.

I tumble through, carried on by the crowd. No one stops me. Once I am outside the station, I hurry down the road towards a wire fence. A tangle of roads and tram lines. Maintenance works. One may see through to the tracks. Ahead of me are four or five train lines. Soldiers are rushing up and down. *Where? Where?* Hurry away, cross the road.

If I get into the street opposite, I won't be seen. Mistake. Soldiers are coming behind me. I must appear calm. I must thinkthinkthink. I dodge into a Courtyard and wait. More shots. The metallic sounds banging, ricocheting. I must not wait for too long. All around me the rats are running. Those soldiers will search all these shops and alleys and lanes.

I walk out towards the entrance of the Courtyard. Far down the street a Man is down, lying in the road. Soldiers are running towards him. Is that Adolf? It could be. Surely it is? Adelheid – Do not look. Appear to be an innocent girl who is simply walking home from the station. Is he Dead? The body is down flat, pressed against the street, doesn't move.

I am in a narrow backstreet, an area of garages, industrial sheds, warehouses, the back entrances of shops. I hurry back towards the station. Remember to look confident. My eyes move along the Doors of a line of garages. I looklooklook. Study the Evidence. Padlocks on each Door. Except one. The wood there splintered, perhaps newly broken ~

After My Death: Car Problems in Kansas, 1949

I recount for you now events taking place in a time after the War. Sister Viktorine was sure that Dr Frankl would come back to Vienna and I show you now that her instinct in this matter was Correct. He did return and we see him now, striding down the Ringstraße, staring about him at a City so changed that he might hardly find his route.

Rubble, checkpoints, queues. Endless building work which filled the air with dust and soot. Chains of men passing bricks in buckets, clearing the old away, constructing the new. It was 1949. Yet another new World was being created although all anyone wanted was the old. Dr Frankl did not go back to his mother's apartment. He did not even visit that area of the City.

Neither did he visit the apartment where he himself had once lived. Nor contact many old friends. It was better not to know. He had come back to Vienna to visit the Children's Hospital and to talk about the possibility of a job. Walking now up the hill to the Children's Hospital as I did that first morning ~

A few days later he will tell Anni of this trip, that conversation unfolding in distant Kansas in America where he and Anni have now lived for three years. Dr Frankl having now a permanent job in Kansas and this time a proper house. Anni even tending the Garden although she did always hate Gardens. Georg has flown back.

The flight itself seeming like a miracle. That Pan Am could transport him so speedily from Tulln (near Vienna) to New York. Yet the conversation not being relaxed as Anni is leaving soon to go to Hays, this being another place which she has struggled to find on a Map.

The Mothers' Union have invited her to speak and she goes because she is needed.

The talk itself might be useful to the Mothers' Union but Anni tends to find the Questions in the parking lot afterwards to be more revealing. Also, often people write in advance with Questions. She always finds herself reluctantly explaining that in New York or in Chicago there might be Doctors who can help.

Usually the raddled and distressed woman who questions her is a factory worker or a cleaner, a Person who cannot travel, who will have no way of seeking such support. Why is it not possible to do more? *I have tried so hard for him. I have done everything that I can. He is loved, so loved. Why are they telling me he must be placed in an institution?*

A woman has written to her from Hays about her son Brian and the problem of sleep. The letter is incoherent. She hopes it says *sleep* not *sheep*. This is not the Point. She reminds herself to Focus. Before she leaves on this trip she must ask Georg ~

She is saying now: Vienna — very ruined? Of course, they have both seen photographs in the press but it is hard to get an overall impression. Certainly, it seems that whole Streets are missing but is that just in the Centre or does the devastation stretch out into the suburbs?

Georg says: Pretty bad. The Streets everywhere blocked. The bread stale. People carrying water from standpipes. So many windows blown out. There was a shuttle bus. I don't know how I would have got there without.

The Hospital?

In the American Zone, mercifully. That makes travel easier — but the strangest thing. You would never know. Despite it all, despite everything we heard. Just as it always was. The crucifix. Do you remember that crucifix? Well, there it was. On the wall. Can you believe it? That one Sister Vik fixed about fifty times.

Dr Frankl takes a gulp of water, coughs. Describes himself travelling from the Hotel Bristol, walking up those apparently same stairs, through the apparently same Door into the Reception and unbelievably there was Hans in that same Office. So good to see him. So good. Not changed at all. Older maybe, but still the same. Like stepping back in time.

He's expecting you to return to Vienna permanently?

Anni knows that she shouldn't have started this conversation now, not when she has to drive to Hays, two hundred miles west, to give this speech. She must really learn to say no. Often she is not paid for her speeches but always there is so much gratitude.

Georg says: Of course, Hans wants me back. He's always made that plain. And, yes, well, I did enjoy being there again. It felt like home, of course. It is.

Even now. Home?

Yes, yes.

So you – we – will go back?

Georg drinks water, stares down the yellow, dusty garden.

Says: Should we discuss this now? I know you are trying to leave. I'm a little worried about the car. Have you started it recently? It's a long drive.

Yes. I know. But I want to ask.

OK. Yes. Well, it is an excellent position he is offering and it has the benefit of being a known quantity. I know all the upsides and downsides of working for him. It is always good to work with someone who thinks in the same way. I mean, that's always been the difficulty here. The approach is different.

No *schizoids in diapers* in Vienna?

No. Definitely not. Thank God ~

Anni knows Georg doesn't want to engage in another conversation about *schizoids in diapers*. The phrase comes from an article that was published in *Time* Magazine over a year ago now. Georg likes to think that the article was just some Idiot journalist making a Story out of nothing. Anni knows it was not.

The article was about the kind of Children who, in Vienna, would have been known as Autistic Psychopaths. The Donald Ts and the Gottfried Ks. Kanner had been quoted in the article, of course, talking about the Mothers and how they show no feeling for their Children. How this results in Cold Children who show no emotion and are incapable of love.

Anni knows it isn't just one or two journalists. This is what happens when people who really know nothing about psychoanalysis begin to apply it to Children. Several of her colleagues – men and women – support that approach. Children must be sent to institutions, saved from their own Mothers.

Anni says now: I don't like the way things are moving. Is there any place here for your work – or for mine? At least in Vienna, people would understand.

Georg says: I know. A big decision. Anyway, I enjoyed the trip. Hans asked me to lunch – and supper. It was such a pleasure to see Hanna. And the Children. Five Children. Can you imagine? I'm pleased for him. Hans still working all hours. Not easy to be married to him, I'd say. Hanna was longing to see the Family Frankl. She has such fond memories of you.

The Family Frankl. Can you be a family when you are only two? Anni doubts it. Does anyone really have fond memories of her? Wasn't she always considered awkward, tolerated only because she was an old friend of Georg? Now who is she? A woman talking to the Mothers' Union, explaining services which don't exist, for sheep or sleep ~

Anni says: You didn't say *anything*, then? You just talked about the Future.

No. No. I didn't. People are trying to rebuild, to move on. Although, of course, Hans did mention his Thesis. I mean, all that work has been buried. Sorry. Unfortunate phrase. Anyway, I was glad he managed to complete his Thesis. Shouldn't you be leaving? Do you want me to check the car?

No doubt Hans is still making use of your Research and mine?

Georg shakes his head: Anni, Anni. Come on. We've been through this before. Hans and I did all that work together. He thanked me very much for my input and he acknowledged your contribution as well. Anyway, that is all done with now. Ideas move on.

Anni asks: Is that how it would be if we went back? Would we just keep our eyes fixed forward? I mean, every time you shook a Person's hand, wouldn't you wonder?

Georg is firm: No. But then I've never been one for that sort of Question. It was a certain period. It is finished with now. Anyway, I thought you wanted to be gone by 2.30?

She is Angry now. Why doesn't he care?

Hotly she says: You are telling me you never wonder? You never feel inclined to ask people in general – people like Hans – who kept their jobs all through the War?

Georg has set his jaw: No. I don't.

Really? Really?

I really never do. Since you press the Point. Since we are on this subject, I'll tell you why. Because, of course, I look at a Man like Hans and I know. He never had the makings of a hero, did he? Do I think he was a brave Man? No, I don't. But I'm not that Man either, Anni. I left when I could, and I travelled first class, and I had excellent references and contacts and I abandoned my elderly Mother to die in God knows what circumstances.

She wishes now that she had not spoken.

Georg continues: I don't want to talk about heroism. I don't think you should either. All of your family are still with us, aren't they? Scattered, yes. Living in poky flats rather than seven-bedroom mansions. But Alive. You know, that woman, the other day?

Anni raises her eyebrows. Which woman? Women everywhere are crying.

Georg saying: Yes. OK. I know. Anyway, that particular one. You know what her eight-year-old son said? *Mommy, when you lived in Germany were you the guard of a concentration camp?* That's how it is, isn't it? Everyone looks at us, don't they?

Anni knows it is true. She feels it every time she steps out of the house.

Georg saying: They are wondering how we survived. Were we spies? Who did we pay? What job did we take? Whose lives did we sell? I cannot stand up to that judgement and I will not judge others. We were none of us heroes. The heroes are Dead. You know that ~

Anni is crying now and she waits for Georg to apologise but he doesn't. He just stares down at her with fierce eyes. He has always said – *Let's not talk of that, let's look to the Future.* He is right, of course, because suddenly all is hate and blame and even Georg is Angry now and wishes that she would shut up and stop asking so many Questions.

THE MATCHBOX GIRL

The Point he is making is correct. What right do they have to judge? They were only ever fourth- or perhaps fifth-level victims. In the hierarchy of loss, they barely register. Stupidstupidstupid. She should never have started this conversation. She picks up her bag, goes out to the car, yanks open the Door, jumps in and turns the key.

A whine, a thump. She turns the key back, waits, tries again. Whinewhinethump. She pauses, then jams the key round once more. The car rattles and shudders, the noise grating in her head. She looks in the mirror, sees Georg watching. Damn him. Since he had warned her about the car then why did he not insist that they try it earlier?

She lays her head against the wheel and weeps. How can she tell him? How can she say? It must be said – now. She opens the car Door and turns to face him.

Says: Georg. I can't go back. I can't.

Oh. Oh. So now you say it. You've spent the last eleven long years telling me about how much better Vienna is, how we can never integrate in America. Now I'm offered a job in Vienna and I'm ready to go. Now you say ~

She sinks back into the car, tries the ignition again. Should she suggest that he should return and she will stay? After all, what is their marriage? She has merely tagged after him causing Trouble. Shouldn't she set him free in order that he can go back? Or should they both stay, surrender, resign themselves to being endlessly remade like a darned patchwork quilt?

Increasingly, despite herself, she has adapted. She no longer reads this Country as though analysing the exterior signs of a mysterious foreign tribe. She no longer asks herself again and again how she could assimilate in a society so fragmented. No longer asks – to what would I assimilate? Instead, finds herself accepting how over-sized it all is, how opaque.

He says: Get out of the car. I'll see if I can start it.

Damn the bloody car.

She says: No. No. There is no need.

She tries again. It will start, she is sure of that. She jams the key around repeatedly. That awful shrieking, clanking noise. Neighbours are looking out, wondering if they should offer assistance. Of course, Georg is Angry with her. What does it matter now if they go back or not? She is too old now for a high-level job. She never finished her PhD.

What is her legacy? Most women could at least claim to have made a Man's Domestic Life run smoothly. She hasn't even done that. In her work – what? What? She has prevented worse things from happening. She has sorted out sleep, or sheep. Is that what they will say when she has gone? The reality is that no one will say anything. Who writes the History of the people who are not heroes ~

Behind her she hears the back Door of the car open. She turns around to see Georg putting his bags – those same bags from Vienna – on the back seat. She says: What are you doing? You are not coming with me. For God's sake. You just got back. It is two hundred miles.

Come on. Get out and let me do it.

He sits in the driver's seat, turns the key once, then off again. Nothing. Tries again. Nothing. Then with a flick of his wrist, he twists the key again and miraculously the car roars. Bloody treacherous heap of junk.

Georg says: Quick. Get in now. Before it cuts out.

She leaps into the passenger seat and the car lurches forward, the engine raging. Georg pulls out of the gate, swerving across the road, his foot hard on the accelerator. The car shudders and rocks as they speed out of the city. Some strange euphoria overtakes them. Burnt fields surround them, the road ahead barren and straight, far out to the horizon.

Georg says: Maybe time for a new car?

They are both laughing. Whooping, hysterical laughter. They know – this is how you go on, how you live. The road unwinds ahead and you travel – on. The wind and the dust blow into their faces. The smell of petrol fumes mixes with the tang of sun-baked tarmac and parched grass. Sometimes you could love this Country. In being a misfit you start to fit.

Anni says: Thank you. You didn't need to come.

Long journey. I don't want you to get lost on the road ~

9.a. The Distraction of Saucepan Lids

I am most tired now of this Writing. I can no longer give consideration to whether I express myself in a manner that is correct. I recall, of course, that those late wartime days were among the worst our Country has ever known yet I personally was often Content. As the spring comes, Sister Viktorine identifies another job for me.

Dr Feldner and his Nephew are not good at Housekeeping but it is not convenient for them to hire a maid. Would I go to their apartment on Sunday after Mass and put things in Order? The flat is situated in Neubaugasse. I know its exact location as I have walked that street many times before and noted the brass plaque on the Door.

Yet now I take a detour to the Rathaus to see the lists of the Fallen. Adolf has not been mentioned. If a Person is shot as a deserter, then they will not be written down. Yet I do not believe that is what has ensued. The image of that padlock stays in my head.

I have also learnt lessons from the situation in which I live. So much of our World is held in place simply by the power of belief. It is the same for both our Führer Adolf Hitler and dear Dr Josef Feldner. Both in their most different ways believe that if something is Performed with enough conviction then it must be so. Battles can be won when they are lost. People can become Nephews because you decide.

Is this Lying? I no longer care.

Within my mind I keep Adolf alive ~

Today when I arrive at the apartment in Neubaugasse, the Aunt of Dr Feldner has come to visit. I have met her before. She lives in Villach where many of Dr Feldner's family also reside but she comes to Vienna often (problems with her teeth). Dr Feldner's flat is a fine apartment with long windows, double Doors, parquet floors, gilt mirrors, oil paintings.

When Aunt Nina visits she usually sits in the main Sitting Room, where three long windows look down over the street, and listens to music on Dr Feldner's gramophone. Yet today she is arguing with Dr Feldner. I hear them as I wash the kitchen windows. Aunt Nina saying: You can't. Everyone will hear.

From my position in the kitchen, I see that Hansi is with them in the Sitting Room. He is thin as a twig for he and Dr Feldner have been eating nothing but cornmeal for weeks. Dr Feldner now insisting: He needs to practise. The gun won't be any help if he doesn't know how to use it. I myself particularly dislike guns but Hansi is a brave lad.

Aunt Nina is most firm: Go to the Woods.

More Dangerous. If people hear gun shots in the Woods, they will definitely investigate. Here there are already many loud noises. Car exhausts etcetcetc.

Dr Feldner has rigged up a board on the mantelpiece. Several pieces of Paper are affixed to make a target. The board does not appear firmly fixed on the high precipice of the mantelpiece and surely any shot might dislodge it? Also, wall lights decorated with crystals, family photographs, a standing light wearing an elegant petticoat. All are at risk.

Aunt Nina is Right yet I know well that once Dr Feldner has an idea fixed in his head – no matter how wild and unreasonable – that idea cannot be evicted. Aunt Nina perhaps knows this because she wags her head dolefully, takes a novel from her bag and withdraws to the small study at the back of the apartment.

Dr Feldner says: We need to Create a Distraction.

Hansi suggests that a heavy object could be dropped.

Dr Feldner says: Quite Right. That is the approach. Adelheid, can you help us?

I am nervous of the gun – or rather averse to the idea of a gun in the hands of either Hansi or Dr Feldner. Both being the types who might accidentally stumble and shoot themselves. Yet I know immediately how this can be managed so I hurry into the kitchen and return with the heavy lid of a saucepan which I hold up in the air.

Dr Feldner says: Brilliant. Lift it up high and hurl it down ~

The Doorbell rings and Aunt Nina responds. This will be Sister Viktorine. She has brought a basket with her which I think may contain a (sawdust and chemical) cake. Also, she is accompanied by Herr Spellbinder. What is he doing here? He has a joke to tell us: How do you tell an optimist from a pessimist? Pessimists learn Russian. Optimists learn English.

Sister Viktorine shakes her head in disapproval but Dr Feldner enjoys this levity. He points out the target, the saucepan lid. (I personally am dreading such noise yet remind myself I must keep my face quite blank.) Sister Viktorine is not surprisingly seized by mortal dread: Josef, Josef. You cannot possibly.

Why not? No Point Hansi having a gun he cannot use.

You can't.

Really? There is no need to worry. Soon we will have tea but let's just get the target practice sorted out first. Stand here, Hansi. I will raise my arm then drop it. Adelheid, you cast the lid down with some force. Fire as my arm drops. Are we ready?

Aunt Nina has now returned to the main room and both she and Sister Viktorine are staring in fixed terror. Herr Spellbinder is quietly gleeful for he loves such disruption. Hansi is vaguely waving the gun in a manner entirely unconvincing. Dr Feldner elevates his arm, asks if we are ready. I raise the lid far above my head. The arm falls. I stretch my hand still higher and throw the lid down.

The gun cracks with such power that the whole building rocks. The chandelier throws up its arms in an attitude of surrender. A lump of plaster drops from the wall. Sister Viktorine is holding onto her jaw as though worried her teeth might drop out. Aunt Nina is standing with her palms pushed forward as though to quell the ravings of lunatics.

Dr Feldner: Good start. But look, Hansi. You do need to look through the sights. Here. Do you see? Right. Ready again.

Sister Viktorine: Josef, Josef. You can't. Half of the street will know. How many times can a Person reasonably drop a saucepan lid?

There are many clumsy people in the World. Maybe if you are worried you could stand at the window? Keep an eye out.

Sister Viktorine shakes her head in despairing surrender but moves to the window. Dr Feldner raises his arm again, the lid bangs and then the gun. This time Hansi has shot the wall next to the fireplace and a hole is blown in the plaster. A china shepherdess who resides on the mantelpiece is pleading for her Life.

Aunt Nina: Really. Really, Josef. Look at the damage.

Dr Feldner: Well done, Hansi. Definitely getting the hang of it.

Then: Are we ready? Let's try that again ~

Hansi must shoot properly. Otherwise, he could be practising all day and the whole apartment would be blown to dust with no skill improved. I take a pen and a piece of Paper from Dr Feldner's desk. Opa taught me how to use a gun. I peer through the sights then draw for Hansi a tiny diagram of how he must line up the square with the notch below.

Dr Feldner: Marvellous. How wonderfully practical Adelheid is.

Bang, bang. The lid, the gun. The music of the two come together symphonically and Hansi hits the target. Since the target is nearly a yard wide this is not a huge achievement, but Dr Feldner is thrilled and Herr Spellbinder shines with delight. Dr Feldner raises his hand in a vigorous salute. Heil Hansi ~

The Doorbell rings. The palms tremble in their pots. The curtains are shrivelling, the chandelier would like to shuffle away. We look over to Sister Viktorine but she shakes her head. Did she not see this Person who is now arriving? Dr Feldner pushes the gun under a sofa cushion, instructs Aunt Nina to sit on it. Herr Spellbinder opens a newspaper.

Sister Viktorine is pressed against the wall, and crumpled up, as though she might faint, but Dr Feldner is quite calm. He orders Hansi into the bedroom. In that bedroom is a large wardrobe but what good will that be if the apartment is searched? I retreat to the kitchen. For some long moments, we hear nothing.

Dr Feldner opens the apartment Door, his voice booms. *Car exhaust. Ca-a-r ex-haust.* No one enters the flat and the Door closes again. Dr Feldner appears, saying most cheerfully: Neighbour. Lovely old chap. Mercifully hard of hearing and badly confused. Even more so now. Tea ~

I am in the kitchen unpacking the basket but Sister Viktorine says that I am to sit down. Herr Spellbinder will assist. Aunt Nina takes up a record, says to Sister Viktorine: Joseph Schmidt? Did you ever hear him? Before the War? Of course, I cannot listen now. The National Socialist Ladies' League of Villach would not be happy. Josef keeps the record here.

She lowers the needle onto the gramophone and the music swoops and soars. Sister Viktorine and Herr Spellbinder are in the kitchen but I do not know why. I have left everything tidy there. Yet suddenly Sister Viktorine does appear from behind the Door with a cake and lighted candles. I had not known it was anyone's birthday.

Then everyone begins to sing and I do not know to whom they sing. *Happy birthday, dear Adelheid.* I do not know What To Do. It is indeed my birthday in just two days. My twenty-first birthday. Yet it had not occurred to me that anyone would make a celebration. Certainly not an elaborate tea party in this most gracious apartment.

Happy birthday. Happy birthday. Dr Feldner swings me around and kisses me. Sister Viktorine hugs me. Dr Feldner gives me a case for needles which is most carefully embroidered. Not new but most pretty. I will enjoy the softness of the velvet fabric. Hansi gives me two small figures he has carved for which Sister Viktorine has made miniature clothes.

As I receive this gift I notice how his face is changed. The sneer is gone and now his eyes are intense, shadowed, pleading. I see also how he must concentrate all the time to keep his hands from shaking. Tea is poured and Dr Feldner bites into the cake: Delicious. Adelheid was so good with the saucepan lid. Immaculate timing. Schmidt could barely match it.

Hansi is still nursing the gun. For a moment the afternoon hangs still, the teapot in the air, the cake on Dr Feldner's lips, his head inclined towards me. Faces all around like lighted candles. Sister Viktorine smiling and stretching her arms wide as though to embrace me, or perhaps the Whole World. In this most Unsafe of situations, I am Safe. Sister Viktorine: This is the Fortress of Friendship and it will not Fall ~

9.b. The Star of Dr A Is Ever Rising

News arrives of the Death of the father of Dr A. Sister Viktorine is Distressed. It is so hard for the Family. What a lovely Man he was. A Man who was devoted to his son. I am uncertain if her account of him is entirely True. Perhaps Dr A's Father loved his son in the way Oma loves me? Was the Father's pride in his son's achievements a support or a burden?

Sister Viktorine is invited to the Funeral and tells of the tranquil place where he is buried in Hietzing Cemetery. A lovely spot. Just outside the City. Such a Peaceful view, a place where one feels the presence of God in every leaf and branch ~

At the time of this loss, Dr A also does receive good news. No more comments are to be made on his Thesis. It is certain that he will receive his qualification. Once again widespread congratulations are made. Everyone is perhaps relieved that they will not be called upon to aid him further. Dr Feldner's *framing and presentation* has obviously solved the problem.

A feeling comes that maybe all will be well. Perhaps our War is at an end. Yet in allowing this thought to enter our minds, we have perhaps tempted disaster? Just a few weeks later we are told that Sister Elena can no longer work at the Hospital as her mother is unwell. She was not able to say goodbye as she had to leave immediately.

Sister Viktorine tells us this with shaking hands and tears gathering. Are the tears the result of Anger as well as Sadness? We cannot know. So many Lies have been told that, even if you heard the Truth, you would not know. Anyway, we don't have to make a Fuss about every Small Thing. Everyone has learnt what I have always known – silence is best.

Even Dr Feldner does not joke any more ~

All around us we feel the presence of the Dead. Sister Maria. Maybe Adolf. Maybe the Altmanns. A waving grey arm which may only be the sleeve of a shirt. In sleep they appear at the side of my bed. In dreams I follow them endlessly down misty alleyways, or woodland paths. If they turn to face me, their faces are masks of metal edged with blood.

The grave can no longer hold all who should be resting there. The Dead call to me and I yearn to follow them. If I accompany them then I might find some final and essential Peace. The soft fabric of the Meeting Room chair. The waving of leaves on a tree or washing blowing on a line. All the Files Correctly Ordered.

Herr Spellbinder is as silent now as everyone else but we all feel his Anger. Sister Elena often helped to cut his toenails since they regularly become infected. His suppressed and seething hatred is directed particularly at Fräulein Eder. He leaves a Dead Mouse on her desk chair, puts the typewriter ribbon on the stove overnight so that it is dried out.

He smells of alcohol, even early in the morning. During the day, on the Radio we hear that victory is close. Our soldiers are surging through Russia, the Führer has a secret weapon which will soon be unleashed. Yet that is not what Spellbinder says. In the late evenings, he continues to listen to the Black Radio, attempting always to identify place names.

Sister Anna is often with him. She is now the only one left of the three Russian Doll Nurses. She was always the smallest and she once seemed Fragile but now she is Fierce. Together they use pins to plot those place names on the map. Herr Spellbinder wants to show me. *Look, look. Do you not see? The pins are moving now in the wrong direction* ~

During the day, Dr A is often out at Meetings. When that happens, Dr Feldner comes to the Hospital with Hansi who assists Sister Viktorine with the Children. This he likes to do, following her smallest instruction. She in her turn smiling at him constantly and praising his work for she knows how much such small kindness does sustain.

One evening I hear Sister Viktorine whispering about where our dear Sister Elena might be, saying: Even if she has been taken to the camps, she will come back.

Herr Spellbinder: No one is coming back.

It is not true. You should not say so.

Sister Viktorine turns to Dr Feldner for support. Often Dr Feldner would indeed say some words to reassure her but now he says: Herr Spellbinder is right. They are Dead.

Sister Viktorine is Angry: So many people. It would not be possible.

Dr Feldner: I do not accept that the people who bring this news are lying. Resettled in Poland? I do not think so. There used to be letters. There are no letters now. Why?

Silence falls. Sister Viktorine waits for someone to support her. Usually, a Person would say *not possible, traitors repeating Lies and Rumours etcetcetc*. Such Words are repeated like incantations, blessings, spells. One can easily mistake repetition for accuracy. Now no one speaks, and Sister Viktorine departs in distress.

I reflect then on Hansi's family. Of course, Dr Feldner is only looking after Hansi until they return. People are still sending parcels to those camps and surely those parcels are delivered? The wires in my mind are buzzing. I must not think these thoughts. I see an image of myself saluting but I cannot raise my hand. The cards are being shuffled again ~

A week later, Sister Anna and Dr Feldner are working through case notes. The hour is far advanced and everyone else has departed home but Herr Spellbinder continues to stack towels in the laundry cupboard. The Radio is playing and the music of a concert comforts us. The normal transmission is interrupted. Who is positioned near the Radio?

From where I stand, I am unable to observe. A new voice sounds. It is the voice of a Man who says that he is a Catholic priest and he is reporting about babies who are being killed in the Vienna Children's Hospital. Sister Anna and Dr Feldner turn to listen but then Sister Anna says: Turn it off. Turn it off immediately.

Dr Feldner reaches his hand towards the Radio and suddenly the voice is booming, the sound of it filling every particle of air.

Dr Feldner is making a Performance as though the switch on the Radio is malfunctioning. We all hurry to exit that area. We must not be seen listening. The voice is still saying – *The Vienna Children's Hospital*.

Sister Anna attempts to pull the plug from the wall: Switch it off, for God's sake.

Dr A appears at the Door: What are you doing?

He is Angry. More Angry than I have ever seen him.

Dr Feldner: Apologies. The switch seems to be jammed.

Why was anyone ever listening to such a thing?

Dr A is moving towards the Radio as though he might smash it.

Dr Feldner turns to look at him and I wait for calming words. Instead: Why not hear? After all. We do know.

Dr A is snarling like a beaten dog: We do not. In the past, perhaps. Now. Now. It hasn't stopped. They just hide it better ~

Dr A's rage is running out of control: Be quiet. I will not have such talk in this Ward. You know who is responsible for this. Listening to illegal channels on that Radio. You know quite well and so do I. This cannot go on. I should have pursued a much firmer line with that Man before. Where is he? Find him. I must speak to him immediately.

Dr A is translucent as ice, his teeth pressed right together. Hansi appears briefly at the Door. He no longer looks ready to defy the Reich with pepper and a paybook. Instead, he is all stretched muscle and brittle bone, appearing like a Person already Dead. He is calculating whether this is the moment for the gun, whether it is safer to stay or to run. Dr Feldner speaks firmly: Hans. Don't worry, I will find Spellbinder. Go home.

Dr A has not become more stable. He continues to appear as a man en route to the grave, with eyes wild and rolling, body stiff and shuddering: Josef, you must understand. You must see my position. You must know. Professor Hamburger is finding more work for me at the Public Health Office. You understand?

Dr A must be kept in his job at any cost. Yet it is clear now that something inside Dr Feldner is ruptured. He can no longer *steer and frame*. This is no longer some mad and mildly amusing Adventure. Instead, he smiles savagely: Well, good for you, Hans. What a great opportunity. Your star is ever rising ~

9.c. A Dog and a Bucket

Theories of Causation are only so many Children's Toys. However, one still considers, one continues to ask – what was finally the process of our unravelling? Our damnation? Dr Feldner and the Radio or perhaps Fräulein Eder? Or was it Professor Hamburger and his enthusiasm for the career of Dr A? Certainly, all these things did play their role.

One may say with certainty that it became progressively more onerous for us to live. Like a juggler we must catch the flying balls againagainagain. Keep them flowing through the air. A high-wire artist far above the gasping crowd, no rope or net to break our fall. Then the day comes. The balls are fumbled, the foot teeters on the narrow wire.

Professor Hamburger saying to Dr A: Good to see Feldner last night. He has been a stalwart of the Ward. Do you not agree?

Oh yes, sir. I could not manage the Ward without him. Also, Sister Viktorine.

Who? Who?

Sister Viktorine.

Oh yes.

Professor Hamburger then continuing: There was, however, some Trouble last night. I noticed as I was walking away from the Opera. After you had departed. I think that young Nephew of Feldner's did not have his Papers. Of course, I helped to sort the matter out but I did speak firmly to Feldner. Are you all right, Hans ~

The conversation is at an end. Except that in that precise moment a boy shoots out of the Ward, screaming and spinning and ducking.

Sister Viktorine comes after him. The boy bangs a red tin bucket. *Stop, Joachim. Stop.* Sister Viktorine tries to arrest him but he charges into the Reception Area, trips, crashes to the floor, the bucket clattering.

Sister Viktorine: I am so sorry.

The bucket. The boy falling. I am back on the beach, all those many summers ago. We have all joyfully clambered through the fence together. Dr A is there with the pram. Hansi and Herbert hold the tennis rackets. We are all cool and loose, sticky with sun and sand. The dog racing around the beach, the handle of the bucket over its neck. The ball sails over the fence.

Dr A is staring into nowhere, his eyes apparently seeing some abomination ahead of him. Something which has nothing to do with the boy wailing on the floor. For an instant, he seems to have lost all sense of where he currently exists. Yet soon he takes control of himself: I will be leaving in just a minute. Meetings. I won't be back later.

There are no Meetings in his diary ~

What transpired in that moment? Of course, I cannot say. Did Dr A see the Sudden Startling Truth of our situation? Surely not – because he must have always known the true identity of Dr Feldner's Nephew. Yet I do not wish to jump to judgement. For what I had definitely learnt in those Wartime Days is how the Brain does both know and not know.

Dr A having always been a Man who could miss an obvious Point. Yet how might I judge? For I also have suffered deep shock on coming face to face with Information which I did always know. Whatever the Facts of the case, he returns to the Ward later that night. A File has been lost. He paces the Corridor, flexes his fingers, his appearance spectral, desolate.

He appears now like a Man with an electric current pumping through him. As You may well expect, I am washing the plates for a secondthirdfourth time. From behind the Door, Dr A's voice drops to a whisper, a hiss: Josef, I must warn you. Hamburger. The Opera. You must find some other solution.

Last night? It wasn't a problem. It was sorted out.

I do not agree. You must review.

This place is Safe.

The voice of Dr A hisses again: Josef, please. Must I make this specific? You are putting your own Life at risk and the lives of many others.

If there is a problem, you must simply claim that you know nothing.

I would not be believed. For God's sake, Josef.

Hans, I'm trying to save a Life.

One Life? What vanity. We have many Children under our care. Many people are employed in this Hospital. I say again – it will not be believed that others did not know.

You will betray me?

No. Of course not. Never.

Hans, Hans. You should never have become friends with me.

Too late for that, Josef. Much too late. I can only tell you. I have Children.

I also. Hansi is my family ~

9.d. We Are Cast Adrift

Three weeks later I walk into the Meeting Room early in the morning and find that the walls have become detached from the building, the roof is swaying and creaking. The tall cupboards and even the velvet chair tip and shift. The sky looms close and accusing at the bursting windows. Sister Viktorine in tears. She is always weeping but this is different.

She saying: Why must he? Why?

Her voice is strangled. She may be crying but she is also Angry. I lay down the tray I am carrying and move towards the Door. My head is unmoored and sailing away and so I hang on tightly to the Door frame although it is treacherously unstable. Is this the moment? Are we now lost? What is the means of this derailment?

Dr Feldner says: He must Serve.

Sister Viktorine speaks in desperation: Who will replace him? How will we continue?

A replacement will be found.

Sister Viktorine: I always thought that he would do his best for us. We have persisted through so many dire obstacles together. He has protected us. He is serving here.

They need Doctors at the Front. This is his Patriotic Duty.

Sister Viktorine: I cannot continue. Our work depends on him.

You must. No choice. The Children need us. He will return.

Why now? Why is he doing this?

Dr Feldner: Excuse me. I need to look for those Files.

They both move towards the Filing Cabinets. I go through into the kitchen and find a chair. I must place my head on my knees and take long sucking breaths. Dr Feldner whispers: I may have pushed him. I have been intemperate and hasty. I have said things. My situation.

The risk he takes is no greater than the risk everyone is taking.

Dr Feldner: No. That is not right. He is closer to Hamburger. He is entirely dependent on him. Anyway, he has done what he can. He is in many ways an exceptional man. But now his Father has died. He has finished his Research.

For him that was all it was? Just Research?

Dr Feldner says: Listen. Listen. You and I have come to know him well over the years. He is a good Man, a good Doctor and someone who is seriously striving to find Answers. But he is not strong and we cannot afford a weak link. The Man knows his own limits.

A few minutes later I see Sister Viktorine enter the Meeting Room. She wipes her eyes and picks up her clipboard. She does not look back as she steps into the corridor. Her head is erect. Soon I hear her organising the morning lessons. I continue with my work but I am deeply shaken and rattled. I want to get away from here. I am not Safe. He has betrayed us.

As the news ricochets around the Ward, everyone is gripped by the same piercing anxieties. Sister Maria and Sister Elena? Who might be next? What of Fräulein Eder who would gladly see any of us arrested? Will I stay at the Hospital if Dr A is not present ~

An announcement is made. The day arrives when Dr A is departing. We stand in line. Professor Hamburger makes a speech telling us of the great service that Dr A has performed for the Reich. Now Dr A makes an even greater sacrifice. In this hour of great need, he is going to Serve at the Front, helping to ensure the safety of those who remain behind in our City of Vienna.

Fräulein Eder wears a winning smile. She has always longed for him to leave. She tells us all how brave he is, how greatly he will be missed. The Children are all led away in a line. Many of them have not known him long and have not seen him often. Dr A is passing down the line of Nurses. All the time I am hearing Sister Viktorine.

Did he ever care? Did he ever care at all ~

Yet that lady shakes Dr A firmly by the hand and thanks him for all that he has done. Everyone is aware that she is making a great effort to behave in a Correct Manner. In reality, she is threadbare with her stuffing falling out. She has always believed in Dr A absolutely. She understands him and she thought that he understood her. Now her Fort has fallen.

Dr A says that he is deeply regretful. He is looking forward to peaceful times ahead when he will be able to return to his work here. He is comforted by the Fact that his many loyal colleagues will continue with his various initiatives. Of course, he will be in touch regularly. If there are difficult cases, the notes must be sent without delay.

Handshake, nod, thank you. Good luck. Thank you.

(Could it be that a Field Hospital at the front is now safer than the Vienna Children's Hospital?) Dr A is positioned squarely in front of me, stretches out his hand: Ah, Adelheid. You also will support Sister Viktorine. I know that I can rely on you. As you are aware, I never give up hope that one day I shall hear your voice ~

After My Death: Disorder in the Year 2010

Some parts of this Story are crooked and stuck down with cheap and ineffective glue consisting of flour and water paste. I am dispirited and desperate now and tiredtiredtired. Yet I must go on. The year is 2010. Our scene is the Wappensaal in our noble Vienna City Hall where Doctors from across the World are gathering to celebrate the Life and Work of Dr A.

In his Youth he was a great pioneer of Autism Research and is acknowledged now to be the Father of Neurodiversity. A syndrome has been named after him. He has been Dead now for thirty years but his name is known throughout the World. His career stretched across half a century and he became the Director of the world-famous Children's Hospital in Vienna. His Children and his Grandchildren are also among those who celebrate ~

Dr Lorna Wing has travelled from London to the Conference. Do you remember her? She is eighty-two years old now and travel is difficult. She remembers that house in South East London, that night when she first read his Thesis. Her dear husband John – gone now – struggled to translate Dr A's words.

So many years ago. Her dear Susie still Alive at that time. She wonders now how she managed to survive those distant days. Now Autism Research provides a career for many, perhaps rather too many, but who can complain? Her aim had always been to raise awareness, to improve services and support. That is what she has achieved ~

She remembers meeting Dr A in 1980. She wrote to him soon after she found his Thesis. She had not expected a reply. She feared that he might be Dead. However, a reply had come promptly and he had generously agreed that he would come to London. He was old then, most old. They had sat together in the canteen of the Maudsley Hospital.

She had been warned that he might be difficult. *Germans, you know.* Yet she was not deterred. Through her work she had learnt how to cope with even those who are most challenging. Is it ever a coincidence that a Person becomes involved in the struggles to untangle the mystery which is Autism?

It turned out that the warnings were unnecessary. Such a mild Man, extremely polite, a good listener. She found that she could agree with him on so many Points. She had questioned him about his Thesis. He struggled to remember. He had written it when he was a Young Man and the circumstances had not been entirely favourable.

She explained how the Thesis had enabled her to understand that maybe Autism, which she had thought to be a rare condition, was actually common. Dr A had also confirmed what she herself had discovered, which was that Intelligence Testing might not be helpful in identifying Autism.

He said: I am flattered that there is so much interest now in that work. It was so long ago now. Also, I realise that people talk of a specific syndrome which matches the Case Studies. Who knows? My dear friend Dr Frankl certainly talked of a series or a scale. Overall, we did not find it helpful to put people in Categories. That was not our purpose.

She poured him more tea. Listenedlistenedlistened.

He explained: I was a pupil of the great Erwin Lazar who created the Curative Education Ward in Vienna as far back as the 1920s. His belief was that diagnosis is not helpful because every child is unique. Difference, not disease. Difference as opportunity.

Dr Wing nods in vigorous agreement. She is warmed by his humility, his obvious compassion, his failure to advance his own work, to trumpet his ideas. Privately, she feels that in his Thesis he overplayed the idea of Autistic Intelligence. Perhaps that was necessary due to the Times in which he worked. When was it? The forties or the fifties?

She asks him why he did not continue that work. His response is vague. *Promoted. Less time for Research. Unfashionable. Psychoanalysis took centre stage.* She agrees. The moment for certain ideas passes and one thinks that those ideas are lost forever. Yet here we are, after forty long years, discussing these exact same questions again.

If we do not write these things down, then later some other poor soul will start this work from the beginning again. He apologises. He is a person who has always been inclined to talk for too long on certain subjects. She assures him that this is not the Case. She does not say that she has enjoyed the sound of his voice, his quiet enthusiasm and certainty.

He says goodbye most politely, thanks her for her time, departs. A year later she will learn of his Death. Two years later Asperger's Syndrome enters the Diagnostic Manual ~

Now the delegates arrive. So much new technology, so many screens and microphones. The room is decorated by diverse flags – those of our Country, our City and the European Union. The long windows are dressed in sheer white drapes, a modern chandelier glitters above. All is dark polished wood and echoing voices.

The coffee is poured and the proceedings begin. Of course, there is always that discussion which the Academics so much enjoy about who discovered Autism. For years, it was Kanner, now Dr A. Was it not strange that two men, on different Continents, divided by War, should have developed such similar ideas at the same time? This they say for they know nothing of the relay race, the baton passed on.

Which is to say that at this date they know nothing of Georg Frankl ~

At the back of the hall is a Young Man who will speak late in the day. He waits his turn nervously although he is entirely sure of his Point. He has warned the organisers of the Conference but he has not been taken seriously. A memorial has been erected to the Children of Am Spiegelgrund. Long ago, a different Hospital.

Late in the afternoon, when everyone is a little drowsy after a good lunch, the Young Man stands up, walks up to the podium and starts to speak. He is mild, dispassionate, elaborates the nature of his Research with confidence. *Of course, one must look at all sides of this question.* Soon everyone wishes that he would keep quiet.

He mentions the names of Herta and Elisabeth Schreiber. Damn this Young Man. This is not Appropriate. What he is saying is deeply insensitive to Dr A's Daughter and to the Grandchildren. Surely it cannot be True? Of course, there have always been those who were never brought to justice. Dr Gross received a state pension until 2005 despite several attempts to prosecute him.

But Dr A? Really? If this is true then why was his work ever allowed to come to international attention? The stain is spreading. The shame is gripping everyone. *Perhaps he did sign Paperwork relating to two Children? But two? This was a Wartime situation.*
Everyone had to do whatever they could to save their own lives. One cannot use contemporary moral standards to judge the past. What might any of us have done in a similar position? Two Children. This they say because at this date they do not know of the Gugging Commission.
Lorna Wing is looking firmly at the floor, her hands neatly folded. She wishes that she had not come. She tries not to listen. She would like to get back to her garden and her detective novels. Afterwards there will be questions. The worst is that she cannot entirely deny knowing of this. Rumours, whispering. Nazis, Collaboration. Was it possible?
She had been asked directly at that moment when Asperger's Syndrome was becoming part of the Diagnostic Manual. The telephone call had come late at night. The documents were going to press. Could there be anything in these Rumours? Perhaps she had been naïve? As an Autism Specialist, it was hardly her business to know.
Finally, she had said what she could say with certainty. *He was a Catholic, a staunch Catholic.* How did she even know that? He had said nothing specific. Yet she could feel it in him. A Person who had some sense of a larger Life, of eternity. She wishes now that she had thought harder.
In her professional Life, she has sometimes made judgements which have had political consequences which she has not foreseen. Dr A may have had no interest in telling a Big Story but others have done the job for him. Of course, one may Question the current

focus on that comforting myth of the awkward eccentric who is brilliantly gifted.

Yet still the Fact remains that the diagnosis of Asperger's Syndrome has allowed her to make the case for services and support for a whole group of people – people who desperately needed such understanding and support – and yet who previously had been ignored as they did not fall within the Autism diagnosis ~

Questions, questions, questions. This Young Man will go on to establish how these desperate circumstances did unfold, and he will set it all down accurately and without venom. Others will take his work, magnify his more sensational discoveries, rob his account of its necessary fog. Keep it big, keep it simple.

I continue to trust the small. In writing this record, I thought to do Better, to tell a Truthful Story. I was present in those times therefore I must surely know more than others do. Yet is this statement correct? Could it be that those who stand closest see least? I ask myself now – What is the difference between Scribe Brunner and the Young Man who stood on the podium that day?

Fact versus Fiction? Perhaps there are merely many and various routes through the past but all lead finally to that Door of Not Knowing? I should have left this task to a Proper Historian. Yet I remember Dr A and his faith in me. *Adelheid, I never give up hope that one day I will hear you speak.* So I am speaking now. I am trying. I ask you, please. Come with me now into those last days. Do not look away ~

10.a. You know a Man Called Fritz?

Who will protect me now that Dr A has departed? Would it be better for me to return now to Oma and the Café? We are told that a suitable Person is being sought to fill Dr A's position. Someone may be sent from Berlin. In the meantime, Professor Hamburger will oversee the work of the Ward. Dr Feldner will take on extra responsibilities.

Fräulein Eder will offer more assistance to the nursing staff and work more closely with Sister Viktorine. All this is quite orderly but Sister Viktorine cannot accept what is now ensuing. She has no energy or enthusiasm. All she talks about is how Dr A has failed us. She allows Fräulein Eder to cancel appointments and to send Children home.

Fräulein Eder should not be involved in any such decisions as she is not a Nurse, yet Sister Viktorine does not challenge her. The Children bicker and squabble. Sometimes actual bitter fighting breaks out in the Corridor and must be suppressed. Sister Viktorine sits in the Meeting Room, sewing, not even saying the Grace of God etcetcetc. ~

I no longer step out to absorb the latest newsreels. No one does attend these any more. Yet all through that damp and dripping spring we hear news of the destruction of the great Cities of the Ruhr. This is the mighty industrial area of Germany and how can they continue with all the factories and the Cities destroyed?

Dresden and Hamburg also, the bombs falling like rain, whole Cities alight. Also, planes fly from Russia now and they destroy factories on the outskirts of our City. Oma and Frau Winkler are equally alight with righteous outrage. For our City is now crowded with foreigners and many are forced to take in refugees from Germany who they do not want. The problem is not shortage of money but rather that there is nothing to buy ~

Soon the Confusion on the Ward is shocking to behold. Dirty sheets lie piled in the Corridor. Dropped crusts of bread are spread on the floor in the Dining Room. Flies gather in the kitchen and washroom. The piano has not been touched in many months. The Children must remain in the School Room and complete their tasks. In silence.

No playing of marbles or running races or card games. The Children concede, as they must, yet the atmosphere is darkly mutinous. The Ward feels like a pan of milk which is close to the boil and which must soon spill over into sizzling and bubbling. One imagines a bitter smell of boiling all about. How much longer can such Anger be contained?

Everything now is decided by Fräulein Eder. She is soon in an even greater vexatious humour as a cupboard Door in the kitchen has opened into her face and her eye has turned black. She always has many stomach disorders (and what does Herr Spellbinder know of this?) ~

As a result, Fräulein Eder is persistent and savage in her persecution of the Children. A boy is made to eat the semolina which he has already vomited. Another is stripped and beaten. A tiny and harmless Girl has her head pushed down a blocked toilet and her plaits snipped off. The Children learn a new prayer. *Lieber Gott, mach mich stumm, Dass ich nicht nach Dachau kumm. (Dear God, make me dumb, so I won't to Dachau come.)*

Fräulein Eder's new levels of venom being particularly directed at a boy called Bertie who is that type of Clever Idiot who she does particularly hate. He is obstinate, brutal and passes his time in organising a Revolution to overthrow Fräulein Eder's regime. He reminds me of Adolf although he is more inclined to act directly rather than manipulate others.

He works with a dwarfish, eggshell boy called Willy and their plans are elaborate. They draw up battle Strategies, discuss ambushes, march up and down the Ward in unison. An armory of weapons is created, although only made of sticks and cardboard. Other Children are recruited and trained, ready for the Revolution ~

When I see how Fräulein Eder does behave with Willy, I am brimming with ghastly forebodings. *Moron, Simpleton, Idiot. They are coming for you.* Who now will protect us? Our only hope is Dr Feldner and his mysterious words – *in the light of our former connections.* Yet he is at the Military Hospital often now. Does he keep away because he knows she can destroy him?

Why does Sister Viktorine permit such Chaos? Such is her silence that you might think that she is no longer present in the Ward at all. She still holds the hands of the Children and tries to help them but it seems as though all the blood has gone out of her. The flesh on her face has drooped and her eyes are often fixed on the floor.

It is well known that her Life is difficult because the friend in whose apartment she has always lived is dying now and so in addition to her work at the Hospital she is obliged to nurse this dying friend as well. Yet her solemnity has more to do with Dr A and his departure. To make matters worse, he writes most often making Enquiries about the running of the Ward.

Are we continuing with the music programme? Bertie? Interesting. Please send the Case Notes. Is Willy becoming more confident? Is his speech clearer? Sister Viktorine reads these letters again and again. When people ask questions, she does not reply. Perhaps she does not know how annoying it is when people don't speak ~

Also, we may no longer look to Herr Spellbinder for help. Ever since Dr Feldner shouted at him about the Radio, he has been most silent. Even though the shouting was not real, it seems he listened. *For God's sake, Man, you will finish up Dead. Please take care. We need you.* Yet although Herr Spellbinder does not Act he is always present.

Whenever you open a Door, enter the Meeting Room, skirt along the Corridor, he materialises, stands dumbly with his hands behind his back. Watches with unblinking eyes and a coiled, reptilian stillness. Does he ask himself (as I do) what the belligerent Bertie really intends? One suspects that his Revolution is more than a game.

Againagainagain, I decide that I must go back to the Café. Fräulein Eder has attempted to get rid of me once and she will try again ~

The Alchemy of Circumstance intervenes. A lad arrives in the Ward. Fräulein Eder is in the process of dismissing him but Sister Viktorine intervenes: No. Wait a minute. Peter?

This is that same Peter who is Lukas's Nephew and works for Oma. Peter saying: Please, Sister Viktorine. I have been sent to get Adelheid. Frau Brunner says that she is to come home immediately.

Is there a Problem?

No, miss. No Problem. Not at all. But she must come.

Sister Viktorine turns to me and gives me permission. I go to the Bunk Room and get my bag. Of course, the Matchboxes wish to accompany me. I do not believe in any such things nowadays. Yet I do take them. All I want is to be outside in the street even just for some short moments.

The morning is luminous, rinsed clean. Summer is at its peak now. Clouds are singing high above as I cross the Josefstadt. Yet when I reach our street, I see that, although it is midday, the shutters of the Café are drawn down. I begin to wonder. I have never seen that before. Even on the day of Opa's Not Funeral the Café was open.

I move towards the entrance which leads into the Courtyard. Above me the dark chandelier glitters. I expect to see Frau Vogt glaring at me from behind her velvet curtain but she is not there. I arrive at our apartment Door and step through the hall, into the kitchen. The Chef is absent. He is Never Not There. Who is doing the cooking?

Through the circular window in the kitchen Door, I see through to the Café but the lights are extinguished. Oma is positioned erect with her back towards me. Everything is swampy and seen through a film of brown. Yet I can discern a familiar shape. Sitting at one of the tables. Actual Opa ~

My bag slides from my hand. I reach to pick it up, hold it against me. Opa raises his hands and laughs, that yelping wild-dog laugh which I remember so well. Oma sees me, pulls the Door open, catches hold of me, pulls me into the Café. My soul has left my body. My breath is paralysed, my eyes painful with staring.

He is here. Of course, I always knew. I always knew. He was Alive and yet still. I cannot understand. After nine long years? He is not the same as he was. Not at all. Scrawny, grubby, stooped. Most of his hair has disappeared but still his laugh is just as savage and joyous as it always was. I know that I am meant to run into his arms.

Yet I am not a Person who ever does indulge in such behaviour and I am too befuddled to do anything except gawp. I remember all the times I have looked for him. I always knew. I was rightrightright. Oma sees the Question in my eyes, whispers: In a prison camp. Escaped. In Czechoslovakia working for the Resistance. Need to be careful. Very careful.

Opa says: Adelheid. Adelheid, my girl. My dear girl. There you are.

He always divines exactly what it is I need to understand. Says: The sewers. Why did they not work that out? How many times did they take the Karl-Marx-Hof and how many times did we fight back? In those ghastly sewers for weeks. Until someone found me a clean suit. Belonged to Mr Gedye. Remember him? Put me in the back of a truck and got me to the border.

What he is saying is right. So many times, as I stood in those allotment gardens, I heard the cry that the building was taken. I saw the troops begin to leave, the guns pulled out. I knew that the building is a warren. Yet I never thought of the sewers. Opa is still talking and I am swept up in his Story. How extraordinary. What a trick.

He is saying: There I was at the border but how could I get across? *Do you know a Man called Fritz?* That was what you needed to say. Many were trying to escape. Then thank God Herr Hansel died at just that time and he was the right height. Walked through one of the green crossings. Took Herr Hansel's Papers and went.

Oma stands beside him and smothers him with kisses. He tips back vodka. She puts the gramophone on. I stand and watch, unable to move, to think ~

Opa is commenting that I am *still not saying anything much? Not a big talker?* I need my Notebooks now. All of this cannot be fitted.

Too Big. I am writing it down Inside my Head but still my brain is bursting and banging. Because everyone thought that he was Dead it was easiest for him to leave everyone with that impression. But nine whole years?

He says: Come, girl. Come. Sit down with me and take a glass. You are of an age now. Not a child now, hey? Nonono most definitely not. Fine young woman you have become. Quite a beauty you are. Come, let me pour you a glass.

I remember then how I loved him. He always believed in me when no one else did. I will be Safe now because he understands. He always has. He is homehomehome. He has arrived at just the moment when he is most needed. He will understand that I cannot remain at that Hospital now. That I am not Safe ~

I seat myself at the table opposite him as I did so often in those past more gentle days. Time has folded up like a concertina. Squeeze everything together – or perhaps crank a handle which may wind us back through the hours so we will be in the World before the Ward, before the shooting of Dollfuß. The World when Opa storms into the School and singes the Headmistress.

Also, he allows me to accompany him – walking through the woods and vineyards at Klosterneuburg Monastery, swimming in the public lido at the Gänsehäufel, or visiting the Prater to watch the great wheel turn. Oma says: At the Hospital, she's highly valued, you know. She still has the Matchboxes. She's always kept the Matchboxes.

I put my bag on the table, take out the Albums. The way that he handles them is so achingly familiar. Gently and carefully. Saying: Good Lord, girl. What a Collection you've got here. A girl after my own heart. Looking after your Oma, a Nurse at the Hospital. I told you. *Don't let the cattle get in the way.* Made us all proud ~

This is the happy ending in the Sentimental Stories I dislike. Yet realrealreal. Opa dons his glasses, bends his head down low, pulls an envelope out of his pocket. I know how this goes. I am too old now to be given Matchboxes yet still I feel the tugging thrill. Opa says: Got these in the camp. People there from all over, although hard to get a smoke, let alone a Matchbox.

I glance, I peer, I stare. I am filled with delight and wonder. These are the Matchboxes I have so long awaited. Beautifully preserved, rare. Only he would know. They will fill the gaps exactly. The Collection now will be balanced. Similar numbers from each area. My Album complete, every space occupied, all neatly Ordered and affixed most straight.

I reach out my hand to touch them. I feel that I must seize them tight in case they evaporate or float away. My hands quiver and my head is starting to thump. I think of Dr A and his Research. All that last-minute checking. A Project he never wanted to finish. What happens when it is done? The World perfect.

Opa: Matchboxes. Imagine. I would have thought you were too grown up for all that. Of course. I would help you. But I'll only be here today. Not safe. I must move on.

Oma becomes sentimental: How I wish you could stay. Just this brief time. Lord knows what this War has done to us all.

Opa proud and grandiose: Yes. New Times are coming, a New World. The Fascists losing their grip. The Workers must Unite to stop these Imperialist Wars. People such as myself, with long experience in these matters, are urgently needed to support the Young ~

The Matchboxes are twisting and swimming in front of my eyes. He doesn't understand. *I would have thought you were too grown up for all that. I'll only be here today.* Oma is still smiling down at him, eyes watery with pride. She doesn't say now that the Man is a Fool, that she is glad that he is Dead. The Mistakes of her Youth strangely quite forgotten.

The playing cards are shufflingshufflingshuffling. When Oma says *I always knew* then she is not rewriting the Story. She did know. She did. All of those people at the Funeral? How many of them knew? How many of them were nodding, winking, raising their eyebrows? Oma and Herr Wächter and othersothersothers.

They did it because he would have been arrested. Or they would be arrested. They did it to Save him, to Save themselves. Shufflecutdealshufflecutdeal. Yet still the Fact remains stubborn and unmoving. Oma tried to have me committed to an institution to stop me from writing down what she knew to be the Truth. The heart-eating eagle now is on the wing.

THE MATCHBOX GIRL

The Matchboxes say what I cannot. They are rising, leaping. Jumping up and down, raging. The pages of the Album flapping. The Elephant is brandishing a truncheon, the Clown is gnashing his jagged black teeth, opening his mouth to swallow me. Opa is still talking about *the Great Struggle*. Same old stuff. Always the World as it should be, not as it is.

Quite soon he will suggest that I might carry a message for him. Go here, go there. Do this, that. Keep quiet. Is it the Big or the Small that matters? I prefer the Small and I am proud to have *no Breadth of Vision*. I can see the Evidence, the Facts, the Blades of Grass. New men but always the same men. Hitler, Stalin, Churchill.

We in this City have been asked to walk forward into a better Future far too many times. We long for stability, for the past, for calm. Will they never stop building their Fabulous Forts and Prosperous Farms? *Look at the Evidence*. What I see is that he never cared. For so long I was told he was Dead.

Now he is Alive but also Deaddeaddead in a way he never was before. *I would have thought you were too grown up for all that*. Who is the child here? *Still not saying anything much? Not a big talker?* What have his years of Talking achieved? Is this now, here, today, thisplacethistimethisfear? Is this my Inheritance? Is this the New World they offer me ~

I raise an Album high and smash it down onto Opa's head. Matchboxes scatter, Opa raises his hands to protect himself. He is too late. I have hit him once and now I hit him againagainagain, smashing the Album down onto his straggly old head. Oma tries to pull the Albums out of my hands. But these people are oldoldold and I am youngstrongcertainvicious.

Oma saying: Adelheid, Adelheid. For God's sake.

Opa saying: Come now, girl.

They rip the Albums out of my hands. I reach behind me and through the cartwheeling mass of descending Matchboxes, I grab a glass. *Always important to know when Not to Stop*. Crack that glass down onto Opa's bald head, see it break in pieces. The blood flows. Oh GodGodGod. I must escape but what happens to the Matchboxes?

He can take them, throw them away. What do I care? You arrange them perfectly. The World is still as Broken and Bewildering and Mean as it always was. What sense? What sense? I run for the Door and break out into the street. I am away from him, away from the screaming Matchboxes. I run and I don't stop.

All around me the City is gasping, the grape ladies on their white pillars raise their hands to their mouths, the trees throw their branches back. All of our City of Vienna knows what I have done. The clouds are smashing into each other. The sky has been shot Dead. Briefly it balloons and then begins to descend in damp folds.

Why are the men always leaving ~

10.b. To War with Cardboard Swords

Who now can Save me? It should be the case that I am now back where I was at the beginning. Where all is Darkness and Chaos and Disorder. For some long moments, these are my thoughts. Yet strangely they soon pass. Once upon a time, I needed Opa to make me into a Real Person and to tell me What To Do.

I do not need that now. I am capable of Independent Thought. I shall never go back to the Café again. I must go to the Hospital. That is my Home. That is the place where Friends will keep me Safe. Even in my deepest Confusion I can find my way there. Dr A has mercifully got his compass to hand. He has drawn me a Map.

When I come to Lazarettgasse, I stare up at those buildings I know so well. This is the Evidence, these are the Facts. The Ward has become worse than the schoolyard. Dr A trusted us to continue his work and we are failing. What is needed is Order and it can be found. I will organise the Matchboxes even though I possess no Matchboxes now.

Even amidst the most tangled Lies, there are patterns and echoes and purposes to be found. Even if there are not, I must believe it to be so. I can survive only if I decide not to know the Truth. Pretending got us into this dire trouble. All I can do now is to Pretend harder. I have to remake the World myself and must do this againagainagain.

Dr A, Dr Feldner, Sister Viktorine. They have demonstrated to me how this can be done. Yes, even the Reich itself has shown me. Blind belief has its Dangers, also its benefits. The Reich can be defeated with pepper. Stalingrad has not fallen. Bertie will organise a Revolution. Dr A is a good Man. I cannot look outside my own person for help now ~

How fortunate it is that I have decided these things, and Organised my thoughts strategically and logically, before I arrive at the Door of the Hospital. For I could never have predicted that, although I had only been gone from the Hospital one hour, yet, even in that time, the situation had disintegrated in ways beyond my worse imagining.

Even as I walk up the stairs, the Doors of the downstairs Wards are opening and shutting and people are standing on the stairs demanding – *What is that noise? What is happening upstairs?* Outside the Door of our Ward a group of Nurses who I do not know are gathering, shaking their heads, listening, rattling at the locked Door.

How am I to get in? Mercifully, through the half glass of the Door, beyond the bobbing heads of the questioning Nurses, I see Herr Spellbinder. He tips his head to one side, pointing with wandering eyebrows. I hurry back down the stairs, dash around the side of the building, find the back entrance and dash up those other blessed stairs.

I know that Herr Spellbinder will have opened the locked Door and I am not disappointed. Yet when I see his face, he is suddenly stricken, beaten, raising the palms of his hands in Despair. The Revolution which Bertie has so long planned has begun. The battle is joined but does not progress towards heroism and victory.

Fräulein Eder is raging. Water splashes, a child is shrieking. I dash into the bathroom. Fräulein Eder is gripping Willy. He is in the bath and she is pinning him down. Is this really happening? All is so vivid that I cannot Pretend to myself that it is not Real. Yet it appears entirely similar to that fantastical and ghastly Story of my Childhood. Water is splattering all over the floor.

Fräulein Eder's face is red and crumpled, her spiky fingers are pushing and pushing. Surely Fräulein Eder will squeeze the life out of Willy? From the Door of the Ward, I hear an insistent banging. Those Nurses from the other Wards are still trying to enter. Most alarmed by the noise, the locked Door, the commotion within ~

This is not a moment for *steering people*. I seize a papier mâché sword but the water has rendered parts of it soggy. I drop it and grab hold of Fräulein Eder's arm. Fury has made her strong. Yet I too am muscular and can fight her with a frightening force. I dig my fingers into her arm and pull against her, my feet slipping on the swamped floor, my teeth gripped.

THE MATCHBOX GIRL

She screams. *Useless Eater. Cabbage. Filthy little bitch.* I am tearing and pulling and hitting but still Willy's head is under the water. Willy might be twelve years old but he is no more robust than a child of six. How long has he been under? I am choking now, struggling to breathe. My head is submerged under the water also.

The banging at the Door of the Ward is frantic now. Fräulein Eder rains blows down on me but to do this she must release Willy and so I pull him up. One of the Children is waving a mop and I lay hold of that. Willy is gaspinglaughingcrying and Bertie is slapping Fräulein Eder around the head. *I will fucking kill her. I will kill the fucking whore.*

The banging at the Door is louderlouderlouder, becoming now most desperate. Fräulein Eder is attempting to depart this scene but Bertie is twisting her sparrow arm most viciously. He sinks his teeth into her wrist. Willy slips on the doused floor and laughs hysterically. *What is going on here? How dare you behave like that? Stop this at once.*

Dr Feldner's face is dark purple and swollen with rage. He must have come up the back stairs. Just as I did. The floor is deluged. The Children are all swamped. I am raining water from hair and shoulders and the mop now falters in my hand. Fräulein Eder is propped against the Door frame, sobbing. The mop also weeps most pitifully ~

The banging at the Door has not ceased. The Noise and Chaos is too much. I must stop the Children rioting. But howhowhow? What are we to do? I am positioned in the Dormitory now, unable to think, yet trying to find dry clothes for the Children. They group together in a huddled mass. Rockshakejibber. I need Sister Viktorine. I am not a Nurse.

Bertie is the worst. His Revolution has failed and it now devours its own Children. *They will send me away from here. I will die. I will die.* He launches himself upon me. I step away. I have always found him disgusting. I do not wish to touch him. But what? What? I close my arms around him and he stops yelling. Immediately the others are on me.

I am pushed back against a bed. This is the Schoolyard. Their hands, their awful hands. Wet and tearful, sticky and smelly. Their stale breath blowing upon me. Nonono. Then I remember, I know and suddenly I am still. I am sitting on the bed, the Children are all around me, pressed against me. Quiet. Quiet. Quiet.

I lay my hand on Bertie's head and stroke his wet, greasy hair. This is what Sister Viktorine would do. This is what I must do. I remember Herta and how I once held her. Yet more bedraggled Children are emerging now and pushing themselves against me. Willy curls up on the bed, holding my uniform in his wizened fist.

His tiny, shrivelled eyes look up at me, full of light and good cheer. Saying: I was Dying and it was lovely. Lovely ~

The Door of the Ward has opened. We know it because we hear the bubbling voices, the echoes of the stairwell. We bow our heads as though waiting for a blow. Surely all now is at an end? Yet strangely I am most calm. I hear a voice – real, decisive, wonderfully familiar: Nothing to worry about. I am dealing with the situation. Please return to your work.

Sister Viktorine has returned. I mean, she has come back to us. She is hereherehere. More here than she has ever been before. Not just flesh and blood but steel. I hear her stride briskly towards the Dormitory. She sees me on the bed, stares poppingly, nods: Thank you, Adelheid. Well done. Thank you.

She has returned. Properly Returned. Calmclearprecise – and kind, always kind. Herr Spellbinder is piling up the wet towels, clearing mops and cardboard weapons away. Dr Feldner calls Bertie into the Meeting Room. I remain where I am and the Children remain blessedly peaceful. How easy this is, how blissfully easy ~

As a result of the Failed Revolution, many things change. Fräulein Eder is in Dr Feldner's Office for some long time while he reminds her again about *our former connections*. I understand nothing of that. I only know that soon Fräulein Eder seems to be permanently ill. Also, she falls down the stairs, knocks out a tooth.

When she does come to the Ward, she does not speak to us. The other thing that changes is that I become a proper Nurse. This is never officially decided. It is simply understood that I will spend more time with the children. Also, Sister Viktorine becomes again her own Reich. We are glad. She is also reading Dr A's letters with care, following his every Instruction ~

10.c. Where Do We Find Eternity?

The World stumbles on. Another summer passes although I have no sense of hours, days, weeks. I make my Own World. You may say that these are Lies. I no longer care. I must live and this is how it is done. Yet also – this they do not tell you. That our spinning World reaches the great peak of its wonder at the moment when it is full of cracks and ready to shatter.

In the autumn of 1943, the deceitful Italians surrender. No one speaks of this news. The Enemy planes now will fly from Italy. We are no longer the air raid shelter of the Reich. In the air some bottled hysteria, some restless, aching pain. The whole City a suppressed scream. Everything echoes like the inside of a drum. Our lives suspended on a silk thread.

In the evenings, I go again now with Sister Anna to the Votiv Kino and we watch the newsreels. The great might of the Reich rolls across the screen. In the dark we watch with our heads tipped back – the bombers and the tanks. Our troops still pressing ahead across Russia. Soon they will reach the Urals and then everything will belong to the Reich.

Every other Country is against us now but they cannot bring us down. People talk most loudly of victoryvictoryvictory. We see and we do not see. The cards shuffling. Againagainagain. Even the sound of feet on the stairs becomes loud and important as though they carry some message about to be announced. We still await Dr A's replacement.

Gradually we realise no one will come ~

In these days Oma often visits the Hospital to spend time with Sister Viktorine. She has been coming ever since I did commit an act of violence with a Matchbox Album. I hide in the Bunk Room and Pretend that I do not know that she is present. She brings the Matchbox Envelopes and the Albums with her and she wants to offer them to me.

That will signal that we are now at Peace yet I do not want to permit her such comfort. She talks most mournfully to Sister Viktorine: Everything I ever did. It was all for Adelheid etcetcetc. I am so proud of her. Of course, I should have told her about her Grandfather but the Danger was too great. The errors of my Youth etcetcetc. ~

I spend many long moments staring out of the windows, or looking down from the Roof Terrace. Even now I love to follow the direction of one street after another. Still thinking and hoping that all the Questions are contained amidst those many floating domes, stacked churches, jumbled skylights and patches of green.

It becomes easier to spend time on this activity of watching because the question of the laundry is problematic. Often the sheets cannot be washed therefore we wash them ourselves in the sinks. Yet where may the sheets be suspended? Herr Spellbinder ties strong pieces of rope under the windows in order that sheets can be made dry.

Sister Viktorine does not like this slovenly approach. *The Vienna Children's Hospital, finest Hospital in the World. Standards must be maintained etcetcetc.* Yet this does give me some time to observe for as long as I like, perceiving the advance of winter and the thick mists which then descend over the City, swaddling us in silence.

Always waiting, waiting. The Future a truncated limb. No longer in existence yet the pain of it always pulsing. Positioned often at the window. Not watching but dreaming. Yet still I was the first to know when one of the Doctors was stabbed by a lunatic with a knife. I saw the commotion as they carried the injured doctor away.

Later we were told that it was Dr Huber who was attacked. He was one of the most senior Doctors in the Hospital. Might there be other lunatics walking the streets waiting to stab Doctors or Nurses? Sister Anna (speaking under cover of the Filing Cabinet) tells us the Man with the knife had come back from the Front to find that his baby daughter had been murdered in the Hospital.

Still people hiss and whisper, insist this is not True.
Why do we not weep? We may not start.
We will be washed away by so many tears ~

Winter comes and everything is starched and white and trembling. All around, one is aware of dead eyes in living people. The Children are transparent, hollow, befuddled. Babes lost in the Wood. Still the letters come from Dr A. Often, in the evenings, Sister Viktorine reads these missives. A field Hospital in Croatia. One cannot imagine the Horror.

Yet Dr A writes long accounts of the scenery, the flora and fauna, the traditions of the local people. This comes as no surprise. This is the man he always was and one views his eccentricities with affection rather than surprise. We know how proud he would be if he should return and walk into the Ward now. Sister Viktorine prays for his safety.

A new Nurse has come to the Hospital called Sister Johanna. She is of a nervous disposition and that knife incident makes her say that she couldnotcouldnotcouldnot. Fear is more infectious than typhus and we all wish she would desist. Sister Viktorine must often sit with her in the Meeting Room, holding her hand and encouraging her to pray.

Saying to Sister Johanna that she must not judge herself so harshly for her Fear: We cannot spend our whole Life trying to Cure the Disease which is Ourselves.

Often Sister Viktorine then calls us all together in the evening. Tells us that *no matter how much is taken from us, we build an altar in our Hearts. We draw on the well which does not run dry.* Seeing her then, I perceive that, without me knowing it, she has become old. Her dark hair now lined with white, her whole body both insubstantial and yet also more solid.

She talks then of Eternity for although the Reich will last for 1,000 years (this she says with the smallest smirk) yet the Kingdom of God never ends. Sister Johanna, collapsed and damp with tears, says — What will Eternity be? Sister Viktorine opines that for each Person, it will be a place that you would most dearly love.

For her personally, the Garden. Others then start to talk of parks and mountains and lakes. For me, they do not know of any place. I could tell them that I love everything, all of it, every leaf blowing on a shading tree, every blade of grass. Sister Anna says that perhaps for me a room full of Files neatly Organised. Sister Viktorine hopes I understand this as a kindly joke ~

This Sister Johanna seems most feeble yet is a caring Person. She goes out *hamstering* at the weekends and brings back delicious mushrooms. She teaches me how to twist straw together to make a long chain. Then she helps me plait such chains together so that I might make a little bag for myself.

She also lends me books. Once I would have considered these books to be Silly Stories. Now I am glad enough to read in the long hours of the night. Yet what I do enjoy more is to listen to the conversations between Sister Viktorine and Sister Johanna. Much like those remembered conversations with Fräulein Weiss.

The Proper Ordering of the World? Is it possible? In this connection, Sister Johanna does talk of her love of History. However, she is also worried because History is about judgement and, when accounts of our own troubled Times are written, how might we be Judged? Is Grillparzer not right to say *we walk behind our own corpse in our lifetime*?

Sister Viktorine is not troubled by such Questions as she has always preferred Stories. Saying: History is surely only the skimmed milk of the past? Everything we might really want to know is absent. Historians only tell you how things should have been done. Any Fool can tell you that – after the event.

Sister Johanna is not happy with this opinion. She values Facts. Stories are really for Children. Sister Viktorine enjoys a few loose ends. The Mystery of Life is that, in our time, we do not know what has Value. We plant seeds and we wait. Yet some seeds lie dormant for many years before they flourish. Therefore, the Work must be enough unto itself ~

At Christmas Herr Spellbinder tunes into the Black Radio. Dr Feldner is with us and Hansi, who has been working across the road in the General Hospital now comes to join us. He smiles most brightly, knots his hands together to stop them shaking. Later, Der

Chef is heard on the Radio. I hurry away as I dislike that voice but still I can hear, even in the Bunk Room.

He is talking again about how the Nazis have all become soft and should be punished for their weakness. Then quite suddenly his voice is disrupted. The racket of a Door being broken down, shouting, shooting. *Schweinehund. Schweinehund.* I am filled with Terror and I run back towards the Radio.

I do know this cannot be Real and yet the Violence does seem absolutely True. I put my hands over my ears. Sister Anna hides behind the Door. Hansi is shuddering. Der Chef has been captured and he will be shot. Sister Johanna is once again reduced to weeping. Dr Feldner says repeatedly that no one is to be agitated as this is merely a Radio programme.

Later that night the Truth of his words is demonstrated. The situation becomes most ridiculous. The same Radio programme comes on again and we hear once again the apparent capture and shooting of Der Chef. Again, I put my hands over my ears even though I know what is the Truth – or perhaps the Many Untruths – of this.

Dr Feldner laughing most merrily, enjoying the programme exceedingly. Hansi now courageously deciding to join with him in this good humour. Dr Felder saying: How very careless. How does one die twice ~

The early months of that last year were rancorous, hushed, taut. Still those same Words are repeated againagainagain. Pflicht, Treue, Wille etcetcetc. (Duty, Loyalty, Will etcetcetc.) Also, soul, community, service. Yet I understand now that the more a Word is repeated the less the reality it describes actually exists. We all of us long to touch something Real.

Perhaps it was those conversations about the Judgement of History. I do not know. Yet I started to dream again and again of a Court of Law. The Judge with his gavel, a crowd of accusing faces all about. I am standing in the witness box. Everyone staresstaresstares. Questions. So many Questions. Why this? Why that? How? How? How?

We are all on trial. All who were not Brave, all who did not speak the Truth when they could have done. All who did not stand up and express their opposition. Why did we not See? Why did we not Act? Now all the accused are as silent as me, unable to utter one

Word. The judge yells at me, at all the many who cower there – *guilty, guilty, guilty.*

The guillotine awaits. The blade will fall and sever our stupidly nodding heads from our futile bodies. I want to explain. Please, please. I can only say. You were not there. You cannot know. Yet all are silent. What Answer may we give? What excuse have we to offer? I wake with strangling iron fingers gripped round my windpipe ~

Not long now. This they say but what will come? Everyone says – *Enjoy the War, the Peace will be terrible.* When the spring comes – quite early that year – it is bursting green and spangles gladly. A weak but straw-gold sun touching everything, like that first summer ten years before. Just as during that distant time, we seem to have strangely little to occupy us.

The days have no contours, no edges. Sister Viktorine spends many hours with the Children in the Garden and I help her. Bertie reads Stories to the younger Children. Those stories no longer seem silly. Instead, they are necessary. After all, how would you use Facts and Figures to explain the World we now inhabit?

Dr Feldner and Hansi are also often with us. Once again, sock relay races are run and marbles spin across the Corridors. There was a time when we all felt some hidden resentment towards Dr Feldner for the Danger he causes. Now all that is forgotten and we enjoy his pranks, games, laughter. We enjoy Hansi too. He belongs to us all. He is the one we can save.

Often, he is out at night with Peter (from the Café) and even Dr Feldner. They paint *1918* on walls (a forbidden reference to the defeat of the last War). Surveillance becomes less strict but punishments become more horrific. Communists are not just imprisoned but beheaded. *(Always too little and too late, then too brutal, too violent.)*

In those days, I enjoy the Roof Terrace or sit in the chair in the Meeting Room, just as I had always relished to do. Discerning each blade of grass unique and spectacular, each ray of sun pierced with such a mellow brightness. That Wartime summer so much Happiness was there. Yet also great seriousness. We knew that this was our last waltz ~

Then breaking into our lives without any warning. A morning of acid Chaos and Fear. I am up early and I see him come. Dr Feldner. At the Door of the Ward. He is the colour of drain water, the back of his hand pressed to his mouth. He has been walking fast, even running. His sparse hair is spiky, his eyes ravaged. He doesn't bother with the Filing Cabinet: I've lost him. Last night. I lost him.

Sister Viktorine is already so pallid but now she is dissolving entirely, merging into the hollow air around her. She stretches out a hand but he pulls away. She opens the Door of the Meeting Room and steers him in. Herr Spellbinder is there. Standing against the curtains, his hands behind his back, endlessly watchingwatchingwatching.

Sister Viktorine: What happened? What happened?

Dr Feldner paces like a wild animal, gasping and shaking his head, his hands waving: Last night. We were stopped at a road block. We've gone through many times. I know the men. Last night – a different Man. They usually don't ask for Papers. I told Hansi to run. I ran but in the other direction. I did hear – I did hear – shots. Not just Hansi firing the gun.

Sister Viktorine says: God save us. Oh, dear Lord, save us.

Dr Feldner continues to shake his head repeatedly as though this knowledge might be dislodged: I didn't dare go back home in case they came. I spent the night on top of the coal box in the entrance hall of our friend's building. Then an hour ago. I went. He wasn't there. He would have come back. He would ~

Dr Feldner has always been breezily calm, purposefully detached. How dreadful it is to see him now, fevered and desperate, his eyes so full of sorrow and pity. Yet also, I am thinking. I know Sister Viktorine is aware. The Truth is that if Hansi was shot Dead then we may be Safe. He had no Papers. No one will be able to identify him.

What if he has been taken Alive? What might be discovered? Sister Viktorine is listing all the places where perhaps Hansi might be discovered. She is going to keep believing. Even though gun shots were heard. Which must surely mean. Dr Feldner told me once that I must never Lie to myself. Yet now we are all Lying to Ourselves as forcefully as ever we can ~

We hear the Door of the Ward opening. Every muscle is stretched to the point of breaking, blood has become stagnant in our veins. *They are coming for us.* This will not be a matter of worms down your shirt, your homework soaked, your glasses stamped on. *Dr Feldner's Nephew.* We will not be believed.

Dr Feldner's voice changes: Ah. Good morning, Fräulein Eder. Bright and early today.

Does she reply? We cannot hear. Dr Feldner begins to speak as though he has been interrupted in a discussion about one of the Children. Sister Viktorine also continues with much Pretending. *Yes, yes, thank you for that advice. I will certainly adopt that approach.* Herr Spellbinder never appears to move at all and yet strangely he has now faded away.

The day begins. The doors, the window frames, the staircase, the floors and beds. Everything is unhinged. We work as though we are machines. Clickingtickingnodding. Sister Viktorine wants to pray but she has no choice except to look as though nothing has happened. She swallows again and again. She must be praying inside her head and I pray also.

I wonder. What can I do to calm her nerves? Why are there always so many Children with so many needs? Children with convulsions, Children with indigestion, Children with rickets. How does one offer comfort in difficult situations? Maybe I could give flowers? I pick garden flowers for Sister Viktorine, organise them into a neat bouquet.

I am a little nervous to present them to her but I surmise this is the right thing to do. Just as I am coming back up the main stairs, I hear rushing and stumbling footsteps behind me. Now. Now. Where can I hide? Yet turning round I apprehend that it is Dr Feldner leaping up the stairs. I move aside and he dashes past.

I also enter the Ward. Yet I am watchful. I keep my eye on the back stairs. Should I run? Is Dr Feldner being followed? Has he come to warn us? Dr Feldner catches hold of Sister Viktorine and twirls her around: I found him. He had gone to our friends in the Sixth District. He had a key but, anyway, they were home. I think we are all right. We are safe.

He pulls her against him and for a long time they embrace like lovers, pressed close. Sister Viktorine registers me and the flowers: Oh look, look.

Her face is radiant. Dr Feldner lifts the flowers from my hands, presents them to Sister Viktorine with a deep bow, like some Grand Operatic Performance. They are smiling stupidly, raising their hands, staring heavenwards. For a miracle has come to pass. Dr Feldner turns to me and I remember that I must smile but I am smiling without even willing it.

He catches hold of me and hugs me just as he embraced Sister Viktorine. The thoughts crowd in on me then. He would have done the same for me, for any of us. *The fortress of friendship never Falls.* There is a difference between a deal (what we may get from a Person) and Friendship. I know that now.

Dr Feldner says: I am going to get breakfast for Hansi. Very late breakfast. He likes a good breakfast. Thank you. Thank you.

Sister Viktorine is holding the flowers and smiling at that other World. At Eternity, at the well that does not run dry, at the never-fading Garden. She sees it close now ~

10.d. Matchbox Bombs and Window Accidents

Safesafesafe. Not safe. Safe. Notnotnot. How can I tell you? I am flattened, bleary, evacuated from myself. The Question starts like this – *How many people were at that road block?* When Hansi was asked for his Papers, when the shots were fired. I do not know. Probably Dr Feldner also does not possess this information. Was one of them Fräulein Eder? I think so.

It was the Monday morning just after Dr Feldner and Hansi had enjoyed such a hearty breakfast together. The disruption started in relation to that same boy named Bertie who had led the Revolution. (Dr Feldner had previously taken some Notes on this case, to be sent to Dr A.) Also, the type of boy that Fräulein Eder does believe to be a fraud.

Now she has said that Bertie must stand facing the wall and he may not move. When Dr Feldner arrives, he questions this and Fräulein Eder reports the boy has only been there half an hour, which is not True. She having also labelled him all the usual insults. *Idiot, Simpleton, Imbecile etcetcetc.* The point being that he has been positioned there longer than three hours.

Herr Spellbinder watching all of this. Not so still now. Fidgeting, seething, his teeth rasping. A conflict does start between Fräulein Eder and Dr Feldner. He emphasises again that she has no role in the operation of our Ward. She is Professor Hamburger's Secretary and she does only his work. Again, he hopes *she will take account of our former connections* ~

We pray this will be the end of the Story but it is not. Fräulein Eder is now in a waspinabottle-suppressed hysteria. Yet Dr Feldner is tranquil as always. He has always underestimated Fräulein Eder. When Dr Feldner tells her again not to touch the Notes, her smile is most merry and savage, saying: How is your Nephew, Dr Feldner? Trouble at a checkpoint?

Herr Spellbinder is close by with the laundry cart when she says this and halts absolutely still. The checkpoint? How does she know? In reality, the Question is not complicated. Everyone knows what Fräulein Eder does with her free time, they know about the fur coat and the parties in the apartment above the Blockleiter's Office.

I would like to consider that this is just one more skirmish in our ongoing War. Yet Fräulein Eder has become less controlled and increasingly deranged for months now. The illnesses, the accidents. There is surely no limit to what acts of spite or betrayal she might commit. A Person must warn Hansi but where is he? If he is at Dr Feldner's apartment, then I can go.

However, it is almost certain that he is not there. Probably he is in the Hospital somewhere. Even Dr Feldner perhaps doesn't know exactly where he is. Dr Feldner cannot go himself as that will be too obvious and he has a list of appointments. Herr Spellbinder also cannot go. He will be missed. Who now can raise the alarm?

I turn to look at Herr Spellbinder and see something I never expected. Fear. The smell of it is on him. Is it Fear for Hansi? Or is it the boy Bertie? Who can know – yet it is clear that Herr Spellbinder's cards have all been played out. His box of tricks is empty. Not just Fear but also Despair. His World depends on Sister Viktorine and Dr Feldner.

Herr Spellbinder's hands will soon be in the Mincing Machine. Bertie's Revolution was the Fake War. This now is Real. Dr Feldner seems paralysed. He does apprehend the severity of the risk but he does not move. Mercifully, I am helped in this dark moment by dear Fräulein Weiss.

Look, she is there, sitting on the bench in the waiting area. *At some point you might be faced with a situation where you would need to stand up for the Truth. If such a moment arrives, you would know. You would just know and you would also understand how to act ~*

Herr Spellbinder's eyebrows are leaping. He is nodding again and again. But what? What? All of my Life I have wanted Order. I have loved Order. Yet I know now. I understand. Disorder now is our only hope. Yet still I do not know what I must do. I am Pretending to be wiping the benches clean, yet I look at Herr Spellbinder's eyes and I follow their lead.

He knows what I am considering and he is saying – *Yes*. Sister Anna has also arrived in this area, pretending to bring Paperwork for Dr Feldner. We need her. She could go and look for Hansi. Eyebrows raised, heads nodding. Her small, sharp eyes churn with plans and strategies. *Create a Distraction. Create a Distraction.*

Herr Spellbinder's eyes are fixed on the plant pot. Why? Why? I cannot deduce. Should I steer some person or start a Revolution? The Answer comes. All those years ago. Sometimes more recently. I have thrown Safety Matches into the side of the plant pot. Safety Matches are not Safe but still this plan must fail for the Matches would be damp.

It is worth trying for Fräulein Eder's cigarette is balanced on the edge of the ashtray. Pretend, pretend. I am avidly wiping the desk with my cloth. In my mind I am wearing the hearth rug and waving the toasting fork. Pretend, pretend. I stumble and while I am finding my feet, the cigarette end falls into the side of the plant pot.

I move away. No one has seen but what is the Point? Nothing happens. Dr Feldner talkstalkstalks to Fräulein Eder but I no longer hear the words. Sister Anna continues to dawdle with a pile of Files. We need something more. What else can I do? Sister Anna needs to get out of the Door without being seen ~

A crackling, a whiff of gunpowder, but no one has even turned to look before a sudden flare of flame, a crackling and gushing, then a massive bang like the sound of a bomb bashes through the Corridor. Pieces of china are blown all about. Smoke clouds everywhere. The wastepaper bin is near the coat stand and that now leaps with flames.

This is the Karl-Marx-Hof. The gun carriages are arriving, the shells are being fired. Walls will fold up, tiles will blow from the roofs. Everyone will be driven out and arrested. People will go missing. I must runrunrun but I cannot. I must not. Instead, I must look as though this is all a total surprise.

Adelheid – Behave as a responsible Person would behave in a situation of conflagration. I run to get a bucket of water. Dr Feldner is handing something to Sister Anna. The keys to his flat. She is out of the Door like ice off a hot plate. The fire rages, sucks, gusts, dances. Briefly, briefly I am filled with a darkwilddelicious pleasure ~

Yet the fire is quickly extinguished by pots and buckets of water. The fur coat on the curling wooden rack singes and smoulders, emits a filthy smell, which is both acrid and animal. Fräulein Eder strides down the Corridor, shoves my shoulder, points her finger: I know. I know. You and that other cretin.

Oh nonono. Not the tram, the marble, the grey sleeve.

Blow her up. Burn her to ash. Kill her. Please, please.

Sister Viktorine is fierce: Really. You left a cigarette burning.

Fräulein Eder: I won't put up with it. I won't.

Sister Johanna: We must get this window open.

Fräulein Eder: No. If you open that, it won't ~

The window has already been opened. Children are whimpering and cowering. Nurses hurry to comfort them. The floor is damp. The plant is badly singed and stands crooked against the Door. China and earth from the pot are spread all over the floor. The coat stand topples and falls, so that the fur is now also covered in water and mud.

Bertie is failing to help with any mopping and instead is lecturing everyone: In order for a fire to start, you need a source of ignition, of fuel, of oxygen etcetcetc.

Herr Spellbinder is busy with a broom, suppresses a look of ecstatic satisfaction. He raises his eyes to me briefly, acknowledging my handiwork. Indeed, you may learn many useful skills in the Curative Education Ward ~

I retreat along the Corridor to that window where I often hang the sheets out to dry. However, my brief moment of Triumph passes immediately. What has been achieved? What if Fräulein Eder now decides to take her revenge on Dr Feldner? I will soon be in Terrible Trouble. Sister Anna has gone to warn Hansi and she may locate him.

But where now can he hide? Fräulein Eder knows. She means to have her revenge upon us. She is unstable and treacherous and extremely furious. She has the power now to destroy all of us. This Game is over. *They have come.* Hansi's face as it used to be – annoying, truculent, brilliant – appears in my mind.

I remember him as a small rebellious boy when we swam in the Danube together. Adelheid – Do not think. Sheets need hanging. At least I may breathe cooler air. As I reach out, my eyes range along the building. I spy Fräulein Eder standing on the distant windowsill trying to manipulate the broken window back into position.

A ticklish breeze is blowing, pulls at the window, makes it hard to grasp. Herr Spellbinder is telling her *be careful.* Saying: I would give you a hand. But regrettably, my knee. That is not Safe. You should not stand up there. Let me.

Bertie is present also. *I can help you. Do take care, Fräulein Eder.* For a moment she turns to look, her foot flicks out, as though she intends to kick him. Her hand fumbles, she tips, her spine arches backwards, her head appears, her legs. A flicker of shoe, of petticoat, hair pins spiking, curls unravelling, a gash of stocking, a hand waving.

Cartwheeling against the radiant sapphire blue of the sky. Falling, tumbling, her feet bashing against a portico below. I crane my neck. She is spreadeagled on the ground, twisted. *Go back to your work, everyone. Go back to your work now. Get away from the windows. Nonono.* This is not. This is not what I am seeing.

In that insect world spread out below, people are staring, pointing, screaming, running. I dash towards the Reception. Herr Spellbinder is shutting the window. Says to me – *Get away. Now.* Nods calmly, pushes the laundry cart away. Shoutingyellingwailing. Sister Viktorine is at the Window where Fräulein Eder stood. I come to a halt beside her.

All around us the Windows open, then bang closed. *Do not let the Children go to the Windows.* A Nurse runs up from the Ward below. *Have you heard? Have you heard?* Sister Viktorine will allow no Gossip. She is closing the shutters. *Go back to work, everyone, now. Carry on. Be quiet. Do as I say. Now.*

Yet everyone is asking again and again – *Where is Fräulein Eder? Where? Where?* Herr Spellbinder disappears through the low Door which leads to the back stairs. I pass into the School Room which is empty now and hurry to the window. The scene below unrolls like a newsreel or an adventure film. People are swarming around, their heads bobbing.

THE MATCHBOX GIRL

A stretcher is being carried out. I hear Dr Feldner. *Fräulein Eder was trying to fix the window.* Down below long black cars, sleek as sharks, glide towards the Hospital. The Gestapo are getting out. A Maths book goes out of a window. Then a whole woman. So many people must have witnessed. Such a crowd of windows. Everyone must return to their work.

All must behave as though nothing has happened. Yet soon those Gestapo are in the Ward: We are looking for Herr Spellbinder. Where is he?

Sister Viktorine saying: The Children. We must have quiet.

Spellbinder? Where is he ~

Down below I can see the single, individual, particular blade of grass that is Herr Spellbinder. He has appeared out of a side Door and is striding towards the laundry van. He has not been seen. The police and soldiers are inside the building. More are arriving now. A group of eight marching up the hill towards the main Doors. A tremendous shout rises up.

Herr Spellbinder has been spotted. Dr Feldner is positioned beside me now. The film unwinding and unwinding and we cannot halt it. We did not intend. Did not intend. Causation is progressing like a train gathering speed and for once, events will lead exactly where they must lead. We see it all. Oh God. Oh God. No.

Herr Spellbinder is in the van and he presses his foot down. The van rocks, roars, speeds. He is driving straight at the column of eight men on the pavement ahead of him. He hits them, mows them down. Skittles falling. Everyone is shooting. The sounds crack and bounce. The van swerves and smashes to a halt, hitting a barrier.

All around men are sprawled on the pavement. Toy soldiers. All fallen down. Herr Spellbinder is yanked from the van. *For God's sake, Man, you will finish up Dead.* I cannot see his face but I know. That loud, maniac laugh. His crooked teeth dancing, his ears jiggling. Howls like a wolf, the noise high-pitched, mournful. A warning, a plea ~

The gun shots have stopped but now one final shattering crack is heard. Herr Spellbinder crumples. Dr Feldner catches hold of me, pulls me from the windowsill. I find myself on the floor, with my back to the radiator. Dr Feldner's face close to mine, all the skin stripped. Only bone and teeth and dark holes of eyes.

Time passes with a pleading slowness. Everything thick and sticky as treacle. Dr Feldner shuts the window, hauls me upright. Places a hand on the windowsill to steady himself. For some long minutes we are there together, silent, my back still pressed against the radiator ridges. Dr Feldner swallowing again and again, his breath jerking.

Feel the bullet smash into our jaws. Hear the explosion of blood and shattered Brain. Entering every corner of the skull. The collapse of Herr Spellbinder's body. Life like electric lightning is passing through us both. Reminding us, insisting. We are still here. I force myself to stand up straight and pull my cap back into place.

Dr Feldner nods, closes up the buttons of his white coat. He pulls me with him into the Corridor. From the Ward we hear Sister Viktorine. She has gathered the Children all around her. She is praying, her head bent. *Now and in the time of our Death.* Briefly, Dr Feldner and I stand and watch. The words seep into us, our hearts begin to still.

The Children are quiet, despite the tumult which still rises from below. Willy says: Fräulein Eder has flown away like an angel. Soon she will be in the land where it is whitewhitewhite and beautiful.

For once Sister Johanna is calm: The brakes on the van failed. They are asking for staff to assist but I cannot. Too much work to do here.

Dr Feldner says he also cannot go. Orders: Adelheid, come. He takes the vodka from the cupboard. I drink and am assailed by startling shock. The kitchen cupboards – now suddenly gorgeous, precious, unique. Herr Spellbinder. The gun. The sky around him arterial blue. Broken sobs, wracked weeping.

Dr Feldner: Adelheid, let me be clear. If you were ever going to speak, this wouldn't be the moment ~

10.e. Children and Blades of Grass

We cannot comprehend the strangeness of God's grace. Hansi was safesafesafe. That is all that I can say. I began this Historical Record to show the Lessons which may be Learnt. Yet now I have nothing to offer. I have no Strategy of Life for You or for myself. I thought that we might at least be Clear on the difference between Right and Wrong. Truth and Untruth.

Yet even that is muddled. We ganged up on Fräulein Eder and put her hands in a Mincing Machine, we pushed a worm down the back of her blouse. We all wanted her Dead. We none of us can know the puzzle of Causation, the workings of *the Alchemy of Circumstance*. Drop a cigarette, a woman flies. Things meant to be Small become Large.

Perhaps for once I may have drawn the Right Conclusion (although sadly this perhaps was mere Accident). Fräulein Eder wanted to tell the Authorities about Hansi, she wanted to tell the Truth. Yet that was a Truth which would have resulted in many Deaths. I have become like Grandmother with the Notebooks. Burning up the Truth. This I cannot unpick.

The days grind onward, as they must. In those months following Fräulein Eder's Death, I am happy. The memory of that day causes me little pain. The Truth is that for so long we had been no more than leaves, blowing and blowing in the wind, chased from one place to the next, the wind always bashing us. Only in that brief moment, we were powerful ~

How can we live in these Times? Sister Viktorine asks most frequently, hands spread expansively, still hoping to catch the Goodness of God as it falls from the sky. This question I am able to answer. The Human Being is not designed to live in a constant State of Fear. No matter how Dangerous the situation, you forget and continue your Normal Life.

You tell yourself diverse Stories as to how the risk is not so great. How disaster will not strike today. You become Split-Minded and you are glad of this. I have my job and I am needed. I Serve. Sister Viktorine still receives Instructions from Dr A and she writes replies. She also forwards him the Case Notes but we know nothing of his circumstances.

The loss of Herr Spellbinder is felt deeply. Dr Feldner attempts to enquire about his Funeral but one cannot ask too much. Initially we fear questions, an interrogation, a Court case. Years before, at the time of the Anschluss, I had asked myself how two people could fall out of a window. Now I ask myself how one could fall? Without doubt, she was adjusting the catch.

Dr Feldner reports to the police station to give a statement. We all know that he will take care not to mention Bertie and that he will scrupulously and assiduously lay all the blame at the Door of the treacherous scoundrel and known black marketeer Herr Spellbinder. That was the intention. *Create a Distraction.*

Sister Viktorine feels that we should at least be able to bury him respectfully but no one has time now for the Dead. They are too numerous. It seems Herr Spellbinder had no Family. I write about him in the Notebook of my head. Never a Clay model. Always our most Disorderly Orderly, the Master of Disaster, the Lord of Misrule. When Anubis weighs his Heart, it will be found light as a feather. Because he was powerless, no one could destroy his power ~

The Question now is everywhere but it is never asked. What will transpire when the Bolsheviks come? *Surely the British and the Americans know that this was never Our War.* But it was Our War. We remain loyal to our tragic Country for its roots grip deep in bone and blood. Defeat is not a possibility. The Führer will never sue for Peace.

News comes that the Opera House will be closed. It is not only music that has Died now. Our Fantastical Capital City must become merely provincial. For in this time all is Berlin. This wreaks more damage on our City than any bomb. Yet still we sweepwashfeedmop and go to Mass againagainagain. I envy the rats who may leave by any drain.

I would not say that I am now fond of the Children but I know how to make myself love them. They are no longer jumbled up together but separate and unique. Otto. Heinrich. Johannes. Kaspar. Liesl. Anna. Maria. Helene. One thousand blades of grass are not a lawn. Children also.

Dr A wanted to know what the meaning is of the moving globules of fat in the bowl of soup. There is no meaning. Each globule of fat deserves attention. Each blade of grass. When you try to impose some sense, some Order, then the globule of fat is less than it was. The Wonder and Mystery is gone.

Dr A did not know this about soup, but he knew it about Children. He knew that if you decide that a Person is this, or that, then you may overlook some other things which are perhaps more Important. You may consider that you understand but, in fact, you are only taking away from that Child the essence of their personality.

All this I do turn over in my mind, as we listen to Bertie reading Stories of other Times. I open the Atlas and show the Children the World except there is no World now. Only this time, this place. Sister Viktorine is luminous. The life inside her shining like the filament of a bulb. We need dreams now and it doesn't matter what dreams we choose ~

We must tape up the windows. The Cellars of the Hospital are prepared. We inform ourselves in relation to air defence. How far can a bomber fly? Five hundred km. What is the load of such a bomber? It's 1,500 kg. If there is Danger, we will hear a two-tone signal (the Cuckoo Is Calling). We may need to alert the block behind as the phone is often not working.

This is a War of annihilation being waged against the German people by implacable enemies. We must be ready to be sacrificed on the altar of the Fatherland. Yet no bombs come and no one believes that they will. The Allies might bomb the suburbs but not the famous Inner Ring of our City. The Führer will protect us. (Or else, Otto von Habsburg.)

The Führer is cunningly concealing a secret army and soon that will be mobilised. Also, poisoned gas will soon be used to defeat our foul and despicable Enemies. Grandmother says this when she comes to the Hospital. Sitting with Sister Viktorine in the Meeting Room, bringing news of the Winkler girls.

Saying: Gerda. Loading guns, if you please. Artillery training for women. Can that be right? Poor Frau Winkler. One daughter unmarried but having babies for the Reich. Another *loading guns*. What is expected of a woman in this World ~

One night as Grandmother is leaving, she stops at the Door of the Ward. I am comforting a crying Child. I hold that Child tight and let her rest her head against me, stroke her cheek. I know how this will soothe the Child. I am a proper Nurse now. Grandmother sees me, shakes her head most sentimentally.

Says: In these hard times, we do learn what is important, do we not? It seems that dear Adelheid's frozen heart has finally come unlocked and she has come to God. That was what I always found impossible. She has never felt even the least affection for me.

I must not fall into the temptation of feeling sorry for Grandmother.

I expect Sister Viktorine to respond with Similar Sentimental nonsense. Instead, she says: I never thought that Adelheid was heartless. I always believed her to be full of love and courage. I am not sure she has changed. We set out to change the Child, but the changes must come within ourselves ~

Another winter ebbs and flows. We live as though in a dream. The days are blurred and gentle. We want nothing, we expect nothing, we feel nothing. One day a crying woman comes to the Ward. This used to happen most frequently but not so often now. Still this woman laments upon Sister Viktorine. Her hair is knotted, her face collapsed, her eyes stinging.

She is Fräulein Eder's Mother: Did she fall? Was it an accident?

I am relieved I do not have to answer these questions. I saw Herr Spellbinder's hand on her leg. I saw Bertie lean across. Sister Viktorine did not. Still the woman is lachrymose. She wants to tell Fräulein Eder's Story. *Suicide. Suicide.* Had Sister Viktorine not noticed that Fräulein Eder was becoming more and more depressed? The accidents?

The woman nods, confides. *A secret, a problem.* She wanted to atone for the Mistakes of her Youth. Whispers: She married a Jew.

Always there in the Paperwork. That new man. A gorgeous fur coat but such presents come at a cost. It was only her work at the Clinic which sustained her. She spoke so often and with such love of Sister Viktorine.

Everyone has a Story now. A Fantastical Story, a Fairy Story.

Let the Witches all be Wicked. I don't want to hear ~

10.f. The Cuckoo Calls

The summer of 1944 is insufferably steamy. The City smells. In June we hear that the Bully Boy British have arrived on the coast of Northern France. It has been stressed that, in truth, the American and British troops are gentlemen and will behave as such. Yet also if we should ever encounter these troops, we must immediately string them up.

September comes and the days are opaque and overcast. Even the sun itself is reduced and evasive. I take my Matchboxes back from Grandmother. She apprehends that this is Peace but it is not. One morning I find that two or three matchboxes have become unstuck. More than that, because the window is open, they have blown away from the Album.

They remain on the table but what I cannot understand is how they could possibly have become unstuck. This makes me worried and I meditate on this question as I go back to work. Soon I am busy with the Children again and the thought goes from my head. Yet also I am noticing that there are no Rats now. Where have all the Rats gone?

That morning Sister Viktorine is contented because she has received a letter from Dr A. Certainly, he must be home soon. We direct the Children out into the Garden so that we can carry out some maintenance on the flower beds. The morning mist has dispersed. Since there has been no rain for several days, some watering is also needed.

I bring blankets and cushions. Some of the smaller Children must sit in the shade with their hats on. I am pouring water and Sister Viktorine has gone to find the wheelbarrow for the weeds. That same tugging wind which has come so often over the summer is rising again. I catch a hat which is blowing from a Child's head ~

A person is waving to us from the upstairs window. A beckoning wave. Their voice calls but I cannot hear. I go towards the Door which leads to the stairs as the Person will descend in order to relay the message. That is how it usually works. Now Sister Johanna arrives at the bottom of the steps in a fluster. Says: The Cuckoo. We must get the Children in.

This is a drill. We have had several practices already but we must behave as though the Danger is Real. We must not commence to let the Children panic or we will never be able to usher them inside. Sister Viktorine tells them that a rainstorm is coming. *Please hurry up now.* I start to gather up blankets and cushions but Sister Viktorine says to leave those things.

We can come back for them later. Sister Johanna starts to take the hands of the smaller Children. They do not want to go. *You can come out again as soon as the rain has passed.* Sister Viktorine begins to sing a song because this is a good way to get everyone to fall into line. All crowding in through the Door. Should we take the Children straight to the Cellar? This is hurriedly discussed. We look around and identify that Willy is not with us.

Sister Viktorine says: I shall go and look.

She steps back into the Garden. Sister Johanna decides she should lead some of the older Children upstairs so that they may collect blankets and pullovers. Supplies of this type have been taken to the Cellar before but then brought back up. No Point positioning them there where they will get damp. For three months they were never needed.

I stare out of the Door and observe Sister Viktorine near the flower beds, calling and calling. I know where Willy will be. The Garden within the Garden that I once so Loved. I run towards that corner and immediately I find him. A bang sounds in the distance. The whine of a plane is starting somewhere far away. The whirringsingingbuzzing.

We have heard planes often before but they are always planes of the Reich. Yet now the Fear is upon us. The moment has come. We are straightforward and calm. Sister Viktorine grabs hold of Willy and begins to lead him towards the Door. He fights back but I catch hold of him also and we pull him. A plane is above us. Willy stares up in terror. No need to worry. The plane will drop Leaflets like white birds ~

Willy has ceased fighting and heads towards the Door. I see Johanna with the older Children, coming back down the stairs. *We must get to the Cellar now. Upstairs. I saw.* More planes now are howling and shuddering overhead. A sudden sickness rising in the gut. Dark crosses outlined against the blue of the sky. The anti-aircraft guns boom.

From the street below people are yelling and children wail. Car horns are blaring. Dogs are barking, footsteps dash. *Get indoors, get under cover.* We join the Children but now the stairs are crowded. Stretchers are being carried down. A woman is crawling on her hands and knees, a Man waves a crutch. Children are cringing, their faces frozen in ghastly horror.

Sister Viktorine: The other building. Did anyone call?

The block at the back. One sees that the windows are open. No signs of activity. Is it possible that they do not know? We can identify the staircase through the long windows and no one is hurrying down. Sister Viktorine will go and verify. She steps out across the Garden. An explosion sounds. Near or far? I cannot tell ~

I remain at the Door waiting for Sister Viktorine. Where has she gone? Surely she only gave the message to the first Person she saw? She should perhaps stay in the other building? The details of the Garden become inflated, restless, urgent. Nodding flowers, a cushion, the wheelbarrow abandoned in the middle of the lawn.

Every blade of grass staring upwards at the swooping black insects darkening the sky. Sister Viktorine emerges out of the Door of the opposite block. She should not cross the lawn now. I should say. I must stop her. Planes are overhead. I tip my head back and see the details of wings and cockpits. Even the rivets which hold them together.

Sister Viktorine should have remained in the other building, gone into the Cellars there. She makes the sign of the cross, smiles brightly, strides out confidently across the Garden. She comes to the blankets and cushions which were left on the grass. *Much better to pick them up now. Many hands make light work.*

THE MATCHBOX GIRL

I should tell her. No. No. No. I run to grab her, pull her inside. I should saysaysay. I gasp, grab my throat. We both twist our heads. Staring, staring. A plane is close, blocking out the light. The sun glares around its black frame. A coin is falling. Spinning, sailing smoothly down. If she had not stopped. If she had not stopped to pick up.

I grab Sister Viktorine's arm and pull her towards the Door. Her face is open wide. Briefly she is that woman I first knew. Light, quick, graceful, glittering. She dodges now across the Garden. Everything screaming – the grass, the air, the windows, the walls. Our heads tipped back. Everything that is. Everything that ever was.

The World vastly varied and luminous and brilliant. Everything separate and known and entirely beautifully brilliantly itself. All light noise pressure space as a wave of sound hits us and a crash smashes straight through our eardrums. Imprinted in skin, bone, the tips of the hair. Fusing with soul and blood. The earth has given way. Falling. Falling.

The sky throws glass bricks roof tiles branches. Papers are floating through the air blown into a thousand pieces. Metal is twisted, marble cracked. Dust pushes into our throats. The force of the blast steals airlightspace. Everything. Gone. Every bone is shattered, everything has given way. Luck, belief, *the Alchemy of Circumstance*.

None can help. *Do try to keep your mouth shut.* The bomb has fallen right down our throats. Exploded inside us. Gone down a drain and blown away and disappeared. Matchboxes gone and so must I. Sister Viktorine has pulled me against her. Whitewhitewhite. Snow ash feather. Allallall most radiantly magnificent ~

After My Death: The Days of Judgement

Sister Viktorine? Did I tell the Story properly? I am finished now, broken in pieces. You may enjoy a few loose ends but I do not. They do not tell you. How our Lives are Totally Opaque and so will ever remain. The toy bricks never became a Farm or a Fort. If only that which is simple could be Right, that which is complex Wrong. It is always the other way around.

I did always say the Wrong Thing. As in Life, so in Death. I know how Difficult it is when you have too many Questions and no Answers. Not every Suitcase leads to a journey. Realism isn't the best way of explaining what is Real. This was meant to be a Proper Story which makes sense, with a beginningmiddleend.

Some stories are too big to be told. Tell me a Word which links to another. You say *Murderer*. I say Doctor, goodness, pneumonia, arm. My Story is no better than Bears, Bicycles, Fairies. Worst of all, I have told it as though it is a Children's Adventure Tale, as though it is funny. Only now, too late, do I find the Proper Words ~

Why did I break my own rule and decide to write, to speak? Because, dear Sister Viktorine, I did not call out to you that day in the Garden. I should have done. Whatever language we may speak – the language of dogs or whatever – we must try. Yet in truth, I long to return Words to their Proper Usage which was to describe those Small Things which have given me pleasure.

May we not weep for those miserable Words pressed into service to perform functions beyond their capabilities? We struggle to be Ordered only to hide our deep Disorder. The glue is spread all across the envelopes, papers, albums and All is Misshapen.

THE MATCHBOX GIRL

Is an Author a Person who defends that Ancient Viennese Vice? Is there an Egyptian God of Uncertainty ~

Stories do not stop just because the people in them are Dead. For yes, on that day in September 1944, you, dear Sister Viktorine, and I were both Dead. Yet the Story that has been told about that day is most Incorrect. None of the Children died, the building was not razed to the ground. Not in that bombing. Another bombing, a later bombing. Yes, many died then.

What of those who survived the War? All I can do is to make their lives into Matchboxes – small, neat, with clear edges. Lay them out accurately and in a carefully considered Order. Glimpses of their Lives. Let me explain it like this. After the War, they started on the Persilschein, which was so named due to a washing powder from America.

It was truly remarkable how many Nazis were cleaned up with Persil washing powder, and having been scrubbed with great vigour, their vests came out glistening white. Many bitter jokes were made about this process but it was, in fact, quite necessary. Intelligent, professional people who could rebuild the Country were needed at that time.

An example of this was Lukas who mysteriously became a hero of the Socialist Resistance and was given a comfortable job in the Bookkeeping Department at the Rathaus where he caused much Paperwork Confusion before he merrily drank himself to Death ~

Diverse Proper Criminals were arrested and tried. Among them Professor Hamburger. He did not go in the tub as he would never become clean. Dr Gross should have suffered the same fate but remained a free man, despite attempts to bring him to justice. Adolf had told me that *nothing would ever stick to Dr Jekelius*. Yet this did prove Untrue.

He became known as the Mass Murderer of Steinhof. He died in a camp in the Eastern Territories. Those who met him there said he was *the best comrade you could imagine*. They reported that *he gave consolation to everybody* and noted that *he lived up to the highest conceivable moral standards*.

Opa and Oma continued at the Café. Since Grandfather was a hero of the Resistance, they moved into a more commodious apartment. A pleasant habitation at the back of our building which looked onto trees. On the walls, in frames, they had many pages of Matchboxes. Opa gave up on Politics because of the betrayal of Yalta.

Peace also has its costs. Opa was not able to visit his family in Budapest even though they were but three hours away. This he could not Forgive. Instead, he finally turned to caring for Oma and they wept many cheerful tears over my loss ~

Dr Feldner's biggest ever gamble paid off. He and Hansi spent the last days of the War wandering the nighttime streets of Vienna with a brush and a tin of paint, still daubing the numbers 1918 on many walls.

Hansi always kept the 177 tickets which served as a reminder of his Wartime visits to the Opera. He later estimated that at least one hundred people in the Children's Hospital knew his true identity and yet no one spoke. In 1950 Dr Feldner formally adopted Hansi who took the name Feldner-Bustin.

Hansi became a neurological surgeon and had three Children and six Grandchildren. Briefly, he did move to America but he could not stay. He had to return to Vienna to be with Dr Feldner. They had breakfast together every day for the rest of Dr Feldner's Life.

Although Dr A declined to write an obituary for Professor Hamburger, he gladly made a speech at Dr Feldner's seventy-fifth birthday alluding in a joking manner to certain daring Wartime Adventures.

When Dr Feldner died in 1973, at the age of eighty-six, he wanted no announcement in the newspaper, no readings at the Funeral, no guests, no music. The Feldner-Bustin family desired to plant a tree for him along the Avenue of the Righteous at the Yad Vashem Holocaust Memorial in Jerusalem. Dr Feldner wanted none of that and his bravery has never been formally celebrated.

Hansi's Children and Grandchildren still live in Vienna. Should You walk down the Neubaugasse You may find them in the apartment where Dr Feldner once lived ~

Maurice, who worked at The Rookery in Aspley Guise, never spoke of his Wartime experiences, but when the County of Bedfordshire decided to investigate the highly secret role that it played in Wartime espionage, a lady from the Council wrote to ask him if he might tell his Story. She was sure that he was part of the bombing raids.

He could not explain about the white bombs. Out of doubt they had bred doubt, and that had opened the crack in the Door through which perhaps some were saved. No talk of Propaganda by Pornography now. How they had jeered at Stafford Cripps. *If this is the sort of thing we need to do in order to win a War, why, I'd rather lose it.* It is all Wrongos now ~

Frau Schreiber was never troubled by such Questions. After the War she met an American and, when that American left Vienna, he took her home with him. The American arranged for Frau Schreiber to take the Children as well – all of them – even though she might have been glad to leave some behind.

In America she was reunited with Adolf who became an affluent and successful Man. Wearing good suits and smelling appealingly of cologne, he married a pretty woman with exceptionally good handwriting who never wore low-cut dresses. He was ever a Genuine Fake and, like me, an Average Level of Coward.

Since he apparently had a Medical Degree from the University of Vienna, he went into the fashionable field of Psychoanalysis where he specialised in the Mother complex. In his Youth, he had been a patient of the great Sigmund Freud. Thomas the Spaceship also went to America and worked on the NASA rocket launch.

Aurel Iselstöger survived until 2008. Although he spent his Life in psychiatric institutions, he never stopped drawing. His sister always insisted that Dr A saved him. When Aurel died, his work was put in a skip but two lady gallery owners in Cologne rescued it. His work has now been exhibited in both Austria and Berlin ~

Georg and Anni Weiss-Frankl finally made their home in North Carolina. They never had Children but were loving parents to many. They continued to bring Child Guidance Services to areas of rural America where such support barely existed. Everywhere Georg went he tried to recreate the Curative Education Ward at the Children's Hospital in Vienna.

His former boss, Leo Kanner, was credited with the discovery of Autism. Apparently, he had known all about it before Frankl arrived. Certainly, Kanner had never heard of that other Austrian chap. *How do you spell his name?* All we can say is that, as the work passed from Frankl to Kanner, its characters changed.

The staff of the Children's Hospital in Vienna had seen originality and spontaneity, Kanner saw isolation and sameness. Vienna saw strands of both disability and genius in their patients' family histories. America saw the Refrigerator Mother, an idea which caused thousands of Autistic Children to be taken from their families ~

After Georg died, Anni moved to the Blumenthal Jewish Home, in Clemmons, North Carolina. Her crocheted two-tone blue capelet won a third-place ribbon at the Dixie Classic Fair. She also made soft toys for local pre-schoolers, stuffed envelopes for charity and worked for Meals on Wheels.

During those years, she wrote of a lane which she loved to walk. On that lane was an oak tree with a strangely misshapen trunk. She liked to look at this tree and see how it had grown tall and strong despite its early struggles. A touching Story, is it not?

Do people always grow sentimental as they get older?

Sadly, I do not know ~

Who actually did discover Autism? Kanner or Dr A? Sister Viktorine, you might have told them that there was no Discovery, just a rearrangement of known symptoms into a new constellation. If only we could Translate, Interpret. Was it science that untangled the knots or merely love? Are they both the same?

Dr A certainly knew your contribution. He always said you were a Genius. Finally, I am glad that you died. You knew too much. That guilt would have grown like a cancer inside you as it did in so many who survived. A generation living in the shadows, never speaking of the past, never meeting anyone's eye.

In Vienna, they keep the records of Doctors but not Nurses. Yet we did Serve, and we know the Value of Service. Sister Viktorine, your Story was too small. It lacked drama, excitement, romance. The seduction of Absolute Certainties. They talk of the banality of Evil but what of the banality of Goodness ~

Sister Viktorine is Answered

In the tumultuous year of 1945, Dr A walks a begrimed road in Croatia. His glasses broken, his jacket frayed, he carries only a small kit bag. He is with five others, all of whom worked with him in the Field Hospital. This group have had little food or water for some days. They are attempting to get home to Vienna but there is no way for them to travel except on foot.

Around them are the skeletons of buildings, burnt-out trucks, men sitting propped listlessly against trees or walls, Children bleating. People queue at a standpipe which dribbles water. Dr A has spoken to the group firmly. They must walk up through the mountains, to the border with Styria or Carinthia.

They need to travel as far away from the front line as possible because the fighting still rages against the Allies and Tito's Partisans. They start to walk, hurrying towards the mountains as the Allies advance. Progress is painfully slow for one Nurse has a sprained ankle. The food runs out and the nights are glacial. The injured Nurse says that she cannot continue.

Yet Dr A mercifully has his compass and, remembering the hiking parties of his Youth, he steers a True course – North North East – towards Vienna. He even suggests a song. Perhaps that tune that Sister Viktorine had previously played? He can't remember the melody. Others can and so they manage to sing with some vigour. Six people, eleven legs. Maybe we are always walking each other home ~

Coming down from the mountains the group head West, having been warned of skirmishes ahead. They finally reach the Austrian border and cross into Carinthia where they surrender to the British. Still there is no way back to Vienna and for three months Dr A must remain at the border. He volunteers for farm work while he tries to get his Paperwork in Order.

Eventually Dr A is allowed to board a train for Vienna. After he alights from that train, he walks towards the Ninth District but he does not go home. Instead, he clambers over the rubble, finds his way to the Hospital. He knows that the Clinic had been razed to the ground. He knows that Sister Viktorine is Dead.

However, he has at least managed to get in touch with Josef. Although Josef can be erratic, he may be relied upon in such a Difficult Matter. *Josef, Josef. You must, you must. Please see that it is done.*

How painful for him to see his City in such profound Disorder. For 12,000 buildings are destroyed, 270,000 homeless. How could one mourn the loss of the Clinic when so much else had gone? Yet he sits on a low wall in the merciless rain for many long moments, staring at the ruins. Decides then. Funds are already being raised to rebuild. It must happen ~

So it was that Georg Frankl found him back in his same Office at the Hospital when he visited from America four years later. How interesting that Dr Frankl seems to have found it hard to respond to letters written by Kanner but easy to reply to Dr A. The Clinic had been recreated, put back together brick by brick, restored *with photographic accuracy.*

Dr A later became the Director of the Clinic with no Questions asked. He continued to work there for fifty years (although no longer considering questions of Autism). He had never been a member of the Nazi Party and therefore his reputation was beyond question. It was not noticed that he had not merely survived the War, he had been promoted ~

What else was discussed on that day in 1949 when Dr Frankl and Dr A were finally reunited? Sister Viktorine, did they speak of you? Perhaps they did not. Dr Frankl probably did not ask where you were buried. One must look to the Future. For many years no one knew where you were laid to rest but now you have been found.

THE MATCHBOX GIRL

Where? It turns out that you were buried with Dr A's parents in that lovely spot in the Hietzing Cemetery. *One may gaze at the distant Woods and the vineyards from there. A place where one feels the presence of God in every leaf and branch.* You asked – *Did he ever care for me?* Maybe now you have the Answer ~

The End

Where now is Adelheid Brunner? Of course, I never existed. I invented myself, just as the Clinic taught me. Don't we all do that? You should be careful of reading Fantastical Stories. Do You have bad dreams? Are You a personality type of *Social Utility*? Do You wet the bed? Of course, you must know that none of the Dead are Definitely Dead.

This is the Notebook I will not burn up. I keep the Record Room neatly Ordered. Still I walk the Streets of Vienna continuing to believe that the Answers lie knotted in the Streets, courtyards, gardens of my City. Can You feel it? My arm brushes the sleeve of Your coat. You follow me to the end of the street but, when You turn the corner, I am gone ~

Are You never done with Your endless Questions? You insist that the Man who hated labels must be neatly labelled. A brilliant Pioneer of Autism Research or a Murderer? Must he always be merely the sum of the Misunderstandings which gather around his name? Perhaps You have only been listening to the parts of the Story which You wanted to hear.

I know how that can happen. The compass has become damp and the needle sticks. Like Grillparzer I must ask – *Love! Hate! Is there no Third?* You assume You have been extending Your sympathy to a Troubled Child but You have been listening to the Defence of an accomplice to Murder. This was never a Detective Story. We already know.

He signed those Papers. He conclusively did.

Herta, Elisabeth. The thirty-five of the Gugging Papers.

A crime is a crime, murder is murder.

The Truth must be that he was an Evil Man ~

This Fact is like one of those pieces of gristly meat I hated to eat. You chew and chew. You try to break the hard edges down. You hope you might conceal the meat in a napkin or a plant pot. But no. You must force it down and it wedges in your throat. You gag againagainagain. You are choking and struggling to breathe.

Understand this – once a person has been Deceived, then that person can never fully be Undeceived. If you admitted the extent of your Error, you would not be able to Trust Your Own Mind. Yet it is also True that, if everyone insists repeatedly that a thing is not there – then finally It Is Not There. Enough. Enough. We did all know. We did. Guilty as charged ~

Cast the first stone if You dare. In Death, I thought I might arrive at some final and essential Peace. It is not so. The Dead are endlessly shuffling in their Graves. There is no New World. The War never ended. Again, the lights are going out across Europe. The bullies are coming now for him, for me, for us.

I am tired. So bitterly, bitterly tired. I hand You the baton. Will You run? Will You run? The Question is not so much about Right and Wrong. Instead, we ask which part of our Ourselves might feel the Difference between the two.

What is that flame within and how might it be kept alight? What is a conscience except the accumulation of the expectations of those who have gone before or who will come after? Cherish the Sacred Art of Phillumeny, listen to the Wisdom of Matchboxes ~

The Children of Am Spiegelgrund will never cease their screaming. All 600 whose Brains are buried now in the Vienna Zentralfriedhof. *Niemals vergessen.* Never Forget. Their skeletal arms, bent and grey, yet still waving and waving. They do not wish to be laid to rest. Fools, fools. Why do you not see? They cry out for the Justice they can never have.

We are all – all – forever stumbling in Frau Altmann's new shoes. Margarete still gaily twirls on the stairs. Safety Matches are not Safe. What we get now is what we deserve. Do not offer us the Insult of Forgiveness. Do not take comfort. Do not feel reassured. No one has been Absolved, Redeemed, Healed ~

Notes and Acknowledgements

This is a work of fiction. However, the research which lies behind this book is extensive and I have attempted to create a story which broadly accords with the information which is currently known about these events. First and foremost, I would like to thank the many people who are on the Autism spectrum, both those near to me and far, who have offered their assistance. I promised anonymity and I will be meticulous in keeping that promise but I fully acknowledge the extent of my debt.

I would also like to thank Dr Maria Asperger Felder. In writing this story, I have invaded the privacy of her family. She did not wish to make any comment on the book but generously wished me well in my efforts. I am truly grateful to her. I also thank academics and practitioners who have been generous with their time and research. First and foremost, Dr Marius Weigl-Burnautzki showed me around Vienna and worked tirelessly in the Vienna archives filling in many research gaps. As my visits to Vienna were curtailed by Covid-19, I could not have continued with this project without his excellent assistance. In particular, he discovered the surprising location of the grave of Sister Viktorine Zak.

The work of Dr Herwig Czech of the Medical University of Vienna (who makes a brief appearance in this book) has been essential to my understanding of these events. His 2018 research paper ('Hans Asperger, National Socialism, and "race hygiene" in Nazi-era Vienna') lies at the heart of this book and his thorough and balanced approach has been an inspiration throughout. I also acknowledge Dr Stephen D. Haswell Todd of the University of Chicago whose brilliant PhD thesis ('The Turn to the Self: A History of Autism

NOTES AND ACKNOWLEDGEMENTS

1910–1944') helped me to place these events in a wider context. Sincere thanks also to Steve Silberman whose book *Neuro Tribes: The Legacy of Autism and How to Think Smarter About People Who Think Differently* first sparked my interest in Dr Asperger. He was most supportive when I was starting my research. Tragically Steve died just as I was finishing this book. I was looking foward to the moment when I could tell him more about Sister Viktorine Zak but, sadly that moment never came. I hope we may yet meet on another shore.

Adam Feinstein's book *A History of Autism: Conversations with the Pioneers* was written before Dr Herwig Czech's revelations in relation to Dr Asperger but was, nevertheless, a useful guide. John Elder Robison at the College of William & Mary in Williamsburg first highlighted the importance of Georg Frankl ('Kanner, Asperger, and Frankl: A third man at the genesis of the autism diagnosis'). He shared his thoughts and knowledge generously. Some of the details in Edith Sheffer's book *Asperger's Children: The Origins of Autism in Nazi Vienna* were also useful to me.

Samantha Dluzak of Norwich University, Vermont, has followed up on John Elder Robison's work ('The Forgotten Pioneers: The Life and Work of Anni Weiss and Georg Frankl'). The biographical details she supplied for Anni and Georg gave life to the American sections of this book. Vienna-based journalist Anna Goldenberg's moving memoir (*I Belong to Vienna: A Jewish Family's Story of Exile and Return*, translated by Alta L. Price) tells the amazing history of her grandfather Hansi Bustin. It provided me with important information both about Hansi himself and also about Dr Josef Feldner.

Dr Judith Gould was most generous in speaking to me of her own invaluable work and also of her dear friend, and pioneer of autism research, Dr Lorna Wing. Dame Uta Frith was the first person to translate Asperger's work into English and those translations remain key to our understand of his thinking. I am also grateful to Susanne Zander of the Delmes & Zander gallery in Cologne for rescuing the work of Aurel Iselstöger and for sharing images with me. Charlotte Beradt's book *The Third Reich of Dreams* (translated by Adriane Gottwald) is an extraordinary collective diary giving an account of the dreams of those living under the Reich. To read it is to come to a fuller understanding of what it was like to live in a regime of extreme oppression.

NOTES AND ACKNOWLEDGEMENTS

I am grateful to Walter Kempowski for his 'small library of the nameless' and the novels which arose from that research. I am also indebted to historian Nicholas Stargardt for his work relating to the German experience of the Second World War and in particular to his skill in honouring the children who lived through that time (*Witnesses of War: Children's Lives under the Nazis*). I must also acknowledge British foreign correspondent and journalist G.E.R. Gedye (1890–1970) who lived through the rise of fascism in Austria and predicted the horrors to come. His book *Fallen Bastions: The Central European Tragedy* is endlessly lively and illuminating. Although Eva Hoffman's memoir *Lost in Translation: Life in a New Language* is not about the Second World War, it gives a brilliantly penetrating account of the dislocation caused by migration and helped me to imagine the struggles that Anni Weiss-Frankl might have faced when trying to create a new life in America.

I have also drawn inspiration from philosopher Ian Hacking (1936–2023) whose work on naming and the named raises so many interesting questions. I have also been inspired by the books of Simon Baron-Cohen and by Joanne Limburg's book *Letters to my Weird Sisters: on Autism and Feminism*. The novels of Hans Fallada and *Night Falls on the City* by Sarah Gainham set a standard which I could never hope to reach.

My dear friend Angela Findlay was writing her courageous memoir *In My Grandfather's Shadow: A Story of War, Trauma and the Legacy of Silence* while I was writing this novel. Our conversations gave me courage and shaped some of my thinking. I was also fascinated and moved by Katrin Fitzherbert's extraordinary memoir *True to Both My Selves*.

Susannah Rickards provided invaluable assistance by reading early drafts of this book. Sally Bayley was also an early and attentive reader who understood Adelheid entirely. Rebecca Abrams and I have stood by each other through some dark times and I am a huge admirer of her endless courage and good humour.

Thanks also to John Mitchinson, Rina Gill, Kathleen Jones, Roopa Farooki, Jacqui Lofthouse, Marina Benjamin, Lorraine Rogerson, Miranda Gold, Anna Beer, Rachel Malik, Kel Portman, Caroline Sanderson, Peter Moseley, Madeleine Bunting, Tamsin Shelton, Houman Barekat, Jude and James Cook, and Neil Griffiths. Emma

NOTES AND ACKNOWLEDGEMENTS

La Fontaine Jackson helped with early translation work. Thanks to Jamie Bulloch, historian and translator of German literature, for his valuable comments and also to Theodora Danek for a sensitive and meticulous copyedit. I am thankful also to Sharona Selby for brilliant proofreading. My wonderful students at Oxford University and Goldsmiths were often an inspiration. My thanks also to Eleanor Birne, Patrick Walsh, Cora MacGregor and Margaret Halton at Pew Literary and to Peter Straus and all the team at Rogers, Coleridge and White. Also, to Allegra Le Fanu, Alexis Kirschbaum and Francisco Vilhena at Bloomsbury. They have all been fearless in their support of this book. Last but certainly not least, my thanks to my husband Stephen Kinsella and to my children Thomas and Hope for all the laughter and the love. It is, of course, standard to include a statement saying that none of these people bear any responsibility for the contents of this book. Given the many controversies surrounding the events I describe, this well-worn disclaimer must be thoroughly emphasised.

A Note on the Author

Alice Jolly is a novelist and playwright. Her writing has been awarded the PEN/Ackerley Prize, an O Henry Prize and the V. S. Pritchett Memorial Prize, and been longlisted for Ondaatje Prize and was runner-up for the Rathbones Folio Prize. She teaches on the Creative Writing Masters at Oxford University.
@JollyAlice

A Note on the Type

The text of this book is set in Bembo, which was first used in 1495 by the Venetian printer Aldus Manutius for Cardinal Bembo's *De Aetna*. The original types were cut for Manutius by Francesco Griffo. Bembo was one of the types used by Claude Garamond (1480–1561) as a model for his Romain de l'Université, and so it was a forerunner of what became the standard European type for the following two centuries. Its modern form follows the original types and was designed for Monotype in 1929.